A PORTRAIT OF TIME

A TIME TRAVEL ROMANCE NOVEL

AISLING MCBREEN

ISBN: 979-8-9921962-2-1

DEDICATION

To my dear friends Dotty and Angel, without whom this book would not have been possible. Thank you for your friendship and support through every step of the writing journey.

AUTHOR'S NOTE

All characters in this novel are fictional. Any resemblance to real people, living or dead, is purely coincidental. However, 1920s Jacksonville is portrayed as accurately as possible—with a little artistic license taken by the author.

PART I: ATTRACTION

ONE: LUKE

I drum my fingers on the Honda's steering wheel and bob my head to *Bohemian Rhapsody*. It's my favorite song, and I know all the words, even if I couldn't hold a tune to save my life. But who's listening?

Pink crape myrtle blossoms flicker past as the crack in my windshield morphs into a stick-figure alien with saucer eyes. I blink once, twice, and it morphs back into a windshield crack.

What the...?

A car horn blares. Panic squeezes my throat as I realize I've traveled two miles—all the way to Naval Air Station Jax—without realizing it. Highway hypnosis, that was it. I zoned out while singing. I straighten the wheel and raise a hand to the driver I almost clipped. Sorry, dude.

I focus on the clog of traffic waiting to turn into the naval base's main gate and the cool spring breeze flowing through my window. I turn on my indicator and check my rearview mirror. The keychain Rubik's Cube on my visor swings as I slip into the right lane. The cube becomes a stick figure, then a cube, then a stick figure again.

Okay, this is getting weird, I think. But it's not like I haven't hallucinated before. Like that one time I saw a carousel above my bed—complete with pink flying elephants and dolphins—after my 21st birthday bash at Slurwood's dive bar. I had vague memories of being carried out of the bar and into an Uber, and painfully clear memories of puking in the back seat and being tossed on the curb a quarter mile from my apartment. What hurt the most was waking up in the morning and discovering I'd left the driver a $50 tip.

I turn my thoughts to the fresh canvases waiting in my studio.

1

They've been calling my name all morning, and I can't wait to get my afternoon tutoring sessions out of the way.

A red Camaro cuts in front of me, and I slam on the brakes. I glare at the driver, and I swear he's a stick-figure alien. I want to give the driver-alien the finger, but I breathe out the anger instead.

My inner rage is long gone, but the alcoholic in me yearns for the bottle that used to live in my glove box. I try to imagine that sweet ethanol smell as I pop off the liquor bottle's cap, but all I can smell is river water and manure.

The river water makes sense, I guess—I'm a half mile from the St. John's, but *manure?*

I crank up the airflow and pass the strip mall where a mattress store has commandeered Aunt Edna's former gallery space. She always said my work would end up in a gallery someday, when I paint my "truth."

But what is my truth? Three years ago, the only truth I knew was how masterful I felt when I created whiskey-fueled paintings. I thought I was creating magnum opuses. But looking back, I see them for what they were. Competence.

Aunt Edna was right. The truth is—and still is—missing from my paintings. But what is the truth about life? That it's fast and fleeting? A cycle of heartbreak? Sure, I can paint a portrait worthy of hanging on somebody's dining room wall. But not one that will usher in a new era of art—or draw "oohs" and "aahs" at gallery openings.

Heck, they aren't worthy enough to be *in* a gallery—Aunt Edna was spot on there. Galleries don't appreciate competence. Galleries want excitement, different, edgy. Will tonight be the night that I paint an edgy masterpiece? Doubtful, given my plans for another portrait. A $500 commission for a local attorney's headshot. Hardly career-making. Maybe if I sketch a stick-figure alien and call it "Stick Figure on White," I'll make a million bucks.

What I need is a muse, although the thought of dating makes me shiver. I haven't had a date in three years, since my breakup with Rose. That disastrous Tinder date doesn't count. When she asked me if cerulean blue was a type of crab, well—I couldn't help myself. I explained to her the different blue color variations in both paintings and real life, how it was vital to understand the difference in pigment composition and chemical properties. For example, cerulean blue is made from cobalt stannite—giving it a chalky appearance, while indigo blue's molecular structure allows light to pass through. After ten minutes, she'd excused herself to go to the bathroom and never came back.

If only I could dig up some inspiration that didn't involve dating. Archimedes in his bathtub. Newton under the apple tree. Luke Campbell driving across a river.

Where the hell is that manure smell coming from?

Bohemian Rhapsody ends, and with it, my good mood. The next song is *Dream On*. Yeah, universe. I've got the message.

My Honda rumbles onto the Buckman Bridge, and I cross the St. Johns River.

I check my mirror, signal for the exit ramp, and suddenly I'm surrounded by stick figures. Dozens of them climbing into the sky, surrounding me with whirls and swirls and chalky walls and black walls and—

The drill whirs. At first, I think I've fallen asleep at the wheel and barreled into roadworks.

But that screeching, high-pitched whine is too close—inches from my face. No, *in* my face. A disinfectant tang mingles with the bitter taste of Novocain in my mouth. Yesterday's Novocain. Today's Novocain. Time fractures like light through a prism.

My body jerks in the dentist's chair, but my mind screams I'm still moving at sixty miles an hour. The vapor-white room tilts and sways like I'm hydroplaning. Yesterday—no, today—I was here, gripping these same padded armrests, tasting this same bitter tang.

The hygienist wore scrubs with bug-eyed aliens—or were they cartoon teeth?—on them. She's wearing them now. I remember commenting on them, will comment on them, am commenting on them in some bastardized time loop.

Blaring car horns. Squealing dental drills.

My stomach heaves as two realities slam into each other: the antiseptic smell of the dentist's office mixing with the scent of brackish river water. The same river that Rose and I watched the Fourth of July fireworks from three years ago, back when she still believed I could change. Back when she said my habit of shuffling my Rubik's cube was a cute idiosyncrasy and not a reason to "grow

3

up and see a goddamn shrink."

Back when she'd hold my trembling hands and tell me everything would be okay. But this isn't okay. None of this is okay.

A dental lamp glares in my eyes, too white and too harsh despite my prescription sunglasses, but my skin still feels the warmth of the sun through the windshield. The vinyl chair presses against my back, yet my foot remains suspended, pressing a gas pedal that isn't there.

Dr. Wong withdraws the drill from my mouth. "Are you in pain, Luke?" he says, voice muffled behind his mask. The same words, the same inflection as yesterday. As today. "I can give you more Novocain if you're feeling something."

More Novocain? No, this has already happened. This was yesterday morning. Oh God, I'm asleep at the wheel.

I'm going to crash. I pinch my thigh. "Wake up, wake up, wake up!"

A panic attack squeezes in my chest as my brain tries to reconcile the impossible. My heart speeds up as if I'm walking in front of a speeding city bus, about to be flattened. Cold sweat coats my body in an icy glaze. My chest constricts, and I can't breathe. I need a paper bag—like the one I hyperventilated into when Rose found my hidden bottles, or the one I was using when Aunt Edna picked me up from the King Street bar, my brain too wasted to comprehend the Uber app—again.

I scramble out of the chair, rip the rubber guard from my mouth, and toss it onto the floor. It bounces once, twice, and hits the side of a stainless-steel cabinet with a plink. The room sways like I'm drunk driving a car, swaying across lanes, and I shut one eye to focus. It doesn't work; my inner ear refuses to accept that I'm standing still and wobbles me into a vertiginous vortex of rubber room and swaying bridge. The fluorescent lights strobe, turning my surroundings into a horror movie disco.

"Luke!" Dr. Martinez steps back, drill in his hand. "What's wrong?"

The room refocuses for a split-second, throwing me into a memory of yesterday's root canal—a procedure that hasn't happened yet.

"I can't—" I grab the doorframe with one hand to steady

myself, my knuckles gripping the plastic as if I'm holding on to a ledge railing for dear life.

"I already did this. Yesterday. Today. I'm driving—" I press my other hand to my ear, trying to stop the world from spinning. I wonder if I'm drunk right now. Was that it? I'd gone to the dentist hammered, and now I'm panicking because, because...

... because the crape myrtle petals are still there, ghosting pink trails across my vision, falling through the air-conditioned office air like pink snow. They smell of spring and sunshine, of antiseptic and blood.

"Mr. Campbell, you haven't had the procedure yet," the assistant says, her cartoon-toothed scrubs mocking me with their googly eyes. "Please sit back down, we can—"

"No." I back toward the waiting room and bump into a side table. A basket of toothbrushes and dental pamphlets tumbles onto the floor. The distant clatter threads through my car radio and mixes with the refrain "Dream on, dream on, dream on..."

"No, I'm not going through this again. I need to..."

I need to wake the hell up.

I rush toward the exit, or it rushes toward me. The same potted spider plants I noticed yesterday, four dead leaves lying on the floor in exactly the same place. The same 2010 National Geographic lying on a vinyl reception chair, turned to a page with a blue iceberg.

Behind me, Dr. Martinez calls my name, but I'm already running—or driving—through the door, desperate to escape the sensation of my foot on the accelerator, sticking to me like old gum on the bottom of my shoes.

The Florida heat hits me like a sticky wall of wet cotton. The sun casts shadows that shift and warp, echoing the displacement in my brain.

A woman walks past in a polka-dot sundress I swear I just saw through my windshield. Nausea rises as I head to the street, my body still convinced it's rumbling over the Buckman.

The ABC liquor store across the street catches my eye, its neon open sign a homing beacon for my alcoholic brain. The craving swells. One drink to steady my nerves, to blot out this undecipherable morning. To blur the edges of a reality that refuses to stay in focus.

My fingers find the three-year sobriety chip in my pocket I received in March, its bronze surface warm and smooth. One thousand one hundred and fifty-seven days of meetings, of counting minor victories, of rebuilding trust. They don't mind if I talk there; at the last meeting I'd rambled on for thirty minutes about how Jack Daniels was the only thing that helped me in social situations. And living without it was like being a turtle without its shell; vulnerable, naked.

My studio. I need my peaceful studio. The one place where I can control chaos. The one place where I can scream and play Duran Duran at full blast and not have to worry about strangers attempting to fix whatever is wrong with me.

It's a fifteen-minute walk, but I take thirty because I keep stopping to press my hands against solid objects—brick walls, lampposts, crosswalk buttons—trying to convince my body that I'm not still in motion. The sidewalk under my feet feels real but looks like river water—brown and undulating. The sun shifts from midday cerulean blue to late afternoon ultramarine to nightfall indigo in the space of one footstep.

By the time I reach the converted warehouse on the outskirts of Riverside, I'm drenched in sweat. My tooth throbs in that ghostly way that happens when Novocain wears off—even though I know it shouldn't be wearing off yet. The familiar smell of oil paint and dust hits me as I unlock my studio door, telling me I'm here.

Whatever "here" means now.

Inside, Aunt Edna's half-finished portrait watches me from the easel, her knowing eyes following me across the room. I've been painting her from her last Christmas photo, capturing her warmth, the way she sat with me through those first brutal weeks of sobriety. She brought me watercolors in rehab because they wouldn't let me have oils. "Seriously?" I'd asked. "You think I'm going to sniff oil paint now?" The idea was so ludicrous, so preposterous, that I'd tried to walk out of that crazy house until Aunt Edna stopped me. "Just give it a week, for me," she'd said. "And paint what hurts." But if I don't know the cause of my current pain, how can I paint it?

I sit down on my studio stool, hands shaking as I take out my phone, canceling any tutoring sessions on my calendar. "Family emergency," I text Tommy's mom, then correct myself: "Medical emergency." Because what else is a repeated root canal on the same tooth? What else is time folding in on itself like wet toilet tissue?

I grab a fresh canvas, slam it onto the easel, and tighten the clamp. As I squeeze paint onto my palette, it transforms into motion, into fear. Cadmium red for the dentist's drill, midnight blue for the car's speed, alizarin crimson for the terror of being in two places—times?—at once. The colors mix and swirl like Slurwood's pool table used to when I drank, but this time it's my canvas that's intoxicating.

The paint flows faster than my thoughts. I blend the titanium white of the dental office into the cobalt blue of the highway. The dental chair twists into the driver's seat; the road lines warp and spiral into scalers, forceps, and suction tips. Two moments, two realities, bleeding into each other on the canvas. The crape myrtle petals become spots of blood, become stars, become moments frozen between seconds.

"I'm not crazy," I whisper to Aunt Edna's portrait, but I can't look at her critical gaze anymore. She's telling me to "Breathe, Luke, or you'll end up in a place you can't come back from." I stand up, grab her portrait, and turn her to face the wall.

As the afternoon light shifts across my studio floor, time bends. I am a man in two places at once, torn in half by two realities.

I am in a place where nothing makes sense except the way the colors collide on canvas.

TWO: EILEEN

I drum my pencil against my notebook, humming *Bohemian Rhapsody* under my breath. The tune's been stuck in my head all morning, an earworm that's coming and going with the persistence of a mosquito. I know most of the words, although I've never been a Queen fan. I guess it's just one of those songs that everyone knows, right?

My hand cramps from sketching, but it's a small price to pay for what could be a career-making discovery. I can already envision the opening of the article I'll submit to the *Journal of Archaeological Science*. Previously undocumented pre-Columbian cave art suggests more expansive migration patterns than formerly thought.

Butterflies flutter in my stomach. If these drawings are what I think they are, then a dry academic article might be the start of something much bigger. I imagine myself describing the figures on *Science Friday*, or watching a BBC crew capture the shifting patterns in HD, or standing on the red circle of a TED stage, explaining how this changes everything we know about indigenous art in the Southeast.

The limestone walls weep with humidity, each drop of condensation catching my headlamp's beam and covering the cave paintings like tiny stars.

I snap a few reference photos with my iPhone before returning to my sketches.

This ancient rock art shouldn't be here—not in Florida, not in a riverside cave system, and definitely not this well-preserved.

Bohemian Rhapsody enters my head again, Freddy Mercury singing "I will not let you go," which is rather appropriate for an earworm. They say that if you want to get rid of one, sing the entire song out loud. But I don't have five minutes and 55 seconds to waste. Every second counts here. I must get these drawings completed so that I can get back to the university on time for Professor Chen's afternoon lecture.

I wipe my graphite-streaked fingers on my Jaguars T-shirt before flipping to a fresh page in my notebook.

The figures are unlike anything I've seen in my research: outstretched forms with intricate patterns that shift in my headlamp's beam, like shadows dancing on water. Their insectile limbs possess a fluid grace that defies anatomical logic. Each six-foot-tall stick figure has a torso no wider than my wrist. The body tapers to an elongated head with no discernible features except for circular indentations where the eyes might be.

What captivates me most are the markings etched into their forms—not crude scratches, but deliberate spirals and concentric circles that radiate outward from central points on their chests. Some figures appear to be stepping through what look like doorways—or a portal not unlike the one from that old movie *Stargate*—their bodies half-dissolved as they cross a threshold into... What?

I can only guess at what these pre-Columbian drawings depict. Other caves? A peyote-induced hallucinogenic state? Time travel? I chuckle at that last absurd thought. I can visualize the polite rejection letter from the Journal.

Dear Miss Nash,

Thank you for your submission. However, our journal does not currently publish quasi-science.

Regards,

The Real Scientists.

I brush the thought away and start humming—

Oh, for goodness' sake. I sing "... da da da da you shoulda put a ring on it..." Earworm, be gone.

I return to sketching the other figures, standing with arms outstretched toward what might be stars or distant suns.

The scratch of pencil on paper echoes off the timeworn walls as I try to capture every detail before I need to leave at noon—in one hour.

As I sketch, I notice something extraordinary. From certain angles, the figures seem to overlap, creating the illusion of movement, as if they're walking forward and backward through the same space. I jot down "optical illusion" and wonder if something in the rock composition—geodes or opal perhaps— might be causing the phenomenon. It could be a trompe l'oeil, although I'm pretty sure that the concept originated in the Renaissance.

Above me, roots from live oaks pierce through the cave ceiling, their tendrils creeping down like blackened stalactites. The roots have destroyed some of the upper depictions, although there's enough on the walls to keep me sketching for a week.

The air tastes of wet earth and limestone, tinged with the mossy hint of river water. Through the cave mouth, the Suwannee flows past, its tea-colored water reflecting the harsh Florida sun. The river's unusually low level revealed this cave today, its limestone walls glowing in the reflected light. Yesterday, I'd explored a different one—a smaller, darker space where my breath had echoed off claustrophobic walls, and the only light filtering through cracks was no brighter than a candle flame.

"One more sketch," I mutter, though I've already filled six pages. My fingers are black with graphite, and my neck aches from two hours of looking up and down from my notebook.

The figures remind me of the Mississippian period pieces I'd studied during my undergrad at UF. But there's something different about them, something that makes my budding anthropologist's instincts tingle. The way the patterns flow into each other, like time-lapse photography of stars wheeling across the night sky.

I've been documenting rock art across the Southeast for three years, ever since that first field trip to Cahokia—once the largest pre-Columbian city in North America—changed the course of my studies. But these drawings are different. The drawings in Cahokia depicted symbols and patterns, but these... these tell a story.

I pack up my supplies with care, each item going into its designated pocket in my waterproof bag—a habit drilled into me by four years of fieldwork and one lost iPhone. I shouldn't have replaced it on my broke-ass student budget, but I need a high-definition camera to capture minute details.

The cave mouth frames a perfect view of my paddleboard, its

blue and white hull tethered where the water has retreated to expose limestone. Spanish moss drapes the cypress trees like gray curtains, swaying in the afternoon breeze. An osprey calls somewhere upstream, its cry echoing off the water.

Standing, I duck under a low overhang, my boots splashing through the water. Suddenly, a wave of vertigo hits. I steady myself against the rock and wait for the pressure in my head to subside. I've had dizzy spells before, thanks to my breakfast-skipping habit, but never one like this. It's like I'm falling, swirling in space, seeing quadruple.

Something is wrong, very wrong—a blood clot? Stroke? But then, minutes, seconds, hours later, the cave comes back into focus.

And the drawings have disappeared.

I blink hard, my heart hammering against my ribs. The wall where I'd spent the last hour sketching stares back at me, smooth and blank as a blank page of paper. No figures. No patterns. Nothing but natural ridges in the rock, worn smooth by millennia of floodwaters.

"What the..." I fumble for my notebook, nearly dropping it in my haste. The pages I'd just filled are blank. Not torn out, but blank, as if I'd never even opened it.

The cave feels wrong, like a familiar room viewed through a periscope. It's smaller, with the ceiling lower, the walls closer. Darker too, like the cave I'd been in yesterday, a half mile further downstream. But even if I had somehow paddled back there without realizing—what was it called when drivers zone out on highways? Autopilot? It was the same, but wrong. Like when you come home and someone's moved all your furniture an inch to the left, or the way my apartment felt after Tarik moved out, taking half our shared belongings with him.

For a time, I thought he could be The One. But now I realize that not only was he definitely *not* The One, but that the idea of another half being out there waiting to be discovered is nothing more than a foolish Hollywood fantasy, fueled by too many late nights eating raspberry white chocolate Häagen-Dazs while crying over *Notting Hill*. But who am I kidding? I still get the sense that he's out there, somewhere—

What am I thinking?

I'm ankle-deep in water in a cave that's all wrong, and I'm daydreaming about Mr. Right? I should slap myself.

I stumble toward the entrance, my head swimming. Too much time in the dark, I tell myself. Too much sun earlier. Maybe mild dehydration—I'd only drunk half my water bottle, too excited by the discovery to remember basic field safety. I had—highway hypnosis, that was it—and I'd paddled back to Monday's cave without remembering, that was all.

But as I emerge into the sunlight, something else nags at me. The water level looks different. Higher. Like it was... yesterday. A great blue heron stands motionless in the shallows where bare limestone had been exposed just moments ago. It regards me with knowing eyes before taking flight, its wings casting rippling shadows across the water. Didn't I see this same bird in the same place yesterday, outside the smaller cave?

My phone shows 11:00 AM. Same as it did when I first entered the cave. But that's not possible—I'd been sketching for at least an hour, watching the sun's angle change through the cave mouth, marking the passage of time like the indigenous peoples might have done centuries ago. I stare at the phone, wondering if I've missed daylight savings. Or crossed into the Central Time Zone. Both thoughts are illogical, and yet I can't think of anything else that could explain my phone displaying the wrong time.

I grab my paddleboard's tether, my academic mind kicking into gear. The evidence doesn't lie—or in this case, the lack of it. My phone shows the same time, as if that hour of sketching and photography never happened. The water level is as I remember from yesterday's paddle, down to the way it laps against the base of the limestone in little wavelets that sound like whispered secrets. Even the protein bar I always bring—and distinctly remember shoving into my pocket—is back in my bag.

My body tells the same story. That ache in my shoulders from sketching? Gone? My aching wrist? No longer aching.

"Okay," I say, forcing myself to focus on my breaths, the way Professor Chen taught me during a panic attack before my first major presentation. I need to approach this systematically.

I pull out my phone and will my shaking hands to steady. I go back inside the cave to photograph the wall—the blank wall I know, with absolute certainty, was covered in ancient art just moments ago. Then I photograph the water level, the surrounding rock formations, every detail that might help me figure out what happened here.

Back outside, I ease up onto my board. The late-morning heat presses down as I paddle to the other cave. I halt after two strokes, disoriented and uncertain if I should paddle downstream or upstream.

I glance around and see the tire swing hanging over the water, full of laughing teenagers who were there yesterday. A blonde-haired girl in a hot pink bikini screams as a skinny boy with too-large trunks pushes the tire out over the water. She screams back at the boy, "Danny, you do that again and tell your momma about your hash stash."

It's the same scene as yesterday. A visual earworm? Is that even a thing?

I realize I am not in the new cave with drawings. I'm back at the smaller cave. The caves must share a passage. I must have walked from one to another in the dark without realizing it, like the time I lost my way in the Mammoth Cave system during my first year of grad school.

But that didn't explain the kids on the tire swing, the empty pages in my notebook, or the way my muscles don't remember an hour of sketching.

Professor Chen told me on my first day in Advanced Archaeological Methods: "History isn't just about what happened—it's about proving what happened." Her words had gotten me through countless research dead ends and helped me with pottery shard assembly, carbon dating, and turning site surveys into coherent narratives about the past.

But what do I do if I don't know what happened?

My hands tremble as I dip the paddle into the water and turn my board around. I need to get back to my car and to campus. I need to research if there have been other reports of... what? Caves that act like wormholes? Cave-induced visual earworms? Temporal anomalies surrounding the Suwannee? The thought feels absurd, but I allow my brain to entertain all possibilities—just like I do when examining an artifact, considering whether a mark is a symbol, a geometric shape, or scratch marks from the passage of time.

As I paddle back to my car, one thought keeps circling through my mind like the osprey overhead: what if I'm not the only one? What if someone else has experienced a jump in time? And if they have, how would I even find them? Reddit perhaps? An obscure blog? The dark web? I don't have a clue.

At least Bohemian Rhapsody has gone.

But then, in pops another earworm. It's another tune, one I'm less familiar with. The words aren't there, except for two words, which must be the chorus—dream on—and I hum the melody. I stop paddling, turning my head toward the sound of...

A drill?

But as I listen closer, it's just the cicadas doing their thing.

I dunk my paddle into the water and glide forward, my mind cycling through unanswered questions: what just happened to me in that cave? Who created those drawings that now exist only in my memory? And most importantly—will they reappear tomorrow, or have I crossed a threshold that can't be uncrossed?

I paddle toward campus with one certainty forming like bedrock: I need to go back to that cave tomorrow when the water is—hopefully—low again. Whatever's happening, the evidence is there—even if it's evidence of my own unraveling.

THREE: LUKE

The canvas won't stop moving.

I've been painting all afternoon, struggling to capture reality splitting apart. The familiar, citrusy scent of the solvent reminds me of the smell of whiskey, and I make a mental note to buy a bottle of odorless solvent as soon as possible. I don't need that reminder, not now when that craving is a hairsbreadth away from blooming into a full-blown need.

Three years since my last drink, only to trade one kind of reality distortion for another. Back then, I drank to blur the edges of the world. Now the world blurs on its own, without my permission.

I should call my sponsor, Greg, but he's at work. Later, after dinner. If I still have an itch.

The dental chair twists through the center of the composition like a tornado, with chrome and leather swirling together like Yin and Yang. My brushstrokes are frantic, desperate—nothing like my usual careful attention to light and shadow. Cadmium red bleeds into cerulean blue, colors I never use together. They don't complement each other, but they capture the violent collision of this morning. Tomorrow morning? I wonder what will happen when I drive over the Buckam bridge tomorrow. I have no intention of finding out. If I don't disappear halfway across the span, I'll have a panic attack.

So, no. Tomorrow I'm staying here in my studio to finish this piece. It's calling my name, begging me for completion.

Around the dentist's chair, I've painted morning light fracturing into afternoon shadows, then back again. I use color combinations that shouldn't work but do: dioxazine purple for shifting time, lime green for nausea and displacement, metallic silver for the cold steel of dental instruments.

The paint is thick, impasto, built up in layers that mirror the way reality stacks upon itself. I've never painted like this before. I've never needed to with portraiture or still life. But thin layers of safe, traditional colors such as Payne's gray and buff titanium couldn't capture reality tearing apart at the seams, then reassembling itself.

I layer transparent glazes over opaque chunks of paint, creating a depth that pulls the viewer in like the vertigo that keeps hitting me in waves. My brush moves faster than logical thought, translating fractured moments into imagery. The dental light becomes a twisted sun, its beam refracting through the shattered moments of my day. The late morning sunlight from my drive bleeds through the harsh fluorescents of the dental office, creating unreal shadows that my hands somehow know how to capture.

I pause for a sip of water from my mug as another wave of vertigo hits. The room spins so violently that if I were standing instead of sitting, I would have fallen to the floor. The smell of manure is so strong I look down at my feet to see if I've lost control of my bowels. But all I see is a dirt road...

I slap my cheek.

... a paint-splattered wood floor.

Once the vertigo has passed, I swear I hear the clop of hooves.

I grab my phone. Its screen is smudged with paint fingerprints.

Within five minutes, my internet search history looks like a cry for help: "time perception disorders," "schizoid episodes," "sudden memory distortions."

The more I read, the more my stomach knots. Early-onset schizophrenia. Temporal lobe epilepsy. Dissociative identity disturbance with comorbid depersonalization-derealization features. The words blur together like wet paint, each diagnosis more terrifying than the last. According to what I'm reading on the Mayo Clinic's website, the last term sounds like the most likely suspect.

Do I feel as if I'm seeing my actions, feelings, thoughts, and self from a distance, like I'm watching a movie? Check.

Am I experiencing the feeling that other people and things are separate from me and seem foggy or dreamlike? Check.

Is time slowing down or speeding up? Check.

There are multiple versions of me living simultaneously. Which "Luke" am I now? Is there another Luke who lived the next 24 hours? Another Luke who's currently enjoying a stiff drink? A Luke who believes he is sane? And is his name even Luke? Is there a Pat, Paul or Peter hiding in the recesses of my brain, waiting for their turn to shine?

Great. Three years sober, and now my mind disintegrates into a textbook case of dissociative pathology.

The irony would be funny if it weren't so terrifying.

I put my cup down and sit in front of my easel, reaching for a small brush to add highlights to the dental tools. The memory of them gleaming under the harsh light is so vivid—will be so vivid?—that I catch my breath when I realize the tools are so perfectly rendered that I could almost grab one and pick it up from the canvas.

Paint drips onto the floor, adding to the Jackson Pollock landscape under my easel. The splatter pattern reminds me of the way time seemed to spray outward when reality cracked, and I stare at it, lost in the chaos of—

A knock at the door makes me jump. My brush flies out of my hand and skitters across the paint-splashed floor. It leaves a smear of white as it slides, like a comet trail through my personal universe of madness.

"Luke? You in there?"

I open the door to find Kristy leaning against the frame, clipboard in hand. Her grease-splattered maintenance uniform mirrors the chaos on my studio floor.

Kristy has known me since before sobriety, before Aunt Edna's death, before everything. The sight of her should be comforting. Instead, I break into a cold sweat. I'm behind on my rent.

Yesterday afternoon—which, if I'm correct, is now today—I avoided her, knowing I was short on rent. My intention was to catch her after tomorrow's—today's—tutoring sessions. If she were to ask me how much money was in my wallet, I'd say, *not the first clue, hon.* I just hope that whatever money I have is still there and not scattered around the dentist's waiting room floor, a windfall for those left in the wake of my hasty retreat.

"Hey, sorry, I know you're working, but—" She stops mid-sentence, eyes fixed on the canvas behind me. "Holy cannoli."

"I know it's different," I say, reaching for my wallet even as she moves past me into the studio. The leather is warm and solid in my hands, grounding me in this moment—at least, I think it's this moment. I open the wallet, and there are six crisp fifty-dollar bills.

I breathe a sigh of relief. "I can get you the rest of the rent tomorrow after my—"

I stop, my brain stuttering over the word "tomorrow." What is tomorrow anymore? The concept feels as twisted as the chair in my painting, as fractured as my sense of now and then. Is this the "now" when I've already handed over the cash, or is this the "then" where I've already done it?

"Luke, this is... visceral. Honest." Kristy tilts her head, stepping closer to the painting.

The motion reminds me of how the dentist had tilted his head, examining my temporary filling. Will examine? Has examined? My temples throb.

"What happened to Aunt Edna's portrait?" she asks.

"I'm taking a break."

"Break? This is a demolition." Kristy gestures at the new canvas, her hand tracing the air in front of it as if she can feel the turbulence I've captured. "The way these lines pull apart but stay connected... and these colors. I've never seen you use colors like this before." Her voice holds a note of concern beneath the amazement. She's known me too long not to notice when something's off.

The dental chair in the painting spins faster under her gaze. The paint is still wet enough to catch the afternoon light in a way that makes it appear to move. Or maybe that's just my head spinning. Again. The room tilts, and I fight the urge to check if I'm still in the car, still in the dentist's chair, still anywhere but here.

"Keep going," she says, ignoring the cash I'm holding out like a shield against her scrutiny. "This one's a masterpiece. Dark as hell, but a masterpiece. It's like... like being in two places at once."

My laugh comes out so shaky it's bordering on hysteria. The truth of her observation hits close to home, like a pick scraping against an exposed nerve in my molar. "Yeah, that's... that's kind of what I was going for."

I press my back against the wall, needing its solidity. The rough texture of the brick catches on my shirt, anchoring me in space if not in time. At least, I hope I'm me. I hope I'm not Pat, Phil, or Peter. "Listen, about the rent—"

"Right, sorry." She takes the cash, thumbing through it with paint-stained fingers. "You're short."

"Fifty. I know. I've got students tomorrow, I'll get it to you then?" The words come out as a question, and that's exactly what it is. I may or may not be here tomorrow. But wherever I am, I hope I'm not sitting in an endodontist's chair on Monday morning at 11 a.m.

I could give her the $47 cash I have in my wallet's zipper, but I'll need that for gas. I say goodbye to the Chipotle veggie bowl I was looking forward to for dinner.

But is that $47 in there? I don't want to check in front of Kristy. If it isn't there, I'll be raiding my penny jar again.

"It's fine. Just don't leave me hanging this time." She makes a note on her clipboard and then looks back at the painting. "Seriously though, whatever inspired this? Hold on to it. This work will sell."

Sell? What does that even mean when "selling" is something that happens in linear time? Paint. Gallery. Opening. Sell.

I think I'm losing my mind, I want to tell her. I think time shattered and took my sanity with it. I think I'm trapped in a loop of root canals and reality shifts, and the only way I can make sense of it is with paint and canvas.

Instead, I just say, "Thanks. I'll have the fifty tomorrow." The promise feels hollow, considering I'm not even sure tomorrow exists anymore.

After she leaves, I think about the certainty of the Mayo article, the way it packaged my incomprehensible experience into neat diagnostic boxes.

I have dissociative-identity-perception whatever it was. And I wonder when Pat or Jim-Bob or whoever is going to take over my mind again and hijack my day.

FOUR: EILEEN

The university library's fourth floor is almost empty this time of day—that dead zone between afternoon classes and evening study sessions. A few scattered students hunch over their laptops, faces illuminated by blue light. The familiar smell of old books usually calms me, but today it just reminds me of all the hours I've spent here researching pre-Columbian art patterns, searching in vain for something I might have missed.

I know I won't find answers here, but heading out to the caves at dusk would be foolish during prime mosquito and alligator feeding time. Besides, my head isn't in the right space to face those caves again today.

The plastic chair digs into my spine like a rock outcropping. Fluorescent lights flicker overhead—classic sci-fi horror movie warning. Except this time, they're flickering after the scare.

After I discovered today is yesterday.

Time isn't just broken; apparently, it's running backward.

I find precisely zilch about temporal anomalies on Google, though what exactly am I supposed to search for? Time distortions in Florida caves? Chronological displacement on the Suwannee? I time-traveled in Florida? Anyone looking over my shoulder would probably speed-dial the men in white coats.

I consider posting on Reddit, but cringe imagining the replies.

No, but I was abducted by aliens.

Yesss! Wanna see my tardis?

You kidding you nutjob?

This can't have happened just to me. Others must be out there. Maybe I should scrawl stick-figure time travelers around town with my number? Right—because nothing says "stable archaeologist" like paranormal graffiti and a direct line to my phone. Hello, felony charges, goodbye PhD.

Professor Chen would be disappointed if she knew how quickly I'd abandoned empirical observation for wild speculation.

So, what do I know for sure? Missing time, missing data, and potentially missing marbles. My internet search history reads like a PhD candidate's spiral into despair: "psychological effects of confined spaces," "factors affecting time perception," "neurological responses to dark environments."

The more I read, the tighter my stomach knots. Oxygen deprivation. Sensory deprivation hallucinations. Stress-induced cognitive distortion. The terms blur like sediment in disturbed water, each explanation breeding more questions. Three years of stress-inducing grad research, and now my mind fractures?

I could call Sandy, my counselor, but what would I even say? I think I'm having a Groundhog Day moment. Or I just lost a day of my life, literally, as in rewound 24 hours. Or how about I've spent the last day looking for fellow time travelers?

Counselors, by law, only press the panic button under a narrow set of circumstances: harm to self, harm to others, or delusions of time travel.

Yeah, nope. I'm not calling Sandy.

I close the browser, look over my shoulder, and refocus on my notes.

I spread my research materials across the study carrel: primary sources on the left, supporting documentation on the right, field notes centered. I arrange the photos I took of the empty cave wall, placing them next to my blank waterproof notebook.

I filled the notebook with sketches just hours ago. If I jumped back in time a day, then did the notebook jump back in time too? I realize the absurdity of my thought process—not just time travelers now, but time traveling notebooks—and cut it off before it takes root.

My phone buzzes with a text from Mr. Ed, my landlord. I tap the screen.

"When can I expect your rent check?"

I frown. But I paid him, didn't I? I try to remember—then check my banking app. Not only did I not pay him, but my balance is a lot lower than I thought.

How did I spend so much this month? I don't remember.

But then I do.

I thought I had extra money from my stipend, so I'd foolishly dropped over $500 at REI on a new paddling outfit, a waterproof bag, and water shoes. What had I been thinking?

I type back, "Sorry, I'll send you $900 right now. Can I get the last $50 to you next week?"

That would leave me with $47 in my bank account for gas and food. Doable, but definitely no wiggle room for Chipotle takeout.

The three dots appear in the chat, lingering for what feels like an eternity.

"Sure."

I exhale, put my phone back on the desk, and try to focus.

I push my waterproof notebook to the side and open my phone's Photos app. As I scroll through them, part of me isn't surprised to find that all the photos of the cave drawings have disappeared.

For a second—not even that, maybe a picosecond or a nanosecond or some other tiny unit of time that makes me not sound like I've completely lost my mind—the most rational explanation is that someone hacked my phone. No, not just any someone. Someone with access to my phone. Someone in the government.

I place my phone down like it's on fire. It hits the carrel with a thwack. A couple of students look my way and before I can allow myself to think they're CIA or FBI or DOGE or whatever government entity is responsible for investigating space aliens, I stand up and stretch.

Because that seems like the sanest thing to do.

I flop back into the chair. Focus, Eileen, focus.

I breathe in deeply and count to five, then exhale and count to five. Inhale, exhale, until I feel as centered as I'm going to get. Then I open my notebook and start writing what I know.

Yesterday—or is it today?—I'd explored the cave system a quarter mile downstream from where I found the drawings. The water level had been higher then, hiding the second cave entrance.

Or had the water been lower yesterday?

I chew the end of my pen, a nervous habit I adopted in grade school and never grew out of. During exam weeks, I chomp through a dozen pens. The one currently in my mouth might last five minutes.

Is this what's happening to me? A bad case of stress?

Sure, stress can make you lose track of time—like when I greeted Tarik at my door in pajamas, having forgotten our birthday dinner plans at the Skywalk. God, that had been mortifying. Three years together, and I'd stood there in my worn Florida Gators pajamas, while he'd been dressed for the nicest restaurant in Jacksonville, birthday flowers in hand.

But losing track of a day differs from having one rewind entirely. Isn't it?

"Think like a historian," I say, Professor Chen's favorite mantra steadying my racing thoughts.

I can still see her writing it on the whiteboard that first day of Archeological Methods, her precise handwriting emphasizing each word. Field research 101: return to the site. Document everything. Establish a timeline. The same process whether you're dating stone tools or proving you're not losing your mind.

My phone shows 6:47 PM. The LED screen's harsh glare reminds me of my headlamp reflecting off the cave walls—walls that had been covered in drawings that now exist only in my memory. If time has reversed, and if it really is Monday, then the drawings will be in the upstream cave tomorrow when the water recedes late morning.

I close my notebook. I'm not getting anywhere here. I should review my notes and prepare to defend my thesis research choice about the connection between river trade routes and artistic development in pre-contact Florida. Instead, I'm about to risk my academic standing to chase vanishing cave drawings.

The elongated forms, the shifting patterns—they'd reminded me of something I'd seen in my pre-Columbian art research, something from that semester I spent studying Mississippian symbolic systems. The memory, elusive and just beyond my grasp, is like a word stuck on the tip of my tongue.

The drawings had been in the upstream cave, the one revealed by the abnormally low water levels. And I know that location matters as much as timing. Context is everything in archaeology—

the difference between a significant find and a meaningless piece of rock.

My phone buzzes—an early reminder for tomorrow's lecture. The device skitters across the carrel like a water bug on the river's surface. Another absence and Professor Chen will drop my grade, no matter how good my thesis might be. The same professor who wrote my glowing recommendation for the summer research grant, who defended my choice to focus on river-based trade networks when the department chair suggested I stick to safer topics. But as I start to pack up, sliding my water-stained field journal into my bag, a snippet of conversation from a passing group of students catches my attention.

"—it's a bit derivative—"

"—like he's painting a breakdown—"

But when I look around to see who's chattering in the library, there's no one there.

A shiver runs down my spine. Is this the universe telling me I'm having a breakdown?

No, it can't be that. Something about those words is familiar, like I've heard that conversation before. But then again, it could have been an auditory hallucination, that seems more rational. Or could it have been a coincidence? There's a pattern here, I know it, and I just have to find its primer.

A primer is the key to understanding sites, artifacts, or cultural patterns—much like how a cluster of trade beads or ornaments can reveal historical trade routes, or how recurring symbols across different regions can suggest long-distance cultural contact.

But right now, physical evidence takes priority. Primers can wait. I need to plan, document whatever I find—or don't find—in that second cave.

The strap of my field bag settles across my shoulder as I stand. I run through a mental checklist for tomorrow morning. Extra batteries for my headlamp, backup phone charger, granola bars, bottled water.

Professor Chen always says every piece of historic art tells a story if you know how to read it. Her voice in my head steadies me as I head for the stairs, my footsteps echoing in the library's cavernous quiet. But first, you must know where—and when—to look for it.

I know the where, but whether I have the "when" pinned down—well, that's another matter entirely.

The setting sun streams through the library's west windows, casting long shadows across the floor. Tomorrow, I'll either prove I'm not crazy, or I'll have to accept that my career in archaeology is ending before it's begun. Either way, I need to approach this like any other field research: with methodology, documentation, and the systematic attitude that got me this far.

Even if what I'm documenting might unravel everything I thought I knew about time itself.

FIVE: LUKE

I'm cleaning my brushes with a borrowed bottle of Klean-Strip odorless mineral spirits when the world shifts.

The morning light stretches and warps, then snaps like a string on a spinning top, bringing with a dizzying wave of vertigo. I am surrounded by the smell of manure, mint mouthwash, and pine air freshener—a stomach-churning combination that makes reality speed up around me.

When my world stops revolving, I'm standing in front of Aunt Edna's portrait. But instead of facing the wall as I left it, it's on my easel. I stare at the charcoal outline. White canvas dominates, accusing me with its emptiness.

No. No, no, no.

I stumble back, knocking over the jar of clean brushes. They clatter across the floor, spattering water across my sneakers.

My hands grip the easel, my knuckles white as I glare at the canvas. The past is changing behind me. Or the present is rewriting itself. Or, more likely, I have that condition the rehab doctor warned me about. It can persist even when sober. What was it called? Alcohol something psychosis. Withdrawal? Related? Doesn't matter.

Hallucinations. Paranoia. Fear. Check, check, check.

But I never had that condition in rehab, did I? Or if I did, would I forget I had it?

No, this is something different. It's that... whatever that dissociative identity thing was. Pat or Paul or Jim Bob or whoever has been controlling my brain and—

My fingertips clutch my AA chip in my pocket. Three years since Rose left, since Aunt Edna helped me into rehab, since I promised myself "never again." The metal is cool and solid and is possibly the only real thing in this room.

The twisting time painting I finished this morning—will finish?—is gone, taking with it the cerulean blue, the ultramarine, the indigo, the cadmium reds of my magnum opus.

I scan my studio in a panic. It must be here. My realism pieces hang on the walls—a landscape of the beach, a study of bald cypress knees, and a portrait of the city mayor. All meticulous studies of light and shadow. Empty canvases line the top of a hanging shelf. Cardboard tubes and boxes lay in a pile in the corner.

I must have put it in my car's trunk. The logic of this thought escapes me, and I can't think of one good reason why I'd stash it there, but it has to be somewhere.

I grab my car keys. I'm heading for the door when my phone chimes with a cheesy bar of *Monster Mash*. Kristy had put it there as a joke on our coffee break last Halloween.

But I'd changed it back the next day to *Beethoven's Fifth*.

I stop dead in my tracks and hold up my phone.

October. But not October ahead. October behind. Five months ago. Before I got that ticket for running a stop sign on New Year's Day, before my molar started throbbing in February, before I disappeared over the Buckman Bridge, before I started Googling "Am I insane quiz" at 3 a.m.

A laugh bubbles up from somewhere dark and hysterical, tasting of last night's egg salad sandwich and fear. Now I understand why Van Gogh cut off his ear. He kept jumping through time until all he could see were cobalt blue swirling skies and distorted chrome-yellow sunflowers. Maybe he had a Jules or Victor or Willem stealing time when he wasn't hallucinating his distorted bedroom in Arles.

The abrupt sense of not belonging in this place—this time, this space—brings on a wave of vertigo again, not dissimilar to the ones I used to get ten shots into the night. I need a doctor. But what kind?

I run through the options, my mind racing like it did in early sobriety. Psychiatrist? Neurologist? Brain tumor specialist? The endodontist's lamp burns behind my eyes, the manure stench clogs my nostrils, the liquor store's neon open sign calls my name.

I should call my sponsor. And say what? *Hey Greg, I think I'm a time traveler.* He'd say, *Hang on, buddy, while he dials for the men in white coats.* Or worse, he'd call—what's that government agency that deals with weird stuff? The FBI? No, that's too normal. NASA? The ones who confiscate moon rocks? Wait—does Homeland Security have a time travel division?

I hesitate, then book an appointment with an online crisis counselor instead. Because I'm having a crisis, right? If I look up "crisis" in the counselor's handbook, I'm pretty sure that it would say, *"The patient believes they are experiencing ten different realities at once and they are about to completely lose their shit."*

My I-Phone screen blurs as I book an online session with TheInstantCounselor.com. But what exactly would I say to a counselor? *Hi, I'm Luke, three years sober, and I think I'm a time traveler?* Would that be a one-way ticket to a padded room? Or was that only if I threatened to hurt myself? I've worked too hard for my sobriety to risk being medicated into oblivion. So yeah, no. I'll stick to symptoms.

My phone buzzes, the vibration jarring against the wooden table.

"Mr. Campbell, where are U?"

Jenny. My high school art student, with her endless questions about perspective and metaphor. We were supposed to meet at Panera—five months ago. The memory of cinnamon buns mingles with manure mingles with minty mouthwash mingles with—

I slap my cheek and think of the monks who slap themselves. Great, I'm a flagellant now. Might as well shave my head, put on the robe, and head for the airport to sing Hare Krishna.

I type back, fingers trembling. "Sorry, medical emergency. Let's reschedule for next Monday, k?"

But would next Monday arrive? Or would I keep sliding between moments like wet paint on canvas?

Oddly, I find myself looking forward to the crisis counselor session in 24 hours. Maybe they can help me make sense of this without concluding I'm having an episode of post-alcohol dementia or whatever that disease was.

I need to calm myself. I need to paint.

My hands are shaking as I reach for a new canvas. I know with sudden clarity that the Fracture piece is not in the trunk of my car. It's in my head, and I must paint it. The image burns in my memory like an afterimage of the sun, demanding to be made real.

The door creaks—that distinctive squeal that Kristy keeps promising to fix.

"Luke? You okay in there?"

Kristy pokes her head in, frowning at the scattered brushes on the floor.

When I see her, I jerk forward in surprise, jabbing a glob of red paint on my jeans.

It's Kristy. But not the Kristy who just praised my new style, calling it "visceral" and "a masterpiece." This Kristy has longer hair, falling past her shoulders in natural brown waves, and she hasn't bleached it yet. This Kristy is still smiling because I haven't fallen behind on my rent. Yet.

"I'm fine." My voice cracks like antique paint. "Just... working through some stuff."

The concern in her eyes reminds me of Aunt Edna in those final days, when she told me to "paint what hurts, then what heals."

"You sure? You look a little..."

"Stressed," I finish for her. "Just stressed. Trying something new." The lie tastes like gym socks in my mouth. No, it tastes like mint mouthwash and manure, and if Kristy—with her pressed lips and time-reversed hair—wasn't standing there, I might have slapped myself again.

Although clearly, slapping my face did not work. The only thing that keeps my sanity from fragmenting into a million pieces across time is this canvas. And Kristy is preventing me from painting on it. I stare at her with my best get-the-hell-out look. All artists have perfected that look. It's like Navajo Code Talk but with glares. I raise a brow. I'm in the zone.

"Okay..." she says, retreating toward the door. "Here if you want to chat, alright? I'm taking a coffee break in an hour."

I wave her away, the gesture too sharp, too jerky. I love Kristy. She's ten years older than me and fifty times wiser. My aunt's friend's daughter, we practically grew up together, and she's a tortured artist as well.

There's never been any romantic stuff there. I suspect Kristy is, well, not into guys, but she doesn't seem to be into anyone. And she certainly isn't into me. We are coffee mates and Jags fans in the nosebleeds, which is all we can afford. And up until a few years ago, we were "baby" buddies. That's what we called the gallon of Jack Daniels we used to buy. A baby. But Kristy stopped drinking before me, and God love her, she got Aunt Edna to nudge me in that direction too.

After she leaves, I press my palms against my temples, trying to hold my fragmenting thoughts together.

"I'm losing my mind," I say to Aunt Edna's unfinished portrait, her charcoal eyes boring into me.

Maybe losing my mind is what it takes to paint time coming apart at the seams. Maybe Van Gogh saw the fractures too—translating them into swirling skies and twisted beds, every moment bleeding into the next until cutting off an ear seemed perfectly reasonable.

I should be panicking. First, slapping my cheek. Then, amputating a body part.

My mind meanders through the logistics of ear amputation. Palette knife? Too blunt. Metal ruler? Not sharp enough. X-Acto knife? Too small. How the heck does an artist cut his own ear off? I seem to recall that Van Gogh had used a razor, but I'm pretty sure that Walgreens only sells safety razors. And if I'm to follow in his footsteps, then I must also locate a local brothel and a maid called Rachel to hand the severed ear to.

I chuckle, wondering if Kristy is standing outside the door listening to manic laughter.

While my brain ponders the issue of how much ear cutting would be considered a bona fide amputation—a lobe? An inch? Half?—my hands are instinctively creating the background on canvas. My brush drags cerulean through crimson, carving depth with strokes that feel like second nature.

And that's the part that stops me cold.

Because this isn't just instinct.

This is certainty.

I didn't develop this style through years of struggle. I didn't push through failures, slowly refining my technique. One day, I was a realist. The next, I was painting fractured time.

My chest tightens as the realization sinks in. My art isn't just changing. Time isn't changing.

I'm changing. I have changed.

The strokes I'm making now? They didn't come from me. Not the version of me that existed yesterday—or seven months in the future, which is technically the same thing now. I didn't learn this. It was given to me. Dumped into my brain like a memory from a life I haven't lived yet.

I stare at the wet paint, my heartbeat loud in my ears. This isn't just about art. This is about something bigger.

If time is rewriting me—if my hands know things before I do—what else will time reconstruct?

SIX: EILEEN

I paddle along the Suwannee as the sun climbs higher in the morning sky. The river's surface sparkles, alive with a shoal of redbreast sunfish, but I keep my focus on the limestone outcroppings.

I've secured my camera in my dry bag, along with my notebook, still missing the sketches from yesterday—or was it today? Professor Chen's lecture isn't until 3:30 p.m.—plenty of time to document everything properly, to follow the meticulous methodology that she's drilled into me since my first year: "Context is everything, Eileen. Location, preservation, surrounding features—document it all."

The academic part of my brain—the part that's earned a 4.0 GPA and chose to spend her twenty-fifth birthday analyzing cave sediment patterns rather than having dinner with her boyfriend— keeps trying to rationalize yesterday's experience. Top of my list: stress-induced fugue state, dehydration, something involving the cave's air composition. But none of those theories explain my blank notebook or my rewound day.

I shake my head. The emotional part of my brain tells me that what I'm doing here is pure insanity. I should have hightailed it to Sandy's office instead of risking another Groundhog Day.

Isn't a persistent angel vs. devil battle in the brain yet another sign that something's not quite right upstairs? I take a deep breath and concentrate on my paddle strokes, my posture, anything but hypothetical what-ifs.

The water level is still unusually low, exposing the cave entrance ahead. Its black mouth, tangled with dangling roots, reminds me of the Tunnel of Terror ride my gran had taken me on when I was nine. I'd screamed and flailed so hard at that gaping mouth with its crazed eyes and rotten teeth that Gran had to hold me down to keep me from jumping out. "It's okay to be scared, sweetie," she'd said. "I'm scared too, and sometimes scary can be fun. Just wait and see."

Well, I wasn't scared yesterday, but now as I tie the board to a tree stump, my sweat-covered hands are trembling.

A mild electric current tingles in the air, and there are goosebumps on my arms. It's nerves, Eileen, that's all, I tell myself. But I look around for a DANGER ELECTRICAL LINE sign anyway.

There are no signs, but I notice the water glows cerulean blue today, vibrant against the dull limestone. I recognize that specific shade from somewhere—Art 101, perhaps? The memory surfaces: cerulean blue originated in 1860. Strange how memory works. I don't remember what I ate for dinner last night, but I can recall the exact birthdate of an esoteric paint pigment. Go figure.

Deep breaths. Check knot. Adjust dry bag. Test headlamp. The familiar routine brings my stress level down a notch.

Time to face my fears. I switch on my headlamp.

I duck inside and wade through six inches of water until I reach the main chamber. My breath catches when I see them: elongated figures with intricate patterns, exactly as I remembered. Not a hallucination, then.

The figures dance across the limestone walls, their designs unlike anything in my thesis research on Southeastern cave art. They remind me of Mississippian-era motifs, but the odd proportions make my archaeological instincts buzz with excitement alongside that ever-present unease.

I pull out my phone and photograph every inch of the wall, each image a piece of evidence I can't lose again. The camera's flash illuminates details I missed before—spiraling patterns that suggest movement, flowing like time made visible.

But is this an exercise in futility? No. I'm simply repeating an experiment to see if I get the same result. If I exit the cave into yesterday again—well, nothing bad happened apart from a healthy dose of vertigo. And if it does happen again, I'll need to try a different approach.

My phone buzzes against my hip, and I almost drop my phone.

It's Professor Chen.

Maybe it's news about my thesis. I double-tap to activate my earbuds.

"Eileen? Got a minute?"

"Of course."

"Listen, there's been a scheduling change. The department wants to move up thesis defenses this semester. You'll need to present three weeks earlier than planned."

My free hand clenches into a fist. "Three weeks? But I'm still finalizing my research on—"

"I know it's not ideal, but everyone's in the same boat. We can discuss it more in class today." She pauses, and I can hear the concern in her voice, the same tone she used after my breakup with Tarik. "You are coming to class today? I don't want to have to drop your grade."

"Yes, absolutely. I'll be there." If I'm not time-warped back to yesterday.

After we hang up, I return to my photographing with renewed urgency. Less time to prepare means I need every scrap of research I can get. If I can prove the drawings are real, if I can document them properly before they vanish again...

The cave air presses against me, thick and damp. The spirals carved into the stone seem to shift in the beam of my headlamp, like the memory itself: out of place, out of time.

I put my camera away, pull out my notebook, and start sketching.

I've drawn one line on the paper when the air pressure changes, like the lull before a storm. Static charges the cave atmosphere. No, it's not the cave that's static. It's me. My stomach heaves as I stagger toward the cave entrance, remembering yesterday's displacement. If I can make it back to my board before—

The world tilts then whirls around me—a Mad Tea Party Ride on water. My head pounds—like the worst caffeine headache ever—and suddenly the humid cave air turns cool. The silence breaks. Clicks. Murmurs. Voices from somewhere.

When the world comes into focus, I'm standing next to an unfamiliar cave wall. I press my hand against the cool rock, trying to steady myself. But it isn't a cave wall. It's the university library wall, with a sheet of paper with an arrow pointing the way to Study Room B.

I yank out my phone and stare at my screen in disbelief. It's 11:47 a.m., October 31st.

Five months ago.

My breath comes in short gasps as I scan the library. Students sitting in carrels, rolling carts with stacks of returned books, a bulletin board with campus flyers. All normal, except... it's five months ago.

Not 24 hours ago. Not a Groundhog Day ago where I fine tune my experiment. It's five months ago. What was I even doing then? Oh, God. Am I going to have to sit through that Advanced Quantitative Reasoning class again and listen to Mr. Singh drone on? Greet Tarik at my door in pajamas? Have a meltdown during finals week?

I feel the panic rising, a quicksand sucking me down, stealing my breath.

Breathe, Eileen, breathe.

In one thousand, out one thousand. In one thousand...

A minute later, I'm calm, although one student stares at me like she's seen a ghost. I close my eyes. That can't be right. I'm not a ghost. She's staring at me because I just practiced my breathing and I look like an oddball, that's all. I open my eyes again, and now she's giving me a half-crooked smile.

"You okay?"

I nod. "Yeah, just catching my breath."

She nods and walks past.

I scurry over to a study carrel and reach for my waterproof bag. But it's not there. Instead, I'm carrying a backpack. Of course. I won't buy that waterproof bag until next March's spending spree at REI. At least I'll have the sense to forgo that financial mistake.

I remove my backpack and sit down. I pull out my lined notebook and a pen. I write, *Why five months? Why am I here?*

Then I write *Cave* and circle it. Whatever is happening to me, that's where the answers are.

But I hesitate to go back there. I might end up somewhere worse than a downstream cave, or a university library.

I check my phone again. Maybe, just maybe, the date is wrong?

I tap the icon for the local news app. My fingers leave damp prints on the screen, but when I blink, they are gone. I scroll through the headlines—which should be about the pile-up on 95 yesterday or the miraculous last-minute Jags win, their first this season. But instead, the headline reads, *Trick, Not Treat: Local Man Arrested for Halloween Candy Tampering.*

Halloween. The headlines are from five months ago. Today.

The archaeological historian in me needs to document everything, establish a pattern, and formulate a logical explanation. The same drive that kept me in the library until 2 a.m. studying water level records now pushes me to understand these time shifts, to map them like the movement of obsidian in Mesoamerican trade networks.

But logic abandoned me somewhere between yesterday and five months ago, and now I'm stuck in a time where my greatest discovery is submerged beneath the Suwannee.

I clutch my notebook. Its blank pages are an accusation. Gran would have known what to do. She always said that history held secrets we weren't ready to understand. I never thought time would be one of them.

SEVEN: LUKE

The crisis counselor's face fills my laptop screen. She's younger than I expected, with watchful eyes and a practiced smile that reminds me of the intake counselor at rehab. "What brings you here today, Luke?"

My finger hovers over the "End Call" button. Its red warning glow begs me to nuke the session. What am I supposed to say? I jumped through time, and now I need to paint my future? I need an anti-time travel prescription? But I maxed out my credit card to pay for this, so hanging up now would be a waste. And I need answers.

"I've been... experiencing some unusual, uh, perceptions of reality." The words taste safe and clinical, like the lemon-scented air freshener Rose used to spray in the bathroom. "Like déjà vu, you know, but a bit more, um..." Insane. "Intense."

She leans in with a professional warmth that radiates through the screen. "Can you tell me more about these experiences?"

In my screen's reflection, the unfinished canvas awaits on my easel. I should be painting, not talking about my feelings with a dime-store shrink. What was I thinking? I could be layering the dental chair, adding shards of light to the background to represent passing time. I could be adding dabs of dioxazine purple and titanium white, perhaps with a hint of quinacridone magenta, for the purple quartz I know was hiding behind the vertigo. I could be—

"Luke?"

"Yes, sorry, it's like..." I pause, choosing my words carefully, testing each one for signs of madness. "... living the same moment twice... but differently. And it feels more... real than... reality." More real than the moments that appear and disappear like a carousel of projector slides. More real than the root canal that I haven't had yet. My hand drifts to my jaw, remembering phantom pain that won't exist for months.

"It sounds like you're experiencing issues with your perception of time. Would you say it feels like time is slipping away, looping, or something else?"

It's time disappearing, adding, twisting, looping, slipping. "Yeah, maybe looping."

"Have you experienced anything like this before?"

Sure, during post-gin blackouts. "No. Never."

She observes me for a beat too long. She's not stupid. She knows. She must have had a thousand alcoholics come through these sessions—people who swore they'd never blacked out, never puked in the gutter outside Wendy's at 1 a.m., never passed out on their front steps—too wasted to get the key in the lock.

"Listen, I know how this sounds. I'm three years sober. I was on meds for anxiety for a while. I—"

The words tumble out like excuses, like the ones I used to make to Rose. I only had two drinks. I'll stop tomorrow. I'm not an alcoholic.

Three years sober, but my knuckles still remember the feel of drywall crumbling under the punch.

I never hit Rose. Never a woman.

But that's just another excuse. I had a temper. Period. The blackouts were the worst part. Waking up to her tight smile, knowing I'd said or done things I couldn't remember.

Every morning, I'd promise myself I'll quit tomorrow. Or on my birthday. Or on New Year's. But the bottle kept calling my name. What's one more drink? One more sip, one more shot, one more day at a time.

After Rose left, I'd done more than punch a hole in the drywall that night. The morning after, our apartment looked like a rock band had smashed it up in a drug-fueled orgy. I had emptied all the kitchen cupboards. Tossed cans and jars left dents puckering the walls. Hurled jars of spaghetti sauce across the kitchen, the cracked plastic jars smearing bloody trails across the linoleum. Frisbeed our Ikea dinner plates, shattering them into smithereens. And then there was the—

"Luke?" the counselor asks.

"Yes, sorry. Just thinking about—" What an asshole I was. "Stuff. Like maybe I'm losing it."

"Are you worried you're having a breakdown?"

"Aren't I?" The question sounds mouselike, like it's squeezing through the narrow space between my clenched teeth.

Her smile softens, and for a moment she looks like Aunt Edna did on that last day in hospice, all gentle understanding and no judgment. "Luke, I don't hear a breakdown. I hear someone trying to make sense of what's happening. How are you coping with these experiences?"

I glance at my paints, already mixed and smeared onto the palette in colors I never used before the time shift—cadmium red screaming against cerulean blue, alizarin crimson slamming into hansa yellow deep, metallic silver clashing with phthalo green. "I paint. It helps make sense of things." Yeah, right. Like how it helped to make sense of Rose leaving, of Aunt Edna dying, of a mediocre art career, of—

"Art can be very therapeutic. Would you like to tell me about what you're painting?"

A dental chair that's also a tornado that's also time ripping at the seams because I survived a root canal—twice—three times? Fluorescent lights that blind me, will blind me, have already blinded me. My Honda's dizzy spin as it disappears over the Buckman.

"It's..." Probably total garbage, a derivative of a painting I already created—next May. "Abstract. Different from my usual style."

"And how does that feel? Working in a new style?"

Ah, I can answer that one honestly. "Natural. Which is the weird part. I've always been a realist. Now I guess I'm a..." Distortionist? Fracturist? Luke Campbellist? I chuckle to myself at the absurd thought that I could start an art movement with a dental chair and a steering wheel.

I shrug my shoulders.

She scribbles a note and smiles. Ah, he's a hobby artist, I bet she's thinking. He doesn't even know what style of art he's creating.

We talk for another twenty minutes, although I'm no closer to understanding myself than when we started the session. She asks the right questions, makes the right supportive noises. Professional concern wrapped in therapeutic technique, like the way my rehab counselor would ask formulated questions about triggers and coping mechanisms. But with each passing moment, the dental chair pulses more insistently in my mind, demanding completion.

After we disconnect, I breathe a sigh of relief and turn to my canvas. Aunt Edna's charcoal outline watches me from the corner of the studio. Five months ago—now—I was still planning the composition, still rooted in structured lines and solid reality. "I'm not crazy," I tell her, even as I dip my brush into alizarin crimson to paint displaced time.

The first stroke is bold, violent, nothing like my careful realism. The crimson spirals across the canvas, and the endodontist's chair pops out like it's 3D. I paint faster, harder, chasing the memory of next May's magnum opus.

I lose track of how long I paint, the same way I used to lose track of drinks.

A knock at the door jolts me out of my fugue. I know it's Kristy before she speaks, the same way I know she'll dye her hair blonde in three months.

"You missed coffee break."

"Sorry, I was in the zone."

Her eyes widen when she sees the canvas. Her hair is still its natural brown, longer than I remember. Her outline shudders and crackles like a hologram with a weak signal. Blond hair. Brown blond brown blond—

She's going to say *holy cannoli.*

"Holy cannoli." She moves closer, head tilted.

And, *this is different.*

"This is... different."

Great. I'm a precog now, as well as a time traveler. I chuckle. Cackle? "Good different?"

"Intense different. Like the chair is... in two places at the same time. How the heck did you get that effect? You've used...wow, I never would have put those colors next to each other. But it works. Where did you get this idea?"

From next May. "Would you believe me if I said it hasn't happened yet?"

She laughs, then stops when I don't join in. The sound hangs between us like a drop of water dangling from my apartment's leaky faucet. "Luke? You okay?"

No. I'm about as okay as Van Gogh when he checked into the Saint-Paul-de-Mausole asylum. "Yes."

"Cool. See you at coffee break tomorrow?"

If I'm still here in the morning. "Sounds great. See you then."

After she leaves, I work until daylight fades. The canvas—or my head—thrums with displaced time, with a fragmented future that hasn't happened. Or maybe it has. Maybe it's always happening, over and over, like impasto layers without end.

I step back, brush in hand, fresh cadmium red dripping onto my sneakers. The dental chair spins on the canvas through time, just as before.

From one angle, it's a masterpiece. A vision of it hanging on a gallery wall flashes before me, before I remind myself that I've been snubbed by every gallery in town.

From another angle, it's a copy, a forgery missing its soul. It doesn't feel like my hands created this—it's like someone snuck into my studio and left their imitation here. But who would copy this mediocre painting?

And from six feet away, it's just an almost-finished piece in need of a touch-up.

"What's missing?" I ask Aunt Edna's portrait, her unfinished features soft in the dying light.

She doesn't answer.

A half-bottle of Jack Daniels would fix the disconnect, restart the creativity, and stop the noise. The liquor store's open sign flashes before my eyes, a steering wheel rotates in the front window, a drill's high whine floats across the lot, a swirling—

My fingers grasp the sobriety chip in my pocket. Three years sober. Three years of meetings, of avoiding drinking buddies, of pounding out art instead of pounding down drinks. I cannot, must not give in now. But maybe just one to take the edge off?

No. I need to recite the serenity prayer— the "sober prayer" as Kristy called it. "God, grant me the serenity to accept the things I cannot change..."

As I recite the prayer, I pull the green chip out of my pocket and into the light. I focus on the number 3 as a reminder that—

My mind goes blank as I stare at the chip between my fingers. It's not a green number 3. It's a red number 2.

"No," I whisper, gripping the coin like it might rewrite itself if I crush it with enough force. I remember receiving the three-year chip just days ago—standing in that drafty church basement. Kristy raised a diet coke in a toast and clapped louder than anyone else as I pocketed the milestone. But that was next May.

And now it's October—again.

Of course. October. My two-year chip. Because it's not March yet. Because I haven't earned the third chip yet. I hold the chip in my palm. It turns from red to green before my eyes. Red green red green...

I drop it to the floor and it tinkles, rolling toward the dental chair piece. When it hits the easel, it spins once more red-green-red before its slow-motion topple. The dental chair spins on my canvas, caught forever in its moment of temporal destruction.

I stoop, pick the chip up, and slide it back into my pocket. It's not a token of triumph anymore. It's proof that the world is broken—and I'm broken with it. As I stand up, I get a whiff of manure and mint. I cackle at the jarring combination.

Manure and mint, cadmium red and cerulean blue, October and May, green chip and red chip. I exist in a world where nothing belongs together—including me.

EIGHT: EILEEN

The campus looks the same—yet different.

Little things catch my eye as I walk from my biweekly morning session at the counselor's office. The missing student center mural that hasn't been painted yet. The green azalea bushes, stripped of their spring flowers. Construction barriers around what will become the new mathematics wing. My feet know this path so well I could walk it blindfolded, but today, each step feels like walking through a movie set.

During the session, I'd hoped for some insight into whatever was causing this—this what? Time-lapse? Temporal distortion? But I couldn't find a way to weave it into the conversation naturally.

Sandy had asked, "How is the meditation going?"

Oh, you know, in between Groundhog Day and library hallucinations I haven't had the time...

Instead, we went over stress reduction techniques. Again.

Academic burnout, she'd labeled it, like my emotional issues were a chipped arrowhead that needed cataloging. "PhD fatigue" led to my meltdown last fall, when I'd tossed my books in the trash and barged into my advisor's office to demand a change of major.

Like that was an option in graduate school. I chuckle—cackle?—at my stupidity. What had I been thinking? I glance around to make sure no one's staring.

I can't say that counseling has been helpful. We circle around the same issues I've been well aware of for years: my overwhelming course load, the constant pressure of maintaining my academic scholarship, and lingering grief over Gran's death last summer. She'd been my rock since I lost both parents within months of each other—Mom in that horrific skydiving accident, Dad from a heart attack that followed four months later. I was only five then, too young to process anything except that my world had collapsed.

And according to Sandy, I'm still processing it. Those rituals with Gran—baking cookies from scratch, drinking peppermint tea on the porch, Sunday afternoon James Bond marathons with cheese popcorn—weren't cherished memories but coping mechanisms that buried my grief instead of addressing it.

Sandy's prescription for what she calls my "emotional backlog" consists of morning meditation, a reduced course load, and a hobby. As if more avoidance techniques are more effective simply because they carry the academic veneer of a counselor whose methodology seems lifted straight from Psych 101.

I'd probably get better advice from a copy of *The Subtle Art of Not Giving a F*ck*.

Despite my skepticism, I took up drawing as a hobby. Instead of documenting everything through my phone's camera, I sketched unique tree bark patterns, complex shadow gradients, and other field trip minutiae that my camera might have overlooked. The practice sharpened my senses beyond just sight—textures, scents, and especially colors, began to reveal their subtle complexities to me.

As I walk, I take in fall's cobalt blue sky, a contrast to the pure cerulean of spring.

I stop dead in my tracks. How do I know that? The specific color names pop into my head as if an artist is whispering in my ear. Aren't auditory hallucinations a sign of schizophrenia? I glance around to make sure no one's looking, and a girl with tight braids and a shuffling gait stares at me. Her eyes narrow and her head tilts—as if I'm out of place, like a Ming vase in the anatomy lab.

I should go home to recharge, to eat, to sleep off this eerie sense of displacement. But I can't risk missing class—not when I don't remember how many I've already missed this semester and not when I need to reorient myself in this timeline.

I pull out my phone and check my calendar. It shows my class schedule for this week. My stomach drops when I see Mr. Singh's Advanced Quantitative Reasoning for MWF. Today, now, it's time for Pre-Columbian Societies.

I pause outside the archaeology lecture hall. Through the

window, I can see Professor Chen setting up her slides. The wall projection says Early North American Trade Routes. Well, at least I don't need to take notes. I've learned this before. The Mississippians built an impressive commercial web between 800 and 1600 AD, linking settlements from Cahokia—modern-day Illinois—to Moundville, which became Alabama. Gulf shells, Great Lakes copper, Appalachian mica, and Rocky Mountain obsidian traveled thousands of miles along river highways and foot-worn paths—a continental marketplace centuries before European contact.

Professor Chen is a constant in this dreamlike world. Everything about her exudes methodical confidence—from her crisp linen blazer to her neat chignon hair bun to the way she arranges her notes in perfect alignment. If I were to tell her what was happening to me, I imagine she would say, *Fall back on your training. Document everything. Look for patterns. Think like a historian.*

But who am I kidding? Of course she wouldn't say that. She'd stare at me like I just told her I had the Holy Grail in my backpack. Is that so, Eileen? How fun! When's the last time you saw your counselor?

Instead, I slip into my usual seat at the front of the class. I arrange my notebook and pens, trying to look like someone who belongs.

Professor Chen begins her presentation on migration patterns in pre-Columbian societies. I've heard this lecture before, taken these notes before. The déjà vu is so strong it makes my head swim. But a detail from the lecture jumps out at me like a neon sign— faded petroglyphs along the Tennessee River, spirals, and humanoid figures whose meanings are still debated.

My hand shoots up before I can stop myself, muscle memory overriding caution.

"Yes, Eileen?" Professor Chen's voice carries that familiar note of encouragement that always made me feel seen, valued.

"Has anyone studied early American depictions of—" Time travel? Temporal displacement? "—of how they depicted unusual passages of time?"

"Unusual? As in...?"

Time travel. Wormholes. Stargate. "As in whether their use of hallucinogens might have led them to believe they were traveling in time?"

"Interesting question. There's no evidence they believed in time travel as we think of it. Most interpretations suggest calendar systems or astronomical maps. Why do you ask?"

Because five months from now, I'll time travel in a cave with preserved drawings. "Just... thinking about local sites." I force my voice to stay steady, professional. "The Suwannee has so many unexplored cave systems. Perhaps there are parallels, uh, I mean, depictions of..." I lose my train of thought and give her an apologetic shrug.

She gives me an appraising look that makes me think of Gran. It's that same mix of curiosity and concern Gran gave me when I told her, at age seven, that I wanted to be an exotic dancer when I grew up. I loved to dance, and to my seven-year-old ears, "exotic" sounded like Hawaii and beaches and storybook magic rolled into one. Gran patted my hand and said, "Dear, we need to have a little chat."

By the look of Professor Chen's raised eyebrow, I'm about to receive the academic version of that same conversation.

"I see. Well, that's a little off-topic, so perhaps we can chat during office hours?"

"Sounds good," I say, my cheeks burning. The last thing I want to do is talk about Florida caves without revealing that one of them might be a time portal.

* * *

After class, I retreat to the library's archaeology section, seeking refuge in its familiar dusty corners and fluorescent-lit study carrels. My laptop opens to the last thing I was researching five months ago—seasonal flooding patterns in North Florida river systems. The screen blurs as exhaustion hits me, and the words warp like ripples on river water.

My phone Da-da-da-DUMs against the wooden desk. *Beethoven's Fifth.* I turn the sound off and check the text. It's from Tarik.

"Does 2 at riverwalk work 4U?"

Right. Five months ago, we were still together. Still about to have that lunch date on the Riverwalk to chat about his "Big news." I remember wondering what the big news could be. A huge grant? An invitation to his parent's time-share in the Maldives? I wore my best honey-colored dress and brought strawberries and gourmet cheese. He showed up with a peanut butter sandwich and told me he'd accepted a job in Seattle.

He'd waited until after he'd gobbled the ten-dollar wedge of Rogue River Blue to tell me he was leaving. "I couldn't turn this opportunity down."

But that was five months ago. Now.

My head throbs with the thought of it. Through the library windows, I watch students cross the quad in the sunshine, living their normal lives in their normal timeline.

I type back: "Can't. Something's come up. Research."

"NP. Everything OK?"

If only he knew how stupid that question was. Sure, just another day working on the flux capacitor.

"Just busy. Rain check?"

I put my phone on the desk and look at the date. It's now November 1.

As much as I don't want to have lunch with Tarik—we've been broken up for months after all—will I change the future if I don't see him? I recall a quote from my freshman Ancient Greek History class, something Agathon said: "For this alone is lacking even to God, to make undone the things that have been done." Is that what I'm doing now? Playing God?

But I can't see how a skipped lunch date would change anything. He's going to break up with me, anyway.

I cover my face with my hands and sigh. My training offers no framework for this, no methodology for navigating the impossible. For navigating five repeated months. And I have no data with which to even start. No drawings. No photographs. Nothing. Without data, I can't begin to trace the origins of the phenomenon. But—

I slap my palm on the desk.

I do know the origin. The Suwannee cave.

But is it even there? What if I've jumped into another dimension where the cave doesn't exist? What if I paddle out there and instead of a cave, I find a riverside park with a gazebo and a

"Keep Out" sign?

It has to be there. I'm five months back in time, not in a *Twilight Zone* other dimension, so it must be there. But whether the water levels will be low enough to enter is another matter. I open a browser tab and search for "water levels on Suwannee."

Tomorrow, I'll return to the cave. Even if I have to rent a diving bell.

NINE: LUKE

My brush hovers over the canvas, cadmium red globbed at its tip. I've spent two days on this piece, but there's still something missing.

I intended to add another feature, but my mind feels disjointed, and I've forgotten what that feature was. I try to make the connection, but a caffeine headache brews behind my eyes. I should make a cup, but I just need to do this one thing. It's there, half-formed in cadmium red, so I was going to paint a...

Nope. That didn't work.

In the center of the painting, behind the endodontist chair, there's a...

Nope. And now the headache has intensified. It's turned from a dull throb into—

Oh no. No, no, no.

I drop the brush on the floor, gripping the edges of my stool as my studio spins around me. As the chair-steering wheel and finished Fracture painting and the brick walls and the white walls and Aunt Edna's charcoal eyes and the azure green eyes and an orange dress shirt—

"—so we'll open at six," a husky female voice says. "We'll have wine and sparkling water. Any last-minute suggestions?"

I stare at my empty hand. My brush, the canvas, my paint-splattered studio—all gone. No, not gone. Ghostly, present, spinning into nothingness like the last remnants of a dust storm. The particles whiz like snow around me, then disintegrate into the void.

I'm sitting in a sleek office chair, surrounded by people in business casual, and the husky-voiced woman with steel-gray hair points at a calendar on the wall. April.

Five months forward. One month before the drive over Buckman Bridge that started all this. Could the Buckman be a time portal? Like, what's the name of that movie with the guys who walked through that Egyptian circle... *Stargate*, that was it...

"Mika?" The woman—gallery director, my brain supplies through the fog—is looking at me expectantly. "Everything good to go for this evening?"

Mika? I blink. Oh, my God. I was right. I have that dissociative perception—no, dissociative disorder—what was that movie called? *Split*, that was it. Dissociative split something?

She's looking at me, waiting for a response. "I... uh, guess."

I guess? Is that the best you can do, Campbell? How about, *Where the hell am I?*

She takes a step back, her eyes widening as they dart between me and her notes. "Oh, I... I'm so sorry... Luke. I forgot for a second that we had, uh, moved Mika's event up to next month." Her hand flutters to her temple, brushing away invisible cobwebs before she attempts a smile that looks more like a wince, her eyes narrowed with confusion. "So, are we good to go for tonight?"

I look at the warping, twisting, shiny silver wastebasket. I'm about to throw up. Whatever is going on tonight, I hope it isn't worse than this. "Could you, uh, just give me the highlights again?"

Highlights. They're surrounding the endodontist chair, backlighting the steering wheel, flowing from the edge of the canvas into—

"The hard opening's at six, but if you can be here at five for the soft opening. We have..." She checks her notes, once, twice. Her face is so tight with confusion that it's going to collapse in on itself at the nose, like there's a vacuum inside her skull that's sucking all the skin in. "Oh, my. I didn't realize we had that many collectors. Well, sixteen collectors will be here at five."

Collectors? For me? I glance around the room—the white walls suggest I'm in a gallery, and I'm the only one here in paint-splattered jeans.

This cannot be real.

I shove my hand into my pants pocket and my fingers close around the AA chip. Is it my two or three-year chip? I can't bring it out without drawing attention, so I trace the coin's face with my thumb. It feels like a two-year—smooth, worn at the edges—but it could be a three.

The familiar ridges warp as reality bends again. The sensation is becoming familiar now, like how a queasy stomach used to warn me I'd had one too many.

I blink at the opening night poster, trying to orient myself. Block letters herald

LUKE CAMPBEL
QUANTUM DISPLACEMENT
APRIL 23, 6-9 P.M.

Gallery show. *My* gallery show. The fluorescent lights overhead remind me too much of the endodontist, and I resist the urge to bolt from the room.

"Wine and sparkling water," I repeat carefully. "Yes, that's..."

Did she even say that? No, she never—

"Correct. Any additions?"

I shake my head too fervently, like she's just asked me if I want an enema. How did I know to say, "Wine and sparkling water"? How do I know she sent me an email last December, asking if I would be interested in gallery representation? How do I know I've painted not one Fracture piece, but ten? How is any of this possible?

"Excellent." The director—Sandra? Sharon?—makes a note. "And you're sure about the title? It's not too late for a last-minute change. 'Quantum Displacement' is rather... sciency."

"The title stays," I hear myself say with surprising conviction. I'd Googled this. At least, I think I must have Googled it. It's not like there was a quantum physicist in my sparse circle of artsy friends. The title fits my work because...

...quantum displacement is the phenomenon of an object or individual shifting between states of existence across different points in time or space often without traversing the physical distance between them it suggests that reality is not fixed but fluid with moments capable of overlapping repeating or reordering due to fluctuations in the underlying quantum structure of time.

Apparently, I've gained fifty IQ points since the trip from my wooden stool to this plastic chair. Is that what time travel does? Turn artists into Einsteins?

But wait, isn't "delusions of grandeur" a sign of schizophrenia?

I'm in trouble, whichever way you slice it.

"Well, it certainly fits the work." She gestures to a portfolio on the table. "Especially the cave motifs. They're quite haunting."

Cave motifs? I lean forward to get a better look at the photos spread across the table. My heart nearly stops. There, entwined in what appears to be my new "signature style" of fractured reality and twisted time, are patterns I've never seen before. Ancient symbols. Stone passages that seem to shift and change the longer you look at them. Elongated stick figures.

What the heck? Stick figures got me a gallery show?

I trace my finger over one photo, and for a moment, I smell limestone and river water. A wave of vertigo hits, and I freeze in place, like I'm playing Red Light Green Light, and staying still will stop the madness.

"Speaking of which," Sandra/Sharon says, "the Jacksonville Arts Journal wants to do a feature. They're particularly interested in the Campbellism angle. Should I set up the interview for after the show?"

My eyes travel in her direction, though I'm still as a human statue. "Campbellism?"

Sandra/Sharon tilts her head and raises an eyebrow. "As in, they want to explore the angle of new Campbellism."

New Campbellism? What the heck is that? An art movement I've never heard of? Some guy with my last name who...

Then it comes to me. The other Luke Campbell, c. 1925. I know this. I make the connection. That artist who disappeared way before Amelia Earhart. But wasn't he best known for his sketches? Wasn't he part of a logging crew? So how—

"Marc—Luke? Are you okay?" A woman's voice, distant. No, not distant. In front of me. Sandra/Sharon. It's Sandra, I'm sure of it. Her name is Sandra.

"I... need to think about the interview, uh, Sandra," I manage. "My work is still..." A dream? A nightmare? There? Not there? "... evolving."

She nods approvingly. "Of course. The mysterious artist angle. I like it."

The meeting wraps up, and the suits file out. I stay rooted in my chair, staring at the—*my*—portfolio. The cave paintings—my cave paintings—stare back. There's something familiar about them, something I can't quite...

A flash of memory: Kristy's hair, long and unbleached. "It feels like being in two places at once."

But she wasn't looking at these cave paintings then.

They didn't exist yet.

Or did they?

TEN: EILEEN

The problem with reliving five months of your life *is la paralysie du choix*. According to my high school French teacher, there's no equivalent phrase in English. But you can roughly translate it as standing in front of fifty doors with no idea which one isn't rigged with explosives.

Should I show up at the coffee shop where I know Tarik will be studying, or ignore him like a door knock from missionary Mormons on Sunday morning? Ghost him or send him a text saying *Hey, we broke up before, so let's do it again?*

The questions swirl as I paddle toward the tire swing marking the darker cave's entrance. It's been one day since I skipped our riverbank lunch. Twenty-four hours of dodging his calls, responding to his texts with maybes. In our original fall timeline, we'd be fighting about Seattle by now. About how he didn't consult me before accepting it. Not that we were going to get married or anything, but communication is necessary in a relationship.

The irony isn't lost on me. Technically, we're still in a relationship. And technically, I'm not communicating with him.

The methodical part of me analyzes the potential consequences of my choices. The thought of going through the motions of a doomed relationship—especially when I have more important things to do, like figure out why I'm here—makes my stomach curdle. But I could be creating a butterfly effect. One minor change now could mean large, unpredictable changes to future events.

Maybe if I ghost Tarik, he'll ghost every woman he ever dates afterward, exacting revenge on womanhood itself. And maybe one of those women will cry on her way to work and cause a sixty-car pileup. Or maybe if I do text him that we broke up already, he'll be so confused and glued to his phone that he doesn't see the city bus barreling toward him when he crosses the road.

I scoff at myself. I am embracing Hollywood physics and going down what Professor Chen calls an "illogical archaeological rabbit hole." Like as an undergrad, when I spent a full day trying to prove that a spiral carving near the river was a Mayan glyph—ignoring the fact that the limestone wasn't native, and the "glyph" was probably made by a bored local with a pocketknife in the '70s. Classic illogical archaeological rabbit hole.

Anyway, I doubt anyone on *The Butterfly Effect's* production team experienced time travel—if that's what this is.

My internet research yesterday evening uncovered a rabbit hole of the physics persuasion. I couldn't understand the articles; they seemed written in Indus Script, not English. Time travel is theoretically possible, according to the laws of quantum mechanics, but that's as far as my Intro to Physics knowledge took me. After that, the article's author droned on about...

...the phenomenon of an object or individual shifting between states of existence across different points in time or space, often without traversing the physical distance between them. It suggests that reality is not fixed but fluid, with moments capable of overlapping, repeating, or reordering due to fluctuations in the underlying quantum structure of time.

I stop paddling and stiffen as if I'm playing a game of Freeze. How on earth had I retained that? I thought I hadn't understood it when I read it yesterday. But now it makes complete sense. A person or object can jump between different times or places without moving through space, because time itself isn't fixed—it can bend, loop, or reshuffle.

My brain must have worked on the problem overnight.

My phone buzzes in its waterproof case. Da-da-da-DUM. Tarik.

I'm tempted to pull out my phone and text, *Sorry, this isn't working. We're different people. Apparently I'm Einstein now, and I have more important things to do rather than listen to you prattle on about Seattle.*

Instead, I resume paddling, focusing on the morning sun glinting off the water. I stop in front of the darker cave and slide off my board. The cave is accessible, but I know from my previous—future?—observations that it holds no answers. Still, I duck inside.

My headlamp illuminates the bare limestone walls, sweeping across ordinary rock. No drawings, no markings, nothing that would even interest a freshman archaeology student.

I pull out my waterproof notebook and note the water level, which is up to my knees. I jot down "bare walls" and tap my pencil on the paper. The algae next to the cave opening isn't important, but I note it anyway. Analysis requires data, and the smallest of observations—or events—could reshape my interpretation.

Cases in point: In *Back to the Future*, Dr. Brown hits his head on a bathroom sink and invents the flux capacitor. In the 3rd century BCE, Archimedes discovers the principle of buoyancy and yells "Eureka!" while soaking in a bathtub. In the 21st century CE, Eileen Nash uncovers the key to time travel while staring at algae growth patterns on her phone during a contemplative bathroom break.

While I can imagine receiving a lifetime achievement award from the Archaeological Institute of America, I'm a realist. An accepted submission to a couple of journals is a more achievable goal—if I can make sense of these caves.

Patterns matter, and every artifact tells a story. I can hear Professor Chen's voice: "Context is everything, Eileen. Details matter. Nothing exists in isolation."

But what's the context here? Algae. Dripping water. Echoing squawks from great egrets outside. A cave that exists in two states—bright and dark, high water and low, past and present twisting together like...

Like something I can't grasp. Okay, so I'm not Einstein after all. But a little clue from the universe would be great right now. What am I missing?

Details matter. I scribble a caret before the word *algae* and write "phthalo green." The color is important, though I don't have the first clue why. Come to think of it, has the universe been sending me clues? What was the sky color I noticed the other day? Sky blue? Sea blue? I draw a blank. Shoot, I should've jotted that one down.

Cerulean. That was it. Cerulean blue.

I write the color name and start to sketch. I draw stalactites suspended like daggers from the ceiling, moss-slicked boulders huddled inside the cave mouth, and water hugging the walls. Next May, I'll be able to see the mineral deposit line. But the water hasn't receded yet. Should I draw it from memory? Uncertain, I scribble a note: add future waterline? Then, I photograph the same area for later comparison.

When I'm finished, I pack my supplies away and wade out to my board.

My phone buzzes again. Da-da-da-DUM. Tarik. I pull out my phone and read the text.

"Hey, know ur busy but quick coffee in am?"

I sigh. I'm going to have to address this issue. If anything, it'll stop the distraction. I'm aware that I'll sound cold, heartless. But a clean break will be best for both of us. It'll free Tarik to make his Seattle plans without dealing with arguments about us. And it will free me to pursue...

The thought that completes the sentence isn't what I expect. It isn't "pursue my thesis" or "pursue the evidence." No, the thought arrives with such sudden clarity that my legs go weak as I'm mounting my board.

Pursue someone else.

Someone I haven't met yet. Someone who knows that cerulean blue is the color of fall skies.

* * *

Through the window, November sunlight casts long shadows across Bold Bean's reclaimed wood tables, so hippy, so Tarik, so different from the harsh March glare I remember—will remember?—from our first awkward post-breakup encounter. I could have sworn the tables were dark oak the last time, not this reclaimed pine with its artisanal knots and carefully preserved imperfections. Just another detail shifted by the time slip, or maybe a memory that never happened.

A barista calls out my order, the steam wand hisses, and a chair scrapes across the tile floor. The ordinary sounds of a coffee shop, but they feel distant, unreal. My focus has narrowed to the cave I'll visit after lunch, to the mystery waiting in its depths.

The barista has made a love heart in the foam of my

cappuccino. I take the wooden stirrer and demolish the shape with a few jabs.

"You look different," Tarik says. "Did you get a haircut?"

He shakes the sugar packet to distribute the sugar evenly, folds the packet in half, and tears the edge. "That way," he once told me, "I get exactly half a pack of sugar." At the time, I thought it was an adorable quirk. But now I want to slap the packet out of his hand.

Always precise. Always measured. Like the carefully curated indie music he plays in his car and the artful way he dishevels his hair. As he stirs, the spoon clinks against the ceramic in perfect three-second intervals, a sound that grates on my nerves like sandpaper. He'll stir for exactly ten rotations before putting the spoon on the table pointing to twelve o'clock.

I clench my fist under the table, unsure of where the anger is coming from. I am not an angry person. Well, if you discount the time I gave the finger to the weekend NASCAR enthusiast who cut me off in a Camaro last week. Or was it next May? Only it wasn't a Camaro, it was a white truck—

A tap on my hand. "Eileen?"

Right, Tarik. "I know you're going to Seattle."

He stops stirring and lifts the spoon out of the cup. Coffee drips onto the table. "How did you...?"

"Does it matter?"

He puts the spoon down and adjusts it toward twelve o'clock with his index finger. "I guess not."

"Tarik." I cover his hand with mine, stilling his spoon fiddling. His skin is warm, familiar, but the touch sends an uncomfortable jolt through me, like forcing matching magnetic poles together. "I don't think this is working."

His long eyelashes flutter behind wire-rimmed glasses. There are no lenses—he says that glasses make him look intelligent. Now they make him look like a pretentious poseur wearing fake glasses.

He pulls his hand away. "What?"

"Us. This." I gesture between us, cataloging the details with precision: his matching cardigan and laptop case, the dog-eared corner of the journal article he's been pretending to read, the PFLAG button he wears for the cool factor, not because he has a gay relative. What did I ever see in him? "I've been feeling it for..." *three months* "...a while."

"Is this about your thesis? Because I told you, I support..." He waffles on about how I've misunderstood this and that. How I'm not thinking straight because I'm not considering this and that.

But I'm not listening. I'm not surprised he's battling to save the dregs of our relationship. My words have short-circuited his mechanisms of control and order. Our relationship is the spoon at 12 o'clock until he tosses it into the dirty dishes bin. If I was the one who took the spoon and threw it in there, he'd have pitched a fit.

"It's not about my thesis." Though the cave drawings that don't exist yet hover in my mind, their swirling patterns as clear as the list of coffee options on the chalkboard. "It's about us. There's just... no spark."

His face falls, then he composes himself. Always controlled, even when I've shoved a wrench into his machinery. "You're right. I was going to tell you it was over today, anyway."

* * *

The afternoon sun beats down as I paddle along the Suwannee. My board cuts through water that reflects the sky like hammered copper. The water is cool as I reach my destination and slide in, sending ripples across the surface that distort my reflection like a funhouse mirror.

I secure my board and check my gear one last time, falling into the familiar pre-dive routine Gran taught me years ago. Secure mask, clear snorkel, quick pinch and swallow to equalize ears.

Ten feet. Four seconds. I can hold my breath for three minutes, so four seconds is nothing. But the gaping mouth of the cave cautions me to stay away, just like The Devil's Eye in Ginnie Springs threatens recreational divers. It's a warning that if I go in, I might not come back out. I might get my shirt caught on a jagged rock or get disoriented in the black water. I might get diver's panic and drown in my desperate attempt to get oxygen.

Oh, for goodness' sake. It's ten feet in a straight line, not a "professionals only" five-mile dive through the Devil's Spring system.

One deep breath, and I duck under.

The beam of my waterproof headlamp cuts through the murk, tannins dancing in its beam like pink snow. I kick forward, counting strokes the way Gran taught me. One. Two. Three. The passage narrows, then widens. Four. Five. My light catches something on the wall—a flash of pigment that looks like a steering wheel. No time to inspect. Six. Seven. The water blackens. Eight—

I break through into the open air and inhale. The cave ceiling arches overhead, and water drips from stalactites in a rhythm that sounds like whispered words. I sweep my light across the walls, my heart pounding against my ribs.

The drawings. They're here. Pigments that shouldn't exist, telling a story I can't yet read.

On the right wall, one of the half-dissolved figures walks through what I'd previously thought resembled the *Stargate* portal. But the bulging outcropping above the ring mirrors the same formation I thought looked like the Tunnel of Terror on my first trip here. I've seen *Stargate* six times, enough to recognize an Egyptian time machine when I see one, but this isn't science fiction. The figure isn't stepping through an alien artifact; it's entering this cave. The artist wasn't imagining possibilities—they were documenting reality. My reality.

But before I can focus on them, the air shifts.

The now-familiar vertigo grips me, the world tilting on its axis like stratigraphic layers sliding against each other in a time-lapse animation. The cave air grows syrupy, tasting of salt and impossibility. I expect a wave of panic—will I end up back another six months? Forward eight months? But the vertigo is warm, welcoming, like a hug from Gran telling me this is where I'm supposed to be.

I can't comprehend what I'm seeing. I'm standing in shoulder-deep water. I'm standing in front of a floor-length mirror. I'm removing my snorkel mask. I'm applying mascara. Water drips turn into echoes, turn into music playing from my phone—a staccato drip-drip-drip mixed with lyrics "Waiting for tonight..." I'm in my paddling outfit—tight shirt, short pants—

I'm in my underwear. Practical white bra and panties from Marshalls. A dress I don't recognize hangs on my closet door. Its deep blue fabric reflects the light like water.

I sit down on the edge of my bed and check my phone. April 23rd, 7:15 PM. I'm back to where I started. Or thereabouts. I think it was mid-March when I first came into the cave, but the timeline is fuzzy, like time is rewriting itself. It was a Tuesday—

Da-da-da-DUM. A text notification blinks. I drop the mascara wand on the bed and grab my phone from my dresser.

No. For the love of God, am I in purgatory? Sentenced to repeat the breakup with Tarik over and over again?

But it isn't Tarik. It's Dave.

Who?

"Leaving now. CU in 30."

Who on earth is Dave? I've seen a Dave in a movie, I think. Tall, chiseled like John Travolta. But what movie was it? Or is this a memory? I can't be sure. Maybe Dave is a study mate. Or a long-lost cousin.

But no. He's a boyfriend. A date? First date? Not sure.

My eyes fix on my reflection, at the unfamiliar emerald green dress waiting to be worn, at the mascara wand smudging my comforter with black streaks. Somewhere in this version of tonight, I'm going to an art opening. But why? And with who?

ELEVEN: LUKE

The tuxedo rental hangs on my studio door like a specter. The polyester blend reflects the light like sunlight on water, like light splintering in a kaleidoscope, like flickering lights on a speeding Ferris wheel. My skin crawls with imaginary insects at the sight.

Two hours until the opening, and I'm being watched.

I walk to the window again and press my palms against the cool glass. Nothing but the usual Friday traffic, people heading home or out to dinner. Normal people. Sane people. But there's someone out there, behind the dumpster or on the corner of King and Roselle streets or on the Chevy Impala parked outside Rooter's Plumbing Supply Co.

Great. Paranoia. Let's add that to the list. Visual hallucinations. Delusional time travel. Delusions of grandeur. Check, check, check, effing check.

How many boxes do I check before I check into Atascadero?

My fingers curl around my sobriety chip but I don't remove it from my pocket. Three years sober, two years sober, doesn't matter. The liquor store, a half mile on McDuff, calls my name like Faust's bargain waiting to be struck. Auditory hallucinations. Awesome. Add it to the list.

I kick over a paint can. I wait for that satisfying pop! of the lid exploding and the titanium white spilling its guts across the floor. But it doesn't happen. Instead, it rolls across the wood floor and comes to an unsatisfactory stop at the kick plate.

I raise my hand to swipe the tubes of paint on my easel onto the floor but catch Aunt Edna's eyes. I completed the portrait six months ago on a Sunday afternoon. It's more than a portrait. It's her. And now, she's looking at me, not with kind eyes but judging eyes. Watchful eyes. Knowing eyes. If portraits could move, she'd be waggling her finger. Now, now, Luke. Take a beat.

I lower my hand.

Screw the online counseling. I need help, real help. I'll get the opening out of the way then head straight for the ER.

Or maybe I'll paint.

I turn away from the window, sit in front of a blank canvas, and sketch an outline of a river, flowing from right to left. It's the beginnings of a landscape and it feels right. But then again, this is nothing like those ten pieces hanging in the downtown gallery. Have I lost that inspiration? Am I back to painting mediocrity?

Thank God I finished enough pieces during whatever manic episode I was having. Sandra told me to expect a sizeable crowd tonight. She also said to ignore the chatter on social media about them being "derivative." Derivative from what, I don't know. Could there be another guy who is bipolar or dissociative identity or schizophrenic—take your pick? Someone else out there who has a blended timeline with a dental chair and car seat? The white coats will descend en masse when they hear that one. They're probably used to "I'm Superman," or "I can shoot spiderwebs from my ass," not "I'm a time-traveling steering wheel root-canal repeater."

I should definitely paint.

I sketch in a woman on the river. A fractured woman split into pieces. There. Not lost. Hidden.

My phone buzzes against the metal table. Another reminder for my counseling session tomorrow. I know I've been going regularly, playing the part of the tortured artist working through "creative blocks" and "anxiety." The memories are there, but it's like I've watched those memories happen on a television show, rather than having experienced them. The past few months are a series of plot points, red herrings, and twists played out on an imaginary TV screen in my head. In between those screenshots are commercial interruptions—a riverside movie set, a horse-drawn wagon, a paddleboard, a brass wedding ring. And the smell of peppermint and manure.

It's nonsensical, like they're inserted memories instead of real ones. I could be in the future now. I could be living in a time where memories are inserted and removed like SIM cards from a phone. Well, whatever SIM card they inserted last is borked, and I want my money back.

I have made my decision. I'll paint tonight. And tomorrow I'll find a real psychiatrist. Someone who can prescribe something stronger than breathing exercises. Someone who won't just nod sympathetically when I describe feeling like I'm being pulled through time like a film reel yanked from a jammed projector.

I put down the pencil and change into my tux. The wall mirror shows dark circles under my eyes and stubble. I should shave. Will shave. Have shaved. The face in the mirror looks less like mine every day.

My phone buzzes. It's Sandra: "Car service will be there in 15. Don't be late to your own opening!"

I straighten my bow tie in the mirror, adjusting it until it sits perfectly centered. I'm trying to look like someone who hasn't lost their grip on reality, like someone who deserves a gallery show, like someone who isn't afraid of what might be waiting in the shadows between paintings.

I lock up my studio. The scrape of the key in the lock sets my teeth on edge. I can't shake the certainty that tonight will change my life. I just don't know if I'm ready for what's coming.

Or who.

TWELVE: EILEEN

I slide into Dave's antique Volvo wagon.

"You look amazing," he says. His blue eyes crinkle at the corners when he smiles. Not cerulean blue like the sky, but Manganese blue—the color at the base of a flame.

"Thanks," I say, smoothing my dress.

This is our third date. Our first was coffee, the second a forgettable indie movie at the New Sun-Ray Cinema on Park Street. I should be eager or nervous. Instead, it's like I'm playing a role in a scene I don't remember agreeing to.

I remember our first meeting at the university library. Except I don't, not really. The memory feels borrowed, like scrolling through a friend's Facebook feed. Me, reaching for the same *A History of Early American Art* book. Him, saying "book jinx." Coffee at the campus café, talking about his love of Kandinsky, my research on pre-Columbian art. All of it crystal clear, yet somehow hollow, like photographs of places I've been to, but with someone else.

"I'm excited as hell about seeing the show," he says. "It's gonna be interesting to see whether it's as derivative as they say."

"Derivative?" The word sparks a flutter of a memory. But I can't place it.

"Yeah, that was the focus in class this morning—while we were working. As I was laying down oil, I kept thinking about the boundary between influence and derivation. If I build a vista using gestural drips, is it dialogue with Pollock—or am I just derivative?"

I nod, pretending I know what he's talking about. That's how it's been all day—pretending. Pretending I'm interested in his academic art dissections. Pretending I remember conversations we've supposedly had. Pretending I'm not constantly thinking about the cave.

I want to tear off the dress, change into my paddling gear, and hightail it back to the cave. But what would be the point? To end up a year from now, a year ago, or somewhere even more far-flung? The 12th Century? The 50th? No, I can't go back there, not until I—

Find out who's looking for me.

I take a deep breath, trying to ground myself. This paranoid feeling that someone's searching for me isn't logical. It reminds me of when I was thirteen and convinced everyone at school was conspiring against me. Back then, Gran wiped custard pudding off my textbooks after bullies smushed my lunch into my book bag, and gave me advice I still carry. "Oh, Eileen. It's okay to have irrational thoughts, but we must act only on those rooted in kindness, love, or logic."

Well, thinking there's someone out there looking for me is certainly not rooted in kindness, love, or logic. It's rooted in craziness.

"You okay?" Dave's hand slides onto mine. "You seem distracted."

Oh, you know, just thinking about time traveling again. "Just nervous about my thesis."

The thought of going under the water again, of what might happen... but I must. Eventually. When the time is right.

I don't belong here. Not in this timeline, not in this car, not with Dave.

"Your cave art thing?" Dave takes the turn toward downtown. "Find anything interesting?"

I bristle at his description of the cave art as a "thing." Hadn't I spent most of our coffee date describing the intricacies of the drawings, how I'd hoped to build my thesis around them? Had I been that much of a blowhard?

I withdraw my hand, pull the visor mirror down, and pretend to inspect my lip gloss. "Still researching."

Another lie. Will I ever meet someone who I can be honest and open with? Doubtful, considering my past choices.

The gallery appears ahead, already crowded with dozens milling outside. Dave finds parking close by, and as we walk toward the entrance, a couple squeezes past us. I catch snippets of their conversation.

"...it's a bit derivative..."

"...like he's painting a breakdown..."

I stare at them over my shoulder.

"What's up?" Dave asks.

"Just got this weird sense of déjà vu."

"Oh, right."

I sigh. Apparently, a discussion about his art, his work, and his interests warrant a five-minute soliloquy—while inquiring about my well-being, my interests, and my life gets the under-five treatment—two words, no follow-up.

He pats my back as we reach the gallery entrance and points inside. "Would you look at that? The compositional elements are so well-balanced—yet there's this underlying tension in the brushwork. See how the light falls across the chair? It's creating this juxtaposition between the mundane object and the abstract..."

As he rambles on, I switch off and shove my way through the gallery door. The sudden wall of sound surrounds me as I scan the room: clinking glasses, overlapping conversations, and pretentious laughter. The waft of cheap perfume mingles with the artificial scent of lit tea lights, all trapped in the stuffiness of too many bodies in too small a space.

I stop dead in my tracks.

On the far wall, illuminated by track lighting, is an imposing six-foot canvas dominated by a dental chair, twisted and fractured like my reality. Behind the chair—I can hardly believe what I'm seeing.

Cave art. My cave art. The same elongated forms and radiating spirals I sketched in my notebook before they vanished.

Dave pats my back again. My body tenses and I flinch away.

"Eileen? You good? We should head over there because that one is remarkable in its..."

His voice fades to background noise. Because now I'm certain of two things.

I'm not crazy.

And I'm not alone.

THIRTEEN: LUKE

The gallery presses in with noise and bodies. Conversations blend into a monotone hum, and I can't distinguish which voices are real and which are echoes in my mind.

"Seriously, he must be insane..."

"...and aren't they hiding over there..."

"...the colors clash too much, I suppose, but..."

The Chardonnay and Malbec bottles huddled on the drink cart glimmer in the lights. The sparkling water is as flat and as inspiring as a primer coat waiting for vibrant color. One glass wouldn't hurt, would it? One glass of Malbec to blend in. I wouldn't even need to drink it, just hold it like a prop in—

A prickle races up my spine, electric and familiar—a prelude to... vertigo? I steady myself against the drink cart and brace for the spin, but it doesn't come. Instead, a voice slices through the chatter.

"Luke? What'll it be?" It's Henry, who's manning the drinks cart. Dressed in a black dress shirt and pants, he holds up an empty plastic cup.

"Uh, sparkling water," I say, more reflex than want.

The spin doesn't come, but the prickle remains. It's not a vertigo warning after all. It's... Spidey sense. Danger Will Robinson. Glitch in the Matrix.

I nod at Henry, who pours me a cup of disappointment. I clutch the red Solo cup—the color of danger, another sign I should flee—and fight the urge to scan the room for the black suit, for the undercover plant, for the slender man who knows I don't belong. I sip the water. Crisp bubbles fizz on my tongue, but I smell manure.

Did I step in dog crap?

A fleck of red paint clings to the tip of my worn brogue. I lift one foot, then the other. The soles are clean. No brown gunk clogging the treads. But—oh, God. My shoes don't match. One is a brogue and the other's a Derby. I don't own Derby shoes. The leather shudders and glitches before my eyes. Derby Brogue Derby Brogue Derby...

A man bumps into me. My cup tips over, dumping sparkling water onto the floor. A sign from the heavens. Chuck that shit out of your glass, Luke, and go get the real stuff.

Henry is there in an instant. He mops up the spill with napkins.

Malbec or Chardonnay? I've never been a red-wine person but Chardonnay's like drinking water. Why hadn't I suggested Jack Daniels as an option back when Karen—

"Sorry, man... Oh, wait. You're the artist, right?"

I look up to find the source of the voice.

"Your work is visceral, man. The way you've layered temporal dissonance with such raw authenticity. The juxtaposition of mundane..."

He's right in front of me—spewing empty art critiques that say everything about technique and nothing about meaning. But I don't see him. He's a blurry outline, a ghost, a charcoal sketch waiting for color.

I see *her* with crystal clarity.

Shoulder-length, burnt sienna hair with cadmium orange highlights. Terra verte eyes with cadmium yellow flecks. Straight spine, square shoulders—like she's accustomed to careful observation, to cataloging details like an artist. Her emerald-green dress hangs on her frame as if it belongs to someone else. Perhaps someone more concerned with gallery openings than whatever has her gaze so fixed on my painting. It's not the casual interest of the other patrons. She's looking at my work like she recognizes it, like she's found something she thought was lost.

The chatter dims, the clinking glasses freeze mid-toast, the dust motes pause in the gallery lights. Because I know her. I know her.

We met at a movie set. Yes, that's it. The vision pops into my head, a long-buried memory dragged to the surface. A Model T car putters past—engine chugging like a sputtering genny—women in dropped-waist dresses and cloche hats window shop while a horse-drawn delivery cart trundles by ringing its bell, the hot stink of manure leaking from the catch bag on the horse's rear—

Horse cart? What the hell? But the memory feels real. As real as the dental chair behind me. As real as the stick figures—no, glyphs—I painted without understanding why. She wore a blue flapper dress then, her red hair cut into a severe bob. Her smile is warm honey, slow and sweet, and impossibly distant.

"Luke?"

I jump and my cup tips. If I'd gone back for a refill, its contents would have sloshed across the floor. Again.

Sandra grabs my arm, her bangles jingling with concern. "Are you all right? You look pale."

"Yeah, I'm fine," I say. And for the first time tonight, I mean it.

"Oh, good. Don't disappear, okay? I've got a serious collector in the decision phase."

"Right on," I say, vaguely wondering why she's talking about a sale like it's a Fortune 500 merger. "I'm not going anywhere."

And I'm sure of that, because as she totters away in her six-inch heels, the whirlwind in my head stills. The whispers in my head fall silent. I'm fixed in place like cured oil paint. I glance down at my shoes—just brogues, steady and singular, no longer flickering between realities. That weird Spidey sense has dissolved into something I haven't felt in years.

Peace.

The gallery snaps into focus—clusters of people with their Solo cups and e-cigs and chattering mouths, bright lights glinting off Henry's perfect white teeth as he pours a Chardonnay for another guest, the canvases glowing in the overhead spotlights. My canvases, my creations. I remember every brushstroke, every dab of detail, every stroke of highlight. I remember adding every spiral, every concentric circle, every glyph.

And her—that dress, that hair, all perfectly realized as though I'd spent a lifetime capturing every detail of her on canvas.

I belong here. I am present.

And so is she.

"...the negative space really draws you in," her friend—date?—blabbers, his voice carrying the tone of someone more interested in hearing himself talk about art than actually seeing it. "The way it creates tension with the..."

I tap her on her shoulder. "Hello." The word comes out with the weight of a thousand questions crowding behind it.

She turns, and her eyes meet mine. They're the exact shade of Suwannee River moss I included in my Time on The Suwannee piece, though I've never been to that river in my life. I chose the shade because it matches her eyes, but that's not possible, is it? We've never met, unless we met at a 1920s reenactment somewhere. Norman Studios Film Museum? Although it's been what—twenty years since my middle school field trip?

"I'm Luke Campbell," I say, extending my hand.

"Eileen Nash." Her grip is firm, professional, but her hand trembles against mine. "We've met before, right?"

Yes, in another life. In another dimension. In my dreams. "I think so. At another show somewhere?"

The boyfriend's hand slices between us. "Dave Lundberg."

I take his hand and give it a light shake, never taking my eyes off Eileen Nash.

"Nice to meet you," I say, although I'm not really saying it to *him*, I'm saying it to *her*.

The blond mop says, "Love your work..."

His words blur into background chatter as I tell myself to stop looking at her. But I can't.

A voice, almost a shout, severs the tie. "Do you want another drink, babe?"

Eileen breaks our gaze and stares at blond mop, open-mouthed. I want to move the stray hair on the forehead behind her ear. I want to take her arm and give her a guided tour, then ask her out to lunch.

Eileen's expression stills, like a cave pool undisturbed by time. "No thank you, you go ahead."

Her eyes return to mine. "I'd love to hear about your inspiration for these cave motifs."

FOURTEEN: EILEEN

When Luke Campbell extends his hand, my world shifts—but not like the cave jumps. This is different. Subtle. Like the bump of an elevator sliding into place.

I grip his hand, but I'm staring into his eyes. His cerulean-blue eyes. I've never seen eyes that shade of dusty blue before, although I have, haven't I?

"Eileen Nash. We've met before, right?"

"I think so, at another show somewhere?"

Not likely, seeing as I go to art shows about as often as I sit in a box seat at Jags games—which is never. But we have met, I feel sure of it. He was dressed in a flat cap and paint-streaked work shirt, sitting in the flatbed of a truck with thin-spoked wheels and a long-handled crank at the front, like a Model T, but longer, dustier. Did we meet at one of those Riverside Park reenactments? No, wrong time period—they do Civil War stuff. Or the Renaissance Fair in Clay County? Definitely the wrong time period. As I struggle to conjure up a memory of a 1920s-era fair, I realize I'm still gripping his hand. And I'm still staring into those eyes.

Dave extends a hand right on top of Luke's and mine. I drop my hand, and the men shake hands.

"Dave Lundberg," he says, as though his name carries importance, as if Luke should recognize the name. *Oh, hey! You're that guy—the one who knows everything about art but can't paint anything meaningful, right? Nice to meet you! Let's grab a beer and chat some more. I'd love to hear your uninvited and pontificating opinions about my work.*

Dave drops the handshake and slithers his hand around my hips and onto my back. It feels like a cobra, testing, coiling, waiting to constrict around me and hiss, *you're mine.*

"Nice to meet you," Luke says, although I swear he's directing his words to me, not Dave.

"Love your work," Dave says. "The way you've evolved from pure realism to this more experimental—" and I want to shrivel through the floor from embarrassment.

Seconds later, Dave's arm tenses against my back. "Do you want another drink, babe?"

Babe? I glare at him, with my mouth open, words set to spill off my tongue. Seriously? Can you stop puffing your peacock feathers and let me ask Luke about the cave symbols in his art? But that's not all I want to ask Luke Campbell about, is it? If I'm being completely honest, I want to ask him why his eyes are the color of cerulean blue, why I feel like I've known him all my life, why there's this intense connection between us like a pair of tangled electrons.

But instead, I say, "No thank you, you go ahead."

Dave's hand remains on my back, his presence as stifling as a rush-hour city bus. I'm acutely aware of how this looks—another grad student fawning over the talented artist. But Luke's cave paintings... they're exact. The patterns I documented, the ones that vanished from my notebook. How could he possibly have seen them?

I turn my attention back to Luke. "I'd love to hear about your inspiration for these cave motifs."

Something flickers in his expression. Recognition? Fear? Before he can respond, the gallery owner whisks him away to "meet a collector." Luke holds my gaze as she leads him away.

"Let's get another drink," Dave says.

"I'm good," I say. Right now, the last thing I want to do is listen to more of Dave's jibber jab, and the first thing I want to do is get his slithering arm off my back.

"I need to use the restroom," I say, already moving that way. "Back in a sec."

Outside the restroom, a neat stack of business cards sits on top of an elegant Greek-style podium. I grab a card. Simple black text on cream paper: Luke Campbell, visual artist. And below that, a phone number. My hands tremble as I tuck it into my clutch.

A woman taps my elbow and for a second, I don't recognize her. But then I do. It is Candace Newell, from algebra in my college freshman year. Her curly dark hair is assembled into a neat bun now, a contrast to the wild mane she sported as an undergrad. She's dressed in a crisp button-down and dark jeans that suggest academia without trying too hard.

"Eileen? I thought that was you," she says, eyes lighting up with recognition. "It's been what—five, six years?"

"Candace, hi! Yes, at least that long. What brought you back to Jax? You went on to Harvard, right?"

"That's right. I'm doing an internship at Kennedy Space Center. Thought I'd come check out the old haunts."

"Wow. That's impressive. Astrophysics, right?"

"You got it. Computational astrophysics." She gestures toward Luke's paintings. "These cave glyphs caught my attention. Reminds me of some theoretical models I've been working with."

"Sounds like interesting work," I say. I don't know exactly what computational astrophysics is, but something clicks. Candace was always scribbling equations in the margins of her notes, talking about how she used simulations to model things like black holes, time warps, or what would happen if two stars crashed into each other.

"What sort of models are you working on?" I ask.

She smiles and says, "Time distortion at the edge of black holes, that kind of thing. Honestly, they're just models right now."

I clutch my plastic cup so tightly it crinkles. "Time distortion?"

"Slowing of time near black holes."

"Ah, I see," I say, hoping that I don't sound as deflated as if feel. It was silly to think that a chance meeting with an old sorority sister would lead to a simple explanation for time jumps. What had I been expecting her to say? Yes, you know—people jump in time near black holes. Remember the expedition to Gargantua last year? We time-warped three astronauts to 1963, stopped the assassination of JFK, and—bonus! They scored a mint-condition 1963 Topps Jim Brown. Can you believe it?

Candace takes a sip of her red wine. "What about you? Still digging in the dirt?"

It's not an insult. Back in our Alpha Chi Omega days, we had nicknames for each other. Mine was diggity-dirt, hers was spacehead.

"Someone's got to do real work down here on planet Earth."

We clink glasses.

"Actually, I'm finishing up my PhD. You know, I got dragged here by..." *my possessive jerk of a date* "... a friend. But the cave symbols in the paintings? They look exactly like some I've found in my research."

Candace's eyes sharpen with interest. "That's a cool coincidence. We should catch up properly." She pulls out her phone. "I'd love to hear more about your work."

We exchange numbers and agree to meet for lunch next week. My gut tells me that Candace might be the right person to ask about bent time—if anyone would understand, it would be the girl who once tried to explain Einstein's Theory of Relativity to our sorority.

FIFTEEN: LUKE

I stare at my text app. The "9am" I typed stares back. No response. That means it's a date, doesn't it?

I wait a minute for a response, then set the phone down on one of the high-top tables. The gallery has cleared out—leaving behind overflowing garbage bins, three flyers on the floor, and a deficit of $25 for the stack of business cards by the restroom door that is now gone. I'd better have made a sale. Otherwise, I'll be panhandling at the I-10 overpass for breakfast money.

Sandra's voice echoes from the back office as she talks with the collector who's interested in the dental chair series. Talking is an evil necessity in this business. It's a necessity because you must explain your art before you can sell it. And it's evil because you have to explain it to a hundred people before you can make a five-dollar profit on a print. During my art studio's open house last July, I talked for twelve hours to hundreds of people streaming through to see what "real" artists do behind closed doors. The sum total for twelve hours of exhausting chatter? I sold an $8 print, which means I earned a grand total of 67 cents per hour.

I need this collector to buy something. And I hope he's not asking about prints. I need to pay my rent. I need to eat. I need gas for my car. But most importantly, I need to have enough money in my pocket to buy Eileen a coffee. And a muffin too, if she wants one. Hell, maybe we'll talk until lunch, and then I'll really have to open the wallet. Even fast food costs fifteen bucks these days.

I pick up the phone again and stare at Eileen's number. It's too late to call, I know that. But I also have an inkling she wouldn't mind. You don't call a woman five minutes after you get her number. I don't want to be a creepy stalker. But I wish we hadn't had to cut our conversation short. Sure, I want to talk about the symbols in my paintings. But I also want to understand what it is about her that makes time reassemble and still when she's in my presence.

"Fantastic opening," Sandra says, making me drop my phone. It thunks on the floor. I pick it up—no cracks. Guess that the Temu screen protector worked.

Sandra stands beside me, her smile bright. "That collector wants the entire dental chair series. Says they speak to him about the nature of time." She laughs. "Whatever that means. But hey, if it sells—"

She said it with the enthusiasm of a car mechanic telling me my car needs brake fluid. "Sorry, but could you repeat that? How many does he want?" I heard ten, but I know that can't be right. That would be fifty grand. Did she say "one"? One sounds like "ten" if your mind is elsewhere, right?

"He wants all of them," she says, still donning that saleswoman smile.

"Great," I say. It registers with me that I just made thirty thousand dollars. It also registers that Sandra is looking at me like I should be whooping and hollering and dancing a jig for selling my entire series in one evening. But I'm too pumped inside, too excited about meeting Eileen Nash in the morning—there's not a drop of room for an ounce more excitement. All I can think about is *her*. The way she had said "cave motifs," like she was trying them on me for size.

"Luke?" Sandra's smile falters. "Are you okay? You seem—"

"Fine. Just tired." I manage what I hope is a convincing smile.

"Great opening," she says. "Come by Monday to get your check."

We shake hands, transaction done, time to skedaddle.

Outside, the April night is cool enough to make me shiver. I unlock my car but don't get in, and stare instead at my reflection in the driver's side window. The man looking back seems present, confident, real. Like the timeline has settled. It's not the guy who was going to paint all night and then head to the ER. It's a guy who's fallen in love at first sight.

My phone buzzes. Kristy: "The opening was amazing! Drinks to celebrate?" There's a juice bar on Park Street, WildTease, where we always go—a bar without the burn, where the strongest drink is mushroom coffee.

I text back: "Rain check. Early morning tomorrow."

Because I have a coffee date with a woman whose terra verte eyes look at my paintings like they're the Mona Lisa and The Creation of Adam and Guernica rolled into one. Because I don't want to show up for our first date with black circles under my eyes and yesterday's shirt.

Because my fractured reality laid breadcrumbs to her door.

I hope I'm not crazy. Or if I am, I hope she's crazy too.

The dental chair painting catches my eye through the gallery window, its twisted chrome glinting in the streetlight. For a brief second, I swear I smell limestone and river water.

I get in my car but don't start the engine. I grab the chip in my pocket and run my thumb over its surface. The metal reminds me that at least some things are real in this timeline, even if I'm too chicken to look at the engraved number. If no one observes the moment, does it even happen? Is the cat alive, dead, or waiting for someone to look? Doesn't matter. Not right now.

But as I turn the ignition, I wonder: when I see her tomorrow, which version of myself will I be?

SIXTEEN: EILEEN

At home, I kick off my Mary Janes and wrench myself free from the restrictive dress. It collapses to the floor in a heap, and I nudge it toward the hamper with my toe.

Luke Campbell's business card sits on my desk, gleaming under my lamp like an artifact I've unearthed. My fingers hover over it, tracing his name without touching the paper. There's a ridiculous dating rule about waiting twenty-four hours before texting a guy—some power play I've never understood. But this isn't just any guy. This is the man who knows where to find more cave drawings. This will be an academic discourse, not a date, right? Besides, he didn't give me his card and ask me to call him—I took his card from that podium. Which means the normal rules don't apply.

I pick up my phone and type,

"Hi, Luke. This is Eileen Nash from your gallery opening. I'm a grad student studying previously undocumented pre-Columbian cave art—"

Too formal. I hit backspace, deleting the jargon.

"... studying cave paintings. Would love to—"

Too eager. I hit backspace again.

"... would like to chat about your inspiration for those pieces. Coffee sometime?"

Do I sound too eager? Too vague? Should I suggest a specific time? Does "coffee sometime" sound like I'm hitting on him? Perhaps I should suggest meeting at the university—

I hit send before I can overthink more. I hope that didn't sound too—

My phone buzzes and my heart leaps.

"Great. When?"

Great? Just "great"? Does that mean he can't wait to meet me? Oh, no, I hope he doesn't think I'm a potential buyer. He'll be disappointed when I ramble on about the rarity of pre-Columbian cave art in the Southeast. Should I call him to clarify? No, that's too forward.

When's best to meet? Tomorrow is Saturday. Dave and I are supposed to go to the farmers' market, but...

But the thought of meeting Dave leaves me feeling cold. There's no way I can act like tonight didn't happen. I can't pretend that his territorial posturing wasn't offensive and embarrassing.

I type, "Tomorrow morning? Bold Bean on Stockton?"

Another immediate response: "9am."

I fall back onto my bed, heart racing. This isn't about Dave. This isn't even about my attraction for Luke, though God knows that's there too. This is about answers. About where Luke saw those cave motifs before he painted them. Wherever it is, I'm going to drive there. Or fly there. I'll fly to the Easter Islands if I have to. And if Luke wants to come along for the trip... well, it's okay to dream, right?

I set my alarm. The butterflies in my stomach promise a night of restless sleep. Some of those flutters are for Luke. The rest beat at the idea of finding the cave motifs somewhere new. I've chased clues through dirt and time but never expected one to have cerulean-blue eyes.

SEVENTEEN: LUKE

The Bold Bean door jingles when I push it open. I nearly bump into a man in cycling gear and mumble an apology as I join the line of a half-dozen people. The café is abuzz with Saturday morning energy—baristas call out orders, milk frothers hiss, chair legs scrape against tile.

I scan the room for Eileen, my heart thrumming between certainty she's here and dread she isn't. Maybe she heard from some mutual friend about that asshole Luke Campbell who used to bar crawl down King Street, hitting on women and starting fights—the shameful highlight reel of my drinking days. Word travels fast in this part of town—Riverside is a village within the city, and the gossip probably reached her as soon as she hit Send on that first text.

But there she is. By the window, coffee cup in hand, notepad open. Flecks of sunlight shimmer with light vermillion tones on her red hair.

She looks up, and I wave flaccidly. I am so out of my depth here. She's a grad student and I'm a nobody artist who might have just had my five minutes of fame. My phone's alarm jolted me awake at 6 a.m., giving me three hours to pace, shower, and iron my "Support Your Local Artist" t-shirt. I considered a button-down but didn't want to look desperate. All that effort and all I can do is give her a limp wave?

She smiles and returns to her notebook. I shift my weight from foot to foot in the endless line. If my knee could bend another thirty degrees, I'd be kicking myself right now. I should have shown up early to buy her a coffee. Instead, I'm standing in line, looking like another lame-ass hipster with a tight wallet. The barista calls me forward, and I order the 20oz with a splash of oat milk and two shots of caramel. Five bucks, but who cares? I'm still up twenty-nine grand from last night. Heck, I might dump in three sugars and enjoy the high.

The barista calls my name, and I grab my drink. I take a deep breath and thread between tables toward Eileen.

"Hi," I say, sliding into the chair across from her. Keep it together, Campbell. Don't scare her off by acting like a lunatic who thinks he's jumping through time. "I, uh, wasn't sure if you'd really be here."

Way to go, Luke. Sound confident.

"I wasn't sure you'd come either." Her voice is soft, uncertain.

My gaze drops to her notebook. "Suwannee Caves" is written across the cover in precise lettering, the pages dog-eared and filled with a color wheel of Post-it notes.

"So, you're studying caves?" I ask, fighting to keep my voice level. Rule one of dating, according to Reddit: Start with them. Ask questions.

"That's right." Her eyes light up, and she turns her notebook toward me. Her finger traces a rock formation sketched in pencil. "I'm focused on previously undocumented pre-Columbian cave art that is a result of karst topography—how water carves pathways through limestone over thousands of years. The river levels have exposed chambers that haven't seen daylight in millennia."

"Cool," I say, as my brain stutters to a halt. I try to think of something intelligent to say, but I've got no idea what "karst topography" or "pre-Columbian" means or how they relate to each other. Something to do with maps before Columbus arrived? "So you, uh, found pre-Columbus maps in those caves?"

She smiles. "Close. But not maps—cultures. 'Pre-Columbian' refers to Indigenous societies in the Americas before European contact."

"So, like the Timucuan?" I pat myself on the back. I've spent enough time walking the trails out on the Timucuan Preserve to know a thing or two about the tribe. One: Jacksonville has a National Preserve named after them and two: well, refer back to One.

"Exactly. The Timucua, the Mississippians, the Calusa—all part of that era, depending on where you're looking. Florida was more active than most people think."

Mississippians? Calusa? No clue, but I make an educated guess about what to ask next. She'd mentioned the glyphs in my paintings, so— "That's really interesting. What have you found so far?"

She flips to a page where stick figures dance across the paper—identical to the ones that appeared in my feverish painting sessions.

My mouth dries up like a mid-summer gully. "These are from, uh... a cave?"

She nods. "I discovered a previously submerged cave on the Suwannee. These drawings were in there."

The figures in my paintings—the ones that came through me rather than from me—are from her caves. Caves I've never seen. Her drawings are detailed to the point of being extraordinary, but I need to see them in color. Did I capture the right shades and tones? "Incredible. Did you take photos?"

She looks at me and it's a question. One that I can't quite decipher, but it's like she's analyzing whether she can trust me.

"They got deleted."

Strange choice of words. Not "I deleted them." But "they got deleted." I wonder if that slimeball date of hers from last night had something to do with it. He struck me as the kind of guy who'd pitch a fit about flirting and destroy her research in a jealous rage.

"Oh," I say.

"These motifs," she says, tapping a stick figure with a spindly head and saucer eyes. "This is going to sound weird, but they're in a cave out by Big Shoals. Have you been there? Or did you see them somewhere else?"

Weird? Hardly. Weird is being surrounded by stick figure aliens while driving over the Buckman—right before you jump into the invisible Delorean. "Uh, neither, really." I wrap my hands around my coffee mug. It's hard to be specific when that'll mean instant rejection. Forget a second date. I'll be lucky if she doesn't check her watch twenty seconds later, or ask the Barista for a "Wednesday Special," which is local code for "Call the cops, I'm in danger."

Instead, I deflect. "Big Shoals. That's out west, right?"

She pauses, staring at me with those terra verte eyes. "Yes. On the Suwannee."

Suwannee, right. Music festival. I think I might have passed the bridge over the Suwannee on I-10, but—"I've definitely never been there."

"So, you haven't actually seen the glyphs anywhere in person?"

"No. Not in real life."

"In a book? Or online maybe?"

I shrug, the coffee suddenly bitter on my tongue. "I don't think so. I'm not a big reader, so..."

Friggin' awesome Luke. Way to go. She's an academic, and you just admitted you don't read. If this even was a date, well now it isn't. You just got in the cart and let the horses loose. This, my friend, is not going to go anywhere. Pat on the back, man.

She leans forward, elbows on the table. "Tell me about your paintings, then." She's so close I can smell her peppermint shampoo, see two tiny freckles below her left eye. "Where did you get the idea for the motifs?"

Truth or deflection? Three years sober means choosing the truth, even when it hurts. Even when it makes you sound insane. "I don't remember painting them. Not really. They just... happen." My fingers twitch around the mug. "Like something else is moving my hands." I meet her eyes, knowing how this sounds. "You must think I'm crazy."

"I don't think you're crazy at all. In fact..."

She appears to be chewing on what she's going to say next. After a moment, the corner of her mouth quirks up. "Aren't all artists a little... out there? I think the way you've depicted them is incredible. The way they seem to... shift when you look at them. What inspired you to do the series?"

"Something that happened to me in the past."

She covers her mouth with her hand and looks me directly in the eyes. "Sorry, I don't mean to pry, but would you—"

My hand jerks involuntarily, knocking over my coffee. The dark liquid races across the table and spills over the table edge to the floor. We both reach for napkins, and when our fingers touch, electricity arcs between us. Not as in the metaphorical kind, but as in—I swear I didn't just feel it. I saw it. Like it was a physical connection. An electric, subatomic connection between us that just needed a touch to spark.

"Sorry," I say on my knees, mopping up the spill. "I'm not usually this clumsy. It's just—" I'm nervous as hell.

She's on the floor with me, a wad of soggy napkins in her hand.

"Listen, I know this might sound strange, but... would you be interested in seeing some real caves? For your art?"

Everything inside me goes still. This is it. The convergence point. The reason for all the jumps and fractures.

"When?" I ask, my mouth dry.

"This weekend?"

"Yes," I say without hesitation. Then, softer: "Please."

We deposit the wet napkins into the garbage and sit back down.

"Do you paddle?" she asks. "As in, paddleboarding."

The question hits me like a sucker punch. Paddle. Water. Jasper.

"No," I manage, as memories flood back. Not now. Not this. "But I took surfing lessons when I was fourteen."

Before the shark. Before Mom's scream. Before the crimson bloom. Before it all plays in my head, on repeat in the dark.

My chest tightens as the familiar panic rises. Three years sober doesn't mean three years without anxiety. I reach for my AA chip, rolling it between my fingers under the table.

I should say no. Paddleboards, water, caves—all of it spells disaster. "I'll need a life jacket," I say, forcing a smile to cover the tremor in my voice, trying not to think about how Jasper's life jacket didn't save him.

She smiles. "Cool. I've got a spare."

The sunlight catches her eyes, turning them translucent. In that instant, I see understanding there. Like she knows me. Like she's seen me at my worst and still stayed.

But that can't be right. Because we just met, didn't we?

EIGHTEEN: EILEEN

The morning sun slants through Bold Bean's windows, turning the steam from my coffee into ghostly spirals. I'm twenty minutes early, my hair damp from a 6 a.m. shower. I changed outfits four times before settling on what I normally wear to field research: jeans, a fitted UF archaeology department t-shirt, hiking boots. No point pretending to be something I'm not.

My leather field notebook sits beside my coffee. I've been trying to sketch the cave patterns again, but they keep coming out wrong. Not exact renditions—like Luke's paintings. Not like what I saw in the cave.

My phone buzzes.

Dave: "Missing u at farmers market."

I turn the phone face-down without replying. Guilt gnaws at my stomach, a stomach-curdling mix of caffeine and anxiety. I know I need to break up with him. The easiest thing would be to ghost him. But that wouldn't be fair, would it? Would it be a better idea to risk an argument over the phone or to have to tell him in person and brace for whatever emotion spills out? Hurt? Anger? Snark?

For now, ghosting seems like the best option until I figure this all out.

No, I can't do that. But what do I say? Hey, you possessive creep. We're done. Don't call me again.

I text, "Hey, Dave, I've enjoyed getting to know you, but I don't think we should continue seeing each other. I'm going through some changes right now that I need to focus on. I wish you all the best."

Three dots appear on the screen, and I break into a cold sweat. I'm not in the mood for a text message diatribe or worse—a phone call. I should switch my phone to silent in case he—

A text appears. "Understand. U too."

Well, I wasn't expecting that. But clean breaks are good. And Luke should be here soon.

A waft of warm air and the rumble of traffic come into the coffee shop when the door opens.

Luke walks in and gets in line. The whole cafe shifts around him—like reality adjusting its focus. He's wearing jeans and an artsy T-shirt. His hair is darker than it looked under the gallery lights, as black as a stick of charcoal. My English Gran would have called Luke a *dish*. I'm not sure what to call him, but those little flutters in my stomach are back. But who am I kidding? They never went away. Not since the previous evening.

Our eyes meet, and he gives me a cute little wave.

I smile and look at my notebook. Play it cool, Eileen. No need to gawk like a groupie.

A couple of minutes later, he's walking toward me with his drink.

"Hi," he says, sliding into the seat across from me. "I, uh, wasn't sure if you'd really be here."

Up close, I can see the shadows under his eyes, the slight tremor in his hands as he sets down his coffee. Last night must have been exhausting—talking to all those people for hours.

"I wasn't sure you'd come either." Ugh. Way to sound like a confident archaeologist, Eileen.

His eyes fall on my notebook, and something flickers across his face—recognition? "So, you're studying caves?"

"That's right," I say, turning my notebook toward him. I tap a map-like rendering of the newly exposed cave chamber, with notated passages shaped by karst erosion—acidic water dissolving the limestone. But he doesn't want to hear all that academic-speak. "I'm focused on previously undocumented pre-Columbian cave art that is a result of karst topography—how water carves pathways through limestone over thousands of years. The river levels have exposed chambers that haven't seen daylight in millennia."

"Cool," he says.

Crap, I've already bored him.

"So, you, uh, found pre-Columbus maps in those caves?"

I'm impressed. Apparently, he knows his history. "Close. But not maps—cultures. 'Pre-Columbian' refers to Indigenous societies in the Americas before European contact." For God's sake, Eileen, stop blabbering.

"So, like the Timucuan?"

I draw in a breath. Not only is this man a talented artist, but he's also smart. That doesn't surprise me, considering the complexity of his paintings. I don't stand a chance: He's an A-lister, and I'm the dork behind the scenes penning the script. "Exactly. The Timucua, the Mississippians, the Calusa—all part of that era, depending on where you're looking. Florida was more active than most people think."

"That's really interesting. What have you found so far?"

What have I found so far? You wouldn't believe me if I told you. But to give an answer to his question, I flip to the page with the elongated stick figures that look exactly like the glyphs on his paintings.

"These are from, uh... a cave?"

That wasn't the response I was hoping for. I was hoping for something more like, *Hey, I've been there!* Or, *Hey! I saw those in a cave in Wales on my trip to the UK last summer.* Or even, *Get out of here! My uncle Ham had a collection of old pottery in his basement with these exact glyphs.*

I nod like a bobblehead doll—passive and silent. I'm falling into old habits, doing what I think a man expects rather than speaking my mind. But I can't speak my mind, can I? "Last week I discovered a previously submerged cave on the Suwannee. These drawings were in there."

He's entranced by the figures on the page. "Incredible. Did you take photos?"

I suck in a breath. Should I lie and say no? Or tell him how they magically disappeared and start a conversation that'll end up with him walking out, shaking his head, and mumbling, *nutcase?* No, as much as I want to tell him, I can't take the risk. I am certain that Luke is going to be an important part of my life, and I'm not going to screw this up before it's begun. His cerulean-blue eyes say "Trust me," but I can't trust myself to find the right words.

I say, "They got deleted." At least that's not a lie.

"Oh," he says.

For a second, I think he's probing my mind. He knows I'm lying. He knows that time doesn't stand still for me. And he probably thinks I'm a quack with a mad scientist lab in a campus basement.

Time for another deflect. "These motifs. This is going to sound weird, but they're in a cave out by Big Shoals. Have you been there? Or did you see them somewhere else?"

He averts his eyes and studies his coffee cup. "Uh, neither, really."

Oh, no. Did I say something strange? I did, didn't I. His next words are going to be, *Oh, look at the time...*

Instead, he says, "Big Shoals. That's out west, right?"

I breathe a sigh of relief. I need more than a sigh to catch my breath around this *dish,* though. I need breathing exercises... in one thousand, out one thousand... but that will not go down well on a first date, will it?

I say, "Yes. On the Suwannee."

"I've definitely never been there."

"So, you haven't actually seen the glyphs anywhere in person?"

"No. Not in real life."

"In a book? Or online maybe?"

"I don't think so. I'm not a big reader, so..."

The flutters in my stomach have turned into swirls of excitement. If he didn't see it in a book or online, then he must have seen it somewhere in person. I can't begin to describe how deflated I would feel if he said he'd seen it in a book. If that were true, then it would mean someone else discovered these glyphs before me, which would mean goodbye, PhD thesis. Maybe if I ask him about his art, he'll remember where he saw them.

I say, "Tell me about your paintings, then. Where did you get the idea for the motifs?"

He leans in, close enough I get a waft of limes and coconut. Luke smells as good as he looks.

"I don't remember painting them. Not really. They just... happen. Like something else is moving my hands. You must think I'm crazy."

"I don't think you're crazy at all. In fact..." In fact, I'm probably a 99 on the 1 to 10 crazy scale. "Aren't all artists a little... out there? I think the way you've depicted them is incredible. The way they seem to... shift when you look at them. What inspired you to do the series?"

"Something that happened to me in the past."

"Sorry, I don't mean to pry, but would you—"

His hand jerks, knocking over his coffee. We grab napkins, our fingers brushing. The touch sends electricity up my arm, and suddenly I'm certain—absolutely certain—that he feels it too. This connection. This intangible thing between us.

"Sorry," he says, as we mop up the spill. "I'm not usually this clumsy. It's just..."

I soak up the last of the coffee spots. "Listen, I know this might sound strange, but... would you be interested in seeing some real caves? For your art?" I'm being too pushy, which is not like me, not like me at all. I wait for his shocked look, his *um, uh, I think I might be busy.*

Instead, his face goes perfectly still. "When?"

"This weekend?" The question slips out. I'm inviting an artist to the caves on... what? A date? A field trip? No, a paddling expedition—with someone who's apparently never been on a board.

"Yes," Luke says immediately, like he's been waiting for this question all along. Then, softer: "Please."

We throw the napkins into the can and sit back down.

"Do you paddle?"

He looks confused.

"As in, paddleboarding."

"No," he says. "But I took surfing lessons when I was fourteen."

His face scrunches up and he looks ten years older, like he's dragged up a painful memory.

The morning sun catches his eyes, turning them Manganese blue—the exact color of a Florida spring. In that instant, I see understanding there. Like he knows me. Like he's seen me freak out a cockroach on a toothbrush or sob at the end of *Titanic* or hurl dishes the day before my period starts—and still stayed.

But that can't be right. Because we just met, didn't we?

* * *

Later that morning, the midday sun streams through the windows at Farmhouse Kitchen, turning Candace's water glass into a prism. She looks different from her freshman algebra days. Her curly hair is pulled back into a bun, and her earrings are simple studs, a jarring contrast to the wild curls and giant hoops from her undergrad years. She's also more confident—the kind that comes from knowing you're brilliant at what you do. The Harvard polish sits well on her—she moves with purpose, her gestures deliberate and fluid as she reaches for her water glass.

"So let me get this straight," she says, setting down her fork, her voice carrying that familiar, precise cadence I remember from study groups. "You found cave drawings that vanished. You think there are connected caves, or... or some kind of anomaly there. And now there's this artist painting the exact patterns you saw?" Her voice is low, careful—we're not the only ones having lunch on the restaurant's sunny patio.

I glance around before answering. A couple in matching bucket hats and flip-flops thumbs through their phones at the next table, oblivious to each other, let alone Candace and me. A blank-faced server weaves between chairs, balancing trays—he's probably counting the minutes until quitting time.

I choose my words carefully. I'm not about to tell her I think I'm a time traveler. "I know how it sounds."

"Actually," Candace leans forward, her eyes bright with the same intensity I remember from study groups, "it sounds like quantum entanglement."

"Like what?" I recognize the words from somewhere—a Netflix show about the universe, maybe? I can hear Morgan Freeman's voice, but I can't make out what he's saying. It's like an earworm transmitted from outer space, the words mostly muddled, the concepts unintelligible.

"It's when two particles connect in such a way that the state of one directly correlates to the state of the other, regardless of the distance between them." She pulls out a napkin and starts to sketch. "Einstein called it 'spooky action at a distance.'"

I think about Luke's paintings, about the way he'd said he didn't remember creating them. About the electricity when our hands touched. "You're a bit over my head. Can you explain that to me like I'm twelve? Physics isn't exactly my strong point if you remember."

Of course she remembers. If not for Candace's help with my physics final, I would never have passed. She'd spent the whole evening before the exam showing me flashcards in my dorm room. They weren't the usual dull flash cards—they were what I called Candace cards: Equations on the front, mnemonic on the back. The card I remember most vividly had "F = ma" on the front and "Force = my anger" on the back. Because when physics jargon accelerates, my anger does too.

"Under certain conditions, two particles can mimic each other, no matter the distance." She draws two intersecting circles. "If your consciousness and his are linked—entangled—you could share your existence, what's called a quantum state. In other words, what happens to you could ripple into his experience—like a resonance across time, rather than a direct signal."

She missed the "explain it like I'm twelve bit," but I get the gist. "So, Luke and I are magic twins. If I sip my coffee, he's doing it too—instantly—even if we're on different planets. It's not about sending messages—it's more like we're sharing a brain."

The idea of Luke experiencing my comings and goings hits me all at once. Stuffing German chocolate cake into my mouth at 3 a.m. Yelling "asshole" to the bicyclist who nearly sent me flying on a crosswalk. Demolishing a bottle of wine after Samuel dumped me. It's so absurd I laugh. Not enough to draw attention, but enough to make me snort.

She throws her head back in that distinctive Candace laugh I remember from sorority parties. "Brain melding? Close enough."

"That sounds a little bit like sci-fi," I say. Or soulmates.

She splays her hands and wobbles her head. Maybe so, maybe not. "They've performed tests on subatomic particles and proved that their states remain connected, even when separated. It's like... if one spins left, the other spins right instantly, no matter how far apart they are. Not exactly sending messages, but the particles stay perfectly in sync. It's a bit mind-blowing, even for me. But then again, it isn't exactly my field."

"Astrophysics, right?"

"Yup. Computational astrophysics. So I know quite a bit about quantum mechanics but... well, I'm just a grad student. Still learning, right?"

I nod. "I don't think we'll ever stop. Learning, that is."

She laughs. "Until we max out our student loans."

"Second that." I try not to think about my 50k in student loans. "So, back to quantum entanglement. I'm not understanding how two particles—jiggling at the same time, miles apart—explains Luke painting things I'm seeing."

She shrugs. "The cave could have scrambled your quantum states. If Luke's information is entangled with yours but unstable, he might be experiencing interference—like a weak signal picking up fragments of your reality."

Fragmented reality? My stomach flips. Should I tell her?

Nope.

"But 'signal' implies a source, right?" I ask.

"Mm-hmm. The cave. It could act like a beam splitter."

"Theoretically, could the cave act as, I don't know..." But I do. I hesitate to make myself sound less... unraveled. "Is this some kind of... uh, temporal displacement?"

"As in, time machine?"

Heat creeps into my cheeks. "I guess, maybe?"

But she's not laughing. She's scrunching her brows as if deep in thought. "Theoretically, yes. Einstein's relativity confirmed that travel to the future is possible."

"And the past?"

"Unproven but possible. Wormholes, rotating universes—"

"Caves?" Oh, that came out wrong. Time-traveling caves? Stupid, Eileen. Stupid. "Forget that, I meant..." But I can't find an appropriate word to finish the sentence.

"A cave could create the right conditions. If there were a localized gravitational anomaly—some kind of extreme warping of spacetime—it could, theoretically, cause temporal displacement."

I lean forward, thinking of *Interstellar*, when Matthew McConaughey pitched into Gargantuan. "Localized anomaly? As in—black hole?"

She waves a hand. "Not a black hole; we'd all be dead. But something similar—an area where gravity is concentrated enough to stretch time. If there was a deep enough fracture in the Earth's crust..." She exhales sharply. "Okay, this is wild speculation. But if something in the cave could distort spacetime, it might create conditions similar to a wormhole."

I swallow hard. "A wormhole."

She shrugs. "If there were an energy source, some kind of quantum fluctuation or exotic matter—"

I blink. "Okay, you're over my head now."

"Let me put it this way. Certain mineral compositions can interact with electromagnetic fields. If the cave walls contained something piezoelectric—like quartz—it could, under the right stress..."

She keeps talking, but I hyperfocus on one word. Quartz. The way the figures seemed to move backward and forward on the cave walls. How I'd considered quartz as creating an optical illusion. It couldn't be a catalyst for time travel, could it?

"...so the short answer to your question is that yes, it's theoretically possible that a cave could produce temporal anomalies. It could explain your vanishing drawings."

"If the cave is producing temporal anomalies, how would you prove that?"

"This will be fun. We need to test this cave. Carefully." She reaches into her bag and pulls out a small notebook. "Do you have any houseplants that you want to get rid of?"

A what? Houseplant? What on earth ...

But it's like Candace can read my mind. Either that or she sees my puzzled expression. My brows are so furrowed they're about to block my eyesight.

"A plant is a simple, observable test subject," she says. "If the cave distorts time, we might see weird growth patterns—faster, slower, or out of sync with the other half, which you should leave at home. Not exactly a quantum experiment, but if we get something strange, we'll know we're onto something."

PART II: DECOHERENCE

NINETEEN: LUKE

The sun hasn't crested the treeline yet, but the Big Shoals boat ramp is already heating up with late morning humidity. My palms are sweating, and not just from the Florida sun. Second-date jitters—if that's what this is—make me feel like a teenager again. I pace the wooden dock, my footsteps hollow against the planks, startling a great blue heron into flight.

I've seen one before. But where? The detail gnaws at me like a misplaced debit card. Important, but not life-threateningly important—just enough to nag. And then it comes to me. Here. I saw it here. I get a snippet of a memory: drinking whiskey in a clearing, a group of guys sitting around a campfire, laughing, and playing cards. I must have been hammered that night to forget an hour-and-twenty-minute car ride.

The last twenty-four hours have also been a blur. As soon as I left the coffee shop, I headed to the studio to paint Eileen. But my jubilation waned quickly as I painted. The more I tried to capture her, the more she fractured into ten Eileens—different clothing, pants, dresses, a hat, no hat, even white gloves in one iteration. She was old; she was young. It's like my mind couldn't settle on what phase of life I was trying to depict.

Then I got that unsettling vertigo again. I smelled manure and peppermint, hallucinated a steering wheel, and Treaty Oak—I swear its limbs were crawling toward me. I ended up taking a twelve-hour nap at 6 p.m., thinking I just needed sleep. That's probably what it was, because here, with Eileen on her way—I hope—I feel a little more refreshed and a lot less broken.

Water flows beneath the dock in slow, swirling ribbons, nothing like the surf that took Jasper. We were out in the pre-storm swell, riding those heavy, unorganized sets. Stupid, really. Those

96

aren't beginner waves. And with that kind of choppy, shifting water, you can't see a damn thing beneath the surface.

I check my phone again: 10:55 a.m. Eileen said she'd be here by eleven with the paddleboards. My AA chip clinks against my keys as I shift my weight. I finally drummed up the courage to look at the chip when I woke up and was relieved to find my three-year chip. Back where I belong. Though the texts and emails congratulating me on the show still feel weird—like they're meant for some other Luke Campbell on a different timeline, not just some ordinary guy who caught a lucky break. I check my pocket again to make sure the chip is still there. It is.

Rose used to hate that nervous habit, the constant fiddling. But thinking about Rose now feels like remembering a different person's life. Three years ago, I would have had a hair of the dog by 8 a.m. Now here I am, about to get on the water after almost two decades, and the bottle isn't calling my name. I hope Eileen doesn't bring a picnic with beer, though. I wouldn't want to have that awkward conversation on a second date. Should I have told her I'm a recovering alcoholic? Nope. Should I have packed lunch? Probably, but my stomach's too knotted to eat, anyway.

A car door slams in the parking lot, the sound sharp against the river's constant murmur. I turn and see Eileen. She unstraps the weather-beaten boards from her roof rack with the certainty of someone who does this a lot. She catches my eye and waves, and warmth spreads in my chest like we've known each other forever. Her smile feels more intoxicating than any drink I've had in the past.

She's dressed in quick-dry shorts and a long-sleeved rash guard, but she looks like an old Hollywood movie star—timeless.

"You ready?" she calls out, and I realize I'm still rooted to the dock, staring at her like a red-carpet fan.

She juggles gear and... a potted plant? It's a spider plant, like the one Rose had in our bathroom, its leaves trailing from its mesh bag.

"What's with the plant?" I ask, moving to help her with the boards. I lift one from the ground and we walk toward the water. It's nearly twice the length of a surfboard and much heavier. I struggle to keep it balanced under my arm, the ends seesawing, while Eileen carries hers effortlessly—as if hers weighs five pounds and mine weighs fifty.

"It's to test the air in the cave." She glances at me through her long eyelashes. "It's about half a mile upstream."

"Test the air?" I take the life vest she hands me, catching a whiff of peachy sunscreen. "I thought they used canaries for that kind of thing."

She laughs, but there's something careful behind it, like she's hiding a secret. "Spider plants are better. Fewer ethical concerns." Her eyes light up when she smiles, and it hits me how natural this feels, like we've spent a lifetime together.

I've never heard of plants testing air quality, but then again, I'm not a PhD student. I didn't even finish up my associate's, though I aced the art classes. There's a lot about this situation that makes little sense. For a start, she's a composed, educated goddess, and I'm either: a/ a delusional nutcase who's one more vertigo attack away from slicing his ear off, or b/ an involuntary time-traveler. But here I am, about to follow this magnetic woman into a cave, hoping there won't be another... episode.

There are a hundred things that could go wrong today—her cracking out a couple of cold beers, me having an attack of vertigo, me transporting back to yesterday at 11 a.m., and doing this all over again. I just need one thing to go right: this date.

While I have no intention of telling her about my alcoholic past or my... unusual perception of time... I should tell her about Jasper. About why being on the water again feels like swallowing glass.

But before I can speak, she's beside me with two life vests. "This one's for you," she says, holding out the hot pink vest.

I raise an eyebrow.

"Unless you'd prefer this one?" She shakes the floral one in her right hand.

And just like that, I'm donning a bright pink vest and deciding to tell her later about Jasper.

Once we're ankle-deep in the water, boards floating in front of us, she kneels to wrap the board leash around my ankle. "This keeps you connected to the board. Different from a surfboard tether—it's longer, gives you more room to move."

She makes it look effortless. She sits on her board, then stands upright in a half-second flat. Her paddle cuts the water in smooth, practiced strokes as she demonstrates, holding position against the current. Ten years of muscle memory from surfing screams at me that this is all wrong—standing straight up on what looks like an oversized longboard.

"Knees first," she says. "Then slowly stand. The river's more stable than ocean waves."

I ease onto the board. It wobbles beneath my weight. My knees shake as I push to standing, arms out like a tightrope walker as the board shimmies from left to right. A flash of panic rises—what if I get vertigo out here?—but I push it down. My Barbie lifejacket will save me.

Eileen paddles closer, steady as a living sculpture glued to her board.

"You've got this," she says softly. "Just keep your core tight and your eyes on the horizon."

The river flows dark and steady beneath us. My heart pounds from the brief glances she sends my way, inspiring me to prove I can do this. For her. For myself.

And then I hear a splash.

TWENTY: EILEEN

A jumping fish breaks the surface near Luke's board. He startles, overcorrects—and suddenly the board slips out from under him and he's in the water. The current here is strong, dark water churning against limestone. Without thinking, I drop my paddle and jump in.

The river is coffee-dark, but I spot him, fighting against the pull of the current, paddleboard floating lazily next to him. His eyes are wide, unblinking, and locked on nothing—like he can't figure out where to go or what to do next. I grab his arm.

"I've got you," I say, treading water. "Let's head to the bank."

He regains focus and stares at me. His face is drenched, but I think I see tears in his eyes. He's shaking, but not from the cold—the water is 72 degrees year-round. He grips my hand. "I thought I was a goner for a second. Thank you."

"You're welcome," I say. "But you wouldn't have drowned. Hot pink lifejacket, remember?"

He looks down at the pink jacket bobbing above the waterline. "Barbie to the rescue."

We both smile, and a sparkle returns to his eyes. His breathing is still ragged though, and his fingers dig into my skin like an arcade claw machine.

We're face to face now, and my free arm wraps around his waist for balance as we drift with the current. Water streams down his face, and I'm struck by how beautiful he looks, like a Greek statue beneath a waterfall fountain. His eyes lock onto mine, and for a moment, it's just me, him, and the lazy river, like we're taking a break from tubing on the Ichetucknee Springs.

His breath steadies, and he leans closer, or maybe I do.

A boat horn blares downstream, breaking the spell. Reality

rushes back: the cave, the spider plant, Candace's warnings about testing the time jumps. Luke dumping into the water. I'm putting him in danger, and he doesn't even know it. Or maybe he does, now that he's drenched.

"The bank," I say, nodding to the right. "We should—"

"Yeah." He holds his gaze for a moment longer, and I try not to think about how right it feels. About how much I want to kiss him.

We break eye contact, grab our boards, and swim to the rocky bank. Luke flops down on his back next to me and looks at the sky.

"I'm sorry," he says. "I should have told you I'm not great with water. Not anymore, not since..."

"It's okay. Everyone has their fears."

He looks at me, something vulnerable in his expression. "I guess I can add nearly drowning my paddleboard partner to the list."

I nudge him in the side. "Seriously? Did you not just see the clutch play?"

"You know your football. I'm impressed."

"I've spent more than a few hours up in the nosebleeds."

"Me too. I'm surprised I didn't notice you up there in the clouds. You'd kind of stand out."

He scrunches his mouth, shrugs.

"Look," he says, turning his gaze to the water. "I need to tell you about Jasper, my brother. The reason I freaked out just then, it's because... that's the first time I've been in the water since... it happened."

"Since what happened?" I ask.

"Jasper was fourteen, I was sixteen. We took a few surfing lessons and then there was this big storm offshore, creating these huge waves, right? Well, we thought we could handle it, so we took our boards out. We were in the water for maybe five minutes." He rubs his forehead with his fingers. He shakes his head from side to side—slowly, like he's pushing the memory into place—then he blows out a deep breath. "A shark pulled him under. That's the last time I went in the water."

"Oh, my God," I say. "I've had this... fear of the ocean for as long as I can remember. I was fine as a kid—loved the beach, swimming, all of it. But when I was seventeen, I was out swimming when someone yelled 'shark'." I shudder at the memory, so vivid it might have happened yesterday. "Everyone scrambled for shore in pure panic. Turned out it was a dolphin, but..." I trail off, realizing that I'm rambling, realizing that I might have missed what he was really trying to say.

"I'm sorry," I say. "I'm rambling. Is Jasper, I mean, did he...?"

He shakes his head, then places his hand on my thigh.

"Oh, no. I'm so sorry." Nice one, Eileen. Blabbing on while you ignored his obvious pain.

"It's okay. It was a long time ago. Weird how you and I are both afraid of the ocean though."

I nod. It is strange. I'm the only person I know who hates the beach. On campus, it's a summer staple—beach cookouts at Hannah Park, volleyball at Atlantic Beach, roasting under the sun on the beach. I never accept those invitations, preferring to stay on campus and read in the shade of the old oak trees.

"I never went swimming in the ocean again. Lakes, rivers, pools—those are fine. But the ocean..." I trail off, noticing how intently Luke is watching me.

"What is it?" I ask.

"Your fear," he says. "It's like an echo of mine."

"Different circumstances, but the same... feeling."

He nods, and the connection between us pulses, almost tangible in the air.

"I've never told anyone about Jasper. Not the details, anyway. I'm not sure why I told you."

Because you freaked out in the water, and you're embarrassed. "Maybe you knew I'd understand," I say, and then, boldly: "Maybe you knew we had a connection."

His eyes search mine. I've gone too far, said too much. Instead of finding the right platitudes for his loss, I flirted with him. I'm an idiot. But instead of pulling away, he reaches up and tucks a strand of wet hair behind my ear. His fingers linger against my cheek, gently stroking down.

"Crazy, right?" he says, and I'm not sure whether he's talking about our joint fear of the ocean or this jarring connection between us.

"Completely," I agree, leaning into his touch.

We're close now, closer than we were in the water. I can see droplets clinging to his eyelashes, the shadows of his cheekbones, tiny gold flecks surrounding his cerulean-blue irises. His gaze drops to my lips and then back to my eyes, a question in them.

My heart hammers so fast, I think it's going to explode. We barely know each other. And yet, there's this inexplicable familiarity between us, like recognizing a well-catalogued fossil, rather than unearthing a new one.

"Eileen," he says, my name a question. His hand cups my face, thumb tracing my cheekbone with such tenderness it makes my breath catch.

I should pull away and remember why we're here—the cave, the experiment, the danger we might be in. But my heart wants to close the distance between us.

Slowly, giving him every chance to back away, I lean forward. Our lips meet, tentatively at first, then with growing certainty. Our kiss is wet and hungry. He tastes of salt, of river water, of peppermint. My world narrows to this single point of contact, everything else fading into insignificance—the river, the cave, my theories about what's happening to me, to us.

The kiss lingers, sweet and warm, until a hawk screeches kee-rah kee-rah overhead. Squirrels skitter through the trees, shaking loose a flurry of catkins. I pull back from Luke a little, my thoughts gradually returning to our purpose here.

"We should get going," I say reluctantly, reality reasserting itself. "The cave is around the bend."

"The cave," he repeats, as if he's just remembering why we're here as well. He glances at my bag, the spider plant still tucked in its mesh. "Your plant experiment."

"Our experiment now," I correct him. I stand, pulling him up with me. "Ready to go see some cave drawings?"

TWENTY-ONE: LUKE

I cut my paddle through the water, each stroke steadier as I find my rhythm. I'm using every muscle in my legs to stay afloat, and I can imagine the pain I'll be in tonight. That would be romantic, wouldn't it? Invite Eileen back to my studio, make out on the couch, and then have my leg seize up in a bitching cramp so agonizing I'll start screaming. Yeah, not such a good idea.

Maybe a nice dinner at Orsay instead. I wonder if they have a bottle of Champagne Salon? $5k bottle? No problem. Not this week, anyway.

As the water splashes around my paddle, my mind drifts to Mom's scream echoing across the beach. The lifeguards had laid Jasper's body out on the sand, his right thigh torn up like he'd stepped on a land mine. My legs wobble, the board tilts, and I clench my core to regain balance. I need to think about anything but that day, right now.

I steal a glance at Eileen, who glides next to me with the current. She's like a ballet dancer on a board while I'm an elephant on a balance ball, struggling to keep up. My balance might improve if I could focus, but I keep thinking about that kiss on the riverbank. I steal a glance at her lips, then quickly focus on the water again. Rewind button, please. A time jump right now might not be so bad after all. I miss a stroke, and my paddle splashes awkwardly.

"You okay over there?" she asks.

"I'm good."

I don't turn my head when I glance over, just my eyes, afraid that one sudden move will dump me into the river again. But then again, another 'rescue' might be worth the dunk.

"We're nearly at the cave," she says.

The cave.

If I see those figures inside—my figures, the ones that came from inside my head, I'm going to feel like Indy Jones discovering the Holy Grail. Do they match the glyphs in my paintings? Did I capture the colors correctly? My stomach rolls with anticipation. It's like I'm in line for the world's scariest, highest, most fun rollercoaster, and the ride's about to begin.

Once we reach the cave, the plan is to float the plant in. She's explained this "air quality test" twice now, but the more she says it, the more it sounds like one of my own rehearsed explanations from my drinking days. Not that I think she's lying. It's more like not revealing the whole truth because you're not sure how the other person would react.

Like when I'd lied to Rose about where I'd been all night. I didn't want to tell her I'd been in the drunk tank with twelve other guys who looked like they had toothbrush shivs in their socks. So instead, I told her I'd passed out at my buddy Alan's place. That lie backfired when she bumped into Alan's girlfriend the next day and found out Alan was on a work trip to Palo Alto. That led to Rachel accusing me of cheating and... well, let's just say it went downhill from there. A few hours of my girlfriend giving me hell for sleeping the night in a drunk tank would have been better than the months of suspicious looks and the Mariana Trench that my lie had created between Rose and me.

I wish I could say I never lied again, but that's not the truth, either.

I do aim for honesty since my breakup with the bottle, but I'm not going to tell Eileen that I think the "air quality" test is questionable science at best and a crock at worst. I know enough about still life to know that if there is a plant that can detect air quality issues, it's certainly not the plant that sat on top of the toilet during my morning audience with the throne. Those leaves would have wilted every morning at 8 a.m. if that were the case.

I'm sure she'll get to the truth, eventually. She's waiting to see if she can trust me, and I intend to show her she can.

"Thinking about the experiment?" I ask.

She nods. "Yes. The cave's just around this bend."

I adjust my grip on the paddle, still trying—and failing—to

mirror her smooth strokes. The return journey will be against the current, which will bring a whole new level of acrobatics. I wonder if it will be faster to dump the board and walk to the car?

Her board bumps against mine, and the cave entrance looms ahead, exactly as I've painted it—a gaping black mouth reminiscent of the Tunnel of Terror ride Aunt Edna tried to take me on as a child. I screamed before we stepped into the boat, convinced the monster's jaws were going to clamp shut and funnel me down to hell. This riverside cave doesn't evoke the same sense of terror, but there's something familiar about it. It's like finding a key in my kitchen odds-and-ends drawer I know I must have used, but don't have the first clue what for.

We're so close now I can smell her peachy sunscreen again, mixing with salt and sunshine, the faintest trace of river water, and something else I can't place but feels like home.

"There's something familiar about it, isn't there?" she asks.

The question catches me off guard. Did she just read my mind? No, she didn't say, *me*. She said, "it."

"Yeah, it's like I've been here before, and forgot, if that makes sense," I say. I want to tell her about the time slips, about how I've painted this cave from both a false memory and lived experience, which makes as much sense in my brain as a steering wheel turning into a dental drill at 60 m.p.h. So I will not lie. I'll pace my fantastic stories. The base layer has to dry before you can slather on the paint.

The cave mouth yawns before us. Water drips from the rocks in a rhythm that sounds like music—or maybe that's just my pulse singing in my ears. I know I should be terrified—of the water, of the cave, of the way I feel around Eileen Nash. Instead, my body is free from tension, and my breathing is slow and steady. It's like I've been heading for this place my whole life without knowing it.

TWENTY-TWO: EILEEN

The scientific part of me appreciates the simplicity of Candace's plan. If the mother plant inside changes—wilts, thrives, grows too fast, or too slow—while the spiderette I left at home stays the same, we have proof that there's an anomaly in the cave. Should that be the case, Candace will persuade a few of her fellow physics geeks to come out to the cave and investigate further. If nothing happens, maybe the anomaly was just that—a transient quantum state of some kind—a temporary wormhole.

But the scientific part of me also thinks the test is too simple, and it's missing an important component. Academic rigor perhaps? A control group? But it's not like I'm used to running quantum experiments with a billion-dollar particle collider. The most expensive tool I work with is a carbon steel trowel I bagged at a garage sale for $10.

While my scientific yin and yang debate internally, the other part of me—the non-rational part—wants to stop paddling and cuddle up with Luke on the riverbank. Go figure, right? I'm on the verge of one of history's most important archaeological breakthroughs—and perhaps its biggest quantum breakthrough as well—and thoughts of Luke are flooding my brain. The memory of his sleek body against mine in the water, his sculptured face inches from mine, the husky way he whispered my name.

I read a *Scientific American* article earlier this year called *The Power of Endorphins*. The author argued that the chemical cocktail released during romantic attachment—especially endorphins—can hijack the prefrontal cortex, leading individuals to sideline academic ambitions, abandon research projects, or make life-altering decisions in service of maintaining an emotional connection to the target. Is that what's going on here? My prefrontal cortex is being hijacked, forcing me to hyper-focus on intertwining with Luke instead of my professional goals?

"Thinking about the experiment?" I ask.

I nod. "Yes. The cave's just around this bend."

My board bumps against his, and the cave entrance looms ahead, the Tunnel of Terror ready for us the take a trip into its dark secrets. We'll kiss when we're in there, I'm sure of that. I shake the thought away.

Luke is looking at the cave mouth with the same look a traveler might have when they see the Grand Canyon for the first time. Awe, and something else. Recognition maybe. His brow is scrunched, his lips scrunched to the side, like he's puzzling through it.

"There's something familiar about it, isn't there?" I ask. We're so close now I could reach over and kiss him, but I don't because that would cause us both to fall into the water again. But that wouldn't be so bad, would it? A repeat of those moments on the bank.

"Yeah, it's like I've been here before, and forgot, if that makes sense."

I want to tell him about the time slips, about how I've sketched the cave from both a false memory and lived experience. But of course, I can't say that, not yet. I'll pace my fantastic stories. Because you can't dig straight to the artifact—you must document each layer before you move on.

"Ready?" I ask, untying the tether I've secured to the plant's container. The water level is perfect—high enough to float the plant in, but low enough that we can enter safely.

Luke nods, shifting his weight to keep his board steady. "What exactly are we testing for?"

"Oxygen levels," I lie smoothly. "Some caves can have dangerous air pockets." The words come too easily, and I hate that. But what if I told him the truth? Hey, want to watch me test if inanimate objects can time travel?

"If it's low oxygen, the plant should wilt. Not noticeably, but I'll be able to tell if it's slightly limp."

I hate lying to him, but I'm counting on the fact that he knows as little about plant experiments as I do about spacetime distortions. He might buy it. I hope he buys it.

I give the plant a gentle push, and it floats toward the cave entrance, its rope like a tether, the only link between two worlds. One minute. That's all we need. I count the seconds silently, watching the leaves wave in the current like tiny green flags. Beside me, Luke's presence is a warmth I can feel even without touching. His artist's eyes track the plant's movement with an intensity that makes me wonder what he sees—what patterns, what possibilities.

The minute passes. I tug the rope, and the plant emerges. It looks the same. No wilted leaves, no accelerated growth. For all I know, Candace's experiment was pointless. But something nags at me—if time moves differently in the cave, why didn't anything happen?

Maybe we were looking at the wrong thing.

Something in my chest loosens. Or tightens. I'm not sure whether I'm relieved or surprised.

"Perfect," I say, maybe too brightly. "The air's safe."

I really hate lying now. Candace's warning about quantum entanglement nags at me. I can't do this. I can't. In fact, what the hell have I been thinking? Lying to Luke is not a great way to start a relationship.

"Would the leaves really wilt in... what, under a minute?" Luke's voice is gentle, curious rather than accusatory. When I turn to look at him, his eyes hold the same knowing look from the gallery, like he can see right through me.

"Look, I need to tell you something before we go in. You might not want to go in when I tell you this, actually."

"Tell me what?"

"The last few times I went into the cave, I lost track of time."

"Oh, that's understandable. It's dark in there, right?"

"Yes, but what I mean is—"

"Like highway hypnosis," he says.

How did he know that? "Exactly. I go in, but sometimes when I come out—"

"You're somewhere else."

I stare at him for a long moment. He knows. "How did you know that?"

We sit on our gently bobbing boards, staring at the cave.

"I had a few episodes of, well, highway hypnosis recently. I wasn't here, obviously. It started on a Tuesday. I was on the Buckman Bridge and 'boom,' I'm at the endodontist's office. In a chair, about to get my tooth drilled."

Something about the way he says "Tuesday" makes me shiver. "How much time did you lose?" I ask, but I already know the answer. He's going to say twenty-four hours.

He takes my hand. "This is going to sound a bit nuts, but I lost almost twenty-four hours."

"Me too." I will not tell him it happened next month. Or that I went back a day, not forward. There's a limit to the amount of crazy a girl reveals on a second date.

"What happened? I mean, did you feel disoriented or anything?"

"That was the strange part. I should have felt disoriented or scared. But I just did what I do—research. Try to figure out why it happened. And it's got something to do with the drawings inside this cave."

He raises his eyebrows and blows out a breath. He squeezes my hand a little tighter. "I didn't, uh, take it so well. I thought I was losing my mind. The only thing I could do to stay sane was to paint."

"That's where your inspiration for the series came from."

"Yes."

"Wow, you're a fast painter."

"Not really."

I realize that neither of us is being completely honest with each other. I take a chance. If Luke and I are experiencing the same time distortions, then maybe Luke is directly connected to this. Which, of course, is silly—he is definitely connected to this, as displayed by the glyphs in his painting. Could Luke be the key to understanding the cave?

"It's happened to you three times."

"Yes. But how did you—"

"Because it's happened to me three times as well."

The look of puzzlement on his face mirrors the puzzlement in my head. I do not know what's happening here. The only thing I know for sure is that the cave holds the answers. There's some sort of localized magnetic area in the cave that distorts time.

"Let's go in," he says.

"You're sure?"

"Yes. I don't know what's happening here, but I think both of us need to find out. At least look at the glyphs. See if they tell us anything, right?"

"Okay," I say.

"But look, if we get... uh. If we get 'highway hypnosis' again, let's find each other. I mean, if you end up in the grocery store and I end up back in my studio, come find me. Or I'll find you."

"Your studio, then. What's the address?"

"Easy to remember. Corner of Rosselle and King. CoRK for short."

"CoRK. Got it." I shake my head. "You realize we both sound a bit—"

"Insane," he says. "I know. Tell you what, let's go into the cave, then get lunch back in town. Do you like Indian food?"

"Love it."

"Then that's a date."

"It's a date. Now let's go look at these drawings."

We paddle into the cave slowly, our boards bumping against each other in the narrow space. The temperature drops as shadows engulf us, and I switch on my headlamp. The beam catches Luke's profile, throwing his features into sharp relief. He looks different here—more focused, almost hungry, like he's searching for something he's seen before but can't quite remember.

"There," I whisper, though there's no real reason to be quiet. My light finds the first drawing, an elongated figure with shifting, spiraling patterns. Luke's sharp intake of breath tells me he sees it too.

"I've painted this," he says, voice rough with emotion. "Exactly this. But I've never—I couldn't have—"

"I know." I guide my board closer to his. "Look at the way the patterns flow into each other. Like—"

"Like time-lapse photography," he finishes. "Moments bleeding together."

We drift deeper into the cave, the drawings surrounding us now—etched into the limestone walls in ochre, charcoal, and faint traces of a mineral-based blue. Spirals and concentric circles stretch across the rock face, their patterns hypnotic, almost vibrating in the flickering light. Human figures appear in sequences, each slightly altered from one to the next, as though caught mid-motion—not hunting or gathering, but reaching, stepping, fading. One figure stands apart, its hand outstretched to a second figure that seems barely there, its outline faint and dissolving into the stone itself.

There are strange, jagged lines that loop around these figures, connecting them across panels, like unseen currents pulling them through time. In some places, the figures overlap, occupying the same space but not the same moment. A figure kneels beside a bundle that resembles a modern satchel, incongruous against the crude hunting tools etched nearby. Another gestures toward a bright orb—not the sun, but something more precise, geometric, with radiating lines like ripples on water.

My academic brain tries to catalog them—placement, preservation, stylistic elements—but Luke's presence keeps pulling me away. The way his breath catches at each new discovery distracts me more than I want to admit. At some point, his hand finds mine in the dim light. The touch feels as natural as breathing.

A strange sensation washes over me, like a sudden shift in air pressure. Luke stiffens beside me, and I know he feels it too. But before I can say anything, the moment passes.

I need a moment alone, an excuse to step away from Luke. Honesty, for once, seems easiest.

"Let's go outside for a minute—I need the girl's room," I say, really meaning I need to find a bush.

"You can wait here?"

"I'll come back out with you. I could use a 'boy's room' myself."

He gives me a knowing smile, like he sees through my excuse but doesn't mind. We paddle out into the harsh sunlight—just as thunder cracks overhead, making us both jump.

"One one-thousand, two one-thousand," Luke counts.

"What are you counting?" I ask.

"That's how you tell how far away the storm is."

"What? No, you're supposed to wait for the lightning first, then count until the thunder."

He smiles and slaps his forehead. "Duh moment." Then his smile fades. "But... I didn't see any lightning."

"We must have missed it." But something nags at the back of my mind. Why hadn't we seen the lightning? I don't remember any storms on the weather app. Then again, Florida storms appear out of nowhere all the time, so I push the thought aside and resign myself to paddling home.

"We should head back before the storm hits," he says.

I know we should—it's dangerous to be on the water—but now that I know the spider plant trick, I can come back anytime.

The wind shifts against my damp skin, carrying the sharp scent of rain. I dig my paddle into the water, but my thoughts are somewhere else.

Tarik would have waited. He would have run the numbers first, built a structured plan, argued for more data. Luke just knows. He trusts my judgment without demanding proof first. He follows me into the unknown, even when it scares him.

That kind of trust is terrifying—too instinctive, too unshakable. Too easy. Tarik was never like that. He made me earn his trust slowly, logically, in pieces I could understand. But Luke just gives it to me, without hesitation, without proof. He trusts me as if it's inevitable. And that terrifies me more than anything.

Because if I lose him, I already know it'll hurt.

I push the thought aside, focusing on the paddle in my hands. Maybe some things aren't meant to be rationalized.

"Want to head over to the state park and grab a bite? See if the storm passes?"

"Sounds great," he says.

That's when I notice the spider plant is missing.

"Shoot, the plant must have drifted back in there. Coming back in with me to get it?" I ask, already knowing his answer.

The cave calls to us both now, a siren song we can't resist. His hand grasps mine again as we turn our boards around, and this time, the touch feels like more than just attraction.

It feels like destiny.

TWENTY-THREE: LUKE

The thunder still echoes in my ears as we paddle back into the cave. Something feels off about that storm—about the missing lightning—but the thought slips away like wet paint running down canvas. Besides, I'm too distracted by Eileen's hand in mine, by how the cave drawings pulse in our headlamp beams. The air feels heavier now, charged with possibility.

"The plant should be just around this bend," she says, but her voice sounds distant, dreamlike. The limestone walls shimmer with moisture, and for a moment, the ancient figures seem to dance in the light. One shape catches my eye—a figure reaching through what looks like a doorway, its form stretching, elongating, as if caught between moments.

The figure's hand stretches beyond the doorway, its outline flickering like an afterimage. It reminds me of my reflection in a still pond—distorted when the water ripples. Or maybe... maybe it's more like the echo of my voice in an empty room, growing quieter, but never really gone. I shiver, wondering why the thought unsettles me so much.

"Eileen," I say, but the air suddenly thickens. That familiar vertigo grips me, the same sensation I felt in the car while singing along to Queen. Reality bends like light through water, and I reach for her.

Pain explodes through my jaw, white-hot and electric. My vision tunnels as the nerve howls, a scream so deep it vibrates in my skull. My knees buckle. I clutch my face, expecting blood, expecting shattered bone, but it's just the damn tooth, the one I've been ignoring, the one I was supposed to get fixed next week—last week? A hundred years from now?

The drill whirs.

No, not a drill. The rhythmic clatter of a film projector, its sound drilling into my skull.

The cave walls still press around me, but they're overlaid with flickering images—women in dropped-waist dresses, men in bowler hats, horse-drawn carriages on unpaved streets. The limestone weeps with moisture that smells like developer chemicals, like coal smoke, like the musty air of a hundred years ago.

My stomach churns as two realities collide: the mineral tang of the cave mixing with the sharp scent of greasepaint and arc lights. The weight of the paintbrush in my hand feels too real to be a dream. How am I here? It's like... like I'm a ripple reaching farther than I should, touching moments I was never meant to exist in.

The rough wool of a suit jacket scratches my neck, yet my skin still feels damp from the river water. My hand clutches a paintbrush that wasn't there seconds ago, will be there soon, is there now. The handle is heavier, the wood unpolished, edges worn smooth by another painter's grip. The bristles are stiff, coarse—natural hair, not the synthetic fibers I'm used to. They resist the stroke, dragging across the canvas with an unfamiliar bite. The backdrop before me pulses in sync with my racing heart, waiting for scenes I somehow already know how to paint.

"Let's move, people! The shoot starts tomorrow." The voice echoes off the cave walls—no, the studio walls. The incandescent work lights glare, too yellow, too hot, but my eyes still adjust to the dim phosphorescence of the cave. Women in period costumes swirl past like the current around my paddleboard, their skirts rustling with a sound like water over limestone.

The man looks puzzled. Stares at his clipboard. "You, uhhh... Campbell! Those backdrops will not paint themselves!"

It's the set designer, bellowing my name. Morris—his name is Morris. I know him from... somewhere.

I blink hard, trying to orient myself as the realities settle. I'm here—wherever here is—but the cave clings to me like I was there a hair of a second ago. My clothes feel wrong, heavy with history. The canvas before me stretches like a blank page in time.

Eileen is gone. I spin around, searching the faces of extras and crew members. But she's been pulled away by whatever current brought us here, leaving only the ghost of her touch on my skin and the certainty that we'll find each other again.

We have to. Because now I understand what's been happening to me—to both of us. The time slips, the cave drawings. We're caught in something bigger than ourselves, something that feels less like madness and more like...

"Campbell! Are you in there? Those clouds won't paint themselves!"

I hold up the brush, its weight as familiar as my AA chip, which is no longer in my pocket, and begin outlining clouds onto the backdrop. Each stroke of the brush feels like it could undo me, like I'm balancing on the edge of something too vast to comprehend. I don't belong here, not really. I'm just an echo of myself, loud enough to be heard, even here, even now.

As I work, I wonder where—when—Eileen is. If I'm an echo, a ripple sent too far, then where is she? Has she been pulled into this current too, or is she searching for me from another shore?

And I pray she's as good at finding her way through time as she is at navigating rivers.

Because somehow I know this is just the beginning. The beginning of spiraling out of control.

TWENTY-FOUR: EILEEN

Luke reaches for me just as reality bends. Just as the significance of the missing lightning hits me. The cave wasn't safe at all. We jumped in time without realizing it. Minutes? Hours? Days? Neither of us checked our phones when we went outside and heard the thunder, which means—

"We have to get out of here," I say.

For a split second, I feel his hand in mine—solid, warm, present—and then he's gone, like ripples dispersing on the river's surface. The cave air thickens, taking on a syrupy quality, with notes of ozone. My archaeologist's brain tries to catalog the sensation, to impose methodology on madness, but time itself seems to resist analysis.

The limestone walls blur, then refocus. No, not limestone anymore. Dark wood shelving. The limestone again. My senses struggle to process the overlapping inputs: the mineral smell of the cave mixing with old paper and leather bindings, the echo of dripping water becoming the soft rustle of pages. A conversation filters through the confusion—two men discussing a film shoot along the Suwannee—though they're dropping the "u" so it sounds more like Swan-ee...

The world settles with a sensation like diving too deep, too fast. My ears pop, and suddenly I'm standing in an unfamiliar room. Observation first, just like Professor Chen taught us. Start with the obvious: floor-to-ceiling wooden shelves laden with documents. The air smells of dust and preservation. My fingers trace the spine of a leather-bound volume—real leather, not the synthetic kind we use in modern archives.

Next layer of analysis: context clues. The women's clothing I'm wearing—ankle-length skirt, high collar, practical but formal. Not a costume—the fabric feels worn in familiar places, like I've been wearing it for months. The electric lights cast a steady yellowish glow, the filaments humming faintly in the stillness. Through the window, I glimpse a Ford Model T rattling past on an unpaved street.

A calendar on a nearby desk catches my eye: July 1925. The Jacksonville Carnegie Library, then—I recognize the seal on the letterhead scattered across the desk. My breath catches as I piece it together: I'm in Jacksonville during the twilight of its reign as "The Winter Film Capital of the World." The evidence is there on the magazine covers, their headlines stark against the glossy print:

Can Jacksonville Compete with Hollywood? Local Filmmakers Say Yes.
Historic Landmarks at Risk? The Price of Movie Magic.
Lights, Camera... Trouble? City Officials Debate Film Permits.

"Miss Nash?" A clipped voice breaks through my analysis. "These magazines won't bind themselves."

I turn, my mind still catching up to my body, and take in the man addressing me. Mr. Havemeyer stands stiffly behind the desk, his sharp gaze framed by round wire-rimmed spectacles. His suit is dark and severe, high-collared and impeccably pressed, with a watch chain disappearing into his waistcoat pocket. He looks as though he belongs in another century entirely—Victorian in demeanor, despite the world rushing into the modern age around him. His salt-and-pepper hair is slicked back with precision, not a strand out of place, and the deep creases bracketing his mouth suggest a man who has long since lost patience with frivolity.

His eyes narrow slightly behind the lenses, assessing me in the way men in authority often do when they suspect a woman of having thoughts beyond her station. "Miss Nash?" he repeats, voice edged with impatience.

"Of course, Mr. Havemeyer." The formal tone feels strange in my mouth, but my body knows this role, my brain knows this man's name. "I'll have the index updated and the latest issues sorted for binding."

I sort through the magazines with borrowed certainty, muscle memory from a life not yet lived. Or have I lived it already? The timeline layers in my mind like geological strata—past, present, and future existing simultaneously. Candace tried to explain quantum entanglement when she was explaining the plant experiment, but this feels different. More like... echoes. Reverberations through time.

Where is Luke?

The thought slams into me with the same jolting clarity as digging at random and striking metal where there should only be stone. My hands tighten around the edge of the unfamiliar desk, its dark wood worn smooth by countless others who touched it long before I was born. If I'm here—displaced in time like sediment carried by a flash flood—then Luke might be here too. No, not *might* be here. He *is* here. I know it with the same unshakable certainty as sensing someone just beyond a doorway, as feeling the weight of an unspoken word before it's spoken. It's the instinct that stills your foot at a green light, the moment of hesitation that keeps you safe as a car blows through the red. A presence just ahead, unseen but undeniable.

The cave affected us both; I'm sure of it. It's the quantum entanglement Candace warned me about. But she was mistaken about that spider plant experiment, and I wonder if it's still in the cave, bobbing in its mesh bag, waiting to be claimed by a new owner. Could Luke still be in the cave, wondering where I've gone? No. I shake the thought away. He's here; I can feel him.

My office at the library feels both foreign and strangely familiar, like a dig site I've only seen in photographs. The morning light streams through windows that are both newer and older than they should be, casting shadows that don't quite match my memory. A strange perfume lingers in the air—not the musty paper smell of archives, but something powdery and floral that makes my nose itch.

I need to see myself, need to confirm that I am still me. Because if I am not, how will Luke be able to find me? My fingers fumble through drawers that feel like they're mine but aren't, searching for anything reflective. There—a small silver mirror propped against a stack of letters, its art déco handle exactly what I'd expect from this era. When I lift it, the weight feels right, like an artifact that belongs in my hands.

I draw a sharp breath at my reflection. It's my face, thank God, but transformed by the decade. My usual practical ponytail has become a fashionable bob, pin-straight and gleaming. Dark lipstick shapes my mouth into a perfect cupid's bow, and my cheeks carry a rosy tint that no modern blush could achieve. I touch my face, and my fingertips come away with a chalky residue that smells of roses and talc.

But Luke—where would he have landed in this timeline? I am certain that the cave must have pulled us both through, our quantum connection ensuring we traveled together. I have no rational basis for this thought; I just feel him close. He's here. Somewhere, But Jacksonville in 1925 is a maze of possibilities. He could be anywhere, probably just as disoriented as I am. But am I truly disoriented? I have a strange sense of belonging, like I've always been here. And the thought unnerves me, churns my stomach, because I know I'm not supposed to be here. I'm not supposed to be here at all.

I set the mirror down with trembling fingers, careful not to crack it. Seven years of bad luck is the last thing I need right now, especially when I'm already navigating the worst kind of temporal bad luck imaginable. I must find him. And to do that, I need to think like an archaeologist—gather data, establish context, map the possibilities. Find the pattern that will lead me to Luke.

"Miss Nash?" Mr. Havemeyer says again, with that tone men use when they think women are being difficult. "Do we need to discuss deadlines?"

"I'll have it ready," I say, but my mind is already racing ahead, plotting coordinates through time like mapping a dig site. Luke's here, but first—magazine catalogs. I have a job to do. I need to fit into this time, this place.

I gather the magazines, the paper rustling like time keeping its own rhythm. I hurry to catalog the stack of magazines. I have research to do.

First step: establish context. Uncover the story behind the artifact. And right now, I'm the artifact—we both are. Displaced in time but leaving traces, like those cave drawings that somehow exist in multiple moments at once.

I just pray Luke understands what's happening to us. And that whatever echo of me exists in this time is strong enough to find him.

Because somewhere between the limestone and the ledgers, between the cave drawings and the quantum echoes, there's a truth waiting to be uncovered. And the archaeologist in me knows that the most important discoveries often come from reading between the lines.

TWENTY-FIVE: LUKE

I'm mixing colors for the backdrop at River City Pictures when another wave hits. Late afternoon sunlight streams through the high studio windows, catching dust motes that dance and blur until I can't tell if I'm seeing the sun or dental lights. My hand freezes mid-stroke, paint dripping from the brush.

Ground yourself. I grip the railing of the scaffolding, my balance shifting as time warps around me. I press my palm against the edges of the rough canvas, feeling the texture of dried paint beneath my fingers. The wooden platform is solid under my feet. Real. Now. But which now?

That's when the tooth reminds me that pain is the most reliable anchor to any present moment. A white-hot poker jabs into my jaw, and I suck air through my teeth—bad move. The cool air hits the exposed nerve and sends lightning through my skull. I nearly drop the brush.

"Campbell!" Morris appears at my elbow. "That backdrop needs to be ready for tomorrow's shoot. Kennedy's already breathing down my neck about the schedule."

I nod, not trusting my voice. The massive canvas before me shows the beginning of a riverbank scene—limestone outcrops, cypress trees, tangled vines. Everything the director wanted for his Suwannee River romance. Except my hands keep wanting to paint something else, something darker. Cave mouths that shouldn't be there keep appearing in the rock face.

"You feeling all right?" Morris squints at me. "You're looking a bit green."

"Just tired." The lie comes easily after three years of covering dizzy spells in AA meetings. I reach for my sobriety chip out of habit, but it's not there. Won't exist for another hundred years. The absence hits like a physical ache, a reminder that this time isn't mine.

Another throb pulses through my jaw, and I can't help the wince that follows. I've been fighting this tooth for days. In 2025, I had an appointment scheduled for next Tuesday. Or was it last Tuesday? The timeline fractures in my mind, each shard reflecting a distinct moment.

Morris narrows his eyes. "That's not tired. That's tooth trouble if I ever saw it."

I try to brush it off. "It's nothing—"

"Like hell it is." He steps closer, lowering his voice. "You've been holding your jaw like it might shatter for two days now. Can't have my best backdrop artist laid up with blood poisoning."

Blood poisoning. Jesus. I didn't consider that a bad tooth could kill you in 1925.

"I know a fellow," Morris continues, already reaching for a pencil stub in his vest pocket. "Dr. Wilcox, over on Laura Street. Nothing fancy, but he's quick and he don't charge like those uptown fellas."

He scribbles an address on the back of a call sheet and presses it into my palm. "Go tomorrow morning, first thing. We can't afford to lose you before the Suwannee shoot wraps."

I stare at the paper, remembering sterile offices, the hum of electric tools, the blessed numbness of modern anesthetics. None of that exists here. The thought makes my stomach turn.

"I don't know if I can afford—"

"Consider it an advance." Morris cuts me off, handing me a few bills. "Now finish that section before you go, and don't bleed on my canvas when you get back."

I pick up my brush again, trying to focus on the simple act of painting. But the studio lights are playing tricks, shadows shifting when I look directly at them. Time is elusive, like trying to catch smoke in my hands.

I think I painted this scene yesterday. Or will paint it tomorrow. Or both.

The edge of the room blurs.

"Campbell!" Morris's voice seems to come from very far away. "What in blazes are you doing to my backdrop?"

I look at the canvas and my heart stops. Without meaning to, I've painted a woman in a modern wetsuit examining the cave entrance. Her dark hair is pulled back in a familiar knot. I blink and she's gone, replaced by the proper period scenery the film requires.

But I know her face. I know that cave.

The room tilts sideways, and I grab the scaffolding for support. I must find her. I need to understand why we're here, why everything keeps shifting. But first I need to remember which time is real.

I think I'm falling.

I think I'm already gone.

* * *

After work, I follow Morris's directions, which lead to a narrow storefront wedged between a tobacconist and a milliner's shop. The gold-lettered sign in the window reads "J.F. Wilcox, D.D.S." with "Extractions & Dentures" in smaller print below. My feet slow of their own accord.

I've never been great with dentists, even in the distant future I came from. But at least there, the tools were sterile, the procedures precise. Here? I think of barber-surgeons and whiskey anesthetics and nearly turn around.

But another stab of pain decides for me. I push through the door.

The waiting room is small and orderly, the kind of place meant to reassure you more than impress you. Worn but clean chairs line the walls, and framed certificates hang in precise rows. A potted fern that's seen better days droops in the corner. The air smells of antiseptic, tobacco, and something medicinal I can't identify.

A woman in a crisp, pale dress with a nurse's cap looks up from behind a small desk. "Do you have an appointment, sir?"

"No, I—Morris from River City Pictures sent me." My voice sounds absurd in my ears, formal in a way I never speak. It's like my tongue knows the patterns of this time better than my brain does. "It's my tooth."

As if on cue, it throbs again, and I press a hand to my jaw.

"Dr. Wilcox has an opening now. You're fortunate." Her smile doesn't reach her eyes. "Your name?"

"Luke Campbell."

"Please have a seat, Mr. Campbell. The doctor will see you shortly."

"Shortly" turns out to be an eternity of ten minutes, during which I flip through a dog-eared magazine from 1923 without absorbing a single word. My mind keeps slipping between times—the sterile blue of my dentist's office in 2025, the limestone walls of the cave, Eileen's face as she reached for me.

"Mr. Campbell?"

I look up to see the nurse holding open a door at the back of the waiting room. Beyond her is a space that looks more like a mechanic's workshop than a medical office. A massive chair of leather and metal dominates the center of the room, surrounded by cabinets and a table of instruments that belong in a museum of torture.

A short, barrel-chested man in a white coat turns as I enter. His mustache is perfectly waxed, his hair parted with architectural precision. "Morris's backdrop artist, eh? Sit down, young man; let's see what's troubling you."

I lower myself into the chair, which creaks ominously under my weight. Dr. Wilcox cranks a lever, and the back reclines with a series of mechanical clicks. A bright light swings over my face—not electric, but a complex arrangement of mirrors designed to direct sunlight from the window directly into my mouth.

"Open, please." His tone makes it clear that this isn't a request.

I open my mouth, and his fingers, encased in thin rubber gloves, probe efficiently. When he hits the bad tooth, I nearly leap out of the chair.

"Ah, there's our culprit. Upper left molar, badly decayed. Been ignoring this for a while, haven't you?"

I make a noncommittal sound. How do I explain that in my time, I'd been putting off a root canal for months, and now I'm paying for it across centuries?

"It'll have to come out." He turns to his assistant. "Prepare for extraction, Miss Harding."

My stomach drops. "Is there any other option? A filling, maybe?" Root canal sounds hellish, but extraction sounds medieval.

Dr. Wilcox chuckles. "Could try to save it, but a man in your position? Extraction's quicker, cheaper, and you'll be back to work tomorrow. "I can't imagine Morris will give you time off for the next few weeks while we work on that gold filling."

The time requirement doesn't bother me. But multiple appointments stretched over weeks in a 1925 torture chamber? Out of the question. My hands are already clammy, and if I spend over ten minutes in this chair, I'll panic and walk out.

I nod sharply. Let's get this over with.

Miss Harding approaches with a tray of instruments that makes my blood run cold. Metal gleams under the reflected sunlight: pliers with serrated grips, something that looks like an ice pick and various other implements I don't want to identify.

"We'll numb you up, of course," Dr. Wilcox says, reaching for a syringe that looks like it could pierce armor. "Not as good as the cocaine we used to use, but the government's rather strict about that now."

I grip the arms of the chair as he approaches with the needle. The syringe is glass with metal fittings; the needle is thick enough to see with the naked eye. What the hell is in that thing? Is it even sterilized? I think about asking, but before I can, his fingers are already prying my jaw open.

"This'll pinch," he warns. He drives the needle directly into my gum.

"Pinch" is a lie. It's a white-hot poker, followed by a burning spread of whatever passes for local anesthetic in 1925. He withdraws the needle only to stab a different area, then another, until my entire left jaw is on fire.

"We'll give that a moment to take effect," he says cheerfully, setting down the syringe and selecting dental pliers from the tray. They look heavy and thick, like he'd borrowed them from a car mechanic. How the hell are those supposed to fit in my mouth?

"Morris tells me the crew is working on the Suwannee River picture. Quite the production, I hear."

I try to respond, but my lip is already going numb, my words slurring. "Yesh, big shoot."

"Remarkable river, the Suwannee. Those caves have been there since before the Indians." He tests the pliers, snapping them open and shut with a metallic click—like a giant scarab beetle faking death. My pulse spikes into heart attack territory.

"Did you know they found prehistoric remains in some of those caves? Man's been seeking shelter in the same spots for thousands of years."

My breath catches at the mention of the caves. Does he know? Can he sense the temporal displacement like static electricity on my skin?

"Time to test," he announces, and before I can prepare, he's jabbing my gum with a sharp instrument. "Feel that?"

I do, but it's duller now, distance wrapped in cotton. I shake my head.

"Excellent. Open wide, Mr. Campbell. This won't take but a moment."

I close my eyes and grip the chair harder. The metal pliers enter my mouth, jamming into my teeth. They close around the offending tooth, and Dr. Wilcox braces his other hand against my jaw.

"Deep breath through your nose, now."

I inhale, and as I do, he twists and pulls with a force that could dislodge a boulder. Pressure—then a sickening crack—then the sensation of tree roots being wrenched from my skull.

My vision goes white, then black at the edges. I taste copper and salt. Time stutters—I'm in the chair, I'm in the cave, I'm in my 2025 apartment staring at a dental appointment card, I'm nowhere and everywhere.

"There we are!" Dr. Wilcox sounds triumphant, holding up what looks like a bloody tooth with black decay eating half of it. "Miss Harding, the gauze, please."

A wad of cotton is thrust into the empty socket, and I'm instructed to bite down. The burning sensation is fading, replaced by a throbbing ache that feels strangely familiar, like a memory of pain rather than pain itself.

"Rinse when the bleeding slows, but not too vigorously. No smoking for twenty-four hours. Come back if the pain worsens or you develop a fever." He's already turning away, washing his hands in a basin. "That'll be two dollars. You can pay Miss Harding on your way out."

Two dollars. Morris had "advanced" me three, and I wonder

how much I'm paid in 1925. I reach for a wallet that feels both strange and familiar in my pocket.

The nurse takes my money efficiently, handing me a small paper packet. "Aspirin powder. Mix with water for pain."

I stumble back onto Laura Street, the Florida sunshine seeming too bright, too harsh after the dim office. My mouth throbs in time with my heartbeat, but the worst of the pain has transformed into a dull, insistent pressure. Blood seeps into the gauze, iron-rich and warm.

The world tilts slightly, reality refocusing around me. Something has changed—not just the absence of the tooth, but something deeper. If I ever make it back to 1925, will that dentist's chair still be waiting for me? Or will I return with a missing tooth? I hope for the latter, but this sense of being lost in time—and sentenced to dental purgatory—seems like the most logical answer. All my past mistakes, my temper, my vile words, following me into dental hell.

I touch my jaw gently, feeling the swelling already beginning. But with that specific agony addressed, for now, I can focus on what matters.

Finding Eileen. Understanding why we're here. And figuring out how to get back to our own time before we become permanent fixtures in a past that was never meant to contain us.

First, though, I need to finish that backdrop. Morris is expecting me back, and in 1925, a man keeps his commitments— even if he's bleeding from the mouth and displaced in time.

TWENTY-SIX: EILEEN

It's late afternoon, and I've finished my work for the day. I have two hours before the library closes, so I peruse the basement archives. The archives from 1924 won't tell me anything about time displacement or quantum physics. But it's data, and data is familiar.

I flip through a bound volume of Florida Geological Survey reports, my fingers tracing the faded type. Professor Chen taught me to start with what I know. The mention of erosion near Big Shoals stands out—an area known for its logging and turpentine production in the early 1900s. The removal of trees and stripping of bark could have destabilized the soil, leading to increased erosion along the riverbanks. Perhaps this erosion exposed the cave system, setting the stage for whatever anomalies I've encountered. Could the disturbance caused by human activity at Big Shoals have triggered the cave's temporal properties? It's a tenuous connection, but it's something. I hold on to it desperately, hoping that following the trail of data might lead me to something more solid than the fleeting echoes of time.

Fact one: I'm in 1925. The evidence surrounds me in a cacophony of unfamiliar familiar things. Through the library's tall windows, I watch Model T Fords and Chevrolet Superior sedans bumping along brick-paved Adams Street, their brass fixtures gleaming in the afternoon sun. A steady stream of pedestrians flows past—men in straw boaters and light wool suits despite the Florida heat, women in dropped-waist dresses with hemlines that would scandalize my grandmother's grandmother. The clip-clop of horses mingles with automobile engines and the distant whistle of a steam locomotive.

Magazines advertising Edison phonographs and the latest

"modern" electric iceboxes, with their bold Art déco illustrations and sweeping, confident lettering, are like artifacts from a museum exhibit I've studied in my archaeology courses.

The library itself feels both foreign and familiar. The reading room where I sit is a testament to the craftsmanship of another time—quartersawn oak tables polished by decades of scholarly elbows, gas-powered brass reading lamps, towering shelves of leather-bound volumes reaching toward a coffered ceiling. The air smells of furniture polish, leather, and paper, underlaid with coal smoke drifting in from the city's industrial district. No air conditioning, just slowly rotating ceiling fans that stir the humid summer air without cooling it.

Fact two: I might not be alone here. If Candace's theory about quantum entanglement is correct—and honestly, that's a big if, considering her plant experiment failure—Luke could have been pulled through with me. The thought sends an odd flutter through my stomach. Part hope, part fear.

Fact three: I do not know how to get back.

A spindly woman in a long, ankle-length skirt that speaks of the previous century's sensibilities passes my table, giving me an odd look. I almost smile—my knee-length cotton dress is perfectly current for 1925. At least my archaeology experience helps me blend in behaviorally—I know how to maneuver around old documents, how to appear studious and academic. Years of fieldwork have taught me how to be invisible while working, how to become part of the background.

I flip through a bound volume of Florida Geological Survey reports, my fingers tracing the faded type. The reading room is quiet except for the occasional rustle of pages and the distant clatter of a librarian's cart.

A sudden, sharp whisper from a nearby table catches my attention.

"... and she just strolled in without a hat. Can you imagine?"

I glance up, drawn by the hushed but insistent tone. Two young women sit at the next table, dressed impeccably—gloved hands resting lightly on the pages before them, their posture flawless. The blonde tilts her head toward the window where a woman in a modest but hatless dress passes on the sidewalk.

Her companion sighs. "Shameful. Ladies should always wear a hat in public."

The blonde sniffs. "Or at least a scarf. If she's from out of town, I suppose that explains it."

I freeze.

I'm not wearing a hat.

Heat creeps up my neck. I hadn't even considered it—I've been careful about my dress length, my shoes, even my gloves, but hats? I'd noticed them, sure, but I hadn't realized they were nonnegotiable.

I glance toward my bag. I don't have a hat, but I have a scarf—plain and folded at the bottom of my belongings. Slowly, without drawing attention, I reach down and retrieve it, carefully draping it over my head and adjusting it beneath my chin.

The blonde woman's gaze flicks toward me, and I brace for another whisper. Instead, she simply returns to her reading, satisfied.

I exhale a slow breath. Lesson learned. Hats—or at least head coverings—aren't optional.

I shift in my seat, suddenly more aware of how every detail of my appearance matters in ways I never had to think about before.

As I resettle, I instinctively lean forward, resting one elbow on the table while I scan the page. The wooden chair creaks slightly beneath me.

Across the room, the older librarian shelving books pauses.

It's barely noticeable—the briefest flick of her gaze in my direction, the slight downturn of her mouth before she continues her work. But something about the moment prickles at me.

I glance around.

The other women in the reading room sit with perfect posture—backs straight, hands lightly resting in their laps or carefully poised over their work. No elbows on tables, no lounging into chairs, no casual, weight-shifted poses.

I subtly pull back, straightening my spine, keeping my movements small and contained.

Hats matter. Posture matters. Even something as small as how I sit can make me stand out. What other social faux pas will I make today? I hope, none.

But even as I straighten my back and fold my hands properly in my lap, it feels unnatural.

In my own time, I wouldn't think twice about how I sit in a library. I'd sprawl if I wanted, lean over my work without a second thought. Now, I have to check every movement, keep my gestures small, controlled, demure. Staying in character isn't just about what I say—it's about every unconscious habit I never knew I had.

How long before I slip up in a way I can't fix?

* * *

The geological surveys spread before me show familiar territory—limestone formations, underground rivers, cave systems. But it's like reading a book where half the pages are missing. The chamber where I found those drawings doesn't exist on the map yet. It is undiscovered, submerged, perhaps both.

I study the contours of the river on the map, following its bends and rapids. The names are the same—Big Shoals, Little Shoals, all the landmarks I know from my research. But the surrounding landscape is different. Where I'm used to seeing conservation areas and state parks, these maps show turpentine camps and logging operations. The river itself is different too—more industrial, with notations about steamboat routes and timber rafts.

I press my palms against the smooth wood of the table, fighting the urge to run outside and search aimlessly. That's not how you conduct research. That's not how you solve problems. Think like a historian, Eileen. One step at a time.

My eyes drift to the small, ground-level window, where slivers of sunlight filter through the dust-streaked glass, casting shifting patterns on the floor as clouds pass overhead.

Jacksonville in 1925 is a city in motion, growing and changing fast. The film industry, though past its peak here, still lingers with notable studios like Norman Studios and a handful of independent productions. I remember reading about this in my Florida history courses—silent film studios, sound stages, and creative people drawn to the constant sunlight and diverse landscapes.

If Luke came through with me, this would be a good place for a gifted artist to find work. I just pray he didn't land in Hollywood, which is quickly rising to replace Jacksonville as America's film capital. If he did, I might never find him.

The afternoon light grows dim, and the librarian begins her rounds, turning on the electric lamps one by one. I've been here for an hour, surrounded by the gentle rustle of pages and the scratch of pencils on paper. The documents have given me a better understanding of 1925 Jacksonville's geography and industry, but not what I really need—confirmation that Luke is here, or better yet, a way home.

The electric lamps cast pools of warm light across the reading room's polished surfaces, so different from the harsh fluorescents I'm used to. Soon they'll be announcing closing time. I need a new strategy, a different approach to this puzzle. Maybe it's time to stop thinking like an archaeologist and start thinking like someone searching for an artist in a city where the film industry is fading.

I trade geological surveys for bound volumes of the Jacksonville Journal-Courier. Professor Chen would approve of this systematic approach, even if my research subject has shifted from cave formations to... Luke. A woman at a nearby table gives me a subtle look as I reach for another volume—right, I need to move more carefully. I've noticed how the other women here drift between the shelves like smoke, their movements gentle and precise. I slow my pace, trying to mirror their grace as my fingers glide across the dates on each spine—June, May, April 1925.

I start with the most recent editions, working backward. My archaeological training serves me well here—the same patience required for cataloging artifacts helps me scan column after column of dense newsprint. The entertainment section charts Jacksonville's fading film industry, as Hollywood's better infrastructure and year-round shooting weather draws studios westward.

The advertisement catches my eye in a Tuesday edition from late April:

"ARTISTS WANTED - River City Pictures seeks talented scenic artists for magnificent Suwannee River backdrop paintings. Experience with natural landscapes required. Apply in person at 107 Riverside Avenue."

The paper crinkles under my suddenly tight grip. Water and light—that's Luke's specialty. The way he captures reflection and shadow... if he is here, this would be perfect for him. But he wouldn't have been here three months ago, in April, would he?

Then again, I shouldn't have been here then either—yet somehow, I melted into a librarian's job like I'd been here for years, not hours.

I copy down the address with trembling fingers, my normally precise handwriting betraying my excitement. Riverside Avenue is barely a fifteen-minute walk from here. The geological surveys still spread across the reading room table beckon to me—there are patterns in the cave system I haven't fully mapped. The academic in me wants to understand the mechanism, to catalog and classify this incredible experience.

But if my theory is right, if the cave somehow pulled Luke through with me, he might be out there in this version of Jacksonville. The memory of his face in the gallery—future gallery?—flashes through my mind. The intensity in his eyes as he studied his own paintings, like he was trying to decode messages he'd left for himself. I must know whether he's here. The cave's mysteries can wait.

I awkwardly return the newspapers to their shelf, trying to behave as demurely as expected. The lack of air conditioning makes the reading room stifling, despite the ceiling fans' lazy rotations.

My cotton dress feels suddenly inadequate armor for this mission. In the library, I can fade into the background, just another researcher bent over old documents. But a woman walking alone into a film studio in 1925? The newspaper's "Help Wanted - Female" section made it clear what jobs were appropriate—stenographers, seamstresses, shop girls. Not women barging into male-dominated creative spaces. I square my shoulders. I've faced down skeptical professors and hostile peer reviewers. I can handle this.

Besides, I'm the one who stumbled into that cave, who set this whole situation in motion. Finding Luke isn't just a priority—it's my responsibility. Whether Candace's quantum entanglement theory is right or not, something connected us through that cave. I have to understand what happened, starting with finding the one person who might be experiencing the same temporal displacement I am.

I gather my notes and rise from the table with careful grace. The librarian nods goodbye, then pauses. "My dear, warm weather, isn't it?" Her eyes flick meaningfully to my bare hands. "Most ladies find gloves helpful when out and about."

I glance around the room, suddenly aware of the pristine white gloves on every female hand. Of course—I fish in my bag. They're simple cotton, but they'll do. I'm grateful they aren't leather, which would be stifling in this heat.

Outside, the relative breeze is almost refreshing after the library's stuffiness, though my gloved hands already feel damp. Riverside Avenue lies ahead, and with it, maybe, Luke.

But my first problem is where to sleep. I'm a single woman in 1925, and a park bench isn't an option—not unless I want to be arrested for vagrancy. Women on their own draw attention, and the last thing I need is a night in jail. I pack my bag and head outside, letting my feet find their way toward...

Ma Perkins' boarding house in Riverside. The memory settles in slowly, like most things about this timeline—the brass room number on the door, the shared bathroom at the end of the hall, the faint scent of starch and lavender in the linens. Ma Perkins' stern face had softened when I mentioned working at the library, and she hadn't asked too many questions. Thank God I'm paid up through the week. I try not to think about what happens after that.

TWENTY-SEVEN: LUKE

The Model TT truck rattles down the logging road, its wooden bed creaking with every jolt. The canvas backdrops I painted are tied down with rope, but I still wince each time the wheels hit a rut. Dawn breaks over the horizon, streaking the sky with pink and gold.

I slept at the movie studio last night, stretched out on a wooden platform with my jacket for a pillow. No one batted an eye when the crew arrived at 3:30 a.m.—they're used to people crashing wherever they can. I barely got two hours of sleep before we left Jacksonville at four sharp, following the lumber routes inland toward the Suwannee.

Six hours sitting in the truck bed has left me stiff and aching, my legs cramped from the constant jostling. Someone up front hums *Old Folks at Home*. They call it the Swanee River here, dropping the "u" like it's excess baggage.

"Christ, we should've left two hours earlier," one of the crew hands mutters. "Road's a mess after last night's rain."

The road finally ends at a clearing by the river, carved out by years of logging operations. Spanish moss covers the cypress trees like funeral veils, and the brown water crawls beneath them. The limestone banks could be any stretch of the Suwannee—unchanged for millions of years, unchanged for millions more.

"All hands!" The location manager, Morton, shouts to the crew already unloading equipment. He's built like a brick warehouse, broad-shouldered and thick-necked, his sunburnt face creased with deep-set lines of permanent frustration. A cigar, long since unlit, is clamped between his teeth as he scans the set like a general sizing up a battlefield. His straw Panama hat sits askew on his head, pushed back just enough to reveal the furrow in his brow that never quite disappears.

"Let's get these sets dressed before the heat kicks in!" His voice booms over the clearing, sending stagehands scrambling to secure backdrops before the morning sun turns the Suwannee into an oven.

I hover near my backdrops, supervising their careful removal from the truck. As the scenic artist, my job is to direct their placement and ensure they haven't been damaged in transit. Something catches my eye—a flash of bright green against the brown water. A spider plant bobbing in the current. My heart stops. It's there and gone so fast I might have imagined it, but I know that plant. Will know it? The tenses tangle in my head like paint running down a canvas.

"Mr. Campbell?" One stagehand pauses. Thomas? Timmons? "You don't look so good."

"Just the morning air," I manage, though my tongue feels thick in my mouth. I scan the shoreline desperately, but there's only the pattern of water against limestone, cypress knees breaking the surface like prehistoric creatures coming up for air.

Eileen's face floats in my mind, clear as a photograph: those intent brown eyes, the slight furrow in her brow when she concentrates. The way she looked at me in the gallery, will look at me, is looking at me—stop. Focus. She has to be here too, somewhere in 1925. I feel her presence like a compass needle feeling north. Maybe if I paint enough of these river scenes, she'll recognize my work, find her way to the studio...

"Is there a university in Jacksonville?" I ask Thomas/Timmons.

"University? Not that I know of. There's some kinda college up in St. Augustine, I think," he says.

Some kind of college? Could Eileen be there? I make a mental note to look for train schedules when I get back to the studio. But could I even afford the ticket? And would they even have an archaeology department?

I remove my wallet from my pocket. Inside, there's a crumpled five-dollar bill, a few coins, and a ticket stub from the Jacksonville Terminal—where to, I don't remember. A folded scrap of paper, smeared with charcoal, holds a rough sketch of the Suwannee's limestone banks. No ID, no library card, nothing to tell me who I am in this time—although I'm apparently still called Campbell. Last name? First name? If I ask too many questions, will people start asking them back?

A sticky breeze ripples the surface of the river, and for a flash I see double—modern powerboats ghosting through the pristine 1925 shoreline, eroded banks overlaying the thick forest. I reach instinctively for my AA chip, again finding only an empty pocket.

The late morning blurs into a series of minor adjustments—directing the placement of backdrops, touching up paint where the canvas got scuffed in transit. The heat builds as the sun climbs, and dark clouds are already gathering in the west. We'll have to wrap up before the afternoon storms hit.

"Campbell!" Morton's voice cuts through my thoughts. "How's the lighting on the morning mist scene?"

I force myself to focus on the work at hand, but I keep catching glimpses of movement from the corner of my eye. Never what I'm looking for. Never who I'm looking for.

By early afternoon, thunder rumbles in the distance. The crew works faster, racing the weather. Somewhere along this river, Eileen is trying to find her way too. She has to be. I just have to hold on to that certainty as time keeps slipping sideways in my head.

No one's driving back to Jacksonville tonight—not unless they want to risk a broken axle in the dark. The real stars—the director, the lead actors—will have beds somewhere, maybe in a town downriver. But the crew? We're staying put. I hear the stagehands talking about bunking down near the trucks, maybe lighting a fire if Morton doesn't bark at them for it. Someone's already unrolling canvas near the riverbank. I sigh and do the same. It's not the first night I've slept under the stars, and it won't be the last.

TWENTY-EIGHT: EILEEN

The receptionist at River City Pictures eyes my gloves with approval, but my solitary presence with suspicion. "Mr. Campbell is on location today," she says, arranging papers with precise movements. "I'm afraid I can't say when he'll return."

"I'll wait," I say, my voice as soft and properly feminine as I can muster. "I'm his fiancée." The lie feels strange on my tongue, but it's the only explanation that would allow a respectable woman to wait alone for a man in 1925.

The receptionist's penciled eyebrows rise slightly. "How... interesting." Her tone is polite, but something flickers behind her expression—amusement, maybe even skepticism.

At that moment, a second woman approaches the desk, her heels clicking softly on the tile. Her blouse is crisp, her hair is pinned in a careful wave, and she carries a leather-bound ledger against her hip. Someone who works here, then. A typist? A secretary?

She leans in, murmuring something too low for me to catch.

Both women flick their eyes toward me at the same time.

It's only a second—quick, practiced—but my stomach clenches. I'm being talked about.

The receptionist hums in response, arranging a few papers with practiced precision. "Is your driver parking his car, Miss...?"

I hesitate only for a fraction of a second. "Nash," I supply. Driver? I look down at my plain dress and practical shoes. I'm not exactly sure what a high-class woman—one that could afford a driver—would wear, but I'm certain it would not be a cotton dress and generic shoes.

"No," I say. "I decided to walk today."

She nods, but her gaze lingers. "You're fortunate that Mr. Campbell is—unconventional. Some might find a visit from an unescorted lady quite scandalous."

My stomach clenches. Unescorted.

I've made a mistake.

A woman—especially an engaged woman—wouldn't arrive alone at a business to wait for a man, no matter how respectable the setting. She would have a chaperone, an aunt, a maid, or a driver lingering just outside.

The correct response would have been to clarify that I wasn't truly alone, that my chaperone was simply occupied elsewhere. But now it's too late. The receptionist has already marked me as improper.

I smooth my gloves over my lap, forcing a pleasant, airy smile. "My aunt had another errand," I say. "I thought I'd simply inquire whether Mr. Campbell had returned yet before she comes back to fetch me."

I wait for her to press further. Then, with an almost imperceptible shrug, she gestures toward the waiting area.

"You may have a seat, Miss Nash."

As I settle onto the wooden bench, ankles firmly together this time, I keep my posture straight and my hands lightly folded in my lap. No unnecessary movement, no signs of nerves.

Another lesson learned. Women don't travel alone—not if they want to be taken seriously.

Holding myself like this, performing a role, second-guessing every word, every movement—it's like walking a tightrope. One wrong step, one careless moment, and I'll give myself away.

I exhale slowly, keeping my face composed. I can do this. I must do this. But the thought lingers: how much of me will be left when I stop pretending?

* * *

The lobby's wooden bench is hard, but I've spent longer hours crouched over excavation sites. Women come and go—secretaries and typists, I assume, their heels clicking purposefully across the floor. Each one gives me a subtle once-over, no doubt wondering about the woman sitting alone, waiting.

"The river shoot should wrap early," I overhear one secretary tell another around noon. "Morton won't risk the afternoon storms with those backdrops."

My heart jumps at the word "river." Could they be filming at the Suwannee? There are several rivers around Jacksonville—the St. Johns, the Arlington, and even the Trout. I strain to hear more without appearing to eavesdrop, but the secretaries move out of earshot. I resist the urge to ask them directly—a proper fiancée would already know these details, and I can't risk drawing more attention to myself than I already have.

Later, I catch fragments of another conversation: "...Suwannee location..." and my hands tighten in my lap. So Luke might be there, at the river where all this began. But even if it is the same stretch of water, I have no way of reaching him. The logging roads would be impossible to navigate without a guide, and a woman showing up alone at a film location would raise far too many questions.

The hours crawl by. The receptionist offers neither conversation nor refreshment, though she watches me like a hawk between telephone calls. I maintain perfect posture, keep my ankles crossed, and try to look demurely eager rather than desperately impatient.

"Quite devoted, aren't you?" she finally comments around four o'clock, her tone suggesting the opposite. "Though one might expect a fiancée to know her intended's schedule."

Thunder rumbles outside. I've been here since morning, and my academic certainty is crumbling. What if I'm wrong? What if Luke isn't here at all? The rain falls, drumming against the windows.

"The film crews often camp on location," the receptionist notes with practiced concern. "And with this weather... well, it wouldn't be proper for a young lady to be walking home alone after sunset. Perhaps you should return another time."

The receptionist's pointed comment about walking alone reminds me of my precarious position. She's right—I've noticed how women travel in pairs or groups after a certain hour, how they hurry home before dusk. I gather my things, mind racing. Now I know where to find him, maybe tomorrow, maybe the next day, but I'll need a better strategy than sitting in the lobby all day.

"Thank you for your concern," I manage, standing with careful grace. I am lost as to what that strategy might be—how does one navigate social protocols that died out decades before I was born?—but at least I know he's here.

Outside, the rain has turned the streets slick. I pause under the awning, watching water stream from the gutters. Behind me, I hear the decisive click of the door being locked. Through the rain-streaked window, I glimpse the receptionist gathering her things, pulling on her gloves, and adjusting her hat before closing her ledger and switching off the desk lamp for the day.

I step into the downpour, my gloves quickly soaking through. As I turn the corner onto Riverside Avenue, the rain is falling too hard, and propriety demands I not run through the streets like a madwoman.

I clutch my sodden notes to my chest and force myself to walk on, one careful step at a time. Tomorrow. I'll try again tomorrow.

TWENTY-NINE: LUKE

The first wave hits as I'm touching up the riverboat backdrop. We've got it propped against a cypress tree at the clearing's edge, and the morning light catches the canvas at just the right angle. My brush is loaded with brown paint to deepen the shadows of the riverbank, but when it touches the canvas, it's cerulean blue. No— brown again. The colors keep shifting, like someone's adjusting a dial between decades.

My stomach growls, reminding me I haven't eaten since the hardtack and beans someone passed around at dawn. The crew's been working since first light, and the humidity's already oppressive, plastering my shirt to my back.

"That better be done for today's shoot," Morton barks as he strides past, clipboard in hand, cigar dangling from the corner of his mouth.

"Yes, sir." My voice sounds distant, like it's underwater. My canvas shows the Suwannee at dusk, but something's wrong with the perspective. I've painted the riverbank with a concrete boat ramp cutting into the water, except it shouldn't be there. Not in 1925. That ramp won't be built for another—

The second wave hits harder. The limestone shoreline lurches sideways, and suddenly I see three versions of the same scene layered on top of each other. The 1925 riverbank bleeds into the eroded shoreline I remember from my own time, and behind that... something else. Something from the future. Or the past? Skeletal trees. Dark water. The air is sauna-like, thick with steam.

I reach into my pocket instinctively, fingers searching for my AA chip. Empty. Of course. The craving hits without warning, a wave more powerful than the time shifts—the sudden, visceral need for the burn of whiskey, the oblivion that would follow. Someone on the crew has a flask; I saw the telltale glint when he thought no one was looking.

"What in God's name is that?"

Morton is behind me now, staring at my canvas. I try to focus on what I've painted, but the images keep sliding around. I've somehow captured all three timelines at once—the pristine 1925 shoreline dissolving into the familiar cypress-lined banks of 2025, and in the background, those strange dead trees reaching toward a sky that looks wrong.

"Those perspectives," Morton interrupts, leaning closer. "The way you've layered the viewpoints... I've never seen anything like it."

"It's... experimental," I manage. My tongue feels thick, and my hands are shaking. Not just from the time slips, but from the gnawing need for a drink. "The layers create depth through—" Through what? What am I even saying?

"Those angles," Morton continues, pointing at the canvas. "The way you've constructed the space... it's unsettling. Almost like the landscape is twisting in on itself."

The clearing tilts again. I grab the edge of the backdrop's wooden frame to stay upright as time slips around me like wet paint. The canvas is taut beneath my fingers, stretched over its frame, the brushstrokes dry but uneven where I touched them up earlier. My vision blurs for a fraction of a second, the painted riverbank shifting between past and present like a mirage.

A stagehand walks by with a thermos, and the smell of coffee mixed with something stronger makes my mouth water. Just a sip. Just to steady my hands.

"Never mind where he studied," a new voice cuts in. "Look at how he's captured the movement. Like the whole landscape is flowing and bending around the river."

It's Lem Kennedy, the director. He wears a vested suit and a fedora, his sharp eyes locked on the canvas. He's pointing to somewhere near where I think the cave must be, though the memory feels slippery, like trying to hold on to water.

Kennedy tilts his head, considering the backdrop. "Campbell, this is something else. I want you on the main backdrop for the river scene. Full creative control. Whatever this technique is, whatever you're doing with space and perspective—I want more of it."

Morton clears his throat, shifting his clipboard under one arm. "That's fine, Mr. Kennedy, but we're on a tight schedule. The sooner he gets it done, the better."

Kennedy waves a hand dismissively. "Good work takes time, Morton."

Morton presses his lips together but doesn't argue. He knows better than to push back too hard in front of the director. Instead, he turns to Luke. "You heard the man. Just don't take all day."

Can I say no? They can't put my work center stage. What if I've already changed history? What if these paintings influence something, alter a future timeline? What if they create a butterfly effect and erase my future self? But I can't tell them that. The clearing is spinning, and I'm seeing double—no, triple—and all I can do is nod.

"Thank you, sir," I hear myself say, as if from a great distance. "I'll start right away."

Morton claps me on the shoulder and walks away, already calling out instructions to the other crew members. But Kennedy lingers, studying my face with an unsettling intensity.

"You look unwell, Campbell," he says. "Like a man being pulled in too many directions at once."

You have no idea, I want to tell him. Instead, I turn back to my canvas and pick up my brush. The paint shimmers, changing colors as time continues to bleed around me. I'm running out of time. Whatever's happening to me, whatever this time instability is doing to my mind—it's getting worse. I need to get out of this place, this year. And I need to do it fast.

"When's the last time you ate something proper?" Kennedy asks, still watching me.

I try to remember. The beans at dawn barely count. My stomach clenches in response. "I'm fine," I mutter.

"Nonsense." He pulls something wrapped in wax paper from his pocket. "Here. Cook packed extra biscuits. Can't have our best scenic artist passing out from hunger."

The biscuit is dense and cold, but I devour it in three bites. The solid weight of food in my stomach grounds me, momentarily pushing back against the disorientation. But it does nothing for the thirst that's building at the back of my throat. Someone laughs nearby, the sound followed by the unmistakable glug of liquid from a bottle.

"I'm going to check the other sets," I tell Kennedy, needing to move away from the temptation. Every step feels like wading through mud.

But somewhere in this unfamiliar version of 1925, Eileen is trying to find me. I have to hold on. Have to stay anchored in this timeline long enough for her to—

The third wave hits, and this time, I see something new. A flash of the future, so vivid it steals my breath: Eileen and I are standing by the river, but the water level has dropped severely. The riverbed is mostly exposed, cracked mud where water should be. The remaining water is stagnant, choked with reddish algae I've never seen before. In the distance, I can make out the skeletal remains of drowned trees. And through the haze, I can just barely read the date on a weather-beaten park notice: June 17, 2035.

I blink, and I'm back by the river, paint dripping from my frozen brush. The vision of that devastated river in 2035 overlays the backdrop I'm supposed to touch up. My hand shakes as I try to continue working, but I can't focus on what Kennedy wants. That future felt real in a way none of my other time slips have. Not like memories bleeding through, but like a warning.

The craving intensifies. It's a physical ache that radiates through my jaw and down my throat. Just one drink. Just to steady myself. To make the edges of reality stop swirling and blending together. There's a tavern in the small town downriver; the stagehands were talking about it last night around the fire. I could walk there and be back before anyone missed me.

"Campbell?" Morton is in front of me, staring. "The main backdrop can wait until tomorrow if you're unwell."

Tomorrow. I don't know how many more tomorrows I have in 1925 before time pulls me somewhere else. But now I think Eileen and I will eventually end up in 2035—and whatever's happening to the river between now and then, it isn't good.

I set down my brush and close my eyes, trying to anchor myself in this moment. The smell of the river. The buzz of insects. The distant shouts of the crew. The persistent, gnawing need for a drink that I haven't felt this strongly in years. I breathe through it, counting backward from ten like Aunt Edna taught me.

When I open my eyes, the world is stable again. For now. But for how long?

THIRTY: EILEEN

The library's reading room smells like leather bindings and floor polish. I've spread the materials across the oak table in careful order—geological survey reports, field notes, a collection of Spanish expedition records. Everything a proper archaeological survey should include.

My back aches from another night on the hard mattress at Ma Perkins' boarding house. The walk to Riverside should help to stretch out the knots in my shoulders.

"More coffee, Miss Nash?"

Mrs. Whitmore appears at my side, coffeepot in hand.

She is a tall, severe woman in her sixties, with an upright posture that suggests a spine as straight as the shelves she oversees. Her iron-gray hair is pinned in a tight bun at the nape of her neck, not a strand out of place. The lenses of her wire-rimmed glasses catch the morning light, making her expression hard to read, though I suspect she can see through most excuses with or without them.

Her dark wool dress is buttoned high at the collar, the sort of modest, practical attire that suggests she has little patience for modern fashion. She smells faintly of ink, as if she's spent the morning tending to old ledgers and straightening stacks of brittle newspapers.

I accept the coffee out of politeness, but her presence makes it difficult to focus. She lingers, watching me with the quiet, patient scrutiny of someone accustomed to spotting forged documents and dubious researchers. I get the sense that Mrs. Whitmore rarely sees young women alone in the archives—especially not ones with a suspiciously well-prepared cover story and an interest in historical anomalies.

"Thank you," I say, keeping my voice light.

She nods but does not move away. Instead, she adjusts the stack of bound survey reports beside me, as if testing whether I truly know what I'm looking at.

"You've shown quite an interest in our records," she remarks, her voice pleasant but cool. "Most visiting researchers come with letters of introduction."

"I see." I force myself to stay focused on the surveyor's journal instead of looking at the wall clock again. River City Pictures won't open for another hour anyway.

Mrs. Whitmore lingers. "I was speaking with Mr. Harrison at the main office this morning. He was quite interested in your research." She pauses meaningfully. "Though he couldn't recall a letter concerning a visiting researcher."

My pen stops moving. I've prepared for this, rehearsed it in my head. "I was sent by the Historical Preservation Society in Atlanta. I can bring the paperwork tomorrow."

"That would be lovely." Another pause. "Though I wonder why Atlanta would send someone to study here without informing us beforehand."

Because I'm from a century in the future. Because I'm following an inexplicable pull toward a man I barely know but somehow can't stop thinking about.

I say none of this. Instead, I decide to deflect, gesturing to the surveyor's journal before me. "The Society is particularly interested in documenting historical changes to the waterways. The film crew's presence at the river provides an opportunity to—"

"Yes, the film crew." Mrs. Whitmore's voice sharpens. "I must say, you seem unusually interested in their activities."

My face heats. Yesterday's visit to River City Pictures did not go well. The receptionist had been suspicious of my story about being someone's fiancée, and Luke hadn't been there anyway. I need a better plan for today.

"Their activities will impact future archaeological studies," I say. "It's important to document—"

"Miss Nash." Mrs. Whitmore sets down the coffeepot. "We sent a telegram to Atlanta this morning. They should have a response for us by this afternoon, or tomorrow morning at the latest. Do let us know if you are able to bring that letter before then."

"Of course," I say, turning back to the surveyor's journal. But something catches my eye—an entry from August 1882. Three surveyors went missing near the limestone caves, found two days later with no memory of where they'd been. The official report blamed heatstroke and disorientation.

I check the clock again. Nine-fifteen. River City Pictures won't open its doors until ten. Plenty of time to finish reading about these disappearances and plan a better approach than yesterday's fumbled attempt at playing a fiancée. I need something more concrete, more official-sounding.

I've spread my research materials across the table, trying to look absorbed in my work while fighting the urge to check the time again.

The surveyor's account isn't the only reference to the caves. A Spanish expedition report from the 1500s describes "doors in the rock that open to nowhere." And in the geological survey notes, there's a curious pattern of local tribes avoiding certain bends in the river, locations marked with careful precision in the margins.

Whitmore's chair scrapes back. She's carrying a stack of reference materials to the front desk. Not the telegram. Not yet.

The telegram from Atlanta will expose my false credentials soon enough. I feel certain that my story was rooted in fact, and yet—part of me feels like I shouldn't be here at all, that maybe I don't exist here at all. I feel like a facsimile of a real person, or a doppelgänger.

I close the surveyor's journal, my mind racing. The cave has been doing this for centuries—drawing people in, making them vanish. And now Luke is caught in its pull because of me.

Mrs. Whitmore walks past again, eyeing my spread of materials. I carefully begin packing them away. I need to get to River City Pictures, but not as anyone's fiancée this time. No more pretending to be someone I'm not—that's what got me into trouble here.

Maybe the truth, or at least part of it, would work better. A researcher interested in the river's history, wanting to document the filming locations. It's not even a lie, really. I do need to understand exactly where they're working along the river, how close they might be to...

I have until this afternoon. Maybe tomorrow morning before I'll no longer be welcome at the library. And then what? Single woman, no job, no formal training, no secretarial or other "womanly" skills to enable me to get a job in 1925. I'll end up on the streets by week's end, or worse.

Time to try River City Pictures one more time.

THIRTY-ONE: LUKE

The Suwannee moves slowly today, dark and heavy, winding through the cypress like it's keeping a secret. I grip my brush, focusing on the backdrop. It needs to match the real thing—the water, the moss, the way morning light filters through the trees. Natural. Real.

Simple.

I paint for hours, lost in the strokes. Blend, shape, repeat. The canvas absorbs my focus until everything else fades—the distant chatter of the crew, the scrape of boots over packed dirt, the muffled curse of someone adjusting a camera rig. The world narrows to my brush, the canvas, the river.

When I step back, everything unravels.

The painting isn't what I remember.

The river is too dark; and the trees on the shore twisted, and skeletal. And in the water—a figure stands, half-submerged.

A woman. Holding a lantern.

My breath locks in my chest. That wasn't there before.

My hands shake. I wipe my palm against my pants, and force myself to breathe. Maybe I just—what? Drifted? Zoned out?

Behind me, the crew keeps working. No one reacts. No one sees what I'm seeing.

I swallow hard and turn back—and it's gone.

The river, the trees, the sky—normal again.

Something cold creeps up my spine.

"Campbell!"

A hand claps onto my shoulder. I flinch, barely hearing the voice over the thudding in my ears. "We need that set finished."

He knows me, but I don't recognize him. The words barely

register. My pulse hammers in my ears.

I nod stiffly, trying to focus, trying to ignore the trembling in my fingers as I reach for the brush.

Then I hear it—two crew members near the rigging, their voices low but sharp.

"You notice how he just zones out? Guy's been off since we got here."

"Yeah. And what was up with that painting? Creeped me the hell out."

"I heard Morton say he's going to make a call when he gets back to Jacksonville."

Call? What call? The police? The insane asylum? Worse?

I grip the brush tighter, heart pounding. They're staring at me now. One of them, a spindly man in a flat cap, spits out a gob of chewing tobacco into a tin cup. The other lights a cigarette. No, he's not lighting a cigarette, he's slicing one finger across his throat. You're dead.

This is bad. Worse than bad.

I have to get out of here.

Before I completely lose my mind.

I drop the brush. Walk away.

Someone calls after me, but I don't stop. I step over roots, past the tents where equipment is stored, away from the shouting. My boots crunch over dry grass and soft dirt.

I'm not running.

But I'm not stopping, either.

I don't know where I'm going.

I just know I need to go.

The crew is watching me, whispering. My hands won't stop shaking. The heat is suffocating, the weight of everything pressing down hard. So I walk—away from the set, away from the river, away from myself.

* * *

By the time I notice my surroundings, I'm deep in the woods, following a rough-cut path where the pines thin out. The smell of fresh-cut timber hits me first—sap, sawdust, sweat.

Then I hear them.

Men shouting. Laughter. The sharp whine of a saw biting into wood.

I step into a clearing and see them—a logging crew working near the river, stripped down to undershirts, boots kicked up on stumps. A few are working. Most are not.

The camp sprawls across a half-acre clearing. A row of shapes hunkers at the tree line, some rough wooden structures, others just canvas stretched over frames. Smoke rises from a stone-ringed fire pit, where a dozen men sit—some eating from tin plates, others sharpening tools, rolling cigarettes, or just watching the work with the slow patience of men used to hard labor. Near the water's edge stands a makeshift dock where logs wait to be floated downstream.

The operation has clear divisions—the sawyers with their massive two-man saws working the largest pines, sweat-streaked men securing cables around felled timber, and younger men clearing branches under the watchful eye of a burly man who paces with a notebook.

One man sitting around the fire ring spots me. "You lost?"

I hesitate. I should turn around. Keep walking. But the way the man says it—not unfriendly, not suspicious, just amused—makes me pause.

"I came from over there," I say, pointing a thumb in the general direction of the movie set. "Just needed some air."

The guy squints at me, then grins. "Yeah, don't we all." He jerks a thumb toward a makeshift camp where a couple of men sit around a bottle of something dark. "Come take a load off."

The rest area is a collection of stumps and upturned crates arranged around a small fire. Several older men occupy the prime spots—logger hierarchy apparent in who sits where. The two Black workers I noticed earlier sit a little apart from the others—not excluded, exactly, but with a distance that speaks to habit more than hostility. Still, they're clearly part of the camp's operation, their conversation easy as they share a pipe between them. One of them catches my eye briefly, his expression wary but neutral, before turning back to his companion.

A mechanical winch—a "steam donkey" according to the faded lettering—sits idle nearby, its operator carefully oiling its gears.

I should say no. I should walk away, find somewhere quiet, get my head straight. Instead, I step forward. And sit down.

Someone hands me a tin cup. The scent of whiskey slaps me in the face before I even lift it. My hands tighten around the cup. The chatter around me fades. All I have to do is lift it to my lips. Just one sip. Just one. The cup stays in my hand. And the moment stretches—long enough for me to decide whether I'm about to fall completely or pull myself back.

"First time out here?" asks a voice to my left. An older man with weathered skin and calloused hands watches me, something knowing in his eyes. His fingers are missing the first knuckle on two digits—a logger's sacrifice to the saw. A faded company patch on his shirt identifies him as part of the Big Shoals Timber outfit. The other men seem to give him a respectful berth. Perhaps he's a foreman.

I set the cup down, untouched. "Yeah."

Behind him, the camp's routines continue—a cook bangs a ladle against a pot, signaling the midday meal coming soon. Two fresh-faced boys, clearly new to the work, struggle with armloads of firewood for the cook's stove. The air smells of pine resin, sweat, tobacco, and something savory simmering in the pot.

"It is something special," I say before I can stop myself.

The old logger laughs. "Been working these waters thirty years. It's just a river."

Just a river. The words echo strangely in my head. To him, the Suwannee is just water flowing over rocks, a way to transport timber, nothing more. He hasn't seen what I've seen—the river in three different times, the cave that shouldn't be there, the woman with the lantern who keeps appearing in my paintings...

"You look like a man who's seen a ghost," the logger says quietly.

My head snaps up. "What?"

"Seen it before. Men come out here alone, start seeing things that ain't there." He taps his temple. "River gets in your head if you let it."

Around us, the other loggers have resumed their conversations, passing the bottle, laughing at jokes I can't follow. A game of cards has started at the far end, men clustering tight around small piles of coins and company script. The hierarchy reveals itself in who deals the cards versus who fetches more whiskey. The younger men—teenagers with fewer calluses and skinnier legs—defer to the veterans with missing fingers and weathered faces.

"There's something strange about this place," I say. "The river, I mean. Have you ever noticed anything... unusual?" My intent was to make small talk, but as the words slip out, I want to suck them right back in. I hope to God the man thinks it's the whiskey talking.

The logger studies me. Then he leans forward. "There's a river bend, 'bout half mile downstream from where your people are filming. Old-timers won't go near it after dark. Say the ghosts of the old Indians still walk there."

My heart thuds against my ribs. "And have you seen it?" In my mind, I'm elaborating, but I don't say it out loud. Ghosts? Have you seen ghosts? Maybe future people? Time warps?

He shrugs. "Seen some strange things out here. Light where there shouldn't be any. Heard voices when nobody's around." He glances at the untouched cup beside me. "But most folks who talk about such things are usually deep in their cups."

"I'm not drunk," I say.

"No." His eyes narrow. "You're something else entirely."

THIRTY-TWO: EILEEN

The reception area of River City Pictures feels different today—less imposing, more irritating. Dust motes dance in the sunlight that streams through the tall windows, catching on the glossy movie posters that line the walls. My cotton gloves stick to my palms in the heat, despite the sluggish ceiling fan that turns overhead. Jacksonville in summer feels like breathing through wet cotton.

I stand at the receptionist's desk, watching as the woman rifles through her leather-bound appointment book with manicured fingers. Her perfume is too sweet, almost cloying in the close air. The same woman as yesterday, with her perfectly waved hair and skeptical eyes that never quite meet mine.

"He's not here," she says, barely looking up as she flips through the ledger. The pages make a dry whisper against her fingertips. "Mr. Campbell's still on location."

The disappointment hits harder than it should. I tighten my grip on my bag, feeling the worn leather handle press into my palm. The strap digs into my shoulder, heavy with notebooks and maps I've borrowed from the library.

"Are you sure?" I keep my voice measured, professional, though inside I'm fighting a rising tide of frustration. Every day that passes is another day Luke remains untethered, lost between times.

The receptionist exhales, her nostrils flaring slightly. The pearl buttons on her crisp blouse catch the light as her chest rises and falls.

"He is at the Suwannee set for the shoot." She gestures vaguely toward the door, a gold bracelet jingling on her wrist. "If you need him, that's where he'll be."

I hesitate, studying her face for any hint of deception. The clock on the wall ticks loudly, marking seconds I can't allow myself to waste. The telephone rings from somewhere deeper in the building, the sound oddly muffled. I don't want to push too hard—don't want to attract the wrong kind of attention—but something about the way the woman says it makes me uneasy. Her dismissive tone suggests she's either tired of my inquiries or hiding something.

"Thank you for your time," I manage, the words tasting flat and unsatisfying.

I turn away, heels clicking against the polished floor as I make my way to the heavy oak door. The brass handle is warm under my fingers. Outside, the midday heat hits me like a physical blow, the air thick enough to slice.

I know where Luke is. He's at the Suwannee set.

The problem is getting there.

I pause on the steps of the building, feeling sweat bead at my hairline. The sky overhead is blue, cloudless, and vast. A trolley rattles past, the conductor ringing his bell as the wheels grind against the embedded tracks. Overhead, the electric wires hum faintly before the streetcar disappears around the bend.

Two women pass by, their wide-brimmed hats tilted against the sun, their conversation a musical murmur that fades as they move on.

I have no car, no way to just pick up and leave. The film set is 70 miles west of the city, deep in the tangle of logging roads and forest that surrounds the Suwannee. The trains don't run in that direction, and the only way out would be to hire a driver—if I had the money to do it. Even if I could afford a ride, I don't know who to trust.

The rules here are different. A woman traveling alone to a remote film set wouldn't just raise eyebrows—it would invite questions I can't answer. No one would believe I had a good reason to go, and even if I found a driver willing to take me, the rutted roads and summer storms could leave me just as stranded as I am now.

I press my hand to the strap of my bag, feeling the reassuring weight of my notes and research against my hip. Sweat trickles down my spine, dampening the back of my blouse. I should return to the boarding house, regroup, think of another plan. But the thought of another night in that narrow bed, listening to the creaking floorboards and Mrs. Perkins's phonograph playing through the thin walls—another night without answers—makes my chest tighten.

I pause on the steps, scanning the street. A man in a tweed suit stands near the lot where the studio drivers wait, shifting impatiently in the shade of a young oak tree. He adjusts his hat, then pulls a folded telegram from his pocket, scanning it with a frown.

A gust of wind catches the paper, flicking the edge just enough for me to glimpse a headline:

River City Pictures—Suwannee Unit.

A film set telegram.

I hesitate, my pulse quickening. He could be going to the Suwannee shoot. Or maybe he's just covering the studio. But I can't ignore a chance like this.

Taking a steadying breath, I square my shoulders and approach. My shadow falls across his shoes, and he looks up, blinking in surprise. His eyes are watery blue, deep-set in a face lined by years of deadlines and whiskey. The press badge on his lapel glints in the sunlight.

"Excuse me, sir. Are you covering the Suwannee shoot?" My voice sounds steadier than I feel.

His mouth twitches slightly around his cigarette. He folds his pocket watch closed and tucks it into his vest. "Something like that," he says finally.

That's all the confirmation I need.

I smile politely, stepping into the shade beside him. The temperature drops by a few welcome degrees. Up close, I can smell tobacco and printer's ink on his clothes, the faint sweetness of bourbon on his breath despite the early hour.

"I'm a researcher with the Historical Society," I lie, the words practiced and smooth. "I'm documenting how Florida is changing with the film industry. I heard the set at the Suwannee is remarkable—authentic period details, innovative techniques."

It's a risk. If he's a real journalist with connections, he might know the Historical Society never sent anyone. But he hesitates, eyes narrowing as he takes me in again—my practical skirt, my sensible shoes, the notebook visible in my open bag. Then his expression softens.

"Well, aren't you the ambitious type?" He scratches his chin, sizing me up. "I'm covering the production for the Tribune. Name's Halley. You wanna tag along? It's six hours of bad roads in a truck that barely has springs. Not exactly a Sunday drive."

Relief floods through me, cool as river water. I extend my hand, remembering at the last moment to use the firm handshake my father taught me rather than the delicate touch expected of women in this era.

"Eileen Nash. I appreciate it more than you know."

Halley's eyebrows rise at my grip, but he doesn't comment. Instead, he gestures toward a dusty Ford truck parked at the curb, its black paint dulled by a thin layer of road dust.

"Driver should be back any minute. We leave in ten." He pulls out a silver cigarette case, offering it to me with a questioning look.

"No, thank you." I watch as he lights one for himself, the match flaring brightly against the shadowed trunk of the oak tree. The smoke drifts upward, a thin white column against the relentless sky.

"I hope you like potholes," Halley says. "Driver says road's worse than a washboard after this week's storms."

I let out a breath, feeling the tightness in my chest ease slightly. Potholes? No problem. I'd go by horse and cart if it meant finding Luke. Halley's offer of a ride is the first real step forward since arriving in this time. I might actually find Luke today, and might finally have a chance to explain what's happening to us both.

If he hasn't already vanished into another time. If his mind hasn't already unraveled completely. If I'm not already too late.

THIRTY-THREE: LUKE

I don't remember deciding to stay.

One moment, I'm taking a sip from someone else's cup. The next, I'm on a rough-hewn log, a tin mug in my hand, two drinks in, the whiskey burning its way down, the metal cool against my fingers.

I'm surrounded by the smell of fresh-cut timber—sap, sawdust, sweat. The logging camp is exactly as I first stumbled upon it earlier today: the half-acre clearing with thinning pines, the makeshift dock at the water's edge, clogged with logs. The operation's divisions remain in place, even as most have stopped working for the evening.

The man I'm sketching leans forward on his knees, watching me work with the quiet patience of someone used to long hours and steady hands. His face is broad, lined from sun and hard labor, his jaw rough with a few days' worth of stubble. A deep scar cuts through one eyebrow, disappearing into the creases of his forehead. His shirt, patched and sweat-stained, stretches over his thick frame, the sleeves rolled high to reveal arms roped with muscle. He smells like sawdust, tobacco, and a lingering bite of whiskey.

"You got me right?" he asks, his voice low, edged with amusement. "Don't make me prettier than I am."

I smudge a line of charcoal, deepening the shadows along his cheekbone. "That'd be a stretch."

The men nearby chuckle, but he just huffs a laugh, shifting his weight. "Didn't think a fancy artist'd end up in a place like this."

"Didn't think a logger would care about a sketch," I counter, tilting the paper to study the lines.

He shrugs, eyes flicking between the drawing and my face.

"Figure I oughta get a portrait done before the trees finish me off."

I finish the last stroke, wiping charcoal from my fingers. He studies it, his expression unreadable, then nods.

"Good enough," he mutters. "Reckon you earned another drink."

He reaches for the bottle, and I let him pour.

The loggers don't ask questions. They work in a world where men come and go, where yesterday doesn't matter, and tomorrow is just another day with the same calluses. The camp has an easy rhythm to it—men passing bottles, sharpening tools, telling stories that grow taller with each telling. No one looks at me twice, like I've always been here.

The same logger hierarchy is evident—skilled sawyers command respect, and older men with missing digits occupy prime spots. Two black workers I noticed during the day keep somewhat to themselves at the group's edge, speaking in low tones. The game of cards that started earlier continues, with men slapping down cards and laughing.

The older logger with the weathered skin and missing knuckles catches my eye from across the fire. He's the one who told me about the river bend where old-timers won't go after dark. Something knowing still lingers in his gaze as he nods in my direction.

The burly foreman I saw earlier with his tally book slaps me on the back, nearly knocking the untouched whiskey from my hand. "You work on that movie, don't you?" His voice is gruff, curious without being intrusive.

I nod, barely registering the conversation. The cup feels heavy in my hand. The chatter of the loggers fades in and out like a badly tuned radio. Some moments are crystal clear, others are just noise.

"Figured. You don't look like a logger." The foreman laughs, the sound warming the air between us. He motions for the bottle to be passed around again. "That director fella paying you boys anything worth a damn?"

I shrug. The truth is, I don't know—ten dollars a week? Fifty?—And I don't care. The paycheck from River City Pictures might as well be Confederate dollars or Roman coins for all the meaning it has. Money from a time that isn't mine, for a job I never asked for.

The camp cook clangs a ladle against a pot, just as he did earlier, to signal the midday meal. A few men rise, stretching sore muscles, moving toward where the evening meal waits. Most stay put, letting the whiskey do its work after hours of backbreaking labor.

Someone refills my cup without asking. The amber liquid sloshes, catching the light from the fire. Motes of dust dance across the surface. I stare at it too long, mesmerized by the way it moves, alive and dangerous.

Just one more drink.

One drink to quiet my thoughts, to drown out the panic clawing at the edges of my mind.

I can feel it building—the pressure, the noise. The memory of the painting that changed under my hands. The woman with the lantern where no woman should be. The creeping suspicion that my reality is not right.

I lift the cup and drink.

The whiskey goes down in a rush—hot and dangerous. It burns a path down my throat, blooms in my chest, spreads like wildfire through limbs that have felt disconnected for too long.

And just like that, the floodgates open.

The loggers don't say much, but they notice. When the bottle comes back around and I take another long pull without hesitation, the old logger smirks, tipping his cup toward me.

"Reckon you'll do just fine."

Someone chuckles. Someone else slaps me on the back, and the bottle keeps moving. The night flows with it.

I drink fast. Faster than I mean to. The cup is never empty for long. The loggers keep it filled, a silent brotherhood of men who recognize something broken when they see it. They don't ask what I'm running from. They just make sure I have what I need to keep running.

The same fresh-faced boys I noticed struggling with firewood earlier now sit at the edge of the gathering, watching the older men with a mixture of awe and trepidation. The mechanical winch— the "steam donkey"—sits idle nearby, waiting for tomorrow's work.

The loggers keep talking, laughing, sharing stories about the river, about women in towns I've never heard of. Someone pulls out a deck of cards, yellowed and soft from too many hands. Someone else sings a song about a miner's daughter, voice cracking on the high notes.

I just drink.

The warmth spreads through my limbs, dulling the static in my head. The sensation reminds me of something—a canvas I painted once, all warm yellows and reds expertly blended, no hard edges, just color and movement.

My hands stop shaking.

The world feels normal. Just one time, one place, one moment flowing naturally into the next. No visions of skeletal trees that don't exist yet. No glimpses of concrete boat ramps that haven't been built. No women with lanterns appearing where they shouldn't be.

And I hate how good it feels. How easy it would be to stay here, in this simple world of drink and stories and honest labor. How tempting to let the whiskey wash away everything I know about time and caves and Eileen.

The whiskey turns into another, then another, and soon the edges of the world blur. My words slur together when I speak—not that I have much to say. The loggers don't notice, or if they do, they don't care. They've seen men drink for many reasons: to forget women, to forget war, to forget debts. What's one more man drinking to forget time?

Because this is what men do.

They work. They drink. They forget.

I tip back another cup, feeling the liquid slip and slide around the rim before catching against my lips. The taste hardly registers anymore—it could be water for all I care. Except water wouldn't leave this blessed numbness in its wake.

At some point, I'm standing, though I don't remember getting up. Someone claps me on the back hard enough to make me stumble, but I catch myself against a tree. I hear myself laughing, though it doesn't sound like me at all.

I'm by the river, staring at the dark water, swaying where I stand. The surface ripples with the evening breeze, catching the golden light of sunset. The Suwannee looks different here—wider, wilder. Or maybe that's just whiskey talking. Logs bob in the shallows, waiting for tomorrow's journey downstream.

Eileen is looking for me.

But it's a distant thought, like a memory from another life. A story someone told me once about a woman who travels through time, who might search for a man who paints rivers and can't stay anchored in one reality. It sounds absurd, suddenly. Impossible. The whiskey makes it easy to dismiss.

I sit back down, the world tilting sideways before righting itself again. Someone refills my drink without asking. I grin, loose and warm, the worry that's knotted my shoulders for weeks finally unraveling.

"Guess I'll stay a while."

And then, nothing.

Just darkness.

THIRTY-FOUR: EILEEN

The drive is long and rough, the truck bouncing over roads that transition from Jacksonville's neat pavement to packed dirt and finally to deep ruts carved through the trees. Halley is squeezed next to me up front, occasionally jotting notes in a small leather-bound notebook, while I brace myself against each jarring bump. The leather bench offers no comfort, the thin padding doing little to soften the jarring impact against my tailbone.

The Florida wilderness unfolds around us in layers of green—first the tamed outskirts of the city, then pine plantations in orderly rows, and finally the wild tangle of cypress and oak draped with Spanish moss.

We stop at a weathered filling station, little more than a shack with a rusted tin roof and a pair of hand-cranked gas pumps out front. The air is thick with the sharp bite of kerosene and the sour tang of old oil, mixing with the swampy scent of standing water nearby. A battered Coca-Cola sign creaks on its hinges, and a stray dog dozes in the shade beneath the porch. Inside, the dimly lit space smells of tobacco, sweat, and something fried—maybe catfish, maybe yesterday's leftovers. The attendant, a wiry man in suspenders and a sweat-stained hat, watches us from behind the counter, a toothpick rolling between his lips as Halley steps out to pay.

The air grows thicker, heavier with moisture as we near the river. I catch glimpses of birds I can't identify, flashes of color against the emerald backdrop. The scent of vegetation and wet earth replaces the city's dust and exhaust.

"Almost there," Halley calls back, his voice nearly lost in the truck's rattle. His face is damp with sweat despite the breeze, his collar darkened and wilted.

We turn sharply, and suddenly the forest turns into a clearing humming with activity. The truck rolls to a stop, and I stand on wobbly legs, one hand steadying myself against the wooden slats of the truck bed. The Suwannee glitters in the afternoon light, dark and secretive, curving away into the trees. Along its banks, the film crew has created a makeshift village—tents for equipment, canvas chairs under hastily erected awnings, lights, and cameras positioned at strategic angles.

The late afternoon set is buzzing with movement—actors in ruffled gowns and high-collared waistcoats lounging between takes, crewmen adjusting cables that snake across the ground like vines, assistants rushing with clipboards and coffee cups. A man wearing a fedora and a vested suit that somehow remains pristine despite the heat, barks orders over the chaos. His voice carries across the clearing, commanding and sharp.

"Get those lights higher! We're losing the shadows on the river!"

But something is wrong.

My eyes scan the busy set, searching for the tall figure I know so well yet have only met twice. Luke should be here, working on backdrops, blending paint, staring at the river with that haunted look in his eyes.

Instead, I see strangers—men in work clothes, women in costume, everyone busy with their own tasks, no one paying attention to me as I step away from the truck.

I approach a young woman holding a leather-bound notebook, her hair pinned severely under a wide-brimmed hat. "Excuse me, I'm looking for Luke Campbell. The artist?"

She barely glances up, pencil tapping against her papers. "Don't know him. Try the art department." She gestures vaguely toward a stretch of canvas tarps near the tree line.

I make my way through the organized chaos, dodging equipment and people with equal care. The ground is soft underfoot, churned by dozens of feet into a mix of mud and grass. When I reach the art department—really just a collection of canvases and paint supplies arranged under a sagging canvas awning—I find three men working, none of them Luke.

"I'm looking for Luke Campbell," I say, holding back the

urgency threatening to creep into my voice. "Is he here today?"

One man, older with paint-stained fingers, squints at me. "Campbell? Don't think he's here today. Might have gone back to Jacksonville on the supply truck."

"But he was scheduled to work today," I insist, remembering what the receptionist had said.

"Lady, I just paint what they tell me to paint," he says, turning back to his canvas.

Frustration builds in my chest as I move from group to group, asking the same question, receiving the same unhelpful responses. The sun settles lower, beating down through the trees, and sweat trickles between my shoulder blades. I shed my jacket, draping it over my arm as I continue my search. There are around a hundred people on the set, and it takes what feels like hours for me to talk to them all. At least, it feels like I've asked everyone, when I finally get a lead.

"Campbell?" A middle-aged man with sun-weathered skin looks up from coiling a thick rope. "Yeah, he was here earlier." He tosses the rope over his shoulder, muscles flexing beneath his sweat-soaked shirt. "Painted for a while this morning, then just... left."

Something cold settles in my stomach. "Left? Where?"

The man gestures toward the dense trees beyond the cleared area where they've set up camp. "Dunno. Just walked off." He scratches his stubbled chin. "Been actin' strange since he got here, if you ask me. Staring at his paintings like they were talking to him or somethin'."

I follow his gaze to where the wilderness begins—a wall of green, impenetrable and vast. The thick, endless Florida forest stretches past the river, deep and unmarked by any path I can see. Luke is out there. Alone. I remember his fear of the water, and I shiver.

My pulse quickens, a hollow thudding in my ears that nearly drowns out the surrounding activity.

"Did anyone see where he went?" I do my best to sound calm and professional, but I can hear the strain creeping in.

A younger worker pauses nearby, setting down a wooden crate filled with equipment parts. "Well, I seen him after the supply truck left, so he didn't go that way." He pauses for a moment, scrunches his mouth, and says, "Some loggers came by earlier. Couple hours ago, maybe. They were headed back to their camp downriver." He scratches his neck, leaving a smudge of dirt. "Maybe he went with them? Not many other places he could have gone out here."

Loggers. Of course. The logging industry was booming in Florida during this period. Their camps would be scattered along the river, using the water to transport timber during the wet season. I remember reading about their operations in the historical archives—rough men living in rougher conditions, far from civilization's watchful eye.

"How far is their camp?" I ask, already calculating how much daylight remains.

The young man shrugs. "Mile, maybe two? Follow the river south. Can't miss it—they've cleared half the forest down there."

I set my jaw, determination replacing the fear that had been building. "Thank you."

I glance back at the truck that brought me here. Halley is deep in conversation with the director, his notebook open, completely absorbed in whatever exclusive details he's gathering for his article. He won't miss me, at least not for hours. By then, I'll either have found Luke or...

No, I can't think like that. I *will* find him.

I slip away from the film set, moving toward the tree line. The shade is an immediate relief from the relentless sun, but the humidity intensifies under the canopy, making the air thick and difficult to breathe. I follow what appears to be a rough trail, likely made by the loggers traveling between their camp and the film set.

If that's where Luke is, I'll find him. Before it's too late. Too late for what, I don't know exactly, but I feel time is running out. For me. For us. But mostly for Luke.

The forest closes around me as I walk, the sounds of the film set fading behind me. Ahead, somewhere in this green wilderness, Luke is lost. And somehow, I have to find him, have to help him remember who he is, when he is.

Before time pulls him away from me again.

The logging trail narrows as I follow the river south, mud sucking at my shoes with each step. Sunset filters through the trees in golden shafts, turning the Spanish moss into glowing veils. Mosquitoes hum around my face, drawn by my exertion and the fading light.

* * *

"Can't miss it," the young man had said. Apparently, he'd never tried to follow a logging trail.

The path splits three ways at a cypress knee that looks like every other cypress knee I've passed. I choose the middle fork, the one that seems most worn, and forge ahead. Fifty yards later, it narrows to nothing, swallowed by palmettos and vines that scratch at my arms.

I backtrack, trying the left fork this time. The light is fading fast, transforming the forest into a labyrinth of deepening shadows. Every rustle in the underbrush makes my heart skip— snakes, alligators, or worse things that have no name. Something skitters across the path ahead, too quick to identify.

"Luke?" I call out, my voice thin and immediately absorbed by the dense vegetation. No answer comes except the mocking cry of a bird somewhere above.

Judging by the encroaching dark, I have been walking for hours. The path should have taken twenty minutes, thirty at most. Despair washes over me, sudden and cold. I'm lost in a Florida wilderness in 1925, searching for a man who might not even be here, who might have been pulled through time again already.

The last of the sunlight bleeds away, leaving me in a darkness so complete I can barely see my hand before my face. I step cautiously, feeling my way forward, each footfall a potential disaster on the uneven ground. My throat tightens. If I get truly lost out here, no one will think to look for me until morning. By then...

A sound to my right—a branch snapping underfoot, too heavy to be a small animal. I freeze, straining to see through the darkness.

"Hello?" My voice shakes. "Is someone there?"

Silence answers, stretched taut with possibility. Then another snap, closer this time. I back away slowly, pulse hammering in my ears. My foot catches on a root, and I stumble, barely catching myself against a tree trunk.

A flicker of light through the trees stops me. At first, I think it's my imagination, a product of fear and wishful thinking. But there it is again—a golden glow between the trunks, steady and inviting. Hope surges through me. The logging camp. It has to be.

I push toward the light, ignoring the branches that tug at my clothes and hair. The trail widens, becomes more defined under my feet, and suddenly the forest gives way to a sprawling clearing. The logging camp spreads before me—a collection of rickety buildings and canvas tents arranged in a loose semicircle. In the center, a fire pit crackles, sending sparks skyward. Men move through the camp like shadows in the fading light, their voices carrying across the clearing in a low rumble.

My arrival doesn't go unnoticed. Conversations halt as I step into the firelight, and a dozen pairs of eyes turn in my direction. I straighten my spine, trying to project a confidence I don't feel.

"I'm looking for someone," I announce. "A painter from the film set. Luke Campbell."

A large man with a beard streaked with gray steps forward, axe handle resting casually against his shoulder. "And who might you be, miss?"

"Eileen Nash." I hesitate, unsure what relationship would justify my pursuit. "I'm... with the production company. Mr. Campbell left without completing his work."

A few of the men exchange glances, their expressions unreadable. One of them, a wiry man with a bushy mustache, leans forward, elbows on his knees.

"You lookin' for Campbell?" His tone isn't quite hostile, but there's something wary in it. "Ain't often we see a lady come all this way for a drunk artist."

"It wasn't far," I lie, pointing to the woods. "A twenty-minute walk from the movie set that way."

The man shrugs. "Just sayin'. Lotta folks pass through here. Some looking to stay. Some looking to run. Never a lady, though."

I straighten, meeting his gaze head-on. I have to think fast. "They asked me to locate Mr. Campbell and get him safely back to the set."

I realize the ridiculousness of my words. Why would "they," whoever "they" are, ask a woman to traipse through the woods? But by the looks of this ragtag crew, they're a fringe society, and maybe they aren't fully aware of social norms like white gloves, crossed ankles, and escorted women.

The bearded man studies me, skepticism clear in the furrow of his brow. Several loggers exchange glances, and a few suppress smiles. They don't believe me.

"Your artist friend's here," he finally says, nodding toward the largest building. "Though he ain't in no condition to paint nothin' right now."

I breathe a sigh of relief, but my heart sinks at the words. "What do you mean?"

A younger logger spits into the fire. "Man can't hold his liquor worth a damn. Traded a sketch for a bottle and drank like the river was runnin' dry."

"He's passed out in the bunkhouse," the bearded man—clearly the foreman—explains. "Been out cold for hours."

Relief washes over me, quickly followed by concern. Luke, drunk. How drunk?

"I need to see him," I say, already moving toward the bunkhouse.

The foreman catches my arm gently. "Now hold on, miss. That there's where thirty men sleep. Ain't proper for a lady to—"

"I don't care about proper," I snap, then catch myself. In 1925, proper matters. A woman alone in a logging camp is already scandalous enough. "I just need to make sure he's all right."

The foreman sighs, releasing my arm. "Jenkins, go check on the artist."

A lanky young man nods and ducks into the bunkhouse. He returns moments later. "Still out cold, boss. Snorin' like a bear."

"You're welcome to wait by the fire, miss," the foreman offers. "But I can't let you into that bunkhouse. Wouldn't be right."

I want to argue, but the stubborn set of his jaw tells me this is a battle I won't win. Not in 1925.

"Fine," I concede. "I'll wait."

"You plannin' to take him back tonight?" another logger asks.

I glance at the forest. Night has fallen completely now, the path back to the film set swallowed by darkness. "No," I admit. "It'll have to be morning."

The men exchange glances again. A woman staying overnight

at a logging camp is clearly not what they expected to deal with today.

"Earl, go fetch Martha," the foreman calls out. "Tell her we've got a situation."

A few minutes later, a stout woman emerges from a small cabin bordering the clearing. She wears a faded cotton dress with an apron tied around her substantial waist, her gray-streaked hair pulled back in a tight bun. She takes me in with a single appraising glance.

"This is Martha," the foreman explains. "Camp cook. Married to Big Jim over there." He gestures to a barrel-chested man sharpening an axe by the fire.

Martha steps forward, wiping her hands on her apron. "Well now, you're a long way from where a young lady ought to be," she says, her voice surprisingly gentle despite her stern appearance. "Can't have you sleeping out here with these drunk fools." She shoots a pointed look at the men, several of whom have the decency to look abashed.

"I got a pallet on my floor," she continues. "It ain't much, but it's clean, and it's a sight better than spending the night out here." She glances at the darkening sky. "Besides, there's rain coming. You'll catch your death out in it."

Relief floods through me. "Thank you, Mrs.—"

"Just Martha will do," she says, already turning back toward her cabin. "Come along, then. I reckon you could use something hot in your belly, too."

Martha's cabin is small but immaculately kept. A cast-iron stove radiates heat from one corner, and the aroma of something savory fills the single room. She gestures to a wooden table with two chairs.

"Sit yourself down. Venison stew's still hot."

My stomach growls loudly, reminding me I haven't eaten since morning. "Thank you," I say as she ladles a generous portion into a chipped enamel bowl.

The stew is rich and flavorful, seasoned with fresh herbs. I devour it gratefully, sopping up the broth with a chunk of dense cornbread.

"Your man's in a bad way," Martha says, settling across from me. "Jim said he came stumblin' in here around noon, traded a fancy drawin' for some moonshine." She shakes her head. "Drank it all in one go, accordin' to the boys. Been unconscious since."

"He's not..." I want to correct her assumption that Luke is "my man," but something stops me. What are we to each other, really? Connected across time in ways I can't explain, least of all to a woman in 1925. "He doesn't usually drink," I say instead.

Martha snorts. "Could've fooled me. Jim said he was talkin' all kinds of nonsense before he passed out. Rivers changin' direction, years jumpin' around like jackrabbits."

I nod, wondering what Luke saw, what visions drove him to seek oblivion in a bottle.

"Men get like that sometimes," Martha continues, misinterpreting my concern. "The drink brings out all sorts of demons. He'll have a head fit to split tomorrow, but he'll live."

"Thank you for taking care of him," I say. "And for letting me stay."

"Couldn't leave you out there with that pack of fools," she says with a dismissive wave. "Most are decent enough, but get a few drinks in 'em and..." She shrugs. "Better you're in here."

After dinner, Martha shows me to a pallet on the floor beside the stove. "It ain't much," she says, laying out a worn quilt and a small pillow. "But it'll keep you off the ground."

I've pulled all-nighters before—cramming for finals, preparing for field expeditions, finishing grant applications. One night without sleep won't kill me. I'll just stay alert, ready to help Luke when morning comes so we can get back to the film set.

Jim returns shortly after, a mountain of a man with surprisingly gentle movements around his wife. He nods politely in my direction before settling in a rocking chair in the corner with a pipe. The domesticity of their evening routine feels surreal after the chaos of my day.

Through the small window, I can see the campfire still burning, hear the occasional burst of laughter from the men who haven't yet turned in. The night deepens around the cabin. Somewhere in the forest, an owl calls, its cry echoing across the clearing.

Martha and Jim retire to a curtained-off section of the cabin, leaving me alone with my thoughts. I'm determined to stay awake to be ready when Luke wakes. I sit up on my pallet, back against the wall, listening to the rhythmic snoring from behind the curtain.

The questions swirl in my mind as I struggle to keep my eyes open. I recite archaeological classifications in alphabetical order, recalling dating techniques, anything to stay alert.

But exhaustion is relentless. My eyes burn,, and my limbs grow heavier with each passing minute. I twist strands of my hair, chew my lip, stretch my legs and arms. The stove's warmth doesn't help, wrapping around me like a comforting blanket.

In the darkest part of the night, when the cabin is filled with soft shadows and the forest is utterly still, I let my head rest against the wall, just for a moment. Just to relieve the ache in my neck.

I don't remember closing my eyes.

I don't remember sliding down the wall, head coming to rest on the makeshift pillow.

I don't remember surrendering to sleep in this strange place, with Luke so close yet unreachable.

But I must have, because the next thing I know, Martha is gently shaking my shoulder, saying something about breakfast, and the men will be up soon. I blink, disoriented, as dawn breaks gray and threatening through the small window.

"Storm's coming," she says, nodding toward the darkening sky. "Better get your man and head back before it hits."

THIRTY-FIVE: LUKE

I wake to the sound of axes.

Rhythmic chopping echoes through the trees, punctuated by distant shouts and the crack of falling timber. My head throbs with each impact, a sledgehammer against my skull. I keep my eyes closed, trying to understand the sounds. Construction, maybe? The new condos going up across from my apartment building?

I force my eyes open, expecting white walls, IKEA furniture, my phone charging on the nightstand.

Instead, I find myself staring at a wood ceiling, stained and patched. Confusion washes over me. This isn't my apartment. This isn't—

The memory hits me in fragments—whiskey, loggers, the film set.

I sit up too quickly. The world tilts sharply, and my stomach lurches in protest. The room spins around me, and I barely make it out of the door before I'm retching into the dirt, my body purging itself of last night's poor decisions. My throat burns, my mouth tastes foul, and each pulse of my heart sends fresh pain ricocheting through my skull.

When I finally straighten, wiping my mouth with the back of my trembling hand, the reality of my situation crashes down on me. I'm in a logging camp somewhere along the Suwannee.

"Rough night, artist?"

I turn to see one logger—the older one with the weathered face—watching me with something between amusement and pity. He offers a tin cup filled with water.

"Thanks," I manage, my voice a raw scrape.

"First time's always the worst," he says, as if we're discussing a carnival ride and not the worst hangover of my existence. "Food's over by the fire, if you can keep it down."

I nod, immediately regretting the movement. The camp comes into focus around me—half a dozen wood buildings, a smoldering fire pit, men moving with purpose, sharpening tools, loading equipment. The river glitters beyond the trees, morning light dancing across its surface.

Wrong. It's all wrong. The Suwannee I know has concrete boat ramps and metal railings, informational plaques about wildlife, an occasional plastic water bottle or chip packet caught in the reeds. This wild, untouched version feels like a painting, not reality.

"Look what I found in the dirt," another logger calls out, approaching with a crumpled piece of paper. "Reckon our artist friend was busy before he passed out."

He unfolds a charcoal sketch, holding it up for the others to see. Laughter ripples through the gathered men.

"What's this supposed to be?" one of them asks, pointing. "Looks like our camp, but wrong somehow."

I try to focus my blurred vision. The drawing is of the logging camp, but not as it appears now. In my sketch, the buildings are crumbling, roofs caved in, nature reclaiming the clearing. Trees grow through what is now the fire pit. Moss blankets the collapsed bunkhouse. It's the camp as it might look decades from now, abandoned and forgotten.

"Don't recall making that," I mutter, the admission bringing fresh waves of shame and confusion.

The younger logger snorts. "Sure you don't. You were scribbling like a madman half the night, mumbling about how things 'should look' and 'will look.' Figured you were just drunk."

"Hey," calls another, "what's with the water level in your picture? River's halfway up the banks there. You expecting a flood?"

They laugh again, passing the sketch between them, pointing out details that make no sense in the present.

"Give it here," I say, reaching for the drawing, but the logger holds it out of reach.

"Nah, think we'll keep this one. Ain't often we get art made special for us, even if it is crazy talk put to paper."

I take a step and stumble, my balance compromised by the lingering effects of the alcohol and the disorientation of being out of time. The old logger steadies me with a surprisingly gentle hand.

"You ought to head back to your movie people," he says. "They'll be missing you."

Will they? I can barely remember what my purpose is here. Painting backdrops. River scenes. Something about a southern romance, or was it a historical piece? The details slip away like water through my fingers.

"Luke?"

The voice cuts through the fog in my mind, familiar and yet unfamiliar simultaneously. I look up, certain I'm hearing things.

But there she is—Eileen—standing at the camp's outskirts, her figure backlit by the morning sun. For a second, she looks like she did on our first date, by the river in 2025, her hair loose around her shoulders, her clothes modern and practical. But then the image shifts, and I see her as she is now—hair cut into a razor-sharp bob, wearing a simple blouse and skirt that belong to this time, not ours.

"Eileen?" My voice cracks on her name. "What are you doing here?" She must be a mirage. A trick of dehydration and whiskey withdrawal. A post-blackout fever dream.

She steps forward, her expression a mixture of relief and anger. "I stayed with Martha last night." She points to a stout woman in a faded cotton dress, rolling dough on a rough wooden table. "I've been looking for you everywhere."

The loggers whistle and exchange glances. "Looks like your lady friend's not too happy," one of them remarks.

I turn away, unable to meet her eyes. She seems real. Looks real. Could she be real?

My muddled mind begins to clear, and shame settles deep in my gut. Not only is Eileen Nash standing in front of me, but she's seeing me exactly the way I never wanted a woman to see me again.

"You shouldn't be here," I mutter. "You shouldn't see me like this."

"Like what?" Her voice is tight with frustration. "Hungover?"

"I'm not hungover." The lie slips easily from my lips. "You have no idea what it's like."

"Then tell me!" She strides closer, ignoring the loggers' interested stares. "Because from where I'm standing, it looks like you're just drinking yourself into oblivion while I've been searching for you for days."

"You want to know what it's like?" My voice rises despite the pain in my head. "Look at that!" I point to the sketch the logger still holds. "I don't even remember drawing that, but there it is— the camp as it will be in fifty years. I see everything at once, Eileen. Everything. This camp now, this camp abandoned, this camp underwater from a flood."

The loggers murmur and look at each other.

Eileen's eyes flick to the drawing, then back to me. "But why get drunk?"

"It was the only way to make it stop!" I run my fingers through my hair, feeling the grit and sweat from a night spent on the ground. "Do you know what it's like to paint things you don't remember painting? To look at a canvas and see a woman in the river who disappears when you blink? To constantly question which decade you're actually in?"

The loggers have gone silent, watching our exchange with uncomfortable fascination.

"Well, isn't this a fine little show?" one of them finally comments. "The artist and his muse having a lovers' quarrel."

Eileen turns on him, eyes flashing. "Give me that drawing."

The logger raises an eyebrow but hands over the crumpled paper. She studies it for a moment, then folds it carefully and tucks it into her pocket.

"We're leaving," she says to me, her tone brooking no argument. "Now."

"Listen to your lady, Campbell," the older logger advises. "Before you embarrass yourself further."

I want to argue, to tell her I can't face the world outside this camp, can't trust myself to function, but something in her eyes stops me. Determination, yes, but also fear—not of me, but *for* me.

"Come with me," she says, softer now, holding out her hand. "Please."

I take her hand. Her fingers are warm and solid against mine. The contact is shocking in its clarity—the first thing that's felt completely real since I woke up. I rise unsteadily to my feet, her grip tightening to support me.

"Thank you," she says to the loggers, her voice carrying an authority that belies her appearance. "For looking after him."

The older logger touches the brim of his hat in acknowledgment. "He's an odd one, your friend. Talks like he's from somewhere else entirely."

If he only knew the truth of that statement.

Eileen's hand squeezes mine, a silent reminder to stay quiet. "He's an artist," she says simply, as if that explains everything. And perhaps, to these men, it does.

She leads me away from the camp, back toward the path that connects to the film set. We walk in silence for several minutes, her hand still holding mine, grounding me in the present moment.

"I'm sorry," I finally say, the words inadequate but necessary.

She stops, turning to face me fully. "Luke, I don't care about the drinking right now. I care that you're falling apart and I wasn't there to help. I care that instead of trying to find me, you ran away."

Trying to find her? The thought slams into me, knocking the wind from my lungs. I had no idea she was even here—or at least that's the lie I try to tell myself. Deep down, I know she's right. Some part of me sensed her presence across the fractured timeline, knew I should have searched for her. But the bottle's siren call drowned out everything else.

I stare at this magnetic woman standing before me, this person I feel connected to across the spans of time, the one who could make sense of it all—of me. And I blew it. Self-loathing rises like bile in my throat. "I didn't think—"

"No, you didn't," she interrupts. "You didn't think that I'm experiencing this too. That I'm also trying to make sense of what's happening to us both."

The truth in her words breaks something loose inside me. "I'm losing it, Eileen. I can't... I can't keep track of when I am anymore. One minute I'm here, painting for River City Pictures, and the next I'm in my apartment in 2025, surrounded by galleries and coffee shops that don't exist yet. I thought the whiskey might help, might make it stop for a while."

"Did it?"

"For a little while. Then I just passed out." I shake my head, hearing how pathetic my own words sound—dull and stupid, nothing but the same tired excuses from another broken alcoholic. While time was unraveling around us, I chose the path I always take: the easy way out. Rather than face whatever cosmic force has entangled us, I crawled back into the bottle. And now morning has come, bringing with it the harsh slam of reality and that familiar whisper urging me to drown it all again.

Eileen's expression softens. "We need to get you back to Jacksonville. Get you cleaned up. And then we need to figure this out—together."

"The cave," I say, the answer suddenly clear despite my muddled thoughts. "Something happened to us in the cave."

She nods, eyes bright with a mixture of fascination and personal concern. "I think it's the key to understanding what's happening to us."

I nod, though I can't think of one logical explanation for what she's talking about. How could a cave have caused this? How can a cave fracture my reality, plant me in a year I have no place being in? I think of the TARDIS in *Doctor Who* and I want to break down into hysterics. I'm a time-traveling doctor, I tell myself. I really have lost my mind.

As we walk in silence, my head pounds with every step, a dull, throbbing ache behind my eyes. My mouth is dry, my throat raw, and the lingering taste of stale moonshine clings to my tongue. Each shift in movement sends a wave of nausea rolling through me, my stomach uneasy but empty. My limbs feel leaden, my joints aching like I spent the night wrestling a bear instead of passed out in the dirt.

The forest gradually thins, giving way to the cleared area where the film set has been established. I can hear the distant sounds of the crew, see the equipment arranged along the riverbank. It all looks strange to me now, artificial against the natural backdrop of the Suwannee.

Eileen stops just before we reach the clearing. "Luke," she says, her voice low. "Whatever happens, whatever you're experiencing, I'm here. We're in this together now."

The words settle over me like a blanket, warm and unexpectedly comforting. This is the first break in my mind's chaos since the whiskey wore off. The present moment, standing beside Eileen at the edge of a film set in Florida—comes into focus with unexpected clarity.

"Together," I repeat, the word a lifeline in a sea of temporal confusion.

And for this moment, I know exactly when I am.

THIRTY-SIX: EILEEN

The forest path between the logging camp and the film set feels longer on the return journey. Luke stumbles beside me, his hand gripping mine like it's the only solid thing in his world. Each time he stumbles on uneven ground, I feel his fingers tighten, a silent plea not to let go.

He's silent now, the burst of emotion from our confrontation at the camp having drained what little energy he had. His confession lingers between us. *I see everything at once, Eileen.*

I wonder what that might be like. To exist in multiple times simultaneously, to see the past, present, and future overlaid like transparent photographs.

The cave's temporal disturbances, if that's what they are, disoriented me at first, but my head cleared within minutes. But is my head really clear? The more I think about time travel, the more I realize how pathological I sound. Even to myself.

I'm a time-traveling doctor now? Hopping into a TARDIS to save the world from monsters?

But Luke? He's an artist along for the ride. He was in the wrong place at the wrong time.

I should never have brought him to that cave.

No wonder he turned to alcohol.

"We need to reach Jacksonville by nightfall," I say, breaking the silence. My voice sounds too loud in the quiet forest. "I have a room at Ma Perkins' boarding house. It's plain but comfortable, and she doesn't ask questions—within reason."

Luke nods but says nothing.

"We can get you cleaned up, find you some fresh clothes. Then tomorrow, we'll figure out a plan." As if I even know where to start with this 'plan.' Going back into the cave is a terrible idea.

They could end up—where? Five minutes in the past? Three hundred years in the future? Could they become separated, Luke's fractured mind transporting him to a Victorian insane asylum? No, I need to figure something out. There's a plan waiting to be found. I just have to gather the evidence and think. Maybe Luke has some insights.

Luke stumbles again, and I steady him with my free hand. He's lost weight since I saw him in the cave, his frame somehow diminished under the rumpled clothes.

"I can't go back to the camp," he says suddenly. "I can't face them. They saw me... they know I..."

"We have to go back," I say. "We're six hours from Jacksonville, and we need a ride."

He shakes his head. "We need money for the boarding house, for the fisherman. My things are at the studio. My paints..." The words trail off, his expression distant, as though he's trying to recall what belongs to him and what doesn't. Or he's trying to sort through what's important and what isn't.

"Luke." I stop walking, turning to face him. The sun filters through the canopy above, dappling his face with shifting light. "Focus on right now. This moment. We'll figure out the rest as we go."

He inhales deeply, and his eyes find mine. For a second, I see clarity there—a welcome glimpse of the man I met at the gallery opening.

"Okay," he says. "The camp then."

We continue walking, the forest gradually thinning as we approach the film set. The sounds reach us before the sight— voices calling instructions, the clatter of equipment being moved, the occasional burst of laughter. Luke's grip on my hand tightens again.

"They're going to stare," he mutters.

"Let them." I square my shoulders. "We'll walk through, get your things, and leave. That's all."

The trees give way to the clearing where the film crew has established their temporary base. Canvas tents and wooden platforms line the riverbank, cameras and lights positioned to capture the perfect angle of the Suwannee. Men in work clothes move purposefully between stations, while actors in period costumes wait in patches of shade.

Our appearance doesn't go unnoticed. Conversations pause, heads turn, eyes follow our progress across the clearing. I hold my head high, my expression daring anyone to comment, but Luke keeps his gaze fixed on the ground, his posture radiating shame.

"Campbell!" A voice calls out, and I feel Luke flinch. A huge man in a vest and shirtsleeves strides toward us, his face flushed with annoyance. "Where the hell have you been? We needed those riverboat scenes finished yesterday!"

"I'm sorry, Mr. Morton," Luke says, his voice small.

"Luke's been ill," I say, stepping in front of him. "Food poisoning, I believe. Quite severe."

Morton's eyes narrow as he takes in Luke's disheveled appearance, the pallor of his skin. "Ill, eh?"

"Nevertheless," I continue, my tone firm, "he's in no condition to work today. We've come to collect his things."

"His things?" Daveson's bushy eyebrows rise. "Now see here, Miss—"

"Nash. Eileen Nash."

"Miss Nash. Campbell has a contractual obligation. He can't just leave."

"I understand completely, Mr. Daveson." I offer my most disarming smile. "And I'm sure once he's recovered, you can discuss those obligations. But right now, he needs rest."

Daveson looks like he wants to argue further, but a commotion near the cameras draws his attention. With a final suspicious glance at us both, he hurries away, already shouting instructions at some unfortunate stagehand.

"That was impressive," Luke murmurs as we continue toward what I assume is his work area—a collection of canvases stacked against a tree, paint supplies neatly organized on a wooden crate.

"Archaeology teaches you to stand your ground," I reply. "Otherwise, no one takes your research seriously."

Luke manages a weak smile, the first I've seen since finding him. It vanishes quickly as we approach his workspace. His eyes scan the canvases, his expression growing increasingly troubled.

"What is it?" I ask.

"These aren't... I don't remember painting these." He touches one canvas tentatively, as if afraid it might disappear. "This one—the riverboat at sunset—yes, that's mine. But these others..."

I look at the paintings. They all appear to be in the same style, but some depict scenes I recognize from our time—the concrete boat ramp that doesn't exist yet, visitors in modern clothing standing on wooden viewing platforms.

"I need to sit down," Luke says abruptly.

I guide him to a nearby crate, helping him lower himself. He puts his head in his hands, fingers pressing against his temples.

"Miss Nash. There you are!" A new voice, cheerful and intrusive, breaks the moment.

I look up to see Halley, the journalist who gave me a ride to the film set yesterday, approaching with notebook in hand. His eyes brighten with recognition when he sees me.

"Found your missing artist, I see." He tips his hat, then surveys Luke with undisguised interest. "Though he appears worse for wear. Late night with the loggers?"

Luke doesn't respond, doesn't even look up. I step forward, physically placing myself between them.

"Mr. Halley, this isn't a good time."

"On the contrary," Halley says, pencil already poised above his notebook, "I think it's a fascinating time. Word around camp is that Mr. Campbell is some kind of artistic genius. I hear someone say he's the new Maxfield Parrish." His eyes gleam. "The readers will eat it up."

"There is no story here," I say firmly. "Mr. Campbell is simply unwell."

Halley's gaze shifts from Luke to me, then back again. "Unwell," he repeats, drawing out the word. "Of course." He tucks his notebook away, but his expression remains avid. "Feel better, Campbell. The art world awaits your next masterpiece."

He saunters away, whistling softly to himself. I can already imagine the column he's composing in his head.

"We need to get out of here," I tell Luke, kneeling beside him. "What supplies do you need?"

Luke lifts his head, his eyes red-rimmed but focused. "Just my sketchbook and the smaller paint kit. The canvases..." He trails off, staring at the unfamiliar paintings. "Leave them."

I gather his supplies—a leather-bound sketchbook, worn at the edges; a wooden box containing tubes of paint and brushes, and a few loose sketches that I carefully fold and tuck into the book. Luke watches me, making no move to help, as though the effort required would be too much.

"Is that everything?" I ask.

He nods, then pauses. "Wait." He rises unsteadily and moves to a small valise half-hidden behind the tree. "My clothes. Now we can go."

I help him to his feet, supporting him with an arm around his waist. Together, we make our way across the clearing, ignoring the stares and whispers that follow us.

"Halley has a truck," I say quietly. "He's heading back to Jacksonville this afternoon. I could ask—"

"No." Luke's response is immediate. "Not with him. I can't... I can't be confined with someone like that right now. Questions. Always questions."

I understand his reluctance. Halley has the relentless curiosity of all journalists, and Luke is in no state for an interrogation. But—

"We don't have a choice, Luke. We can ride in the back of the truck together. I'll promise him an interview tomorrow in return, once you're feeling better."

Luke shakes his head. "Eileen... I can't..."

I chuckle. "Ever made a promise you didn't intend to keep?"

He stares at me as if I'd just asked him to recite the forty-seventh prime number. Then I understand his expression. Luke knows exactly what it means to tell white lies. And he's possibly more well-versed in it than I am.

We hold hands, and for now, that connection is enough to steady us both as we leave the film set behind, moving toward an uncertain future—or past—or whatever awaits us at the cave.

THIRTY-SEVEN: LUKE

The boarding house is quiet in the late afternoon, sunlight filtering through lace curtains to cast intricate patterns on the wooden floor. Eileen sits across from me on a faded armchair, her eyes never leaving my face as I finish explaining everything—the dental chair, Aunt Edna's portrait, the gallery showing that hasn't happened, has happened.

I shouldn't have told her. The words spill out. The confession that sounds insane. Time jumping. Several realities interwoven and superimposed. Living in 1925 and 2025 simultaneously.

"So the first jump happened before we met," she says carefully. "Before the cave."

"Monday morning. I was heading to a tutoring appointment and suddenly I was back in the dentist's chair, twenty-four hours earlier." I run a hand through my damp hair, freshly washed and still carrying the scent of Ma Perkins' pine soap. "Then five months back to October, then forward to April."

Eileen's expression is one I've seen before—clinical, analytical—the same expression the rehab psychiatrist wore when I described the hallucinations that accompanied my spiral into alcoholism three years ago.

"You think I'm crazy," I say flatly.

"No." She leans forward, elbows on knees. "I don't."

But she should. Now that I think about it, the cave isn't the cause. Maybe I'm the cause. My fractured mind has somehow bled through to reality, and I've dragged this beautiful woman along for the crazy ride. We're in some kind of mass hallucination, or, what do they call it? Stockholm Syndrome? Maybe in reality I'm still in 2025, and I have convinced Eileen that we can time travel.

"Luke." Her voice cuts through my spiral. "Look at me."

I force my eyes to meet hers.

"I believe you," she says. "I believe you because the same thing happened to me."

My head feels better from the hangover; the pounding has reduced to a dull ache behind my eyes. Being around Eileen, it feels like she's the only fixed point in a universe of shifting possibilities. I'm sure she's going to call 911 and Baker Act me any minute, but instead, she tells me her secrets.

"I was in the cave on the Suwannee," she begins. "Drawing. Cataloging. It was Tuesday, 11 a.m. Then suddenly, it was Monday, 11 a.m., and I was sitting in a different cave—one I visited the previous day." She pauses, watching my reaction. "Then five months back. I'm in the library. I haven't even broken up with Tarik yet."

The room tilts around me, not from alcohol this time, but from the weight of what she's saying. I want to ask her who Tarik is, but by the "yet," he sounds like an ex. And an ex is somehow... good.

I can't explain why, but I feel a pang of jealousy at this Tarik, even though he isn't in the picture—yet. I'm not about to wear my heart on my sleeve and tell her—what exactly? That I'm falling for her? Will fall for her? Have fallen for her?

"You jumped through time too," I whisper. "Before we met."

She nods, her expression earnest. "The same pattern as you. The exact same jumps."

"But you're not—" I gesture vaguely at my head, at the chaos I've been trying to describe.

"Falling apart?" She finishes for me. "No. I'm not."

"Why?" My question is laced with an unwanted note of desperation. "Assuming we're both, you know..." I can't say *jumping through time*. It feels ludicrous, like it would feed my delusion. Yet, being around Eileen, I realize that since this morning, since she found me in the logging camp, I haven't felt fractured at all. I feel sane, whole. Except for the time travel thing, that is.

"Why are you handling this so well when I can barely tell what day it is?"

Eileen stands and crosses to the window, her silhouette outlined by the golden light. For a moment, she looks like she could belong to any era—timeless, somehow. When she turns back to me, her eyes are filled with a mixture of compassion and scientific curiosity.

"I have a theory," she says. "It's about quantum entanglement. Well, it's not my theory, really. I have a friend, Candace. She's studying to be a computational astrophysicist."

I almost laugh. That explains a lot. Not. Quantum entanglement? She might be speaking Greek, for all the sense that makes to me. "Of course. Quantum physics. Why didn't I think of that?"

"I'm serious, Luke." She moves to sit beside me on the narrow bed, close enough that I can feel the warmth of her arm against mine. "Candace told me. In quantum mechanics, when two particles become entangled, what happens to one immediately affects the other, no matter the distance between them."

"And you think we're... what? Quantum entangled?" The idea is so absurd that I should dismiss it immediately, but given everything that's happened, I listen. Quantum entanglement or not, I feel like I've been waiting for this woman my whole life. She's the puzzle piece I didn't know was missing.

"I think when I entered the cave for the first time, something happened. We hadn't met yet, but... maybe..." She takes a deep breath and covers her mouth with her hand. "Maybe we're connected in some way?"

I recognize the words, but my brain translates them as, "Maybe we're soulmates." Maybe it's the way she's looking at me with those brown eyes. Maybe it's the way her lashes flutter when she looks at me. Or perhaps it's the pounding of my heart in my chest every time she speaks.

"And I think because I initiated it—because I was the one who disturbed whatever temporal anomaly exists in that cave—if we're connected, then maybe you're experiencing the same thing."

"Spooky interaction," I murmur, the term clicking into place with an eerie familiarity. I know this—maybe from a documentary, some Netflix series about the fabric of the universe? I can almost hear Morgan Freeman's voice narrating it, but the words are just out of reach, looping in my mind like an auditory mirage, distorted and unintelligible.

Entanglement. That's what it is. A phenomenon where two particles, no matter how far apart, exist in a shared quantum state. One moves; the other mirrors it instantly, as if distance doesn't matter. Spooky action, Einstein called it, as if even he couldn't quite accept the implications. If particles could be linked across space, could they also be linked across time? I want to say all of this out loud but hesitate because I'm not even sure that's a real fact. I could have gotten it from a B sci-fi movie.

"What one particle does, the other does too."

Her eyes widen slightly. "Yes, exactly. How did you—"

I shrug my shoulders. "No clue. I must have read it somewhere?"

But the words feel foreign—like a language I didn't know I spoke until it spilled from my mouth. The term spooky interaction rings through my mind, crisp and complete, as if it had always been there, waiting for me to remember it.

No, I'm an artist, not a physicist. The last time I picked up a science book was probably in high school. I must have seen it during a late-night Netflix binge.

Yet, the words fit too perfectly. The knowledge slides into place, not as a memory, but as something else. Something outside of me.

Maybe I will fall apart. Maybe I already have.

The explanation hovers between us, steeped in near-incomprehensible jargon yet fitting perfectly into the jagged puzzle pieces of my experience. I want to believe the science—want to believe there's a rational explanation for why I'm unraveling—but years of therapy and AA meetings have taught me to be wary of convenient explanations for my broken mind.

The moment stretches between us, something new and fragile taking shape. Then, because I need to know, I ask, "Do you really think this makes sense? Or are you humoring the crazy artist who got drunk at a logging camp?"

Her answer is to reach out and take my hand, her fingers lacing through mine. The contact is electric, immediate—like completing a circuit. The fractured edges of my perception seem to smooth, just a little.

"I believe," she says, "that something extraordinary is

happening to us both. And I believe we need each other to understand it."

I'm floored. Not just because of her theory, which is either brilliant or completely insane, but because she's sitting here at all, holding my hand instead of running as far away from me as possible.

"Why did you come looking for me?" I ask, my voice rougher than I intend. "At the film set, the logging camp. Why not just... go back to 2025 and forget any of this happened?"

She considers this, her thumb absently tracing circles on the back of my hand. The sensation grounds me in the moment more effectively than any meditation technique I've ever tried.

"Because from the moment we met at the gallery, I felt like I knew you," she admits. "Like there was a reason our paths crossed. And then when we both ended up here, in 1925—" She gives her head a slight shake. "It couldn't be a coincidence."

"No, it can't."

"And I'm not even sure I can get back to 1925. The time jumps in the cave...minutes, days, months, years. They seem random. Chaotic."

"Not chaotic," I correct. "Just unpredictable. Chaos theory isn't about randomness—it's about hidden order. Even in systems that seem erratic, slight differences in initial conditions can create vastly different outcomes. If we find the underlying pattern, we might predict where—or when—we land next."

She looks astonished, like I've just shown her a quantum Rosetta Stone. "What? You just went over my head, Luke... how do you know that?"

"I uh..." I have no idea. The words just spilled out.

But even as I say it, the logic feels too certain, the explanation too complete.

This isn't a memory—it's an answer that appeared, fully formed, in my mind.

I scramble for an explanation. A woman told me. A scientist. I spoke to her... But that doesn't feel right either.

When did I speak to a scientist?

I grip the chair arm as if I can anchor myself to something solid. Was it a long time ago? Or was it a long time in the future?

Can I even trust my moonshine-deprived brain right now? The thought digs in, sharp and unrelenting. I know what withdrawal feels like. I know what hallucinations feel like. This isn't that. But it's still something I can't explain.

We sit in silence, the weight of possibility settling around us. Outside, the sounds of Jacksonville in 1925 filter through the open window—automobile engines, distant conversation, the clop of horses' hooves on pavement.

"So what now?" I ask finally.

"I think we need to understand it better," Eileen says thoughtfully. "Let's start by writing what we know. Then go from there. If you're right, maybe we'll see a pattern?"

We sit together as the light shifts, casting longer shadows across the room. I'm still not convinced that we aren't both losing our minds, that this isn't some elaborate shared delusion. But I begin to feel something like hope.

Eileen Nash is the only thing in this fractured universe that feels solid, undeniable. She isn't just real—she's the missing piece; the gravity pulling my scattered reality back together.

She grabs her journal and leans back beside me, our shoulders pressing together—a simple touch, like an unspoken promise. The afternoon melts into evening, our voices weaving through the quiet, filling in the gaps of who we are, who we were before all of this. And I realize that perhaps for the first time in 1925, I exist fully in a single moment, anchored by the woman beside me.

Somewhere between our tangled stories and the hush of the fading light, I share my sobriety struggles—the nights clawing at walls, the quiet war I fight every day. I tell her about my three-year chip, how I turned it over in my fingers like a worry stone, how the weight of it in my pocket kept me tethered when nothing else did. I don't have it now, but sometimes I swear I can still feel it there, like a phantom limb.

She doesn't flinch, doesn't judge. She listens. And then, slowly, she leans into me, as if to say, *I see you. I'm not going anywhere.*

THIRTY-EIGHT: EILEEN

The boarding house room feels smaller as the evening light dims. I sit with my journal open on my lap, pen poised over a fresh page, approaching this problem the way I would any research problem: systematically, with evidence and analysis. Luke is beside me on the narrow bed, his shoulder pressed against mine, the warmth of his presence both distracting and comforting.

"Let's start with what we know for certain," I say, drawing a firm line across the top of the page. "The dates and times of our jumps."

I write the first entry in my neat, precise hand:

JUMP 1: Tuesday, March 11, 2025, 11:00 AM → Monday, March 10, 2025, 11:00 AM 24 hours backward Luke: Driving → Previous day's dental appointment Me: Cave drawings → Previous day's different cave.

"It's strange to see it written down like that," Luke murmurs, his eyes following my pen. "Makes it seem more real somehow."

I nod, understanding exactly what he means. The act of documenting transforms the unbelievable into data, something that can be examined and understood. It's what I've always done when faced with uncertainty—create order from chaos.

"The second jump," I prompt.

"Monday afternoon to October," he says. "Five months back."

I add the next entry:

JUMP 2: Monday, March 10, 2025, afternoon → October 14, 2024 ~5 months backward Luke: Studio painting dental chair → Studio with Aunt Edna's portrait Me: Cave → Library before Tarik breakup.

His eyes linger on Tarik's name, but he doesn't ask. Instead, he says, "Then the jump forward to April—to the gallery opening."

JUMP 3: October 2024 → April 12, 2025 ~6 months forward Luke: Counseling/studio → Gallery show preparation Me: Cave → Preparing for date with Dave.

"Dave," Luke says. "The dude with the wandering hand."

I laugh, remembering how much Dave's hand on my lower back felt claustrophobic.

"And then we met," I say softly, the memory vivid despite all that's happened since. "At your gallery opening."

"The strangest first meeting in history," Luke says with a small smile. "I felt like I'd known you forever."

I feel heat rise to my cheeks and focus intently on my writing to hide it. "Then we went to the cave together."

JUMP 4: April 13, 2025 → April 13, 2025 (Same day? Hours later?) Cave exploration → Cave after spider plant experiment.

"What was that one?" Luke points out. "I don't remember that."

"It's a theory," I say. "Remember the storm that came on suddenly? The lightning we didn't see? We could have jumped without knowing it. To that afternoon, maybe? Or a different day?"

He nods. His expression tells me he thinks it's a sane explanation. As sane as a discussion about time travel could be. "And then the big one," I continue. "Into the past."

JUMP 5: April 13, 2025 → July 17, 1925, 100 years backward Luke: Cave with me → Movie studio painting backdrops Me: Cave with Luke → Library indexing magazines.

I sit back, studying the timeline we've created. Five jumps, seemingly random in their distance and direction. Forward, backward, hours, days, months, a century.

"There's something else we should track," I say, flipping to a fresh page. "How each of us experiences the jumps. You said you see everything at once? Multiple realities layered on top of each other?"

Luke shifts beside me, his knee bumping against mine as he leans closer to see what I'm writing.

"It's like... living in multiple times simultaneously," he tries to explain. "I'll be painting a backdrop for the movie, but I can also see what the scene will look like in 2025, with concrete boat ramps and tourists. Sometimes I blink and things that were there a second ago aren't anymore."

I write this down, then describe my experience: Disorientation at first, but quickly oriented to new time/place. Clear perception of a single timeline.

"There's something else too. I see other images. Maybe from the future. Places I haven't been. Things I haven't seen."

"Like what?"

"The Suwannee, I think. 2035? 2040? There's green algae and skeletal trees, like that dead forest up on Jekyll Island."

I nod, recalling a walk with Tarik along Jekyll Island's shore—the so-called Driftwood Forest. Not really a forest, just the bones of one, the result of erosion and dying trees slowly surrendering to the sea. The afternoon had been meant to be romantic. Tarik had told me he loved me, pressing a crumpled rose into my palm, its petals crushed from sitting too long in his pocket. I told him I loved him too, but I should have seen the signs then. A love declared on a landscape of loss was never meant to last.

"And now we're here," I say, looking up from my notes. "Together in 1925."

"But why?" Luke asks "Why us? Why these specific times?"

I turn to a third page and title it "Theories."

Quantum entanglement - connected across spacetime
Cave contains temporal anomaly/portal
Pattern or purpose to the jumps?

"What if there's no reason?" Luke asks suddenly. "What if it's just random? A cosmic glitch?"

I shake my head. "I don't believe that. In archaeology, when we find artifacts in unexpected places, it's rarely random. There's usually a pattern we haven't recognized yet."

I tap my pen against the paper, thinking. "When I was in that cave the first time, I was drawing petroglyphs—ancient symbols carved into the rock. Some of them looked like astronomical charts, tracking celestial movements."

"What if they weren't just tracking stars?" Luke suggests. "What if they were mapping something else? Time shifts, maybe?"

The idea sends a shiver down my spine. I write it down: Cave petroglyphs—possible time map?

We continue like this for an hour, documenting everything we can remember, every strange coincidence and connection. The journal pages fill with our shared history—a timeline that defies conventional understanding of cause and effect.

As the room grows darker, I light the small lamp on the bedside table. Its warm glow casts Luke's face in soft shadows, highlighting the sharp line of his jaw, the furrow between his brows as he concentrates. Even in this state—exhausted, recovering from his drinking episode, unstuck in time—there's something magnetic about him. Something that pulls me toward him in ways I can't entirely explain.

Luke leans closer to my journal, scanning the timeline we've created. His finger traces the dates, the durations, the circumstances. There's something methodical in his movements, his artist's eye searching for patterns others might miss.

His finger stops at the third jump entry. "Wait. Look at this. October to April. Six months forward, roughly. And before that, March to October. Five months back."

"So?"

"So what's six minus five?"

"One," I answer automatically.

"One month," Luke says, excitement building in his voice. "We jumped back five months, then forward six. A net gain of one month from our original time."

I frown, not seeing his point. "That could be a coincidence."

"Maybe. But look at the cave jump." His finger moves to the fifth entry. "We jumped back one hundred years."

"I don't understand what you're saying."

Luke takes the pen from my hand, flips to a fresh page, and starts writing numbers.

"The first jump: 24 hours back. The second: 5 months back. The third: 6 months forward. Net change from our original timeline: 1 month forward. The fourth jump was just hours. Let's call that negligible. And then the fifth jump: 100 years back."

He draws a series of calculations on the page:

-1 day

-5 months

+6 months = +1 month (from original point)

- a few hours. Days?

-100 years

"What if," he says slowly, "the jumps aren't random at all?

What if each one builds on the last, compounding the effect?"

I stare at his calculations, my mind racing to follow his logic. Mathematics has never been my forte. "It looks right, but, well, we have so few data points." And the only way to get more data points is to jump in time more—a prospect that terrifies me. What if we jump to a time before the cave existed? Or after it has been destroyed by erosion and rockfall?

"It's like a mathematical progression." His eyes are bright now, focused in a way I haven't seen since we arrived in 1925. "The first jump is small—just a day. The next is bigger—months. Then we jump forward, but not quite back to where we started. Then the massive jump backward."

"I'm impressed," I say. "So you're a left-brain, right-brain thinker?"

"No," he says. "Math was never my strong point, but I know this sequence. I've seen it somewhere. Heard it somewhere. That scientist—a woman told me. Silver-white hair, wild, like storm clouds unraveling. Her name is Carmen? Kristine?"

I shrug, about to suggest Candace, but no—he's never met her. And she definitely does not have silver hair.

And the math—something feels off. I wish I had my phone to double-check the numbers. I silently curse myself for relying on calculators instead of working things out by hand. The calculations seem simple, but I know better—I can barely balance my bank account without Excel.

Luke taps the pen against the paper, thinking. "What if time isn't just linear? What if it's more like... coordinates on a map? We're not just moving forward and backward in a straight line. We're moving across different points in a more complex system."

I consider this, remembering the petroglyphs in the cave. The ones that looked like star charts but could have been mapping something entirely different.

"The cave," I say. "The drawings on the wall. They could be showing these coordinates, these points in time where the... the fabric of time is thinner, maybe?"

Luke nods eagerly. "Yes! And maybe there's a reason we ended up in 1925. Something we're supposed to do here."

"Like finding each other?" I suggest with a small smile, thinking he's probably watched too many sci-fi shows—like me. I draw in a deep breath, logic telling me we can't possibly be living in a *12 Monkeys* spin-off, destined to stop a plague. Or in an episode of *Quantum Leap,* stuck here until we fix something wrong.

"We did that in 2025," he says, smiling back. "But hey, maybe you're Sam Beckett and I'm Al. And we're here to fix something before it destroys lives."

My mouth gapes open. "I was just thinking that. *Quantum Leap...* you watched it?

"Every episode," he says. "My guilty pleasure."

Our eyes meet, and in that moment, I feel something shift between us—a recognition, a connection that transcends our impossible situation. His hand covers mine on top of the journal, his fingers warm as they intertwine with my own.

"There's something else," he says, his voice low. "When I'm with you, like this—" he squeezes my hand, "—everything settles. The fracturing stops. I see only one time, one place."

"Like I'm anchoring you," I whisper.

"Exactly like that."

"Luke," I say urgently, "I think you're right about the pattern. And I think there's more to it than we understand yet. But there's something else we need to consider."

"What?"

"If there's a mathematical progression to these jumps, that means prediction is a possibility. And if we can predict it—"

"We can control it," he finishes.

Hope flares between us, bright and unexpected. At long last, since finding myself displaced in time, I feel something beyond confusion and fear. I feel purpose.

"We need to go back to the cave. Not yet—not until we understand more. But eventually. It's the key to all of this."

Luke nods, his eyes never leaving mine. "Together."

"Together," I say, and the word feels like a promise.

Outside, night has fallen completely. The sounds of 1925 Jacksonville have quieted to occasional passing automobiles and distant laughter. Tomorrow, we'll have to figure out how to exist in this time—how to support ourselves, how to blend in until we can find our way back.

But tonight, in this small room with its faded wallpaper and narrow bed, I feel strangely at peace. As if we've been granted a reprieve from the chaotic swirl of time to simply be—two people, connected across the impossible, trying to find their way home.

Or perhaps, in some strange way, already there.

THIRTY-NINE: LUKE

When I wake, I'm momentarily confused by the unfamiliar ceiling, the firm mattress beneath me. The distant clatter of hooves against brick-paved streets mixes with the occasional rumble of an automobile passing outside.

Then I feel the warmth beside me, and everything—where I am, when I am—rushes back with startling clarity.

Eileen sleeps soundly, her body curved away from mine but still close enough that I feel the gentle rhythm of her breathing. We're fully clothed, having fallen asleep in the early hours after exhausting ourselves with theories and calculations. Her journal lies open between us, pages filled with her neat handwriting interspersed with my own hurried scrawl.

I carefully shift onto my side, propping myself up on one elbow to study her. In sleep, the sharp intelligence that animates her features has softened, replaced by a vulnerability that makes my chest tighten. Her dark hair fans across the pillow, one strand falling across her cheek. I resist the urge to brush it away, not wanting to wake her.

She's beautiful. Not in the conventional, magazine-cover way that Rose was—all calculated angles and precisely applied makeup—but in a way that feels more genuine, more alive. There's a determination in the set of her jaw even in sleep, a kind of quiet strength that draws me to her like gravity.

I wonder what would happen if we stay in this timeline. It seems I have the makings of a movie art career. Maybe I could go to Hollywood. Make it big. Now that Eileen is with me, I am sure her grounding presence will keep me sane. No more fractured reality, no more seeing multiple timelines layered over each other. Just one life, in one time. With her.

And 1925 doesn't seem so bad. I don't miss cell phones and collection calls. I don't miss traffic fumes and contentious elections and the internet. Life seems simpler here. The air tastes cleaner somehow. The colors are more vivid, as if everything hasn't yet been dulled by decades of mass production and digital reproduction.

As an artist, there's something pure about this era. No Adobe Photoshop, no digital shortcuts. Just hand and eye and paintbrush. The craft still respected for what it is—craftsmanship. Not that I'm some purist who thinks technology ruined art. I own—owned?—a digital tablet and used it happily. But there's something to be said for creating in a world where people still marvel at the skill of rendering reality by hand.

But mostly, it's the silence. The stillness. The absence of a hundred digital voices clamoring for attention, the relentless ping of emails, the constant weight of notifications I can't keep up with.

Here, no one expects anything from me. No calls from creditors. No emails from galleries questioning whether my work is "commercial enough." No social media dissecting my paintings, demanding I explain my own mind. Just me, my brushes, and a world that still marvels at what the human hand can create.

The thought of jumping to another time terrifies me. What if I try to go back and instead of this—disorientation—what if I completely lose my mind? What if I end up so broken that I pull a Van Gogh and slice off my ear, or my nose, or worse?

I feel so close to being completely disassembled that I need this stability of time. Not forever, just now. Just for a few weeks, a few months, however long it takes for me to get the courage to—

Time travel.

The words sound ridiculous, like I'd summoned them from H.G. Wells. The longer I stay here with Eileen, the more I'm feeling like me. And I'm not sure I'm ready to let that go.

But what about Eileen? What's it like to be a woman archaeologist in 1925? I know women aren't exactly running the show in most professional fields. I've seen enough period films and historical paintings to get the sense that a woman in archaeology might have to work twice as hard just to get half the recognition. Would she be happy here? I don't know what her life is like in 2025, though I get a sense that her work *is* her life.

Eileen stirs, her eyelids fluttering as she transitions from sleep to wakefulness. I quickly avert my gaze, not wanting her to catch me staring, but I'm not fast enough.

"Morning," she murmurs, her voice husky with sleep. "How long have you been watching me?"

"I wasn't watching," I lie, then immediately backtrack at her raised eyebrow. "Okay, maybe a minute or two."

She stretches, wincing slightly as she works out the kinks that come from sleeping fully clothed on a too-small bed. "How's your head today?"

"Better." And it is. The hangover has faded to a distant memory, replaced by a clarity I haven't felt in days—maybe weeks. "Something about being around you... it's like everything comes into focus."

A faint blush colors her cheeks, and she busies herself with straightening her rumpled clothes. "We should get some breakfast. Figure out our next steps."

* * *

Despite the boarding house's modest appearance, Ma Perkins sets an impressive table. The parlor doubled as a dining room, with five small tables arranged to accommodate her various guests. We're directed to a table by the window, where sunlight streams across a starched white tablecloth.

"Coffee?" A young girl, no more than sixteen, approaches with a polished percolator and a pair of ceramic cups, steam curling from the spout

"Please," Eileen and I say in unison, then exchange a small smile at our synchronicity.

As the girl pours, I take in the room. A middle-aged couple sits at one table, heads bent over a newspaper they share between them. At another, a gentleman in a neatly pressed suit reviews what appears to be business correspondence while methodically working his way through a plate of eggs. The final occupied table hosts three young women, secretaries or shop girls perhaps, who whisper and occasionally glance our way with poorly concealed curiosity.

"I suspect we're the subject of some speculation," Eileen says quietly, following my gaze to the trio of women.

"Small-town gossip transcends time periods, I guess."

She smiles at that, adding cream to her coffee with a steady hand. "So," she says after taking a sip, "what's on your mind? You've got that look."

"What look?"

"Like you're turning something over and over. Examining it from all angles."

I laugh softly, caught out by her perceptiveness. "I was thinking about staying. Here, I mean. In 1925."

Her spoon stills against the rim of her cup. "Staying?"

"Just thinking about it," I clarify quickly. "Not decided or anything. But... what if we did? Would it be so terrible?"

"The girl returns with two plates, each piled with eggs, bacon, thick slices of toast, and a side of sliced tomatoes. A small dish of preserves sits between us, next to the sugar bowl and cream pitcher.

"Why would you want to stay?" Eileen asks, genuinely curious rather than dismissive.

I take a bite of toast to buy myself time, organizing my thoughts. "I don't know. It feels... cleaner here. Simpler. And if I'm going to be an artist anyway, does it matter which century I do it in? Actually, seems like I do better in this one. Apparently, I start a whole movement."

Her eyes study me over the rim of her coffee cup. "You'd give up everything? Your life in 2025? Your friends, your apartment, your modern medicine?"

"What am I really giving up?" I counter. "A studio apartment I can barely afford? An art career that's just taking off but might fizzle out in a year? Friends who..." I trail off, realizing how pathetic it sounds to admit that my social circle has shrunk dramatically since getting sober. Rose took most of our mutual friends in the breakup, and I've been so focused on staying clean that I haven't exactly been hitting the social scene.

Eileen sets down her fork. "Let me ask you something. If it weren't for the time jumps, would you have ever considered living in the past?"

"No," I admit. "But I never thought it was an option."

"And what about me?" she asks, her voice softer now. "Where do I fit into this fantasy of yours?"

The question takes me by surprise. In my mind, we've been a package deal—wherever one goes, the other follows. The fact that she might have her own preferences, her own life to consider, hasn't fully registered until now.

"I just assumed... I mean, we're connected, right? The quantum entanglement thing. The way being near you stabilizes me." I run my fingers through my hair, frustrated by my inability to articulate what seems so obvious. "And I thought maybe you'd like it here too. The simplicity of it."

She laughs, though there's no mockery in it. "Luke, I'm an archaeologist. My entire career is built on modern technology, scientific methods that don't exist yet. I use ground-penetrating radar and carbon dating and digital mapping. How would I practice my profession in 1925?"

"I hadn't thought about that," I confess, properly chastened. I had thought about it, of course, but I'd assumed she could still practice archaeology in 1925, an Indiana Jones style dig with mini shovels and colanders, not one with ground penetrating radar and digital mapping.

"And as a woman?" She crosses her arms. "In 2025, I still face challenges in a male-dominated field. But at least I have legal rights, professional standing. Here? Women only got the vote five years ago. I couldn't even open a bank account without a husband's or father's permission."

I wince, seeing how self-centered my thinking has been. "I'm sorry. You're right."

"I'm not dismissing your feelings," she says, reaching across the table to briefly touch my hand. "I understand the appeal. There's something seductive about the past, especially for an artist. But it's a fantasy, Luke. A romantic notion that doesn't account for the realities of living in a time that wasn't designed for people like me—or you, for that matter."

"What do you mean, people like me?"

"You're a recovering alcoholic who just had a relapse," she says bluntly but kindly. "In 2025, that's a medical condition with treatment options. Here? You'd be considered weak-willed or morally corrupt."

The truth of her words hits me with a jolt. I imagine trying to explain my addiction to a 1925 doctor, being prescribed whiskey as a tonic for nerves or sent to some primitive sanitarium. No understanding of the brain chemistry involved, no supportive community of others who've walked the same path.

"If my math is right—" I begin, then correct myself, "and to be honest, it's more of a gut instinct rather than a mathematical certainty—if we jump again, we'll 'undo' the last jump. Give or take a few years."

Eileen looks intrigued. "What makes you say that?"

"I don't know. It's just a feeling." I tap my temple. "But here's what I do know: I'll talk to a scientist about chaos theory. I have the memory, which tells me it will happen. Has happened. Has to happen."

She smiles. "On any other date, if someone told me they'll talk to a scientist in the future, I would have walked out the door. But there's something about you," her smile widens, "that tempts me to stay. Maybe for one more cup of coffee."

I laugh, too loud, garnering looks of disapproval from the next table. I lower my voice. "And I also know that one of my paintings gets sold at Sotheby's."

The image flashes in my mind—a canvas I've never painted yet somehow remember seeing, my scribbled signature in the corner, being auctioned for more zeroes than I've earned—will earn—in my entire life. "Which painting, I don't know. I just see my scribbled signature. If I stay in 1925, I'll never sell a million-dollar painting. A couple more reasons to go back."

"A million dollars?" Eileen's eyes widen. "You didn't mention that part before."

I shrug, embarrassed by how self-aggrandizing it sounds. "I'm not sure if it's real or just... I don't know; a fantasy my brain cooked up. But it *feels* real, like a memory."

She considers this, pushing her empty plate away. "So if we go back to 2025—or thereabouts—you become a successful artist. And if we stay here, you become a success of a different kind."

"Looks that way."

"What about me?" she asks, a question that seems to contain

multitudes.

"I don't know," I admit. "I don't see your future like I see fragments of mine. Maybe because you're not fractured like I am."

She nods, accepting this. "We need more information before we make any decisions. But—"

I complete her sentence. "The only way to get more information is to return to the cave."

She nods. "We need a plan. A plan to reconnect if we get separated. Any ideas?"

"Yes," I say, and I feel like I'm exactly where—and when—I'm supposed to be. "I do."

FORTY: EILEEN

My mind keeps turning over Luke's suggestion to stay in 1925. There's a part of me that understands the appeal—the way his eyes light up when he talks about the "authenticity" of this era, as though the past holds some purity that's been lost in our time. But he's not thinking it through. Life isn't simpler here—it's just differently complicated, and for someone like me, severely limiting.

I can't stay. I won't. And I need Luke to understand why.

After breakfast, I spread my journal across the small table in my boarding house room, flipping through the notes we made the night before. Luke had pointed out the pattern in our jumps, but the more I examine it, the less certain I feel.

"If we're tracking the progression correctly," I say, tapping my pencil against the page, "the jumps are increasing in magnitude. A day, then months, then a hundred years."

Luke leans over my shoulder, his breath warm against my neck. "Which means the next jump should take us forward—back to 2025."

"Or further," I counter, trying to ignore the flutter in my chest when he stands so close. "What if we overshoot? End up in 2175? Or undershoot and land somewhere in between?"

"You think the pattern might not be as predictable as I'm suggesting."

It's not a question, but I nod anyway. "I want more data. In any scientific experiment, you'd never draw conclusions from such a limited sample."

Luke moves away, running a hand through his hair. Without product or modern styling, it falls in soft waves across his forehead. It suits him.

"We don't have the luxury of waiting," he says, echoing my

own thoughts. "We need to act. Unless you're considering—"

"I'm not staying here, Luke." My voice comes out sharper than intended. "Neither of us belongs in 1925."

He doesn't argue, but something flickers across his expression—disappointment, maybe. Or relief. I can't tell.

"We need a contingency plan," I say, softening my tone. "If we're separated during a jump, we need to find each other."

Luke nods. "I was thinking about that. The cave might not always be accessible—flooding, construction, collapse..."

"A landmark, then. Something that's existed for centuries and will likely continue to exist."

"Treaty Oak," Luke says immediately. "Jacksonville's oldest living thing. It was already ancient in 1925, and it'll still be standing in 2025. Or 2075."

The suggestion is perfect. I've never been especially sentimental about trees, but I know the massive, sprawling oak in what will one day be Jessie Ball duPont Park. It has survived logging, hurricanes, urban development.

"Treaty Oak," I say. "If we lose each other, that's where we meet. Every Saturday at noon."

"Every Saturday," Luke repeats, as if committing it to memory. "Noon."

He turns toward the window, his profile outlined against the morning light. "We should head to the cave today. The sooner we try to jump, the better."

I hesitate, studying the back of his neck where his hair curls slightly at the collar. Something doesn't sit right.

"What if we don't jump forward at all?" I ask quietly. "What if the pattern isn't as predictable as we thought? What if the next jump is bigger than we expect?"

Luke turns back to me, his eyes searching mine. "Like where?"

I don't answer, but the possibilities hang between us. What if we land in prehistoric Florida, before human habitation? Or in a future where climate change has rendered the region uninhabitable?

"We need to be smart about this," I say finally. "If we're wrong, we could end up somewhere we can't survive."

Luke watches me carefully, then nods. "So we prepare. As

much as we can."

Instead of rushing to the cave, we spend the day gathering supplies. It's not easy—most of what we'd want for true emergency preparedness doesn't exist yet, or would draw too much attention. Still, we manage: a sturdy knife, matches in a wax-sealed container, basic first aid supplies, a compass, and a stash of canned goods, dried fruit, and hard biscuits. We spend a sum total of $4.55, which leaves us with less than $2 between us.

By the time the sun slants through the windows, we have everything packed into two canvas bags. The plan is simple: return to the cave, retrace our steps, and see if the next jump follows the pattern.

And if it doesn't? Then we'll figure it out—together.

I'm checking our supplies one last time when Luke moves to stand beside me, close enough that our arms brush. The contact sends a current through me, and when I look up, his eyes are on mine, intense and questioning.

"Eileen," he says, a whisper on his lips.

The gap between us closes, charged with something I haven't allowed myself to acknowledge until now. His gaze drops to my mouth, and I lean toward him, drawn by a gravity I don't understand but can't resist.

He reaches for my hand, fingers intertwining as he leans closer. My heart thunders in my chest, and for a split second, the complications of our situation—the time displacement, the uncertainty, the fear—fade to background noise.

The sharp rap on the door shatters the moment.

We spring apart like guilty teenagers as Mrs. Perkins's voice calls through the wood. "Miss Nash? You have a visitor."

Luke and I exchange a confused glance. No one knows we're here—no one from this time, anyway.

I open the door to find Mrs. Whitmore standing in the hallway, her tall figure rigid with indignation, her wire-rimmed glasses catching the light. Behind her, Mrs. Perkins hovers anxiously.

"Miss Nash," Mrs. Whitmore says, her voice as cold as her gaze. "I thought I might find you here."

My stomach sinks. "Mrs. Whitmore, I can explain—"

"Oh, I'm sure you can," she interrupts, looking past me to

where Luke stands. Her eyes widen slightly, taking in our private room, the unmade bed, our proximity to each other. Her lips press into a thin line of disapproval.

"The Atlanta Historical Society has never heard of you, Miss Nash," she says crisply. "They have no record of any researcher by your name, nor have they commissioned any study of Florida's waterways."

Mrs. Perkins makes a small sound of distress. "Miss Nash, you told me you were here on academic business—"

"I am," I start, but Mrs. Whitmore cuts me off again.

"Whatever your actual purpose in Jacksonville might be," she says, her gaze flickering meaningfully between Luke and me, "I suggest you not bother showing up at the library again. Academic institutions have standards to maintain, and fraud is not tolerated."

The accusation stings, even though it's technically true. I've been lying about who I am since I arrived here.

Luke steps forward, his voice smooth and conciliatory. "There's been a misunderstanding, ma'am. Miss Nash is assisting me with historical research for a series of paintings. Any confusion about her credentials is my responsibility."

Mrs. Whitmore's expression doesn't soften. "And you are?"

"Luke Campbell. I'm an artist with River City Pictures."

Her eyebrows rise slightly. "The movie painter? The one who's been causing such a stir with his... unusual ideas about the future?"

Luke's smile tightens. "My work sometimes involves speculative elements, yes."

Mrs. Whitmore sniffs. "That explains a great deal. Artists." She says the word like it's a diagnosis. "Well, Mr. Campbell, Miss Nash, I've said what I came to say. Good day."

She turns with military precision and marches back down the hallway.

Mrs. Perkins lingers, her expression troubled. "Miss Nash, I don't allow... impropriety in my establishment. If you and Mr. Campbell are not married, then I'm afraid—"

"We'll be leaving today," I assure her quickly. "Thank you for your hospitality."

When the door closes, Luke lets out a long breath. "Well," he says with a wry smile, "I guess that's the timelords giving us a nod in a certain direction."

Despite everything, I laugh. "The cosmic forces of the universe, working through a disapproving librarian?"

"The universe works in mysterious ways." His smile fades, replaced by something more serious. "But she's right about one thing—we can't stay here. Not just in this boarding house. In 1925."

I nod, relieved that he's finally accepted it. "Then let's go find our way home."

We gather our bags and slip out of the boarding house, careful to avoid Mrs. Perkins. The afternoon sun bathes Jacksonville in golden light as we head to the movie studio, where we hope to find transportation back to the Suwannee.

As we walk, Luke's hand finds mine again, and this time, I don't pull away. Whatever comes next—whatever time we land in—at least we won't face it alone.

FORTY-ONE: LUKE

The movie studio is just a quarter mile from the boarding house. The morning air is thick with humidity, promising another scorching Florida day, and sweat already prickles my hairline as we walk.

"We should be able to catch a ride with one of the supply trucks heading out to the set," I explain to Eileen, trying to sound more confident than I feel. "They make daily runs."

Eileen nods, but her expression remains skeptical. "And if they won't take us?"

"They will," I say, even as doubt gnaws at me. "I'm still technically employed by the studio."

The words sound hollow even to my own ears. I haven't been back since my drunken episode with the loggers, and I have a sinking feeling that my absence hasn't gone unnoticed. But what choice do we have? We need transportation, and we don't have the money to hire a driver.

The River City Pictures office sits in a converted warehouse, its once-industrial façade now adorned with painted movie posters and promotional photographs of their stars. I pause at the entrance, steeling myself.

"Let me do the talking," I tell Eileen, who raises an eyebrow but doesn't argue.

Inside, electric fans push the hot air around without actually cooling it. The reception area is sparse: a few wooden chairs, a dusty philodendron that's seen better days, and a desk where a young woman with penciled eyebrows—Margaret—flips through papers with bored efficiency.

She barely looks up when we approach, her pencil tapping an impatient rhythm against the blotter.

"I need to check when the next supply truck leaves for the Suwannee set," I say, trying to sound casual.

Her fingers pause their tapping, but her eyes remain on her paperwork. "You're not on the list."

A chill runs through me despite the heat. "What?"

Now she looks up, her expression flat and uninterested. "You're not on the crew list. For today's transport."

"There must be a mistake," I insist, leaning closer. "I'm working on the backdrops for the river scenes."

She sighs, making a show of flipping through a clipboard of papers as she eyes Eileen with an expression that might be recognition or suspicion. Her finger runs down several typed lists, stopping about halfway down one page.

"Says here you were let go." She looks up, already moving on mentally. "Next!"

No one is behind us, but the dismissal is clear. My heart pounds against my ribs.

"Let go? There has to be a mistake. I received no—"

"Listen, Mr. Campbell," she cuts in, "I just say what they tell me. If you want details, you'll have to take it up with Morris."

Eileen steps forward, placing a gentle hand on my arm. "And where might we find Mr. Morris?" Her voice is calm, reasoned.

The receptionist sniffs. "He's on vacation. Until next week."

We're standing on the hot sidewalk moments later with no job, no transportation, and no way forward.

"Well, that's that," I say, running a hand through my hair. "We're stuck."

Eileen's eyes narrow as if she's turning over a problem. "Not necessarily. Remember those loggers you stayed with?"

The memory brings a flush of shame to my face. "What about them?"

"Logging companies are always hiring. The work is brutal, but they provide transportation to the camps." She pauses, watching my expression. "And those camps are often near the river—near Big Shoals."

The implication sinks in. "You want me to get a job as a logger?"

"I want us to get to the cave," she corrects. "And right now, this might be our only way."

She's right, of course. Without transportation or money, our options are severely limited. And logging camps are typically located in remote areas—including, potentially, near our cave.

"Fine," I say. "But what about you? They don't hire women for cutting timber."

A smile plays at the corner of her mouth. "No, but they do hire women as cooks and for other domestic work. I can handle that."

Before I can protest, she adds, "We'll pose as a married couple. Newlyweds desperate for work."

The word "married" sends an unexpected jolt through me. I try to ignore it, focusing on the practical aspects of her plan. "Do you even know how to cook for a logging camp?"

She shrugs. "I can learn. Besides, it's just until we reach the cave."

* * *

An hour later, we're standing in the hiring office of the Suwannee River Lumber Company. The place smells of sweat, sawdust, and tobacco. Rough-looking men wait on wooden benches, while a harried clerk processes paperwork behind a scratched counter.

When our turn comes, I step forward with more confidence than I feel.

"Name?" the clerk asks without looking up.

"Luke Campbell. I'm looking for work as a laborer."

This gets his attention. He studies me skeptically, eyes lingering on my hands, which lack the calluses of hard labor.

"You ever swung an axe, Campbell?"

"I have," I say. "Just firewood. But I'm a quick learner and I work hard."

He snorts. "Everyone says that. What kind of work you done before?"

"I'm an artist," I say, then quickly add, "but I've done plenty of physical work. Set construction, loading, carrying..."

He doesn't look convinced. "We need men who can chop firewood and clear brush all day without dropping from exhaustion."

"I can do it," I insist, desperation creeping into my voice.

"We—I really need this job."

His eyes shift to Eileen, who stands slightly behind me. "We?"

This is the moment. I reach back and take Eileen's hand, pulling her gently forward. Her fingers intertwine with mine with such natural ease that for a moment, I almost believe our charade.

"My wife and I," I explain. "We're newly married and need the money to start our life together."

The clerk's expression softens marginally. "Congratulations," he says automatically, then shakes his head. "But I can't hire a man with no experience, especially not one bringing a wife to camp."

Eileen steps forward, her posture shifting subtly. Suddenly, she looks less like a modern scientist and more like a determined young wife from the 1920s.

"Sir," she says, her voice taking on a slight Southern lilt I've never heard before, "I understand your concern. But my husband is stronger than he looks, and I'm a hard worker myself. I can cook, clean, mend—whatever your camp needs."

The clerk hesitates. "We do need a cook's assistant at the Suwannee camp. Last one quit without notice. But it's rough living, miss. Not suitable for a lady."

"I'm tougher than I look," Eileen says with a smile that is somehow both demure and determined. "And we don't mind rough living if it means we can be together."

I squeeze her hand, playing along. "We'll take any work you have, sir. We're not afraid of hard labor."

The clerk sighs, clearly wavering. "The pay ain't much. Especially for a greenhorn."

"Whatever you can offer," I blurt. "We just need a fresh start."

He studies us for another long moment, then nods reluctantly. "Alright. We got a truck leaving tomorrow at six a.m. sharp. Don't be late—it won't wait for you."

He shoves two forms across the counter, barely glancing at us. "Name, job, and sign here—this just says if you get yourself killed, it ain't the company's fault. Sign at the bottom. You'll start as a swamper—cutting brush, dragging logs, whatever needs doing. Prove yourself, and maybe we'll let you handle an axe. The missus can help in the cookhouse."

Relief floods through me. "Thank you, sir. You won't regret

it."

"Better not," he mutters, already turning to the next person in line.

Outside, Eileen and I exchange looks of cautious triumph.

"That was impressive," I tell her as we walk away. "I almost believed we were married myself."

She laughs, the sound bright in the heavy afternoon air. "I've studied enough historical periods to know how to act the part." Her expression sobers. "But we still have a problem. Six a.m. tomorrow is a long time from now, and we can't go back to the boarding house."

She's right. After Mrs. Whitmore's visit and Mrs. Perkins' disapproval, returning there isn't an option. And we have nowhere else to go, no money for even the cheapest hotel. We have $3.95 to our name, so at least we can eat. At a no-frills lunch counter near the rail yard, we spend $1.50 on two plates of eggs, biscuits, and grits, washing it down with weak coffee. The place smells of frying bacon and pipe smoke, the air thick with the murmur of working men fueling up before their shifts.

FORTY-TWO: EILEEN

The lunch counter is a cacophony of sounds—plates clattering, voices murmuring, silverware scraping. I push the last bit of grits around my plate, watching as Luke devours his biscuit with the fervor of someone who hasn't eaten a proper meal in days. Perhaps he hasn't.

We're down to less than three dollars after this meal. Barely enough for another meal, much less a place to sleep. I catalog our options methodically, the way I would approach a difficult excavation—careful, precise, evaluating each possibility.

"We could try the mission on Adams Street," I suggest, keeping my voice low. Places that offer charity don't exist in the same way they will a century from now. In 1925, seeking help means subjecting yourself to sermons and separation—men in one dormitory, women in another. "Though we'd have to split up for the night."

Luke pauses mid-bite, his eyes finding mine with unexpected intensity. "No. We stay together."

There's something in his voice—a certainty, an anchor in shifting sand—that makes my breath catch. Before I can respond, he sets down his fork and stands abruptly.

"I'll be right back," he says, his eyes on something across the street.

"I thought you just said, 'We stay together,'" I say, chuckling.

"Two minutes," he says. There's a glint in his eye that tells me he's up to something. He drops his voice to a whisper. "If you see me acting crazy, just come over and grab my hand."

I twist in my seat to follow his gaze. A pawnshop, its windows crowded with musical instruments, watches, and other surrendered treasures. Before I can ask why, he's moving through the diner, dodging a counterman wiping his hands on his apron as he barks an order to the cook.

Through the window, I watch Luke enter the shop. He moves with purpose, like he knows exactly what he's going for. The disorientation that clouded him at the logging camp seems gone, replaced by a focused energy I find both reassuring and perplexing.

While he's gone, I grab my small notebook—the one personal item I kept through our hasty departure from the boarding house. I turn to a fresh page and study the map of our temporal jumps, seeking a pattern. The first jump: 24 hours back. The second: 5 months. The third, to the gallery opening, was approximately—

"Penny for your thoughts?"

I look up, startled. Luke slides back into his seat, a strange half-smile playing at his lips.

"Just going over these jumps," I reply, closing the notebook. "What did you need at the pawnshop?"

He shrugs, a deliberately casual gesture that doesn't match the light in his eyes. "You'd be surprised what you can get for two dollars."

"Our last two dollars," I remind him, though there's no real reproach in my voice. Whatever he purchased, he looks radiant.

"Worth every penny," he says cryptically, pocketing something small before I can get a proper look. "Trust me."

Trust. Such a simple word for such a complex concept. Yet, I do trust him, despite everything. Despite that I barely know him, despite his recent spiral, despite the impossible situation we're in. There's something between us that transcends logic—a connection I can't explain but can't deny either.

"Always the mysterious artist," I say. "Are you going to tell me what you bought?"

"All in good time." He drains his coffee cup and then sets it down with a decisive clink. "We need to figure out where we're going to sleep tonight."

The reality of our situation settles over us again. No money, no lodging, a 6 a.m. departure tomorrow that we absolutely cannot miss.

"We could walk all night," I suggest, though my aching feet protest at the mere thought. "Keep moving until it's time to meet the truck."

Luke shakes his head. "You need rest. We both do, but especially you."

"I'm not fragile, Luke," I say, perhaps more sharply than I intended.

"I know that." His eyes soften as they meet mine. "You're possibly the strongest person I've ever met. But even strong people need sleep."

There's something in his gaze that makes me feel both seen and protected, without a hint of the condescension so typical of this era. It's like he's looking at me from 2025, not 1925—seeing me as an equal, a partner in this impossible journey.

Outside, the afternoon heat is oppressive. We walk without clear direction, passing storefronts with painted windows advertising everything from ladies' gloves to automobile parts. The city buzzes around us—streetcars clanging, people moving with purpose while we drift, untethered. Automobiles bleat their horns—harsh, brassy bursts that cut through the din.

"What if we don't make it back to 2025?" I ask suddenly, voicing the fear that's been growing since our encounter at the studio. "What if the cave doesn't work how we think it will and we're stuck here?"

Luke is quiet for a minute. "Then we adapt," he finally says. "We build a life. Together."

Together. The word hangs between us, weighted with possibilities. In another context, with another person, I might dismiss it as mere sentiment. But here, now, with Luke—it feels like a lifeline.

"I don't belong in 1925," I say, though the conviction in my voice wavers. "The work I want to do, the life I want to lead—it's not possible here."

"Isn't it?" Luke stops walking, turning to face me fully. "You're brilliant, Eileen. You'd find a way to make your mark, even here, even now. Maybe you could, I don't know, seek what's his name... Challenger?"

I laugh. "Challenger is a paleontologist. And he's fictional. Arthur Conan Doyle."

He scrunches his brow, then says, "I knew that. I meant—"

"Well, there's Gertrude Bell. But she dies next year. And Leonard Wolley, he excavated Ur, but he was... is... notoriously difficult and arrogant, so joining his dig will be almost impossible, especially as I know next to nothing about ancient Mesopotamia. Plus, he's British, so unless we can cough up enough cash for a transatlantic ticket—"

I stop talking because Luke seems somewhere else entirely. For a second, his face is blank, unreadable. But then again, maybe he's bored with my monologue on archaeological history.

"Sorry," he says. "I was thinking of something else. But, but you could do it, right? It's not completely impossible. If anyone can do the impossible, it's you."

His faith in me is startling, almost disorienting in its intensity. I allow myself to imagine it—staying in this time, building a life from scratch. With him. Would it be so terrible?

Yes, whispers a voice in my head. You'd be constrained, diminished, forever fighting against a system designed to keep you in your place.

And yet...

"Let's focus on getting to the cave," I say, pushing the thoughts away. "One step at a time."

Luke nods, but there's something new in his expression—a certainty, a decision made. Whatever he's thinking, he keeps it to himself as we continue walking, our shadows stretching longer as the afternoon begins its slow transition into evening.

We find ourselves in a small park, resting on a bench beneath the shade of a magnolia tree. The scent of its waxy leaves mingles with the city's smells—coal smoke, horse manure, cooking food from nearby restaurants.

"We could..." Luke begins, then hesitates.

"What?"

"We could go to Treaty Oak. Spend the night there."

I feel my eyebrows rise of their own accord. "Sleep outside? Under the tree?"

As Luke makes his case, I warm to the idea. There's poetry to it—seeking shelter beneath the old oak that will stand as our meeting point across time. And practically speaking, we have few other options.

As we discuss the logistics—taking turns keeping watch, making sure we don't oversleep—I study Luke's profile. There's a certainty in him now that wasn't there before. Whatever he found at the pawnshop, whatever decision he'd made, it transformed him.

And I find myself grateful for it, for him—this strange, beautiful constant in the chaos of our fractured timeline.

The sun begins its descent toward the horizon, painting the sky in shades of amber and rose. We rise from the bench by unspoken agreement, beginning the walk to Treaty Oak and whatever the night might hold.

"Whatever happens tomorrow," I say, my voice surprisingly steady, "I'm glad we're facing it together."

Luke's smile is like the breaking of dawn—sudden, warm, illuminating. We hold hands, our fingers intertwining with effortless ease as if they've done this a thousand times before.

Perhaps somewhere in the tangled web of time, they have.

FORTY-THREE: LUKE

The ring burns a hole in my pocket. It seems absurd to propose to a woman at a lunch counter. To a woman I barely know, yet feel I know completely. I decide to wait for the right moment. But part of me feels the right moment has already happened.

"We could..." I hesitate, the idea seeming absurd even as it forms.

"What?"

"We could go to Treaty Oak. Spend the night there."

Eileen's eyebrows rise. "Sleep outside? Under the tree?"

"Why not? It's warm, it's not going to rain, and it seems fitting somehow. Our designated meeting spot across time becomes our shelter when we have none."

She considers this, then nods slowly. "It could work. But we'd have to take turns keeping watch—for safety, and to make sure we don't oversleep and miss the truck."

"I can stay up," I offer immediately. "I'm used to pulling all-nighters when I'm working on a painting."

"Luke, you need rest, too. We can take shifts."

"I can sleep in the truck tomorrow. Tonight, you rest."

Something flickers in her eyes—gratitude, maybe, or something deeper. For a moment, the surrounding air is charged with unspoken words.

"Thank you," she says simply, and I'm not sure if she's thanking me for the offer of keeping watch, or for something larger—for following her into this temporal madness, perhaps, or for believing her when anyone else would have called 911.

The rest of the day passes in tense waiting. We stroll along the riverfront, lingering near the docks where workers load crates onto steamships, the scent of salt and tar thick in the humid air. We sit on a bench in Hemming Park, watching the city move around us—newsboys shouting headlines, trolley cars rattling past, women in smart hats hurrying between shops. A peanut vendor calls out his wares, and an elderly man reads the newspaper on the next bench, shaking his head at the headlines. We say little, both too aware of the hours stretching ahead, the uncertainty of tomorrow.

The ring in my pocket grows heavier with each passing hour. As the afternoon light softens into golden hues, I realize the moment has arrived—not because it's perfect, but because it feels inevitable.

I lead Eileen to a quiet corner of the park, beneath the canopy of a sprawling oak that casts dappled shadows across her face. My heart pounds in my chest, a strange mix of certainty and terror coursing through my veins.

In my mind, I rehearse what I think she wants to hear—something practical, logical. Given our circumstances, we should appear genuinely married. The ring was only two dollars, but it will make our story more convincing.

The words form and dissolve on my tongue, hollow and wrong. This isn't about convenience or appearances.

And then, like the fractured timeline we're living in, something shifts. The moment seems to overlay itself with infinite other versions—past, present, future—all converging on this single point in time. I've done this before. Will do this. Am doing this now.

Without conscious thought, I kneel before her, one knee pressed into the soft earth. The simple brass band gleams in my palm, catching the late afternoon sun as I hold it up to her.

"I want to spend the rest of my life with you," I say, my voice steadier than I thought possible. "Will you do me the honor of being Mrs. Campbell?"

Time suspends itself. The park sounds fade away—no trolleys, no newsboys, just the sound of my pulse in my ears and the soft catch of Eileen's breath. Her eyes widen, reflecting surprise that melts into something deeper, something I recognize because I feel it too.

Her face transforms, illuminated from within by a joy so pure it steals my breath. She doesn't speak—just nods, a single, decisive motion that contains worlds of meaning.

I slide the ring onto her finger with trembling hands. It fits as though it was made for her—another impossible coincidence in our impossible story.

When she pulls me to my feet, the world tilts and realigns. Her hands frame my face with a tenderness that anchors me to this moment, to this timeline, to her. Our lips meet, and everything else falls away—the uncertainty, the fear, the displacement.

The kiss feels like coming home. Like the universe has been leading us to this moment across time itself. Like despite all the chaos, we've found the one thing that was meant to be.

* * *

In the evening, we arrive at Treaty Oak. The tree stretches its limbs wide, draped in Spanish moss, creating a natural cathedral of branches. In 2025, it will be surrounded by a park with benches and interpretive signs. Now, in 1925, it stands on a quiet stretch of private land, untouched by the city's growth but not yet formally protected.

We find a relatively secluded spot among its sprawling roots, sheltered from view by the massive trunk and curtains of hanging moss. Eileen arranges our meager belongings to create a makeshift pillow, then sits with her back against the trunk.

"You should try to sleep," I tell her, settling down nearby. "We have a long day tomorrow."

She nods but makes no move to lie down. Instead, she stares up through the branches at the darkening sky. "It's strange," she says softly. "This tree has been here for hundreds of years. It'll still be here a hundred years from now. The continuity... it's comforting somehow."

I follow her gaze upward. "A fixed point in a changing world."

"Exactly." She turns to look at me, her face shadowed in the gathering dusk. "Like you."

The words catch me off guard. "Me?"

"In all this chaos—jumping through time—you've been the one constant. The one thing that makes sense." She looks away quickly, as if embarrassed by the admission.

I want to reach for her hand, to pull her close, to tell her she's been my anchor too—the only real thing in a world that keeps shifting beneath my feet. But fear holds me back—fear of complicating what's already impossibly complex.

"Try to sleep," I say instead. "I'll keep watch."

She hesitates, then nods, lying down on the grass. "Wake me if you get tired."

"I won't get tired," I promise, knowing it's probably a lie.

The night deepens around us, the sounds of the city fading into the occasional distant car horn or shout. Under the canopy of Treaty Oak, it's easy to forget what year it is—1925, 2025, or some other time entirely.

Eileen's breathing eventually slows and deepens as she drifts into sleep. In repose, her face looks younger, the determined set of her jaw relaxed, the furrow between her brows smoothed away.

I pull out my sketchbook—the one thing I made sure to grab from the boarding house—and draw her by the light of the moon filtering through the branches. The familiar motion of pencil on paper calms me.

I'm so absorbed in capturing the curve of her cheek, the sweep of her lashes, that I almost miss the approaching footsteps. But something—instinct, perhaps, or heightened awareness of our vulnerability—makes me look up just as a beam of light sweeps across the ground nearby.

A night watchman, his flashlight cutting through the darkness as he makes his rounds.

I close my sketchbook silently and slide closer to Eileen, placing a protective hand on her shoulder. If he finds us here, we could be arrested for vagrancy, or at the very least, moved along.

The light sweeps closer, illuminating branches just yards from where we hide. I hold my breath, willing the watchman to pass by without noticing us huddled among the roots and moss.

Eileen stirs beneath my hand, her eyes opening to meet mine in silent question. I press a finger to my lips, then point toward the approaching light. She nods in understanding, her body tensing as she prepares to... what? Run? Hide? Fight?

The watchman pauses, his light lingering on the base of the tree. My heart pounds so loudly that I'm certain he must hear it. Eileen's hand finds mine in the darkness, her fingers cold but her grip steady.

For a moment, time seems suspended—the three of us frozen in a tableau beneath the oak. Then, mercifully, the watchman moves on, his light swinging away as he continues his patrol.

We remain motionless until his footsteps fade into the distance. Only then do I release the breath I've been holding, my shoulders sagging in relief.

"That was close," Eileen whispers.

"Too close," I agree. "He might come back."

She sits up, suddenly fully awake. "Should we move?"

I consider this, weighing the risks. "No," I say. "If we stay deeper in the shadows, we should be safe enough. And moving now might attract more attention."

She shifts to sit beside me, her back against the trunk, our shoulders touching.

"I'll stay up with you," she says, cutting off my protest with a raised hand. "I'm awake now, anyway."

I should argue, should insist she get what rest she can before tomorrow's journey. But selfishly, I'm glad for her company, for the warm press of her shoulder against mine, for the chance to talk with her in the quiet intimacy of the night.

"Tell me about your life," I say softly. "In 2025. What were you doing before all this happened?"

She smiles. "Trying to build a career. Worrying about my thesis defense. Dating men who never quite..."

"Never quite what?"

"Felt right," she says. "I'm sorry, I shouldn't be talking about exes."

"It's fine," I say. "I've had my share of... 'never quite felt right' myself." I don't tell her why Rose left. What would be the point? That person, that violent drunk, is not who I am now. The thought of smashing walls in front of Eileen makes me shiver, and it deepens my resolve never to drink again.

I am a changed man—a changing man—and Eileen is the catalyst of that change. I could lean forward, close those few inches, press my lips to hers. It would be so easy. But what if I'm misreading her? What if I'm just another man who doesn't quite feel right?

And even if she does feel this connection between us, what

then? We're trapped in a time not our own, racing to get back to a cave that might send us anywhere—or nowhere. What kind of future could we possibly have?

The moment stretches taut with unspoken words and uncrossed distances. Then Eileen breaks the tension, looking away with a small, self-conscious laugh.

"Listen to us, talking about dating problems when we're time travelers sleeping under a tree, running from night watchmen," she says.

I smile, letting her retreat from the edge we'd approached. "Life finds a way to be complicated, no matter what time period you're in."

She leans her head against my shoulder, the gesture casual yet intimate. "At least we're complicating it together."

Together. The word wraps around me like a promise, warming me despite the cooling night air. Whatever happens tomorrow—whether we make it to the cave, whether we jump through time again, whether we find our way back to 2025 or end up somewhere else entirely—right now, at this moment, we're together under Treaty Oak.

And in some way, that's what matters most.

FORTY-FOUR: EILEEN

The truck rattles over every rut and pothole along the primitive road, jostling us against each other and the wooden benches. I'm squeezed between Luke and a heavyset man who reeks of tobacco, while across from us, three other new hires stare blankly ahead, exhaustion etched into their weathered faces.

Luke dozed off about an hour into the journey, his head eventually finding my shoulder. I don't move to wake him, even as my arm grows numb from the weight. He stayed up all night at Treaty Oak, keeping watch while I slept, and the dark circles under his eyes are a testament to his exhaustion.

"Your husband don't look like logger material," the tobacco-scented man comments, eyeing Luke with skepticism.

"He's stronger than he looks," I reply, the lie coming easier the second time. "And he's a hard worker."

The man grunts, unconvinced. "Soft hands. City hands." He says it like an accusation.

I bristle at his tone but force a smile. "Everyone starts somewhere."

"Not everyone finishes," he replies ominously, then turns to stare out of the back of the truck.

The morning sun climbs higher as we travel further from Jacksonville, the landscape gradually transforming from sparse settlements to untamed wilderness. The road changes to a bumpy dirt backroad, then disappears entirely, leaving us to follow what amounts to a glorified trail through the forest.

Luke stirs against my shoulder, blinking awake as the truck hits a violent bump. He straightens, wiping a hand across his mouth, looking momentarily disoriented.

"How long was I asleep?" he asks, his voice rough with sleep.

"A few hours," I tell him. "We're getting close, I think."

As if to confirm my words, the truck slows. Through the trees, I catch glimpses of the Suwannee River, its dark waters reflecting the midday sun.

The camp comes into view as we round a bend in the trail—a scattering of rough wooden buildings nestled in a clearing, smoke curling from the central cookhouse. A man stirs a pot outside, then pauses mid-motion, squinting toward the truck. I can only imagine his relief—finally, someone else to take over this so-called woman's work. Around him, men haul timber, swinging axes over their shoulders, their voices carrying over the steady thunk of hammering and the rasp of saws. Along the riverbank, felled trees lie stacked and waiting, stripped and ready to be floated downstream.

It's not the same camp where Luke had his drunken episode—a small blessing, given how that ended. But it's close enough to Big Shoals that I can feel a flutter of hope in my chest. We're getting closer.

The truck lurches to a stop in the center of the camp. The driver, a grizzled man with a perpetual scowl, turns to address us.

"Everybody out. Report to the foreman's cabin." He points to a structure slightly larger than the others. "He'll assign your bunks and duties."

We climb down stiffly, stretching limbs cramped from the long journey. Luke's hand finds mine as we walk toward the foreman's cabin, a brief squeeze that communicates both reassurance and anxiety.

The foreman is a bear of a man named Holt, with hands as rough as tree bark and a voice to match. He looks us over with practiced efficiency, assigning bunks and roles with rapid-fire instructions.

"Campbell," he barks, consulting a crumpled list. "You're a swamper. Report to Jenkins after you stow your gear." His eyes shift to me, and something in his expression softens marginally. "Mrs. Campbell, you'll be helping Clara Mae in the cookhouse. Women's quarters are behind the mess hall."

And just like that, we're separated. Luke is led toward the men's bunkhouse while I'm directed to a smaller structure near the cookhouse where the few women in camp are housed.

"I'll find you at dinner," Luke says in a hurried whisper before we're pulled in opposite directions.

Clara Mae turns out to be a stout woman in her fifties with ripped arms and a no-nonsense attitude. She eyes me suspiciously as I enter the cookhouse, her hands continuing to knead a massive mound of dough without missing a beat.

"You ever cooked for fifty men before?" she asks without preamble.

"No," I admit, seeing no point in lying. "But I'm a quick learner."

She snorts. "We'll see about that. Wash your hands and start peeling those potatoes. We've got hungry men to feed at six."

Clara Mae works me hard, but also shares information freely—including the camp's schedule and routines. I learn that the night watchman makes rounds only around the perimeter of the camp, leaving the path to the river largely unwatched after dark.

By the time the dinner bell rings, my hands are raw from peeling what felt like a hundred potatoes, and my back aches from stooping over the worktable. But I've earned a grudging nod of approval from Clara Mae, who concedes that I "might have some use after all."

I also have the beginnings of a plan. We'll slip away at dawn when the night watch ends, but before the day shift begins in earnest. There's a gap of about thirty minutes when the camp is at its quietest, with most men still asleep and the previous watch too tired to pay close attention.

The loggers file in for dinner, a rowdy procession of sweat-soaked men eager for food and a brief respite from their labor. I scan the crowd for Luke, spotting him toward the back of the line. His face is streaked with dirt, his shirt clinging to him with sweat, but his face lights up when he sees me.

We manage only a brief exchange as I serve him a plate of stew.

"How are you holding up?" I ask, ladling the thick mixture onto his plate.

"Fine," he says, though the tightness around his eyes tells a different story. Manual labor is clearly taking its toll on him. "You?"

"Fine," I echo, matching his brave face. "I think I've located the cave area on a map in the foreman's office. It's about three miles west of here."

Luke's eyes sharpen with interest. "How do we get there?"

"I'm working on it," I murmur as the line pushes him forward. "Meet me behind the cookhouse after dinner."

He nods almost imperceptibly, then moves on.

Night falls with a chorus of insects and the occasional distant splash from the river. I wait until Clara Mae retires to her private room at the rear of the women's quarters, then slip out into the darkness.

The air is thick with humidity, the stars obscured by a haze that promises rain by morning. Perfect, I think. Bad weather will help cover our tracks.

Luke is already waiting when I reach our meeting spot, a shadowy alcove between the cookhouse and a storage shed. My breath catches at the sight of him—not from attraction this time, but from concern. He leans heavily against the wall, barely able to stand.

"Luke," I whisper, rushing to his side. "Are you alright?"

He attempts a smile that comes out more like a grimace. "Just some blisters. And maybe a pulled muscle or two. Nothing serious."

I take his hands in mine, turning them palms up in the faint moonlight. They're raw and blistered, the skin broken in several places. The hands of an artist, now brutalized by labor they were never meant for.

"This is my fault," I say, guilt washing over me. "I should never have suggested—"

"No," he says. "This was our only option, and you know it." He winces as I accidentally press against an angry blister. "Besides, it's only for one night. We'll be gone by morning, right?"

I nod, sharing the plan I've formulated. "There's a gap in the watch just before dawn. We'll head west along the river. The cave should be about three miles downstream."

"How will we find it in the dark?"

It's a valid question. The landscape is different in 1925—fewer landmarks, no trails marked by modern hikers. No swinging tire

232

with rowdy kids.

"There's a distinctive bend in the river just before the cave. We'll navigate from there."

Luke nods, then stifles a groan as he shifts position. "And if we can't find it?"

I squeeze his forearm, careful to avoid his injured hands. "We will. We have to."

We finalize our plan: meet by the river at 4:30 a.m., just before the watch changes. Head west, staying close to the water for guidance. Reach the area by sunrise, locate the cave, and—hopefully—trigger another jump.

"What if it doesn't work?" Luke asks the question we've both been avoiding. "What if we can't jump again?"

The possibility hangs between us, dark and ominous as the night sky.

"Then we try something else," I say with more confidence than I feel. "But for now, this is our best chance."

He studies my face in the dim light, then reaches up to tuck a strand of hair behind my ear, his touch gentle despite his raw hands. "Why are you so sure we'll make it back?"

The question comes as a surprise. I was certain he was sure too, but as I look at his quizzical expression, I realize he's unsure. And why would he think we would make it back when I don't even know what's driving this certainty inside me? Is it scientific reasoning, or something else entirely?

"Because," I say, "I refuse to believe the universe would bring us together across time only to strand us apart from everything we know."

The words hang between us, laden with implications I'm not sure I'm ready to acknowledge. Luke's eyes hold mine, searching for something—certainty, perhaps, or permission.

"Eileen," he starts, his voice rough with emotion.

Before he can continue, a shout echoes from the direction of the men's bunkhouse—followed by raucous laughter and the thud of a slammed door.

We spring apart instinctively, the moment broken. Reality crashes back—we're in a logging camp in 1925, planning an escape at dawn, with nothing guaranteed but the attempt itself.

"4:30 by the river. Don't be late."

He nods, disappointment flashing briefly across his features before he schools them into determined focus. "I'll be there."

As I watch him disappear into the darkness, heading back toward the men's quarters, I wonder what he was about to say—and whether I'll ever get to hear it.

FORTY-FIVE: LUKE

I stay awake all night, my body a catalog of pain. Every muscle protests as I ease myself from the narrow bunk, careful not to disturb the sleeping loggers around me. The blisters on my hands have hardened overnight into stiff, painful patches that crack and weep as I pull on my boots.

Outside, the world is wrapped in the deep blue of predawn. The air smells of impending rain, a heaviness that weighs on my lungs as I slip between shadows toward the river. The camp slumbers on, unaware of our planned escape.

Eileen is already waiting by the water when I arrive, her slight figure almost ghostly in the fading darkness. She's tucked her hair under a cloth cap, wears loose work trousers, and carries a small bundle I assume contains some meager supplies.

"You made it," she whispers, relief clear in her voice.

"Did you doubt me?" I try for lightness, but the pain in my back and shoulders makes my voice tight.

She notices immediately, her eyes finding mine in the gloom. "Are you going to be able to make it? It's at least a three-mile hike. It's dense vegetation, so two hours, maybe three."

"I'll crawl if I have to," I promise, and mean it.

She nods once. "Let's go. Stay close to the tree line—it provides cover but keeps the river in sight for navigation."

A wooden crate topples over as I brush against it, sending an empty tin cup clattering onto the dirt. I freeze. Eileen sucks in a sharp breath beside me.

A cough. A shift in a nearby tent. Someone stirs, muttering sleepily.

Eileen grips my wrist, fingers digging into my skin. We wait, the tension stretching unbearably. Then, after what feels like an eternity, the muttering stops. The camp falls still again.

She exhales slowly. "Let's move."

We move silently along the bank, the soft mud swallowing our footfalls. The eastern sky gradually lightens, revealing a low blanket of clouds that promises the rain I've been smelling since dawn. The river flows beside us, steady and uncaring of our temporal plight.

I take a step forward, and my foot sinks. Fast.

The riverbank is worse than I expected, with more mud than solid ground after the night's storms. My boot vanishes into the muck, and when I try to pull it free, I lose my balance, barely catching myself before I go down completely.

Eileen turns, eyes widening. "You okay?"

I nod, though my heart is pounding. We can't afford to slow down, but every step through this mess feels like dragging my body through quicksand. And I can already tell—I'm leaving deep tracks behind us.

I keep half an eye on the water, where half-submerged logs might not be logs at all. Alligators are out here—I know that much—but Eileen moves with the calm of someone who understands them. When I get too close to the bank, she murmurs a warning. "No sudden movements. No splashing. And if we see one, back away slow." She says it as if she's reciting a fact, like this is just another part of survival. But I notice she keeps her distance from the water, giving the river a wary respect. I do the same. The last thing we need is to surprise something with more teeth than sense.

We've covered perhaps a mile when the first drops fall—fat, warm splashes that quickly intensify into a steady downpour. Within minutes, we're soaked through, clothes clinging uncomfortably to our skin. The rain is both a blessing and a curse—it covers our tracks and masks any sound we might make, but it also turns the forest floor slick and treacherous.

Eileen presses on with dogged determination, her eyes fixed on the path ahead. I follow, gritting my teeth against the protest of my muscles and the stinging of rain on my raw hands. Time becomes meaningless, measured only in painful steps and the gradual brightening of the sky behind its veil of clouds.

Finally, after what feels like hours, the sound of rushing water reaches us—different from the steady flow we've been following.

"The shoals," Eileen says, catching her breath. "We're close."

The terrain grows rockier as we approach Big Shoals, the river narrowing and quickening over a series of ledges. The rain has intensified, making the rocks slippery and the path treacherous.

"Be careful," I say as Eileen navigates a steep section. "One fall here—"

My warning comes too late. Her foot slips on the wet stone, and she pitches backward with a startled cry. I lunge forward, catching her arm before she can fall completely, but the sudden movement sends a bolt of pain through my strained back.

We both end up on our knees, breathing hard, rain plastering our hair to our faces.

"Are you okay?" I ask, still gripping her arm.

She nods, her eyes wide with the adrenaline rush of the near-fall. "Thanks to you."

We stay like that for a moment longer than necessary, rain streaming down our faces, her pulse hammering beneath my fingers where they circle her wrist. Then, with a shared nod, we help each other to our feet and continue on.

The landscape grows more familiar as we near the cave's location—a particular formation of rocks, Eileen tells me, a distinctive bend in the river that has withstood a century of erosion. Despite the rain and the changed surroundings, I feel a growing certainty that we're heading in the right direction.

"There," Eileen says suddenly, pointing to a rocky outcropping partially hidden by vegetation. "That's it."

My heart leaps at the sight. The cave entrance is narrower than I remember, half-concealed by plants that won't be cleared away for decades, but it's unmistakably the same place. I feel it like a homing beacon in my gut.

We approach cautiously, both remembering what happened the last time we entered. The rain lessens slightly as we reach the shelter of the overhanging rock, allowing us a moment to catch our breath and prepare.

"What do we do?" I ask, suddenly uncertain now that we've reached our goal. "Just... walk in?"

Eileen nods her head. "I think we're past the point of doing anything but."

"Together?" I ask, offering my hand despite the pain of my blisters.

She takes it without hesitation, her fingers cold but her grip firm. "Together."

We enter the cave slowly, allowing our eyes to adjust to the dimness. Water drips steadily from the ceiling, creating small pools on the limestone floor. The air grows cooler as we move deeper, the sounds of the rain and river fading behind us.

The passage narrows, then widens into a chamber I recognize despite the century of difference. This is where it happened before—where we found ourselves translocated in time without warning or explanation. Drawings of little stick men dot the walls, reminding me of Egyptian hieroglyphs. Not that I've ever been to Egypt, or seen any hieroglyphs in person. But these are old drawings for sure, something that seems more fitting for the walls of The Smithsonian rather than a backdrop to a Floridian cave.

We stop in the middle of the chamber, still hand in hand, uncertain what to do next. Do we simply wait? Perform some action? Speak an incantation? The rules of whatever phenomenon that controls these jumps remain frustratingly opaque.

"Now what?" I whisper, my voice echoing slightly against the stone walls.

Eileen squeezes my hand. "I don't know. Last time, it just... happened."

Minutes pass in tense silence. Nothing changes. No disorientation, no shift in pressure, no sense of movement through time. Just two dripping-wet people standing in a dark cave, waiting for a miracle neither understands.

"What were you going to say to me last night, before we got interrupted by those loggers?"

My cheeks heat up. Last night, it seemed natural to tell her I was falling for her. To lean in for a goodnight kiss. But here, with my legs shivering and my stomach lurching and waiting for time to swallow me whole? Not the time. But then again, how much time did we have left?

"I was going to tell you that—"

Am I repeating myself? I am. I already told her. Have told her.

No, will tell her.

I glance at the walls and my stomach turns. The drawings—they're changing.

Figures that weren't there before emerge in ghostly outlines. Others flicker, distorting as if the stone itself is reconfiguring. The stick figures with outstretched hands ripple like reflections on water.

The tremor begins with a deep, guttural vibration that radiates from the walls. No, not the walls—something deeper. Something underneath time itself.

My thoughts halt abruptly as a tremor runs through the ground beneath our feet. Dust and small fragments of stone shower down from the ceiling as the vibration intensifies. No, not dust and stone. It's as if the cave is disassembling before my eyes.

Eileen says, "I think it's—"

Happening?

The trembling increases, the walls of the cave seem to ripple like liquid, and I lose the sensation of Eileen's hand in mine. The pool at the center of the chamber glows with an eerie blue light. It's so intense that it's painful to look at directly.

"Luke!" Eileen cries, her voice distorted as if coming from a great distance.

The blue light engulfs me, blinding in its brilliance. I feel a wrenching sensation—as if my body is being pulled in multiple directions simultaneously. There's a roaring in my ears, a sound like the ocean and a freight train and a car horn combined. Pressure builds in my head, behind my eyes, in my chest—as if I'm being compressed into a space too small to contain me.

Then, abruptly, release. The pressure vanishes, the light fades, and the roaring stops.

I stagger forward, disoriented, blinking away afterimages of that blinding blue light. Cool air fills my lungs—air that doesn't smell of cave dampness or river mud or Florida rain.

It smells of exhaust fumes, hot concrete, and the city.

My vision clears slowly, revealing not the dim interior of a limestone cave, but the glaring brightness of a sunny day. I'm standing in the middle of a street—a busy, modern street with cars and buildings and—

The blaring of a horn slams into my consciousness. I turn, still dazed, to see a city bus bearing down on me, its driver's face a mask of horror as he realizes he won't be able to stop in time.

Time slows to a crawl. I should move, I know I should move, but my legs won't respond. My mind is still catching up to the impossible jump—from cave to city in an instant.

The bus looms larger, impossibly fast yet paradoxically slow in that strange, stretched moment before impact. I have time to notice route number 12 on its digital window display, the glare of sunlight on its windshield, and the way the metal front swallows everything in its path.

I have time to realize Eileen is nowhere in sight.

I have time to think: This is how it ends.

Then time snaps back to normal speed, and the bus is upon me.

FORTY-SIX: EILEEN

The world spins and twists. A strange blue glow envelopes me as Luke's hand is torn from mine. My ears fill with a roaring sound like waves crashing against rocks, like the rushing of the Suwannee River amplified a thousandfold. Pressure builds throughout my head and torso, through every cell of my body until I think I might shatter.

Then, a sudden release.

I stumble forward and catch myself against something solid—a wooden podium. My vision clears to reveal a half-empty lecture hall, with people filing toward the exits with hushed whispers and disapproving glances. Some are shaking their heads.

I blink, disoriented. Where's Luke? I look around but don't see him.

A large projector screen hangs behind me, displaying images of cave drawings—spirals, loops, stick figures walking in impossible directions. I recognize them instantly: the same symbols from our cave at Big Shoals.

My trembling fingers swipe at the podium's embedded interface, its glass surface coming to life with a faint pulse of light. The date in the corner reads April 17, 2035.

Ten years too far. My mind races as I try to comprehend the temporal displacement. We were aiming for 2025, not 2035. And where is Luke?

The title slide of my presentation glows on the screen: "A Portrait of Time: Temporal Displacement in Prehistoric Cave Art." Fragments of memory surface—not new memories being formed, but existing ones finally accessible, as though they've been waiting for me to catch up to them.

I gave this lecture today. I argued that these cave drawings weren't depicting celestial events as commonly believed, but experiences of time travel. Dr. Abernathy from Biology had interrupted, his voice thick with academic condescension: "So you say that these drawings suggest primitive cultures believed in time travel?"

My response—"Not just believed. They actually time traveled."—had triggered the exodus. I scan the emptying room, searching desperately for Luke's face among the departing academics.

He has to be here. We entered the cave together. We traveled together. He has to be here.

But the rows of seats empty until only one person remains—Candace. She sits in the front row, her notebook open, looking at me with an expression of genuine interest rather than dismissal.

"That was quite a statement, Dr. Campbell," she says, smiling.

Dr. Campbell. The name feels both familiar and strange. I've been Dr. Eileen Campbell for... how long? My head throbs as conflicting timelines attempt to reconcile themselves.

I steady myself against the podium. "Have you seen Luke?"

Candace blinks, apparently surprised by my urgent tone. She taps the side of her glasses, a faint digital overlay reflecting in her lenses. "Luke? No, he sent me a message earlier saying he might be late."

She frowns, scrutinizing my face. "Are you okay? You look like you've seen a ghost."

"I was in the cave just moments ago, with Luke..."

She approaches, her familiar confidence now tinged with concern. "You're overworking yourself. Are you still seeing that counselor?"

Counselor? That's right. Still prone to overworking. The burnout last summer.

I nod. "Yes. I just—" I stare at Candace, waiting for her to have the "Aha" moment, waiting for her face to lose that look of concern and light up as she realizes what's been happening to me. To Luke. To us.

But she says, "That audience reaction was harsh, but you know how academia is about boundary-pushing theories." She touches my arm lightly. "Listen, you're onto something real, even if they can't see it yet. I've proved that time travel is possible... we just need that one push for proof."

I stare at her, pieces clicking into place. "You're a quantum physicist?"

Candace gives me a strange look, head tilted slightly. "Have been for years. Since that plant experiment, remember? It came out of the cave with a different colored pot. Well, that's what you told me, but of course, there was no proof."

It did? But I remember it differently. The plant came out unchanged. It bobbed in, then bobbed out, not a leaf out of place. Could this timeline be... be what? Rewriting itself? Changing events dynamically? Or maybe I'm getting the times and days confused. It's been 45 years, so—

And then I remember. Red, purple, then blue. The spider plant we'd left in the cave as a test. Candace touching the plant in my apartment, her eyes widening as she listened to my story.

But back then, I'm sure she apologized for the "silly experiment." A "grad school experiment," she'd said. Then something about how she hadn't realized the implications of negative quantum time. Or had that conversation happened at a later date? I am not exactly a neurology buff, but I know memories can blend over time, creating a collage of memories that feels like one memory. Is that what this is?

I remember her looking at Luke's paintings. Her changing her major the following semester, abandoning anthropology for physics. Her Ph.D. dissertation on quantum displacement. Years of late nights in her lab, building models that might explain what happened to us.

To us. To Luke and me.

"Where is he?" I ask, my voice breaking. "Luke. He should be here."

Candace's expression softens. "Maybe he got caught in traffic? You know how he hates missing your lectures."

I lift my left hand, and there it is—a simple brass wedding ring, worn thin by years of wear. Not the pawn shop ring from 1925— or perhaps it is—but something more permanent, more established. The sight of it triggers a cascade of memories.

Luke and I getting engaged under Treaty Oak in 2027, the same place where we slept that night in 1925. His hands trembling as he slid the ring onto my finger, magnolia petals drifting around us in the spring breeze. Our wedding in 2028, held in Luke's gallery space—walls adorned with his time fracture paintings, soft Edison bulbs casting warm light across exposed brick, the scent of jasmine and vanilla hanging in the air as we spoke our vows beneath an arch of wild Florida flowers. Candace in her pink matron of honor dress. Luke's friend Kristy in a matching bridesmaid dress. The weight of history and the future pressing down on us, making the moment feel both infinite and fleeting.

Our life together. Our small apartment near the river. The morning light filtering through curtains as Luke sketches me on the easy chair. The arguments about his studio rent, my research grants, whose turn it was to wash dishes. The reconciliations that followed, sometimes sweet, sometimes passionate, always centering us back to what mattered.

But these memories feel like photographs from someone else's album—familiar yet distant. Because I also remember the cave, the blue light, Luke's hand being torn from mine just moments ago. The violent displacement through time.

"Candace," I say, my voice wavering. "When did you last see Luke?"

"Yesterday? At dinner? You both came over, remember?" She narrows her eyes. "It was last night, right?"

I nod automatically, but I'm not sure if "last night" even happened, beyond getting no sleep in a logging camp. A terrible sense of dread is building inside me. If Luke and I both came back to 2035, and we're married—have been married for ten years—then where is he now?

I gather my materials with shaking hands, shoving a stack of handwritten notes—scribbled equations, time fracture diagrams, a worn copy of my research paper—into my bag. My sleek, ultrathin tablet slips in next, its glowing edge flickering as it folds shut. A compact AI recorder, still blinking from the lecture, follows. "I need to go," I tell Candace. "I need to find Luke."

"I'll walk out with you," she offers.

As we exit the lecture hall, I scan the corridor outside, searching for Luke's familiar silhouette among the dispersing crowd.

Nothing.

He's here somewhere. I feel him. We made it to 2035 together. A few years off from where we hoped to land, but still. We made it.

But as we approach the parking lot, doubt creeps in. Did he make it back with me? Or did something go wrong at the moment of transition? Was he sent somewhere—somewhen—else?

I touch my worn brass wedding ring. The weight of it should be comforting, a tangible connection to Luke. Instead, it feels like the only remaining evidence of a life I'm not sure I actually lived.

"Eileen," Candace says as we reach my car, her voice gentle. "Are you sure you're okay to drive? You seem... distant."

I force a smile. "Just disappointed about the lecture. I'll be fine once I get home."

Home. To Luke. He has to be there.

He has to be.

FORTY-SEVEN: EILEEN

It is Saturday, noon. The April sun hangs directly overhead, casting minimal shadows across the sprawling branches of Treaty Oak. I shift on the metal bench, smoothing my dress—the blue one Luke always liked—and check the time on my wristband for the fourth time in ten minutes.

I'm meeting Candace at Treaty Oak for lunch. The same place where Luke and I got engaged. The same place we took shelter during that long-ago night in 1925. This tree has become our anchor point across time, a fixed star in our fractured journey.

Deep in my heart, I know Luke is out there somewhere. Parts of our history together shine with perfect clarity in my mind—our first meeting at the gallery, our time in 1925, moments of connection that transcend ordinary experience. Yet the decade since our return feels dreamlike, filled with half-formed impressions and events I struggle to place in sequence. Still, one certainty remains: Luke will find his way back to me. I just don't know when.

Three days have passed since my disastrous lecture. Three days of returning to an empty apartment. A day of calling Luke's phone only to hear his cheerful voice instructing me to leave a message. And then, a signal letting me know the phone is out of service, like it never existed. Three sleepless nights cycling between terror, hope, and the peculiar double consciousness of remembering two lives simultaneously.

Candace arrives, her slender figure weaving through the Saturday park-goers—young couples on benches, children climbing the protective barrier around the oak's massive roots, tourists capturing AR memories with flashy gestures. She carries a small basket that releases the aroma of fresh bread as she sits beside me.

"You look like hell," she says.

"I haven't been sleeping."

"Still no word?"

"No," I say, accepting the sandwich she offers. Candace and I have had many conversations this week about Luke. She knows that many of her memories are fractured: Luke in one place. Luke not in the same place. She's the only one who believes me, who accepts both versions of reality without questioning my sanity.

"I've been thinking about quantum time," she says, unwrapping her own lunch. "About it being like a liquid rather than a line."

I nod, watching a nearby child chase a prismatic bubble-drone. "In the cave drawings, time isn't depicted as linear. It's loops, spirals, branching paths."

"And my quantum modeling supports it." Candace's eyes light up with scientific fervor. "I think I'm on the verge of something, Eileen. A quantum mechanics breakthrough."

"Like what?" I ask.

She retrieves a small projector from her bag, activating it with a flick of her finger. A complex equation hovers in the air in front of her, symbols twisting and reforming. "Luke's fracture series was the key. The way he painted time—it's like he could see the quantum state directly."

The holographic display shifts to one of Luke's paintings—a man in multiple positions simultaneously, fragments of the same moment experienced from different perspectives. I remember watching him create it in our apartment, his hands flecked with paint, his eyes distant, as if seeing beyond the canvas.

"These paintings aren't just art," Candace continues. "They're visual representations of quantum superposition. Luke wasn't just painting what he imagined; he was painting what you both experienced—perhaps what you still are experiencing."

Her words spark a flare of hope in my chest. "So you think he's alive? Somewhere?"

"I think—" She hesitates, closing the projection. "I think 'alive' or 'dead' might be oversimplifications for what's happening to him."

The conversation pauses. I watch a couple walking hand-in-hand along the path, their laughter carrying on the breeze. Around us, life continues its ordinary rhythms, oblivious to the temporal anomalies Candace and I discuss like weather patterns.

After a moment, Candace activates her embedded phone with a casual wave of her palm. The subtle glow beneath her skin indicates headlines scrolling across her field of vision. I've never bothered with news subscriptions—between juggling research grants, lecture preparations, and my increasingly frantic search for evidence of similar temporal displacements in ancient cultures, I barely have time to eat, let alone follow current events.

"Anything interesting?" I ask, more to be polite than from genuine curiosity. My thoughts remain fixed on Luke, on the cave, on the impossible task of finding someone lost in the fabric of time itself.

"Climate migration numbers up again, fusion breakthrough in Geneva," she recites absently. Then she perks up. "Oh, new archaeological finds in the Amazon Basin that the retreating rainforest has revealed. Might interest you professionally."

Another time, I might have been excited. Now I just nod distantly, thinking how I'd trade every archaeological discovery on Earth for one more moment with Luke.

"Oh, wow," Candace says suddenly, her tone shifting. Her expression changes, a frown creasing her forehead. "Remember that artist you used to date?"

My stomach clenches. The sandwich turns to ash in my mouth. Used to date?

"Luke," I manage. My fingers dig into the bench, knuckles whitening against the metal.

"Wait..." She shakes her head, blinking rapidly. "That's weird, because I remember being your maid of honor." She stares at me, confusion clouding her features. "That's right, isn't it? You guys got married—"

"In another timeline," I finish for her, my voice flat.

She covers her mouth and says "Oh."

I can see it in her eyes before she speaks. My chest constricts. The world narrows to Candace's face, everything beyond her blurring into insignificance. My hands tremble, and a chill spreads from my core outward, leaving my fingers numb. The taste of copper floods my mouth as I bite the inside of my cheek.

"I am so sorry," Candace says, her voice barely above a whisper. "It says Luke Campbell died this week after he was hit by a city bus."

Time stops.

The children's laughter fades. The drone's buzzing silences. The rustling leaves still. Everything around me freezes into a perfect, terrible tableau.

The bus.

The bus I saw bearing down on him through his eyes in my nightmares. The city bus, route number 12, its front grille growing impossibly large in those last seconds.

My lungs refuse to work. My heart forgets to beat. The sandwich falls from my numb fingers.

"Eileen?" Candace's voice seems to come from miles away. "Eileen, breathe."

I can't. Because if I breathe, if I move, if I acknowledge what she's just told me, then it becomes real. As long as I remain perfectly still, we exist in the moment before—before the news, before the loss, before the world shatters irreparably.

But time refuses to stop completely.

"Show me," I finally whisper.

Candace hesitates, then passes her palm over to project the article. The holographic display shows Luke's face—his gallery headshot from last year's exhibition. Below it, the headline: "Local Artist Luke Campbell Dies in Tragic Accident."

Wednesday. The accident happened on Wednesday—the same day we entered the cave, the same day I landed in my lecture hall.

"I knew it," I say, my voice strange to my own ears.

Candace slides closer, her arm around my shoulders. "What do you mean?"

"When we were in the cave, during the time shift, I felt his hand torn from mine. I landed in the lecture hall, but Luke... " My voice breaks. "Luke must have landed somewhere else. Somewhere in the path of that bus."

"Eileen—"

"It's not right," I interrupt, a sudden fury replacing the shock.

"The timeline is wrong. We were supposed to come back together. Something went wrong, and now——" I look at my wedding ring, the brass suddenly dull in the sunlight. "Now history is rewriting itself around his absence."

I stand abruptly, my sandwich falling to the ground.

"Where are you going?" Candace asks, rising to follow me.

"The cave. I have to go back there."

She grabs my arm. "Eileen, no. We don't know what caused the displacement. We don't know if it'll happen again."

"Luke is already dead," I say, the words burning my throat. "What does it matter?"

"It matters because——" Candace stops, her expression changing. She presses her fingers to her temple, grimacing slightly. "That's odd."

"What?"

"I just had the strangest——" She blinks rapidly. "I have a memory of Luke calling me this morning. About meeting us here for lunch."

Hope surges through me. "He called you? Today?"

"But that can't be right. The news article——" She stares at her palm screen, then at me, confusion etched across her face.

A sudden breeze stirs the oak's leaves, sending dappled shadows dancing across the ground. The world feels less solid somehow, as if the edges of objects have become slightly blurred, reality itself uncertain.

"The fractures," I whisper. "Like in Luke's paintings."

Candace nods slowly. "If he exists in a quantum superposition—neither fully here nor fully gone—then observation itself might be affecting his state."

"The more we look for him——"

"The more we force reality to decide about where and when he exists," she finishes.

I sink back onto the bench, my mind racing. "So what do I do? Keep looking? Stop looking? Go to the cave?"

Candace shakes her head. "I don't know. But rushing back to the cave isn't the answer. Not yet. We need to understand what's happening first."

I close my eyes, trying to center myself. When I open them

again, the world seems slightly different—the light a shade warmer, the breeze a touch softer.

"We'll figure this out," Candace says, taking my hand. "Between your archaeological insights and my quantum physics, we'll bring him back."

I nod, though uncertainty gnaws at me. Because while Candace sees this as a fascinating scientific problem, I see it as something more primal, more desperate—the unraveling of my life, thread by precious thread.

"Let's go back to my lab," she suggests. "I want to run some new simulations based on your cave drawings."

As we gather our things to leave, I cast one last glance at Treaty Oak, its sprawling branches reaching toward the edge of the park. How many lovers has it sheltered? How many promises witnessed? How many tears are absorbed into its roots?

And somewhere in the tangle of time, did Luke and I really stand beneath it, ring in hand, future bright before us? Or is that memory already fading, a ghost of a timeline that never quite solidified?

I touch the rough bark one last time, a silent promise. I will find you, Luke. Across time. Across everything.

PART III: ENTANGLEMENT

FORTY-EIGHT: EILEEN

I sit beneath Treaty Oak on a Saturday morning in June 2070, my arthritic fingers tracing the worn brass of my wedding ring. Thirty years of Saturdays. Three decades of the same ritual.

The oak has grown more gnarled with age, much like my hands. Metal supports now brace its heaviest limbs, a network of cables and biodegradable injection sites marking human intervention against time's relentless pull. The city installed a protective barrier around the root system fifteen years ago when saltwater intrusion threatened Jacksonville's oldest trees.

"Can I help you with something, ma'am?"

A park docent approaches—young, maybe early twenties, with the eager helpfulness they always have. They rotate these kids every few months, so none ever recognizes me as the woman who comes every Saturday without fail.

"No, thank you. Just enjoying the shade."

But that's not true. I'm searching, always searching. For Luke.

The city has transformed around this patch of green. Glass and carbon-capture buildings tower where modest structures once stood. The air is hotter now, despite the atmospheric regulators the coastal cities installed in the 50s. Beyond the park's edge, pedestrians navigate the Saturday morning crowds, their neural implants guiding them through traffic and conversations alike.

None of them is Luke.

My tablet chimes—a message from my niece. Not my biological niece, of course. After Luke vanished, I married my research instead of remarrying. My Saturdays at Treaty Oak became my dates. But Candace's children became my family by choice, by love. Sometimes it seems that everything is connected, that certain people were meant to meet. That some people were

253

meant to live together, to die together. That, I feel, is the fate of Luke and me. He's out there somewhere, waiting for the right moment for us to reconnect.

"You still at the tree, Aunt Eileen?" Hannah's message reads. "Remember, dinner's at seven. The whole family's coming."

I send back a simple confirmation. She knows where I am. They all do. They've stopped asking why.

Candace, of course, is the only one who understands that quantum entanglement doesn't just describe particles. Sometimes people become entangled too. Somewhere, somewhen, Luke Campbell still exists—that his disappearance in 2040, or 2035, or 2025—wasn't an ending but a continuation. At least, she nods and comforts at the right moments. And Luke's disappearance turned her research focus from computational astrophysics to quantum mechanics.

For me, the search took another form. I buried myself in the cave drawings, in the way ancient civilizations depicted time—spirals, loops, branching pathways. The cave wasn't unique; I found traces of similar images etched into stone in Mexico, in Turkey, in the ice-carved walls of forgotten Siberian caves. Some cultures had gods who existed outside of time. Others painted figures who seemed to walk forward and backward at once.

At first, my colleagues humored me. Then they dismissed me. Eventually, they ignored me altogether. My papers became footnotes in conversations about "fringe archaeology," a cautionary tale of what happens when a once-serious academic chases myths. I let them say what they wanted. I know what I saw.

Despite our separate lifelong research, Candance and I are no closer to finding Luke. But he's here somewhere. I can feel him here at the tree. Now, then, and in the future.

At first, I remembered losing Luke in 2035.

That was what the newspapers said. That was what the world believed. That was what *I* believed.

But over time, the details blurred. Mutated. New memories surfaced—ones where we had more time, where we had five full years together, where I lost him in 2040 instead.

I remember our wedding... I think. The scent of magnolias, the way Luke's hands shook when he slid the ring onto my finger. Or was it jasmine? And wasn't it me who hesitated? No—he laughed, didn't he? Said something about how time always had a way of bringing us back together. Or did I imagine that part?

I remember lazy mornings in our apartment, sunlight pooling across the floor as Luke painted, but the colors shift each time I recall them—sometimes ochre, sometimes deep blue, sometimes shades I don't think exist.

Candace had theories, of course. She always did. She used to tell me that Luke was never fully anchored, that his probability never truly collapsed into reality. That while I was looking for him, the past was still in motion, rewriting itself to fit what was coming next.

Which was true? Did I grieve him in 2035? Or did I watch him vanish five years later?

Or is reality still deciding?

"Excuse me."

I open my eyes to find a young man standing before me, maybe thirty, with a tablet and stylus instead of the neural interfaces most prefer now.

"I'm researching the Campbell art movement for my dissertation," he says. "You're Dr. Eileen Campbell, aren't you? Luke Campbell's wife?"

A familiar ache spreads through my chest, though I'm uncertain whether Luke and I even got married in this timeline.

"I am. How did you know where to find me?" I ask, looking around.

"Uh, your niece. She says you come here on Saturdays for lunch."

I close my eyes and silently thank Hannah for not saying the truth. Oh, sure, you'll find her at Treaty Oak, where she's been sitting for the last thirty years, waiting for her long-lost love to appear like a genie out of a bottle.

"How can I help you, Mr...?"

"Allan," he says. "Allan Proctor. I'm an MFA student at Jacksonville University."

And let me guess. Another art student wondering if my Luke borrowed from his namesake, the legendary founder of Campbellism, who vanished in 1925. The same tired questions about derivative work and coincidental connections.

"I wondered if you might share your perspective on his later works?"

I freeze. Something about the way he says 'later works' unnerves me.

"Particularly the 'Quantum Leap' series," he continues. "The pieces from the 2050s. The ones that predicted so much of modern quantum theory."

My breath catches. The 2050s?

"I'm sorry, but..." I shake my head. "Luke has created nothing since 2040. He—"

"Disappeared," Allan finishes for me. He glances down at his tablet. "Yeah. That's what some records say. But others... conflict."

He hesitates, fingers swiping over the screen. His brow furrows.

"I've found references to retrospectives in 2055. An auction listing in 2061. A lecture in New York in 2062. But when I checked the provenance on the later works, the paper trail just... stops. As if they appeared from nowhere."

"You're telling me history can't decide whether my husband has been gone for thirty years?" I say flatly.

He exhales a sharp laugh. "Yeah. Pretty much."

I press a hand to my temple, exasperated. But then he says something else, something that stops me cold.

"The Campbell market has been going crazy the last few years," Allan continues, scrolling through his notes. "His 'Temporal' series is selling for upwards of $20,000. But his original logging camp drawings? The ones from 1925?"

I already know what he's going to say.

"Those sold at Sotheby's for twenty million dollars."

I laugh bitterly. "Of course they did."

Allan hesitates, glancing back at his tablet. "What's strange, though—" He frowns. "The Luke Campbell from 1925 is regarded as a genius, the founder of Campbellism, a pioneer who defined an entire movement. But the later Luke?" He shakes his head. "His work was dismissed as derivative—critics said he was riding on the coattails of his predecessor."

He looks up at me, brow furrowed. "But that doesn't make

sense, does it? They're supposed to be the same person."

There it is. The flicker of recognition, the awareness that history is fractured, still smoothing itself out, still unsure how to tell the story of a man who lived everywhere and nowhere at once.

"Depends on who you ask," I say lightly, watching his face. "Some historians claim the later Luke was merely a follower of the original Campbellist school—someone mimicking the genius of the past. Others?" I pause, letting the silence stretch just long enough. "Well. Others wonder if they were always the same man."

Allan blinks. "But... that's impossible. Isn't it?"

I shrug. "You tell me. You're the researcher."

History is still folding itself into shape, still smoothing out the contradictions. Still deciding.

"If there ever was a paradox," I say finally, "it's right there. 1925 artist Luke Campbell disappears, and his works fetch millions. 2040 Luke Campbell disappears, and his works fetch a fraction of that. There's no logic in it, of course."

I glance up at Allan, giving him a small, knowing smile.

"It's as if the art world lives by the non-rules of quantum mechanics."

He frowns slightly, but before he can respond, I add, "That nothing is ever truly lost. Just temporarily unobserved."

Allan watches me for a moment, as if trying to decide whether I'm profound or just old. Then he nods politely, thanks me for my time, and walks away.

After he leaves, I gaze at the aged bark of Treaty Oak. My gaze drifts to the exact spot where Luke carved our initials thirty-five years ago. The bark has grown around it, swallowing the edges, but the mark remains. Or does it?

It's barely there—so faint that a casual observer would see nothing but a knot, a distortion in the wood, as if time itself were trying to erase us.

I am considering not coming back next Saturday. My body is tired. My mind, despite remaining sharp, yearns for rest. Maybe it's time to stop waiting. Maybe it's time to let go.

I struggle to stand, my knees protesting. The sun feels warmer than usual against my face. I look around one last time, taking in the tree, the park, the city beyond—all changed, all continuing without Luke.

"Goodbye," I whisper, to the tree or to Luke, I'm not sure.

I've taken three steps away when the air before me shimmers, like heat rising from asphalt. A distortion, a warping of light. I freeze, breath caught in my throat.

The shimmer intensifies. For an instant—just an instant—I see him. Luke. Not aged as I have aged, but exactly as he was in 2040. Our eyes meet across thirty years of waiting.

Then he's gone again.

But I know what I saw. I've seen this before, and I will see it again. I am the observer, according to Candace. I am the one keeping his quantum state from collapsing entirely. As long as I watch for him, as long as I wait beneath Treaty Oak, he exists somewhere in the quantum foam of possibility.

I turn around and return to my bench beneath the old, gnarled oak.

I will be back next Saturday. And every Saturday after that.

Because somewhere, somewhen, Luke is looking for me too.

FORTY-NINE: LUKE

I am nowhere. I am everywhere. I am fractured light scattered across a broken mirror.

Time doesn't flow around me anymore—I flow through it, or perhaps it flows through me. The distinction hardly matters when you've become unmoored from reality itself.

I see Jacksonville as it was, as it is, as it will be. Buildings rise and crumble before my eyes. People age, live, die in a heartbeat. I feel like I'm being pulled apart, my consciousness stretched across decades, centuries even.

The only constant is her. Eileen.

She sits beneath Treaty Oak, her hair now silver, her hands weathered by time. When I reach for her, the world bends away, warping like heated glass. Sometimes I can almost touch her— almost. I've learned to push myself toward her, to concentrate every fragmented piece of my being on her form. On rare occasions, I think she sees me.

My existence has become a series of snapshots, disconnected from one another:

A street corner in 2035—I'm crossing toward the café where Eileen waits. Then darkness, displacement.

The logging camp in 1925—whiskey warming my throat as I sketch what would later be called "early Campbellism."

Our apartment in 2038—Eileen asleep beside me, her breath steady against my chest.

Treaty Oak, over and over again, across decades. Eileen sitting. Waiting. Aging.

I wonder sometimes if I'm real. If I ever was. Or if I'm just the universe's way of observing itself, a consciousness without a body, a thought without a thinker.

Is this death? Or something altogether different?

"Dr. Campbell?"

A voice. Not directed at me, but at her—Eileen. I watch as a young man approaches her beneath the tree. I strain to hear their conversation, to connect with this moment more firmly than others.

"I'm researching the Campbell art movement for my dissertation," he says.

I painted those pieces. Or will paint them. Or have always been painting them. Tenses become meaningless when you exist outside of linear time.

He asks about the "Fracture" series. I remember creating those—paintings of timelines splintering, of moments existing simultaneously, of the cave on the Suwannee River where it all began. I painted them before we went to—or after we returned from—1925, it doesn't matter anymore, or perhaps I painted them in a time that doesn't exist—trying desperately to make sense of what had happened to us. Or will happen to us. To capture what I was seeing even then—the fraying of my connection to a singular timeline.

I didn't know then that I was painting my future. Or my past. Or both simultaneously. But now I understand completely.

Eileen answers him, her voice steady despite the pain I can see in her eyes. "You're telling me history can't decide whether my husband has been gone for thirty years?"

I want to tell her she's wrong. I haven't been gone for thirty years. I've been painting what I saw, what I felt, for an eternity. The understanding came later, after I'd been torn from time's fabric, after I became whatever I am now.

I see Candace too—Candace at thirty, at forty, at seventy, working on equations that describe my fractured existence better than my art ever could. In some moments, I can even see her presentations, hear her lecturing about quantum consciousness, about observation and reality.

"Looking at something changes it," she tells a rapt audience in a timeline I can barely grasp. "Reality isn't something fixed, but something we built by watching, waiting, remembering." I couldn't understand her then. I do now.

I am the observed and the observer. This is what Candace tried to explain, back when I was still fully real. That the moment we are seen, we are defined. That looking for someone keeps them from being lost.

I watch Eileen watch for me. I see her coming to Treaty Oak, week after week, year after year. I see myself by her side for each moment. Her constancy is both my anchor and my prison.

I see what would have happened if she had stopped—if one day she had walked away from Treaty Oak and never returned. My consciousness, such as it is, would have dissipated. I would have ceased to exist in any meaningful way.

But she never stops. Even now, as she considers it—I can feel her weariness, her doubt—she stays. She returns to her bench. She waits.

And I continue to exist in this halfway state, suspended between being and non-being.

I gather myself, focus my fractured awareness into this moment, this place. I push against the barrier separating us, straining against the quantum membrane that keeps me from her.

For a moment—just a moment—I am fully measured, observed, defined. Eileen sees me, and that makes me real. The scattered fragments of my existence pull together, locking into place.

I see her directly, not through the veil of scattered time. Our eyes meet—steady, searching, knowing.

I try to speak, to reach out, but the connection is already fading, slipping through my grasp like light bending away from a horizon. Before she can hold onto me, before I can hold onto myself, the universe decides otherwise.

I'm being pulled back, stretched thin across a thousand moments once again.

But in that brief connection, I understood something. Something profound about existence itself.

Reality is not fixed. It's not immutable. It's created in the spaces between observers and the observed. It exists in the connections we forge, in the persistence of memory, in the stubborn refusal to let go.

If Eileen is waiting for me, I exist.

If I am reaching for her, she has purpose.

We are entangled beyond time, beyond space, beyond conventional understanding. Not just our particles, but our very consciousness.

The cave was just the beginning. It opened the door to something much deeper, something weaving through the fabric of reality itself.

I will find a way back to her. Not just in glimpses and shimmers, but fully, completely. I don't know how yet, but I will.

Because somewhere, somewhen, we belong together.

And time, for all its power, cannot change that.

FIFTY: EILEEN

I wake up early, feeling the weight of my decision. Today will be my last Saturday at Treaty Oak. I've already packed up the bench supplies I keep ready—the small cushion for my back, the thermos of tea, the book I never actually read. After thirty years, it's time.

Hannah calls as I'm about to leave.

"You're still coming for dinner tonight, right?" Her voice carries the same gentle concern it always does, carefully avoiding any mention of my Saturday ritual.

"Of course," I say. "And Hannah?"

"Yes, Aunt Eileen?"

"Thank you. For understanding."

She's quiet for a moment. "You're saying goodbye to him today, aren't you?"

I don't answer immediately. After decades of everyone tiptoeing around my Saturday visits, it feels strange to acknowledge it so directly.

"Yes," I finally say. "I am."

"I'll pick you up afterward. Just call when you're ready."

The morning is unusually clear for June in Florida. Climate shifts have made our summers brutal, but today feels like a reprieve—cooler, less humid, the sky an impossible blue. Perhaps even the weather is acknowledging my farewell.

The park is quiet when I arrive. No docents approach me today; perhaps they sense something different in my demeanor. The bench—my bench—sits empty beneath Treaty Oak, waiting for me one last time.

"Hello, old friend," I whisper, running my hand along the oak's gnarled trunk.

The bark feels different somehow—warmer, almost vibrating beneath my palm. I chalk it up to my emotional state, to the significance of this final visit.

I settle onto the bench, my bones protesting as they always do. Thirty years of Saturdays have carved grooves into this wood that match the curves of my body. I wonder who will sit here after me, if they'll feel the imprint I've left behind.

"I can't keep doing this, Luke," I say to the empty air. "I think even you would understand that."

My words drift into silence. No one answers, of course. No one has answered for thirty years.

I close my eyes, allowing myself to remember. Our first meeting at his gallery opening. The cave at Big Shoals. 1925. Our return. Our brief, beautiful marriage. His disappearance. The decades of research with Candace, trying to understand what happened, trying to find Luke.

And the cave. I went back, of course. How could I not?

At first, the river still ran strong, carving its way through limestone as it had for thousands of years. But time has a way of erasing things. Year after year, the waterline crept lower, the clear rush of the Suwannee thickening into green algae, then shrinking to a trickle. Now, it's barely more than a stagnant stream. Another thing lost to time.

The cave is still there. Waiting. But without the river, it looks wrong—like a doorway without a house attached.

I stood at the entrance, staring into the dark, trying to force myself to step inside. But I never did. Because God knows what that would do to Luke, or where it would send me. Or if it would take me anywhere at all.

Candace sent in a robot once. The robot saw nothing. No anomalies. No distortions. No hint of what had happened to us.

That was when I stopped looking for proof.

But my own research never stopped, either. I spent years asking the same question in a thousand different ways: Were the cave drawings simply describing myths? Or were they depicting something real?

Candace's words echo in my head, "Keep waiting, Eileen. The math says it's possible."

But that was twenty years ago. She stopped telling me to wait back then. But she didn't tell me to stop either.

I stand up, my decision firm. One last touch of the tree, one final goodbye, and I'll call Hannah.

I place my palm against the tree's bark, feeling the rough texture beneath my skin.

"Goodbye, Luke," I whisper. "I've loved you across time. I hope that was enough."

I turn away when something shifts. The air tightens, pressure building in my ears like the moment before a storm. A shimmer dances at the edges of my vision, heat rising from the ground in distorted waves.

It's familiar. The spirals, the branching paths, the figures walking forward and backward in the same moment. I once thought those depictions were metaphors—artistic flourishes. Now, I wonder if those ancient artists were simply trying to paint what they saw.

Static electricity raises the hair on my arms. The distortion intensifies, the air bending—literally bending—like space itself is warping around a central point in front of me. My ears pop. A low hum builds, vibrating through my chest, through the ground beneath my feet.

I should be afraid, but I'm not. Something in me recognizes what's happening before my conscious mind can fully process it.

The distortion folds in on itself like origami. Light fractures around the edges, splitting into prismatic colors. The humming grows louder, more insistent.

And then—

Luke is here.

Not a glimpse, not a shimmer, but Luke himself. Solid. Real. Standing before me with the same bewildered expression he wore that first day in the gallery when he saw my cave drawings merged with his dental chair painting. He reaches for me, his hand trembling. When his fingers touch my cheek, they're warm. Real.

"Eileen." His voice is exactly as I remember it. "I found you."

The world seems to hold its breath. For thirty years, I've imagined this moment, dreamed it, calculated its probability with Candace's equations. And now that it's here, I find I have no words.

So I do the only thing that makes sense. I step forward, into his arms, and hold him.

After all this time. After all the Saturdays. After all the waiting. Luke has come home.

* * *

We sit beneath Treaty Oak, side by side, on my bench. I've not let go of his hand since the moment he appeared, afraid that if I break contact, he might dissolve like morning mist. The initial euphoria of reunion has given way to something more complex—a tangle of emotions I can't fully unravel.

"You haven't aged," I say, studying his face. The same face I've seen in dreams for decades. The same dark eyes, the same expression of gentle concentration when he's puzzling something out. "Not a day."

"And you've lived thirty years without me." His voice breaks on the words, his fingers gently tracing the lines time has etched into my face.

The tenderness in his touch triggers something unexpected—a flare of anger. I pull away slightly, surprising us both.

"Thirty-five years," I correct him, an edge in my voice I didn't intend. "Thirty-five years of waiting. Of wondering. Of sitting on this bench every Saturday like a fool."

But had it been that long? I'm no longer sure. It feels like we've been apart for decades, and yet it feels like he was here yesterday.

His face falls. "Eileen—"

"Do you know what it was like?" The words tumble out now, unstoppable. "To wake up every Saturday morning, hoping today would be the day you'd return? To gradually watch everyone decide I was delusional? To see pity in their eyes when I refused to accept you were gone forever?"

I hadn't planned this, hadn't even known these feelings were simmering beneath the surface, but now they pour forth like a dam breaking.

"I missed so many moments I'd imagined sharing with you," I say, my voice catching. "All the discoveries, the milestones. I kept expecting to see you walk through the door, and you never did."

Luke's eyes glisten with tears. "I'm so sorry. If I could have found my way back sooner—"

"I know," I interrupt, softening. "I know you would have. It's not your fault. It's just—" I struggle to articulate the contradiction twisting inside me. "I'm overjoyed you're here. And I'm furious that you weren't."

A memory surfaces, unbidden—sitting alone in my office after receiving tenure, the achievement hollow without him to celebrate it with me. The silence of my apartment that night, no one to toast with, no one who truly understood what it meant.

"I never left our apartment," I tell him, the words coming easier now. "I kept expecting the memories to fade, but they only grew stronger. Sometimes I'd wake up thinking you were just in the next room."

Another memory—my fiftieth birthday. Candace had organized a small gathering. Everyone carefully skirted around the subject of Luke, concerned that mentioning him might shatter me. I had smiled and thanked them, and later sat alone looking at old brochures and newspaper clippings from Luke's art show, mourning not just what was lost but what might have been.

"There were good times too," I say, gentler now. "I've had a meaningful career. Made discoveries about the cave drawings that challenged conventional thinking. Candace pursued quantum physics and convinced me there might be a scientific explanation for what happened to us. We never stopped looking for answers."

Luke listens, drinking in every word, every detail of the life he missed. I see hunger in his eyes, the desperate need to recover lost time, to understand the woman I've become in his absence.

"You never gave up on me," he whispers.

"I almost did. Today. That's why—" I gesture vaguely around us. "That's why you're here now, isn't it? Because I was finally letting go."

He nods slowly. "Candace's observer effect theory."

I look at him, surprised. "How do you know about that?"

"I..." He hesitates, looking confused. "I'm not sure. It feels like I've been... everywhere, Eileen. Watching moments of your life. Fragments of conversations, decisions, discoveries. As if I was spread across time itself."

"As long as I was actively looking for you, expecting you—"

"I was in superposition—everywhere and nowhere," he finishes.

The scientific explanation doesn't diminish the miracle of it. If anything, it makes it more profound—the universe bending its own rules to bring us back together. But I also feel a sharp stab of guilt. If my decision to stop waiting brought him back, what would have happened if I'd given up sooner? Or never stopped looking at all?

"I don't know if this is real," I admit, voicing the fear that's been lurking at the border of my consciousness. "If you're really here. Or if you'll stay."

A family passes by our bench, a young mother pointing out the massive branches of Treaty Oak to her wide-eyed child. The little girl breaks away from her mother and runs toward us, stopping just short of our bench. She stares at Luke with unabashed curiosity.

"Your hair is the same as my dad's," she announces, pointing to the slight wave in Luke's dark hair.

Her mother hurries over. "Emma, don't bother the nice people," she says with an apologetic smile.

Luke grins at the child. "That's a very nice compliment. Thank you."

The girl beams before being led away by her mother. I feel something uncurl in my chest. He's real. Others can see him. Touch him. He's not just visible to me.

"I've imagined this so many times," I continue once they've gone. "Dreamed it. Hallucinated it during those first desperate years. How do I know this isn't just another dream? That I won't wake up alone again?"

"You don't," Luke says. He takes my hand again, his thumb brushing over my knuckles. "Neither do I. I've been... fragmented for so long. Scattered across time. This could be another fragment."

The admission should frighten me, but instead, it comforts. This Luke—solid and warm beside me—understands the uncertainty of existence in a way the Luke of my memory couldn't have.

"We'll have to learn each other again," I say, the realization both daunting and exhilarating. "I'm not the same woman you left behind."

"And I'm not the same man," he agrees. "But some things don't change." He lifts our joined hands. "This. Us. Whatever else shifts, this remains constant."

I want to believe him. Part of me already does. But thirty-five years of scientific training has taught me to question, to doubt, to look for evidence.

"My life has patterns now," I tell him. "Routines. Habits formed over decades alone. I don't know how to... how to be with someone again."

Luke turns to me, his expression suddenly curious. "You still clean the kitchen sink before leaving for work, don't you? 'Clean house, clean mind,' your grandmother used to say."

I stare at him, startled. "How could you possibly know that?"

He shrugs, looking equally confused. "I... I'm not sure. It's like I've lived a ghostly version of your life alongside you. Some memories are clear, others feel like dreams I can barely recall."

The idea is both comforting and unsettling—that even while separated, some part of him witnessed my life unfolding. That I was never truly alone.

A memory flashes through my mind—our wedding day, Luke's hands shaking slightly as he slid the brass wedding ring onto my finger. The way the afternoon light caught in his hair, turning the edges golden. The promise in his eyes, the certainty that we would face whatever came next together.

But the memory feels strangely distant now, like viewing it through frosted glass. The edges blur, details shift, and rearrange themselves. Was his tie blue or gray? Did we have flowers or candles on the tables? The harder I try to focus, the more the image seems to dissolve. It's like a whiteboard gradually being erased, leaving only ghostly impressions behind.

Another memory—the first anniversary I spent without him. The small cake I bought anyway, the candle I lit, the wish I made. This memory too, feels uncertain, wavering between sharp clarity and fuzzy incompleteness. Year after year, the same wish, until eventually... did I stop? I can't quite remember now.

And now, impossibly, that wish is fulfilled. But the fulfillment itself is changing what I wish for, what I remember wishing for.

"Hannah is expecting me for dinner," I say, breaking the spell of memory. "She's going to be... I don't even know how she'll react to you."

"Will she recognize me? Remember me?"

"She never knew you. She's Candace's daughter—born five years after you disappeared. She calls me 'Aunt Eileen'."

A shadow crosses his face—the first of many moments where the reality of lost time will strike him anew, I suspect.

"So much lost," he murmurs.

"So much still to come," I counter, surprised by my optimism.

I stand, pulling him gently to his feet beside me. "Come on. Let's go back to the apartment first. I should call Hannah and prepare her. And you should see where I've—where we've—been living."

As we walk away from Treaty Oak, I can feel the weight of thirty-five years lightening with each step. Not gone—those years will always be part of me, part of us—but transforming into something new. Something shared.

I glance back once at the empty bench. The place where I've spent so many Saturdays waiting.

Luke's hand is warm in mine as we make our way through the park. I still half-expect him to vanish with each step, to dissolve like a mirage when tested too thoroughly. But he remains solid, real, present.

"Across time," he says softly, echoing our old promise.

"Across everything," I finish.

And for now, that's enough. The rest—the complications, the adjustments, the reconciliation of parallel lives—will come later. For now, it's enough to walk beside him, to feel the familiar rhythm of his steps matching mine, to know that whatever comes next, we face it together.

After thirty-five years of waiting, we have time.

FIFTY-ONE: LUKE

I stumble forward, my feet suddenly solid against the ground. Gravity pulls at me with unfamiliar, yet familiar, weight. The world around me is sharp, defined—no longer the blur of overlapping timelines I've existed in for... how long?

My thoughts are my own again. Singular. Focused. The countless fragments of consciousness that have been me-but-not-me are gone, collapsed into this one reality, this one moment.

I am whole.

Yet the very completeness is overwhelming. After existing everywhere and nowhere, the sudden specificity of being here, now, assaults my senses. The breeze against my skin feels like sandpaper. The birdsong from overhead drills through my eardrums. Colors are too vivid, edges too sharp. My vision pulses with each heartbeat, the world expanding and contracting in nauseating waves.

I reach out to steady myself against the shock of it, my hand finding Eileen's shoulder. The contact is electric—skin against skin, actual touch after an endless void of almost-connections. The sensation sends a jolt through my system, anchoring me when everything else threatens to dissolve.

"Eileen." Her name feels solid in my mouth, the syllables taking physical form on my tongue.

But as my vision clears, as I really see her, my chest tightens painfully.

Her face, once smooth and youthful, is mapped with lines. Her hair, once full of color, is silver white. Only her eyes remain unchanged—the same intense gaze that captured me at the gallery opening a lifetime ago.

How long have I been gone? Years? Decades? Minutes?

Time has no meaning when you've experienced it all at once. I remember being in the cave with Eileen yesterday, our hands clasped as blue light engulfed us. I remember stepping in front of a bus—the impact I both did and didn't feel—not a violent bang but the clapping of cosmic hands, a magician's trapdoor, a splintering pane of glass. I remember watching Eileen sit beneath this very tree, growing older while I remained suspended in quantum foam.

I have a memory—our apartment by Memorial Park. The way the afternoon light spilled through the floor-to-ceiling windows, catching the edges of Eileen's books stacked haphazardly on the coffee table. Electric cars hummed by outside, their movement effortless, sleek, soundless. The city felt alive, pulsing, always pushing forward. But then—

Another layer presses in.

A different version of our apartment slides into focus. The furniture is rearranged, as if shifted by invisible hands. On the wall hangs a painting I don't remember painting, but I know it's mine— I can still feel the brush in my fingers, the gentle pressure of each brushstroke.

My vision shifts again. A tablet sits on the counter, its display glowing faintly with a message I don't recall writing. Through the windows, the world outside has transformed—sharper, cleaner, more efficient. Self-driving cars glide by, no longer bound to roads as I knew them.

Another shift—something ultra-modern appears, technology beyond what I could have imagined before I... before I what?

Before I disappeared? Before time unspooled around me?

I try to place myself in one of these memories, to anchor myself in a singular moment, but they keep shifting. Folding. I remember a voice—Eileen's?—calling my name, but from where? From when?

The disorientation is physical. My stomach lurches as if I'm falling from a great height. Sweat beads on my forehead. My lungs can't seem to get enough air—each breath feeling shallow, insufficient. The solid ground beneath my feet might as well be quicksand.

I reach for a memory, any memory, to stabilize myself. What is real? What actually happened?

I remember the logging camp of 1925. The smell of pine sap and sweat. The weight of the tree trunks in my hands, blisters forming and breaking on my palms. The burn of whiskey down my throat as I sketched that grizzled logger. That happened. I know it did.

But I also remember a gallery opening in 2052. Eileen beside me, both of us in sleek eveningwear, champagne flutes in hand as critics praised my "retrospective vision." Her hair with silver streaks, then her hand in mine as we navigated the crowd. Did that happen? Could it have?

I remember watching Eileen from outside of time—seeing her work late into the night, seeing her sit beneath this tree Saturday after Saturday, seeing her grow older while I remained untethered. I was everywhere and nowhere, observing but never taking part. A ghost haunting my own life.

"Luke?" Her voice breaks on my name, and I hear both joy and disbelief in it.

I touch her face, my hand trembling. The skin beneath my fingertips is paper-thin, delicate. Evidence of years I haven't lived.

Decades.

The realization crashes down on me like I've been struck by a falling tree. Decades have passed for her while I've been... elsewhere. Everywhere. Nowhere.

"I found you," I manage to say, though I'm not sure how I did. I only know that the endless floating—or was it seconds?—the disjointed existence I've been trapped in has finally stopped.

She steps into my arms, and I hold her, feeling how much smaller she's become. Frailer. But her embrace is still strong, still fierce with determination.

Around us, the world continues as if nothing miraculous has happened. Carolina chickadees call from Treaty Oak's branches. Distant voices carry from other parts of the park. A warm breeze stirs the leaves overhead.

But everything has changed. I am here. I am now. I am singular.

My memories of the in-between are already fading, slipping away like dreams upon waking, yet they leave impressions— emotional fossils buried in the sediment of my consciousness. I remember glimpses—Eileen sitting beneath this very tree at different ages, the logging camp in 1925, our apartment in 2038. I remember seeing her speak with a young man. Yesterday? A week ago? Time has no meaning in the place I've been.

The strangest part is my body. I look down at my hands—hands that should have aged, should have weathered, and spotted with time. Instead, they're unchanged. The same hands that held Eileen's hand in the cave the day of the bus accident. I am a temporal anomaly—thirty-five years out of place, a living anachronism.

"How long?" I ask, my voice hoarse.

She pulls back just enough to look at me, her hands still gripping my arms as if I might disappear again.

"Thirty-five years," she says. "It's 2070, Luke."

2070? Thirty-five years. The date echoes in my mind but refuses to take shape, to become real.

"Thirty..." My voice breaks. I stare at her hands holding mine—hands that have turned pages, created art, grown older without me there to witness it. Hands that have lived a life I was supposed to share.

I've missed birthdays, anniversaries, ordinary Sunday mornings, percolating coffee, tidying up the apartment, watering the plants. Fights and reconciliations. Moments of triumph and despair. All the small, precious seconds that make up a lifetime together—gone in what felt to me like the blink of an eye. So why do I remember them?

2070. I try to comprehend it. When I last existed fully in a single moment, augmented reality was just becoming mainstream. Climate adaptation was a growing industry. The first lunar base was being constructed. Now? I've skipped forward almost half a century.

And Eileen has lived every minute of it without me. While I've been suspended in temporal limbo, she's experienced decades of life: joy, pain, growth, change. She's a woman I both know intimately and don't know at all.

I remember a conversation never had, a moment never lived. Eileen, in middle age, her hair just beginning to gray, telling me about a breakthrough in her research. The pride in her voice as she described finding a connection between the cave drawings and Candace's work on quantum displacement. I heard her, saw her, but couldn't reach her—like I was pressing my hand against the thick glass separating us.

I remember watching her receive her doctorate, wanting to applaud but having no hands to clap. I remember her crying alone on our anniversary, wanting to comfort her, but having no arms to hold her. Present but absent. Close but unreachable.

My chest constricts, breath coming shallow as the magnitude of what I've lost—what we've lost—finally hits me. Years that should have been ours vanished into the abyss between quantum states.

"I wasn't there," I whisper, the words inadequate for the canyon of absence between us. "All those years, Eileen. I wasn't there for you."

The world continued without me while I drifted through the intangible foam of existence. And she waited. She aged. She lived in linear time while I existed everywhere and nowhere.

I feel the weight of a wedding band on my finger—solid, familiar. The cool metal warms against my skin as I twist it absently. Was this ring always here? Did I marry Eileen in some timeline I only half-remember?

A memory flickers, half-formed. A baby girl—Harriet? Henrietta? I see her laughing, growing, reaching for me with small hands. I can almost feel the gentle weight as I lifted her up, see her toothless smile, hear her delighted gurgles. The memory feels real and not-real simultaneously, like all the quantum possibilities of a life I both lived and didn't live.

My daughter? No—a niece. But the certainty wavers, the details shifting like light on water. Did she ever exist? Or is time still deciding?

I remember being in Barcelona with Eileen, though I've never been to Barcelona. I remember a knee injury from falling off a ladder, though my knee is perfectly fine. I remember teaching Hannah to paint when she was ten, though I'm only meeting her today.

These false memories feel as substantial as my real ones—perhaps more so, because they're sharpening while my fracture-state recollections blur. I can almost taste the bergamot tea Candace served me in 2045, yet my memory of floating through timelines is already dissolving.

"I don't understand," I say, though part of me does.

During my time... away... I've absorbed knowledge that shouldn't be mine. Quantum mechanics. Candace's theories. The mathematics of observation and reality. Knowledge that floated through the ether where I existed, that I somehow grasped despite having no formal training in physics.

"Candace used to say she thought you could be in superposition," Eileen says, as if reading my thoughts. "Not fully here, not fully gone. Candace and I... we tried to understand it. To bring you back."

I remember Candace too—younger, then older, working at equations I shouldn't comprehend but somehow do. I remember watching over her shoulder as she developed the theory that would eventually explain my state of being. I couldn't speak to her then, couldn't tell her she was on the right track. I was just an observer, not a participant.

"Is she...?" I can't finish the question.

"Yes, she's still alive," Eileen says gently. "And I can't wait for you to meet her. You inspired her life's work."

The park bench is behind us. I sink onto it, my legs suddenly unable to support me. Eileen sits beside me, her hand never leaving mine.

"What happens now?" I ask.

The question encompasses everything. What do we do when I haven't aged, and she's lived a whole life without me? What happens to a man out of time, born in one century, living briefly in another, now thrust into a third?

I am thirty-five years old in a body that hasn't lived those years. I've witnessed decades I haven't experienced. I'm simultaneously old and young—time-worn in mind but untouched in body.

"Now," she says, squeezing my hand, "we go home."

Home. The word resonates strangely. My home—our apartment—should be long gone. But it isn't. It's here. Now.

The world I knew, already shifting in 2025, should be unrecognizable in 2070. But it's not. Not entirely. I see a young girl on a skateboard—no, a hoverboard—tapping at a neural implant above her left ear. The technology is unfamiliar, but the carefree joy on her face is timeless. Some things never change, even as everything around them does.

"I kept your things," Eileen says, seeing my expression. "Your paintings. Your clothes. Everything I could."

I nod, unable to speak past the lump in my throat.

"The world is different now," she continues. "But we'll figure it out. Together."

Together. After thirty-five years apart. After I've remained fixed in time while she's lived through decades. The space between us should be vast—an entire lifetime stretched between her world and mine.

And yet, as we hold hands, I feel it collapse. The years, the waiting, the lost time—it folds inward, compressing like paper drawn into a single point. The impossible distance between us shrinks to nothing.

"We will always find each other," I say, remembering how we reconnected across time before. "Across time. Across everything."

She smiles, and I see the younger Eileen overlaid on this older version. Same smile. Same spirit. Same determination.

"We do," she agrees. "Though I think we're done with time travel now."

I laugh, the sound startling me with its normality. "God, I hope so."

We sit for a moment in silence. I look up at Treaty Oak, marveling at how little it's changed compared to the city skyline beyond. In my fractured memories, I've seen this tree at many points in its life—and in many possible futures. But now I'm anchored to one timeline, one reality.

"I know why I came back today," I say.

"Why?"

"Because today was the first day you truly stopped waiting. To let me go."

She turns to me, her eyes bright with unshed tears. "The observer effect."

"Exactly," I say. "As long as you kept waiting, kept watching for me, I remained in superposition—both here and not here. But when you finally accepted I might never return..."

"The waveform collapsed," she finishes, the physics somehow making perfect sense to us both now. "You had to fully disappear before you could fully return."

I nod. That's what Candace thought might happen.

"I didn't believe her," Eileen continues, as if reading my mind. "I kept waiting anyway."

"For thirty-five years."

"For thirty-five years," she repeats.

I study her—and see the cost of those decades in every line on her face. But I also see the strength, the brilliance, the stubbornness that is quintessentially Eileen.

The disorientation hasn't fully lifted. My senses still feel too sharp, too present. But now there's something else alongside the confusion—a growing certainty. I am here. I am now. I am real.

The fractures are healing. Reality is solidifying around me, accommodating my presence after decades of absence.

"I'm sorry," I say. "That I wasn't here."

She shakes her head. "You were. Just not in a way either of us understood."

I feel the truth of this. Even in my fragmented state, I was always reaching for her, always trying to find my way back.

She brushes her fingers through my hair, pausing. "You have a gray hair above your ear," she murmurs, her voice touched with something between wonder and amusement—like I'm thirty-two again, and she's noticing the first one.

I let out a breath, neither laughter nor a sigh, just something in between. The weight of time is different now. Lighter. Not something lost, but something we still have.

"What do we do now?" I ask again, but this time the question is different. Not filled with despair, but with curiosity. With possibility.

She stands and holds out her hand to me. "First, we call Hannah to pick us up. She will not believe this. Then we figure out how to introduce you to a world that thinks you've been dead for decades."

I take her hand and rise. "Sounds simple enough."

Her laughter fills me with lightness. "Nothing about us has ever been simple, Luke Campbell."

I look at our joined hands—hers weathered by time, mine unchanged—and feel a strange sense of peace settling over me. Whatever comes next, we'll face it as a couple. Across time. Across everything.

"Let's go home," I say.

As we leave Treaty Oak, we leave behind an eternity of waiting and an empty bench that will never be sat on in quite the same way again.

FIFTY-TWO: EILEEN

Hannah's expression when she pulls up to Treaty Oak is impossible to categorize. She steps out of her sleek electric car with the same efficient grace that Candace always had, though Hannah's features are softer, less angular. Her dark hair—a mix of Candace's curls and her father's straighter texture—falls in gentle waves just past her shoulders. Unlike her mother's analytical intensity, Hannah's warm amber eyes hold a gentler intelligence, now clouded with confusion as she approaches us. At thirty-four, she carries herself with the confident poise of someone established in her career, dressed in a simple linen dress that suggests both practicality and style.

She looks at Luke for some time, confusion and recognition battling across her face. A slight crease appears between her brows—the same expression Candace would get when confronted with a perplexing equation. It's like she's caught between two versions of the same past. I don't know how this works—if certain memories change all at once or if people just stop questioning the gaps.

But I know this: Luke wasn't here before. And now he is. And reality is still catching up.

Hannah's face remains locked in that furrowed-brow expression, her lips parting like she wants to say something but can't find the words.

She steps back, glancing between me and Luke, her confusion deepening. "I—this isn't—I don't know what's wrong, but something isn't right."

Her fingers go to her temple like she's trying to press a memory into place. "You... you were at my high school graduation," she says slowly, then shakes her head. "No, that can't be right. You weren't."

She takes another step back, swallowing hard. "I remember you. But I don't remember you."

Then, as if some internal switch flips, the hesitation smooths away. The tension drains from her face. She nods once. "Never mind. That's silly. Of course you were there."

"Uncle Luke," she says finally, then frowns. "I—"

She stops, shaking her head as if to clear it, her silver earrings catching the afternoon light. Her gaze flickers between us, landing on our joined hands.

"I'm sorry," she continues, "I just... felt like I've always known you, but that's not right, is it?"

Hannah's gaze lingers on Luke. Whatever contradiction her brain is registering, it dismisses it as unimportant. She remembers Luke being here, so of course he must be.

I wonder if she even sees him as I do—unchanged from 2040—or if her mind has already aged him in ways I can't perceive.

I squeeze Luke's hand. We'd prepared for many reactions—shock, disbelief, suspicion—but not this strange half-recognition. But then again, isn't this what happened to us in 1925? Sliding into a timeline that we didn't belong in, greeted with a sense of half-belonging, and garnering odd looks from those around us?

"Hannah," I say carefully, "this is Luke. My husband."

"I know," she says, then looks puzzled by her own certainty. "I mean, I've seen photos, of course. You're exactly how I... remember you?"

Luke steps forward. "It's nice to meet you," he says, extending his hand. "Again."

Hannah laughs nervously, shaking his hand. "This is weird. I keep having these... flashes. Like you taught me to paint when I was ten?"

In the car, Hannah chatters about dinner plans, occasionally glancing at Luke in the rearview mirror with that same mix of familiarity and uncertainty. "Mom's been cooking all day. She's making that lasagna you like."

Luke raises an eyebrow at me. Hannah has never met him before today.

"With the extra basil?" Luke asks.

"Yes!" Hannah says. "That's it exactly!" Then her smile falters. "Wait, how did I know that?"

The world isn't just accepting Luke—it's actively rewriting itself to accommodate him. But the edits are incomplete, imperfect. Like a document with tracked changes that haven't been fully resolved.

At Hannah's house, things become stranger still. Hannah's best friend Meredith greets us at the door, her eyes widening when she sees Luke.

"Mr. Luke!" she says, embracing him without hesitation. Then she pulls back, confusion clouding her features. "I didn't know you were coming. When did you get back from... from..."

She can't complete the thought. There's nowhere in her memory for Luke to have returned from.

"It's complicated," I say, touching her arm gently.

Inside, family photos line the hallway. I stop short, staring at a picture that wasn't there last week—Luke and I at Hannah's college graduation. I've never seen this photo before. Luke wasn't there. He couldn't have been.

Yet there he is, smiling beside me, wearing a blue shirt I recognize from 2038.

"What is it?" Luke asks, following my gaze.

"You weren't at Hannah's graduation," I whisper. "That was 2059."

Luke studies the photo. "But I remember it. Sort of. Like a dream I had."

More inconsistencies emerge throughout the evening. Hannah's boyfriend, Charlie, claps Luke on the shoulder. "Still got that vintage Mustang? Man, I'd love to take it for another spin sometime."

Luke has never owned a Mustang.

Later, Hannah scrolls through her phone and shows Luke a social media post. "Is this your painting? It just went viral on ArtSpace."

The image shows a work I've never seen before—unmistakably Luke's style, but executed with techniques and materials that didn't exist in 2040.

"When did you paint that?" I whisper to Luke.

"I didn't," he says. "At least, I don't think I did. Or maybe I did." He shrugs his shoulders like I just asked him for the forty-seventh prime number. Again. When did I ask him that? The memory is fuzzy, distant from decades ago.

Records are materializing, creating a digital footprint for Luke that extends beyond his disappearance. At dinner, Meredith mentions an art retrospective from 2055 that featured Luke's work. "You gave that wonderful speech about temporality in art. The Times called it 'prophetic'."

Luke and I exchange glances. He was floating in quantum superposition in 2055, not giving speeches.

After dinner, while the others clean up, I pull out my tablet and search for Luke Campbell. Results flood the screen—exhibition reviews from 2045, 2052, 2060. A faculty profile at Jacksonville University showing him as a professor emeritus. Medical records. Tax filings.

But there are inconsistencies. One article places him in New York for a 2050 exhibition, while another has him teaching in Florida during the same period. His medical history shows treatments for conditions he never had. Employment records overlap impossibly.

I refresh the database. A review of his 2052 exhibition is gone. In its place, a 2053 interview appears. It's like watching reality rewrite itself in real time, each correction introducing new errors.

I watch as the system struggles to settle on a single version of history, but the contradictions remain. Luke both was and wasn't here for the last thirty-five years.

* * *

"It's retrocausality," Luke tells me as we sit on Hannah's back porch later that evening. "Not just probability collapse."

"Meaning?"

"In quantum mechanics, when a particle finally occupies a definite state, it doesn't just affect the present—it affects the past as well. The universe is trying to create a coherent timeline that includes me, but it can't resolve all the contradictions."

"So, you were here, but not here, these last decades."

Luke watches the sunset, his face illuminated by the orange glow. "Exactly. My waveform collapsed when you stopped actively maintaining my superposition, but my existence is rippling backward, creating memories and records that didn't exist before today."

"Just like in 1925," I say. "People accepted us, but something always felt off to them."

He nods. "We fit, but not perfectly."

Hannah joins us on the porch, handing us each a glass of wine. She studies Luke thoughtfully.

"I keep remembering you at events I know you couldn't have attended," she says. "Like Dad's memorial service. I have this clear image of you standing beside Aunt Eileen, but..." She tilted her head as if weighing her words. "And there are photos of you in our family albums that I swear weren't there before."

"Memory is tricky," I say, not quite lying.

"Wait," Hannah says suddenly, eyes narrowing. "Weren't you at my dad's retirement party? The one at the riverside restaurant?" She hesitates, doubt creeping in. "No... that's not right. I'm thinking of someone else..."

Luke smiles. "Maybe in another life."

By the time we leave Hannah's house, something has settled. The inconsistencies remain, but they're less jarring. Reality is still adjusting, still accommodating Luke's presence, but the process feels less frantic, less disjointed.

In the car on the drive back to my—our—apartment, Luke stares out the window at the changed cityscape. He frowns. "I feel... off. Like I haven't fully landed yet."

I squeeze his hand. "Candace would say it's just residual something."

"Quantum oscillation," Luke says. "My probability is still settling into place."

My smile is faint. "So you could still disappear?"

"Not if I have anything to say about it."

"Will it ever stabilize?" I ask. "Or will you always be a glitch in the timeline?"

He takes my hand. "Candace would say the waveform will eventually reach equilibrium. Given enough time, the universe will construct a coherent narrative that includes me. The contradictions will smooth out."

I think about the decades spent waiting for him, about quantum entanglement, and the stubbornness of the universe.

"I say it doesn't matter," I tell him. "Reality is overrated."

He laughs, and the sound sends warmth through me. "You sound like a true physicist. Maybe you missed your calling."

As we drive through the night, the city lights reflect off the windows, creating an effect that reminds me of Luke's fracture paintings—reality, split and recombined, never quite the same but beautiful in its complexity.

"We're going to be okay," I say, more to myself than to Luke.

He squeezes my hand. "We always are. Across time. Across everything."

Some things, it seems, remain constant even when reality itself is in flux.

FIFTY-THREE: LUKE

Candace's home sits on the edge of Jacksonville, nestled among live oaks nearly as old as Treaty Oak itself. The house is modest but beautiful—a low-slung Craftsman with solar panels and a garden that seems to blend seamlessly with the surrounding wilderness.

"She's been expecting you," Eileen says as we park in the driveway. "Not like Hannah and Meredith. She's known all along that this might happen."

"Because of her work in quantum physics?" I ask, a knot forming in my stomach.

Eileen squeezes my hand. "She's spent decades trying to understand what happened to you."

My fingers tighten around the door handle. The last time I saw Candace—from my perspective, not the timeline's—she was explaining quantum entanglement over lunch at Farmhouse Kitchen in 2038. Young, brilliant, full of theories about particles and probability.

Now, like Eileen, she's in her seventies.

Eileen doesn't knock. She simply opens the door, calling out, "Candace? We're here."

"In the sunroom," comes the reply.

We follow a hallway lined with framed academic awards and photographs. Many feature Candace receiving prestigious scientific honors—the Breakthrough Prize in Fundamental Physics, the Wolf Prize. In one, she's shaking hands with someone I don't recognize, but who clearly holds some important office based on the formal setting and the flags in the background.

I stop abruptly, my breath catching. In nearly every group photo, I'm there. Standing beside Eileen, looking progressively older in each image. At conferences I never attended. Award ceremonies I never witnessed. Family gatherings that happened while I was... elsewhere.

"I don't understand," I whisper, tracing my finger over a photo where gray streaks my temples.

Eileen tugs me gently forward. "Come on. She'll explain."

The sunroom is awash with afternoon light. Candace sits in a comfortable chair, surrounded by tablets and holographic displays showing complex equations. Age has slowed her movements, but not dimmed the intelligence in her eyes. Her once-dark curls are now a cloud of white, framing a face lined by time but still animated with the same intensity I remember.

She looks up as we enter, and for a heartbeat, she freezes. Her eyes widen slightly, and she draws a sharp breath.

She just... stares. Like she's running a calculation in real time, an equation too complex to solve.

"Luke," she finally says, barely above a whisper. Her gaze drifts over me, flickering between recognition and disbelief. "You—"

She stops herself. The hesitation lingers just a second too long, as if something in her mind is shifting to accommodate what she's seeing.

Her throat moves in a swallow before she exhales, slow and deliberate. The scientist in her takes over. "Right on time," she says at last. "I just made tea."

Eileen gives my hand a squeeze before letting go to embrace Candace. I remain rooted in place, watching as Candace pours three cups of steaming amber liquid.

"Bergamot," she says, offering me a cup. "You always said it reminded you of that winter in Barcelona."

I've never been to Barcelona. Have I? A flash of memory—streetlights reflecting on rain-slicked cobblestones, Eileen laughing under a shared umbrella. I blink it away.

"Thanks," I manage, taking a seat across from her. My hands tremble slightly as I accept the cup. I take a sip, and the taste unlocks something—familiar, comforting, impossible.

"This is..." I set the cup down abruptly, spilling droplets onto my jeans. I don't wipe them away.

Candace studies me. "It's like watching water ripple outward from a stone," she says, gesturing with weathered hands. "Reality's adjusting around you."

"What do you mean?"

She leans forward to straighten a spoon that doesn't need straightening. "Think of reality like fabric. When you disappeared, it tore. Now that you're back, it's mending itself—creating a new pattern that includes you throughout the past thirty-five years."

"That's impossible," I say, my pulse quickening. "I wasn't here." But it is possible, isn't it? That conversation I had with Candace in 2045 about superposition. She made me the same bergamot tea, and we were eating... finger sandwiches? Scones?

"From your perspective, no." Candace touches a holographic display, and it swirls into a new configuration—lines of blue light intersecting, diverging, merging again. "But reality is more fluid than we once believed."

"Is that why I saw myself in your photos?" I ask. "Why Hannah recognized me?"

Candace nods. "The timeline is rewriting itself to accommodate your presence. I remember both versions—you disappearing and you staying." She taps her temple. "Two overlapping realities."

My leg bounces nervously under the table. "So everyone's memories are just... changing? That's convenient."

"Not convenient," Candace corrects, leaning back. "Necessary. The universe abhors contradiction. It's like a river finding an alternative path after a landslide. The water always flows downhill, but the route adjusts."

I've heard this same theory before. We've had this same conversation before. Not the exact conversation, but the same ideas. My head throbs and I can't remember exactly when, but—

Eileen, who has been quietly watching this exchange, leans forward. "Will his memories change too?"

Candace tilts her head, considering. "That's harder to say. Luke wasn't living linearly like the rest of us." She picks up her tea and studies the surface for a moment. "He might get glimpses, fragments. Dreams that feel too real."

I flex my right knee, suddenly unsettled. "Like what?"

"Like injuring your knee five years ago," Candace says, gesturing to my leg. "I remember you falling from a ladder while painting. You walked with a slight limp for months."

My stomach twists. I press my palm against my perfectly healthy knee, feeling a phantom ache that was never there.

"This is insane," I mutter, standing abruptly. I pace to the window, watching a hummingbird dart among Candace's flowers—here, gone, here again in rapid succession. But it isn't insane, is it? Insanity is swirling in no-man's-land in a demented quantum cube for what seems like an eternity. Insane is watching your wife sit under a tree every Saturday for decades, then disappearing back to a logging camp, a 1925 movie studio, a café in Barcelona.

But if reality is this malleable, if time can be rewritten so thoroughly...

I turn back. "Could I go back?" The question bursts from me. "To 2035? When I stepped in front of that bus? I could prevent all this—Eileen wouldn't have to spend thirty-five years waiting. And I wouldn't spend thirty-five years in limbo."

Eileen stiffens, her knuckles whitening around her teacup.

Candace sets her cup down with deliberate care. "No, Luke." The words fall like stones. "That's precisely what you cannot do."

"Why not? If reality is so damn flexible—"

"Because you've finally been measured," Candace interrupts, her voice gentle but firm. She rises, crosses to a bookshelf, and returns with an antique glass paperweight. She sets it on the table between us. "Think of yourself as a particle that was suspended—neither here nor there, everywhere and nowhere."

The paperweight's solid presence is a strange comfort.

"Now you've landed," she continues, tapping the glass with her fingernail. "You've been observed, fixed in this point of time. Going back to the cave would unmeasure you—like dropping this into acid and watching it dissolve."

I sink back into my chair. "What would happen?"

Candace reaches for Eileen's hand, a silent communication passing between them.

"Best case? Nothing," Candace says. "The cave might not respond to you now."

"And worst case?" I press, though the chill climbing my spine tells me I already know.

"You'd scatter," she says quietly. "Like dust in the wind. But without Eileen's thirty-five years of patient observation holding your particles together, there'd be no anchor to bring you back. Or worse—parts of you might land in different times, fragmented forever."

The room falls silent except for the soft hum of Candace's displays. Outside, shadows lengthen across her garden. The hummingbird is gone.

I close my eyes, remembering the disorientation of being scattered across timelines. The terror of seeing but not touching, of reaching but never grasping. The endless, maddening drift through moments and memories.

"You're saying I'm stuck here," I say finally, opening my eyes. "In 2070."

"I'm saying you've been given a miracle," Candace corrects, her voice softening. "Don't push your luck."

Candace exhales, glancing at the holographic display. "Honestly, I don't think reality is done settling yet."

"Meaning?" I ask.

"You might keep seeing small shifts. A conversation you swear didn't happen. A memory you don't recall making. Some things will feel... off."

She shrugs. "Or maybe one day, everything will feel seamless, like you were always meant to be here. Hard to say."

FIFTY-FOUR: EILEEN

The drive back to the city is quiet, the familiar skyline I've watched develop decade by decade, growing larger against the darkening sky. Streetlights flicker on, creating a constellation of human-made stars below the deepening indigo above us. I glance at Luke, watching him take in the buildings that must seem to have sprouted overnight from his perspective—or have they? Memory feels slippery tonight, shifting beneath my thoughts like sand under the tide.

Luke's profile is etched against the twilight—firm jaw, those artist's eyes that never miss a detail. I've always loved watching him observe the world. The way he slightly narrows his eyes when something captures his attention. The barely perceptible tilt of his head. So familiar. So precious.

"Are you disappointed?" I ask finally, breaking the silence, my voice sounding older than I remember it. "That you can't go back?"

His fingers drum a gentle rhythm on his knee—a habit of thirty-five years, yet somehow it seems both old and brand new. He watches the city lights reflect off the water, his eyes tracking patterns that I've long recognized as the fractured and reassembled reality that inspired his fracture series. The same eyes that have looked at me across breakfast tables and gallery openings, across decades of shared life.

"Part of me wanted to fix things," he admits, the confession soft, almost swallowed by the purr of the car engine. "To spare you those decades of waiting."

Waiting? The word catches in my mind like a burr. What waiting?

"They weren't wasted years," I say, memories cascading

through me—vacations in Kyoto, that terrible fight in Rome, Luke teaching Hannah to mix paints, our twentieth anniversary under the Northern Lights in Yellowknife.

Yet alongside these memories flows a parallel current—lonely Saturday afternoons beneath Treaty Oak, empty holidays, a half-finished painting gathering dust in a studio I couldn't bear to clean out. Both streams feel equally real, equally mine.

"I lived my life, Luke. And now I get to share what's left of it with you."

Something in my words seems to reach him. He extends his hand across the console and takes mine. I feel the strange contrast of our skin—his still young and smooth, mine paper-thin and marked by decades. But wait—his hand isn't as young as I thought, and I'm not sure why I thought so. There are familiar calluses on his fingertips from holding paintbrushes, and the same writer's bump on his middle finger. The small scar across his knuckle from when he cut himself building Hannah's treehouse twenty years ago.

Yet when I blink, his hand seems smoother again, the scar gone.

His touch is gentle, as if afraid I might break, yet hungry for connection. The warmth of his palm against mine sends a current of comfort up my arm, grounding me when everything else feels unmoored.

"Forward from here," he says. The setting sun catches the silver strands at his temples—or is his hair still all dark? For a moment, I can't be sure. "Across time. Across everything."

Our old phrase. The words that carried us through good times and bad, through all the strangeness of our lives together. I tighten my grip on his hand, feeling a smile touch my lips.

"Forward," I agree, though a whisper in my mind wonders why my husband is acting strangely tonight. Then again, Luke has always been different, out there, painting about fractured time and quantum entanglement, subjects that he—and Candace—have explained to me many times, but that I cannot quite grasp. The thought curls through my consciousness like smoke, then dissipates.

The car hums beneath us as we cross the bridge, its surface vibrating gently against the soles of my feet. The scent of Luke's cologne—sandalwood and something uniquely him—fills the small space between us. It's the same scent he's worn since—when? Since I bought it for him last Christmas, or since that gallery opening where we first met?

Both memories feel true.

As we cross the bridge into the city—a city we've watched transform together over the years—I sense something settle between us. It's like I've been waiting—have been waiting for something.

The thought disappears as soon as it arrives, like morning dew under sunrise.

I don't feel like I'm waiting. The sensation of anticipation that's been my constant companion fades, replaced by something I haven't felt in—weeks? Decades?

Completion.

He is here. He is now. And that's enough.

The city embraces us, its lights reflecting on the windshield like the fragments of time in Luke's paintings. Past and present, memory and reality, all colliding and merging into this one perfect moment.

Forward.

FIFTY-FIVE: LUKE

My neural implant chimes softly, the sound reverberating pleasantly inside my skull rather than disturbing the quiet of our home studio. Kristy's message materializes in my field of vision. Her familiar avatar—that decades-old photo from when she dyed her hair bright purple—pulses to show urgency.

"Luke, Horatio stopped by your downtown studio again. Rent's overdue. Again. He's threatening to reprogram the door scanners if you don't transfer funds by tomorrow. Honestly, after fifty years, you'd think you'd have figured this out."

I chuckle, setting down my brush. Some things never change. Half a century of renting the same Riverside studio space, and somehow the rent payment is always the last thing on my mind. The new pieces, the upcoming retrospective at MoMA, the commission for the International Space Station's observation dome—these consume my thoughts, not mundane financial transfers.

"Something funny?" Eileen's voice drifts from the doorway of our home workspace.

I look up to see her leaning against the frame, her silver hair caught in a loose bun, wisps framing her face. Age has only enhanced her beauty, each line a story, each silver strand a memory we've shared.

"Just Kristy," I say, gesturing vaguely at the message still hovering in my peripheral vision. "Reminding me I've forgotten to pay rent for the downtown space. Again."

Eileen's laugh is soft, familiar. "The more things change, the more they stay the same. Remember that first year? When I had to loan you money because you spent your rent on that ridiculous amount of cobalt blue?"

"Best investment I ever made," I protest. "That series put me on the map."

"Hmm." She crosses our converted sunroom studio, careful not to disturb my organized chaos of supplies. Her movements are slower now, but medical nanotech keeps the arthritis at bay—for now. "I thought marrying me was your best investment."

I catch her hand as she passes, pulling her gently down for a kiss. "That wasn't an investment. That was a miracle."

She smiles against my lips. "Smooth talker. Always have been."

We've been together for what feels like forever. Sometimes I try to remember a time before Eileen, before this life we've built, but those memories feel distant, faded, like paintings left too long in the sun.

"I've been thinking about our anniversary," she says, perching on the edge of my work table. "Fifty years. Golden. It should be something special."

"London?" I ask, the idea coming from nowhere and everywhere at once. "We could revisit the Tate. See what they've done with the place."

Her eyes light up. "London would be perfect. We haven't been back since that conference in '45."

Images flash through my mind—Eileen against the backdrop of Tower Bridge, rain-slicked streets, bergamot tea in a café overlooking the Thames. We were happy there. We've been happy everywhere, really.

"I'll make the arrangements," I promise, already mentally shifting funds from the MoMA commission to cover a luxury trip. "No expense spared for my muse."

Eileen runs a finger across my liver-spotted hand. "When did this happen?" she says. "Just yesterday we were young."

"Speak for yourself. I'm still young at heart."

"And everywhere else, it seems," she says. "Still maintaining two studios at your age."

I glance around at the canvases that surround us in this intimate home workspace—some finished, most in progress. The larger pieces stay in Riverside, but I've always preferred working on the more personal projects here, where I can be close to Eileen.

My eyes drift to the far wall, where Aunt Edna's portrait hangs in a simple frame. It's the only piece from my early days that I've kept visible—never quite finished, the edges deliberately left in that sketched, liminal state between fully realized and merely suggested. Her eyes, though, those I painted with precision and care. They follow me around the room, kind but unflinching, the way she looked at me during my angsty teenage tantrums.

I knew I wanted to be an artist back then. Aunt Edna had seen my teenage drawings of landscapes: felled trees, black rivers, men sawed in half, split into fragments.

"These are good," she would say. "But..."

There was always a "but," back then. Never more than a "good." And usually some nugget of wisdom, such as "The truest art comes from the clearest mind, Luke. You should control the emotion you put on the paper."

She looks down at me from the portrait, and I wonder if she would be proud of me now. Or whether she would look at my fractured paintings and say, "They're good."

My style has evolved over the decades, but the core has remained constant: fractures in time, reality split and reconfigured, moments flowing into each other like tributaries joining a river.

Eileen teases, "Are you going to finish up in time for dinner? Or should I expect you after dessert?"

"Time moves differently when I'm working," I say. "You know that."

She nods because she does know. She's always understood me better than I understand myself.

My neural implant chimes again. This time it's not Kristy, but a notification from an art blog. I subvocalize the command to display it, and the text appears before me:

Campbell's latest work continues to draw comparisons to the mysterious early 20th-century painter who shared his name. Critics argue that his fracture techniques are derivative of the Campbell who vanished in 1925, whose few surviving works show remarkable prescience...

I dismiss the notification with an annoyed thought. These comparisons have followed me throughout my career—some critic or historian always pointing out similarities between my work and that of some obscure artist-cum-logger from a hundred years ago. I've searched the archives, of course. There are superficial similarities, yes, but my work is inspired by quantum mechanics, by Candace's theories about time and observation, by my own lived experience.

Not by a long-dead namesake who painted a few canvases before disappearing into the mists of history.

Still, I know where the criticism comes from. In a world where AI-generated art floods the market—where algorithms train on centuries of artistic history to produce 'new' masterpieces—I remain one of the few who still drags pigment across canvas. I've been called a relic, a stubborn traditionalist. A few critics call it rebellion, as if I'm making a statement by refusing to let a machine synthesize my vision. But I don't paint to defy anyone. I paint because it's the only way I know how to see the world.

"What is it?" Eileen asks, always attuned to my moods.

"Just another comparison to that other Campbell," I sigh. "The one from the 1920s."

A strange expression flickers across her face—something between amusement and recognition—before it settles back into affectionate exasperation. "People always want to categorize art, to find influences and predecessors. They can't accept that some visions are unique."

"Or that great minds think alike," I add, returning to my canvas. The piece I'm working on shows a single moment fractured across multiple timelines—a technique I've refined over decades.

"Dinner in an hour," Eileen says, pressing a kiss to my temple. "Hannah and Max are coming over."

"I'll clean up before they arrive," I say.

She raises her eyebrows and smiles. "Famous last words."

After she leaves, I lose myself in the painting again. Time slips away, as it always does when I work.

* * *

Before I know it, the gentle chime of our home system announces visitors.

I clean my brushes methodically—a ritual I've performed thousands of times—and head to the kitchen. The familiar scent of grits and biscuits greets me. Comfort food of the highest order. Eileen stands at the counter, brewing tea. She prefers the slow process over the rapid-infusion capsules most people use now.

"Bergamot," she says, handing me a steaming cup. "Your favorite."

The aroma strikes me like a physical force—comforting, familiar, yet somehow poignant. I've always loved bergamot tea. Something about the citrus notes centers me and reminds me of happy times.

Hannah has already arrived, her son Max in tow. At thirty-five, Hannah is the spitting image of her mother Candace in her younger years—brilliant, analytical, with a warmth that belies her scientific precision. She's followed in her mother's footsteps, pushing the boundaries of quantum physics at the University.

Max, now fifteen, has his grandmother's curls but my eye for color and composition. He's shown promise as an artist since he was old enough to hold a brush.

"Uncle Luke," Hannah greets me with a hug. "You look tired. Working too hard as usual?"

"The canvases don't paint themselves," I reply, an old joke between us.

"Unless you're using those new neural interface brushes," Max chimes in. "Then they practically do."

"Traditionalist," I remind him, tapping my chest. "Hand to brush to canvas. The way art was meant to be made."

Hannah peers into the pot on the stove, wrinkling her nose slightly. "Eggs, grits, and biscuits again? Seriously?"

"It's your uncle's favorite," Eileen says, setting plates around our kitchen island. "Has been since before you were born."

Hannah rolls her eyes good-naturedly. "Why do you like that stuff so much?" she asks me. "It's so... 20th century."

"It's my grandmother's recipe," I say. But the moment the words leave my mouth, something shifts. The kitchen lights seem dimmer for just an instant, as if the past is pressing in around the edges. I hear the rhythmic clop of hooves on pavement, the faint murmur of a lunch counter in the heat of summer, the scent of tobacco and frying grease.

My grip tightens around my mug. The moment stretches, impossibly layered, like wet paint smearing across decades.

Then, just as quickly, it's gone.

Eileen watches me from across the kitchen island, head tilted

298

slightly. "Luke?" she asks. A single word, gentle, but laced with something else. Concern, maybe. Or recognition.

The moment passes, the strange dissonance fading as quickly as it came.

"Hmm," is all Hannah says, accepting a plate from Eileen.

We eat together, talking about Hannah's research, Max's college aspirations, and the upcoming anniversary trip to London. Normal family dinner conversation, comfortable and well-worn, like an old sweater.

After dinner, while Hannah helps Eileen with the dishes, Max corners me in the living room.

"I've been thinking about Jacksonville Art Institute for junior year," he says, a hint of nervousness in his voice. "Mom wants me to pursue quantum physics, but..."

"But art calls to you," I finish for him.

He nods, relief clear in his expression. "Did you ever feel torn? Between what was expected and what you wanted?"

The question triggers something—a distant memory, perhaps, or a dream. For an instant, I see flashes of another life: thick calluses, healed blisters, embedded dirt, and resin stains. A different path I might have taken, one without paint-stained hands and the freedom to create.

"Everyone faces choices," I say, shaking off the strange vision. "The trick is recognizing when you're making them. Some people drift through life taking the path of least resistance, never realizing they had options."

"That's deep, Uncle Luke," Max grins, the tension leaving his shoulders.

"Wisdom of age," I wink. "And speaking of wisdom, your grandmother Candace called earlier. She's got some new theory she wants to discuss with you at the university next week."

"She always does." Max sighs, but his eyes light up. Despite his artistic leanings, he shares his grandmother's fascination with the fundamental nature of reality.

Hannah and Max take the evening shuttle back home—no more highways, no more steering. Just coordinates, a soft chime, and a seamless glide through the city's mag-lev corridors.

Later, Eileen and I sit on our balcony overlooking the St. Johns

River. The city skyline gleams, taller than I remember from the days before augmented architecture made building design an AI-driven art form. Across the river, the automated ferry hums silently, a ghostly light trailing behind it. It's a testament to how much has changed since we first met. Was it at a gallery opening? I remember the moment our eyes connected across a crowded room, the instant recognition, the feeling that I'd found a piece of myself I hadn't known was missing.

"Penny for your thoughts," Eileen says, her hand finding mine in the darkness.

"Just thinking about how lucky I am," I reply. "The life we've built. The family we've gathered around us. The art I've been allowed to create."

"Allowed?" she asks, turning to face me. The moonlight catches the silver in her hair, transforming it into a luminous halo.

"Meant to create," I amend. "It feels like... destiny, sometimes. Like everything that's happened was always going to happen."

Her fingers tighten around mine. "Do you ever wonder about the roads not taken?"

Again, that strange flash—a dental chair, a steering wheel, a cave. A sense of displacement, of time unmoored. But it fades quickly, like ripples in a pond, leaving only the solid certainty of this moment, this reality.

"No," I say. "This is where I was always meant to be."

I pull her closer, breathing in the scent of her—still the same after all these years, still home.

"Besides," I add, "any other road wouldn't have led to you."

She laughs. "You're still charming me after fifty years."

"Planning to charm you for at least fifty more."

We sit in comfortable silence, watching the lights reflect on the water. Time passes differently in moments like these—both instantaneous and eternal. Like my paintings, like Candace's equations, like life itself.

I take Eileen's hand, feeling each bone, each vein, each callus earned through decades of living. My thumb brushes over her wedding ring, the brass worn thin from half a century of wear.

And I vow to never let go.

EPILOGUE: LUKE

The wind carries fresh fall air through the open French doors as I rise from the balcony chair, stretching my arms before heading inside. The scent of bergamot still lingers in the air, comforting and familiar.

Something pulls me toward my desk. A loose drawer—barely ajar, like someone had just been there.

Frowning, I tug it open. A few old brushes, a scattering of charcoal, an empty sketchpad. And something else.

A small, round chip tumbles onto the floor, clicking against the hardwood.

I pick it up, turn it over in my palm. The worn plastic is imprinted with a number:

1 MONTH.

I blink. Something stirs—a memory, not quite my own.

Not mine, I think. This was... someone else's. But who?

A flicker—a night in 2020? 2021? A bar, a promise, a relapse, or maybe a rescue. A past that shouldn't exist.

I slip the chip into my pocket.

When I join Eileen in the living room, she is arranging fresh flowers in a vase—jasmine and gardenia—filling the kitchen with their sweet scent. My gaze falls to her hand as she trims a stem, to the brass ring she wears. It looks antique, worn paper-thin from decades of wear. Something about it tugs at me—a memory just out of reach, blurred at the edges.

She looks up and pauses when she sees my expression.

"What is it?" she asks, setting down the scissors.

I hesitate, then pull out the sobriety chip. "Found this in my desk drawer."

Eileen takes it, her fingers brushing mine. I get the familiar buzz of a connection, even after all these years.

She studies the plastic disc, a faint crease appearing between her brows. "That's strange. Whose is this?"

I don't tell her I think it's mine, because I don't know for sure. Memories have a way of doing that—receding, clouding, blending like watercolors on a palette left out overnight.

Eileen places the chip back on the counter. "Maybe it was inside that vase I got at the flea market."

I nod, thinking that was a more reasonable explanation than having a memory gap about AA meetings. The chip catches the evening light, casting a small prism onto the wall. For a moment, I stare at the prism, wondering how a plastic chip could cause light to fracture in such as unexpected way. I turn the chip over, and the prism disappears as though it was never there.

As night falls over the city, I stand on the balcony again. Eileen joins me, her hand finding mine with the ease of decades. The city lights spread before us, each one a moment, a memory, a timeline branching infinitely outward.

I turn to study her profile in the lamplight—the curve of her cheek, the way she absently turns that antique ring on her finger. Something wells up in my chest, inexplicable and overwhelming. If someone asked me to explain why I love this woman, I couldn't find the words. It feels bigger than memory, deeper than reason.

"What are you thinking about?" she asks softly.

"You," I say, and mean it in ways I don't even understand.

ABOUT THE AUTHOR

Aisling McBreen grew up in the United Kingdom and spent her adult life working as a journalist, chasing stories across continents and deadlines. Now retired to the warm coast of Florida, she devotes her time to writing novels and caring for a small menagerie of rescued animals. When she's not at her desk, you'll likely find her in the garden with a cup of tea, a pen behind her ear, and a dog at her feet.

www.ingramcontent.com/pod-product-compliance
Lightning Source LLC
Chambersburg PA
CBHW070651180626
46817CB00006B/2328